BPP-03697 © Antioch Pub.

The King of Colored Town

By the Author

A Tinker's Damn, 2000

Darryl Wimberley

The
KING
of
COLORED
TOWN

The Toby Press

First Edition 2007
The Toby Press LLC
POB 8531, New Milford, CT 06776-8531, USA &
POB 2455, London WIA 5WY, England
www.tobypress.com

ISBN-IO: 1 59264 181 4, ISBN-13: 978 1 59264 181 9, *hardcover*

A CIP catalogue record for this title is
available from the British Library

Printed and bound in the United States by
Thomson-Shore Inc., Michigan

To the many graduates of Kerbo School

Prologue: 1993

I've never seen the dogwoods so white," he remarked, this pale man in dark raiment, the ferryman who would soon, before my people and others, lower Joe Billy to his well-earned Beyond. "Whitest I believe I've ever seen," he repeated, nodding to a window that afforded a view of the courtyard outside. "The dogwoods. You remember? Those lily-white blossoms?"

As if any absence from my home-place would be sufficient to disacquaint me with dogwood trees or their ermine display. Though in fact the dogwood tree's blossom never really seemed to me to be white at all. I can remember springtimes sultry as only summers in northern Florida can be, when the blossoms of the dogwood trees seemed positively febrile. I can remember days when, seeing my big-toed feet shuffling from beneath the hem of my feedsack dress, I imagined that the blooms lining my sandy path were no more than blisters of pus, a yellow seeping.

A weeping wound, my grandmother used to tell me, could be salved with a liniment of dogwood leaves and it was not uncommon for the dogwood to be used medicinally, its bark boiled to counter a fever or ague, its blossoms burned or poulticed for a headache, or, especially during revivals, to cast out demons. My mother was the subject of one such exorcism. For her special affliction. There was no cure for Corrie Jean, but that did nothing to tremble the faith of her congregation. Count your blessings, people said. Move on.

Thus preserving the potency of their faith in the dogwood tree.

I was in Washington when I got the call about Joe Billy. A telegram, actually. It seemed so old-fashioned. I had been invited to the White House to perform for President and Mrs. Clinton and had arrived for rehearsal when, as they say, the word came. I went on with the concert, and remained for the short reception afterward. The President and First Lady were very gracious. He's a real music lover, showed me his saxophone. I was driven back to my hotel in style along a boulevard brilliant with the blossoms of cherry trees.

It is hard to imagine a setting more glorious than our nation's capitol in spring with the cherry trees in full display, but I have always been partial to dogwoods. And it seems to me now, looking out of this house of death to the dogwoods nestled beneath its gingerbread eaves, that my experiences are punctuated by the blossoms of *Cornus florida*. The sagging, worm-eaten building where I began my education, the only school in colored town, was wreathed in a grove of wild dogwoods. Miss Chandler would warm your behind if she saw you knocking the blossoms off those arbored limbs.

And the train station, where I first saw Joe Billy, was framed at its dock by a pair of dogwood trees, reaching each to each on slender, thwarted trunks to form a proscenium over the Pullman car from which Joe Billy made his theatric entrance, practically sailing from the car's interior onto the loading dock, dropping his cardboard case to the pinewood deck. His leering guitar. Standing there like a millionaire. Barely seventeen. Hair pomaded back on the sides like Sammy Davis. Shirt opened two buttons down his chocolate chest. Wrangler jeans too new to be faded pulling tight over slender haunches. Quick and vibrant and short. His eyes, set close, bulged from their sockets in a constant state of astonishment or amusement or provocation, always eager to see everything, anything, that might offer a fight, a fuck, or diversion.

2

First place I made love was girdled by dogwood trees. And that other time. Where love had no part. They stretched me out between a pair of dogwoods. A full moon beamed through those blossoms. Whiter than any white you've ever seen.

"I see a stiss." I nodded toward the coffin where Joe Billy's youth and age lay arrested.

It was an aluminum coffin. Reminded me of the passenger coach that brought us Joe Billy, that car a much diminished version of the Pullmans originating in Chicago and locomoted all the way to the Sunshine State, stopping in Tallahassee for a change of line, and again at Perry, the final L.O.P. & G. feeder skirting the Gulf Coast on silver rails to pass tobacco fields and dairy farms and forests of hybrid pine before finally arriving at Laureate.

This was the town, the sultry place where Joe Billy's youth had been sapped and where, his age spent, he was prepared for transport once again in a metal berth bright-shining as the sun. The coffin was lined in red. In satin. It looked like a coffee table for a whorehouse. Joe Billy would have laughed at that, had he been alive to see it. Had he been able to see.

"There's a stiss thowing," I formed the words once more on dry lips. I still have trouble, occasionally, shaping words. Doesn't affect my playing anymore; a double-reed is more familiar to me by now than a lover's kiss. But speaking I am apt, still, to lisp or mangle or mispronounce and so I am inclined, even now, even when I know I have elocuted perfectly, to blame myself for another's misunderstanding.

"Through the eyelid. There. It thows," I pointed, and the undertaker's disgruntled cough told me I was onto something.

"Sorry, Miss Cilla. We couldn't get it to stay closed."

I laughed aloud.

"'Couldn't get it'?! The man's dead, for God's sake."

"Well, yes, ma'am. Certainly. But that lid just would not stay down. And with the eyes—"

"I know about the eyes, Edward."

He didn't like that. It would have been all right if I'd addressed him as, say, 'Mr. Ed'. Or certainly 'Mr. Tunney'. But to call him 'Edward', just as if he was my employee, which at the moment he definitely was, did not sit well with the white man who had been settling colored people into the sandy loam of Lafayette County at outrageous prices for decades.

"How much for the coffin?" I asked.

"Twelve and a half." He might have been pricing melons. "'Nother fifteen hundred for arrangements. Not including flowers."

"Why don't we just cut some dogwood?" I offered mildly. "Like you say. They're awful white this year."

White blossoms to frame a black man. I straightened abruptly from the casket. Even in mortis Joe Billy seemed to threaten mobility. A laugh. A curse. Nobody could predict what Joseph William King would do in life. Nor even, apparently, in death. But there were no eyes beneath those recalcitrant lids so badly tailored. The eyes had been gouged out not long after he had been put in prison. The fourth year? The fifth? To my shame I knew I could not precisely recall.

"Be something like fifteen thousand altogether," Tunney continued his mercantile train of thought, all pretense at consolation dropped.

"It's prepaid, Edward. We had a contract drawn."

"That's right. Thank you for reminding. So there's a discount of—"

"Why don't you just send a bill?" I suggested. "I guarantee I'll beat whatever the County's paying."

He didn't like that either. To be reminded how cheaply a man dead from prison could be interred. What the County would render in that circumstance. There would be no dogwood blossoms over those graves, or any other lily, you could bet. But here I was, come from out of town to pay top dollar for a nigger's interment.

No sign of gratitude escaped Mr. Tunney's well-masked countenance, only an unvarying smile stretching like a rictus. A plain of flesh caked with makeup, like a woman's face. Or a corpse's restored.

"Dogwood blossoms," a chuckle burbled through that pan of dissemblance. "You sure can pull a leg, Miss Cilla."

"No. Dogwood is what I'd like, I think." I turned away abruptly. "A bunch of blossoms over the casket. And the gravesite, too."

"Fine, then."

"And do something about that stitch, Edward. It's sloppy."

A crimson tide threatened to destroy his pallor.

"Yes, ma'am," was all he said.

I gathered my shawl over my well-wrought suit, passing through a cloying veil of velour to reach an uncurtained anteroom devoid of mourners. Through that chamber, down wide, limestone steps to a deserted, Sunday morning street and rented car. My feet appeared much larger to me than they should in their dark, Italian pumps. I pulled an ungloved hand roughly over my eyes. When I looked up I beheld a row of dogwood trees.

They formed a perfect line on the far side of the boulevard, a brace of symmetric limbs lightly garnered in moss, extending to display bowls of white blossoms that waved gently, like a bevy of beauty queens in a homecoming parade, carried to and fro in the train of a salty breeze. The car was near, now. I fumbled in my purse for the keys.

"Joe Billy, Joe Billy!!"

The words burst through tortured lips.

"I am so sorry."

Chapter one

*But if ye will not drive out the inhabitants
of the land before you; then it shall come to pass,
that those which ye let remain of them shall be
pricks in our eyes, and thorns in your sides, and
all shall vex you in the land where you dwell.*

NUMBERS 33:55

They hadn't of burned that church, maybe none of the rest would of happened," Joe Billy used to say, and I wanted desperately for that to be true. After all, had it not been for that business with the churchhouse Joe Billy certainly would never have left his neighborhood in Tallahassee for Laureate and Colored Town. He would have remained without doubt in French Town, living with Mama Fanny, sipping iced tea beneath her mimosa.

Enjoying his music. Watching the world go by.

There was a time when there had been much to see. Through the forties, French Town had bustled with activity, a segregated enclave of Tallahassee with a population descended from Old South slaves, their unchained progeny now owning businesses and property. Shops and stores pickled the streets in that era, and commerce was lively. But by the sixties, French Town had duplicated the slide

7

to poverty common to practically every community of color in the South. Banks would not loan money to businesses desperate to expand. Laborers became increasingly unskilled. Children dropped illiterate out of inadequate schools. Drugs were sold in virtually open markets where once melons and green beans were displayed, and pimps and prostitutes stalked where families once proudly labored in their own concerns.

None of that mattered to Joseph William King. Only thing Joe Billy cared about was a good time, and in that pursuit enjoyed a degree of freedom that would have been impossible for me to comprehend. Life with Mama Fanny was, to put it mildly, unsupervised. Fanny let her son leave school at fifteen without a moment's balk or censure. Let him stay out as late as he liked, sleep in as long as he liked. She didn't even pressure Joe Billy to get a job, though as it happened his afternoons were occupied, with meager compensation, at Meitzer's Music Shop.

Mr. Meitzer, an old Jew, ran the place. It was there that Joe Billy learned the thousand delicate skills necessary to keep a saxophone healthy, or tune a piano, or string a violin. The old meister restored guitars as well, and this was the only labor Joe Billy ever truly enjoyed. He loved to hold a guitar, any guitar. Loved the shape of a guitar. Like a woman, he used to tell me. That hourglass architecture. The curve of a guitar like a finely shaped hip. Or that fine place where the belly narrowed to a waist and then out again. Wood sanded and finished smooth and soft as skin. The sound hole was situated for a variety of interpretations. A gash, a hole. A mouth, a scream. A navel. A cunt.

Violins and cellos, even banjos made their way to Meitzer's shop, but it was the guitar that was Joe Billy's conjure woman. The long play of the hardwood neck. The nut. The bone. Bridge and saddle.

He tried to play, of course. Even in exile in Colored Town he tried to keep it up, poring almost every night over chord books and spinning 45s on the record player I stole, trying to imagine himself the next B.B. King or Robert Johnson. Devil and Blues. But hours and hours of practice taken with blistered fingers demonstrated that his talent would never rival B.B.'s or Bob Johnson's. Still, Joe Billy found a way to use the guitar in the service of a different kind of imagination.

It started in Tallahassee with his own guitar. Joe Billy inherited his first instrument, a Gibson, from Daddy Meadows, that six-string not so much bequeathed as left behind when the strapping pulp-wooder abandoned his wife and their four-year old burden to strike out from south Georgia for parts unknown. The guitar got packed with Joe Billy and Fanny for the trip to Tallahassee where it was duly reinstalled—along with Fanny's maiden name. Joe Billy grew up a King, the Gibson his only link to a putative father.

According to Joe Billy, the similarity between a woman's body and a guitar's light-framed anatomy struck him just about the time of his first erections. But he was a little older, fifteen or so, when, stealing a sample of acrylic paints and lacquers from the high school's auto shop, he retreated with his Gibson to a closet-sized bedroom for his other purpose. It was there that Joe Billy found his true expression. In something less than a week Fanny's fatherless boy had conformed the surface of his inherited guitar into the image of a voluptuous woman.

She was lying on her side, this female, a nude torso stretched along the axis of the guitar's leering neck and exposed in bold, primary colors on the surface of the instrument's polished body. The soundhole situated her navel. Raven hair played in damascene tangles over the naked round of the guitar's shoulder to display a sensual hip. A kind of bracelet fell in linked motes of turquoise or jade in a shallow arc from her wasp's waist toward the pubis lasciviously suggested below, a G-string dimly realized from visions of Biblical whores, Aholah and Aholibah, say. Or Jezebel.

One evening Joe Billy took his guitar to French Town hoping to jam at a local blues establishment. Tully's Lounge was never as successful as, say, the Red Bird Café, but was still, locals insisted, a venue for serious artists. The Adderley Brothers, Cannonball and Nat, were said to have played at Red Tully's place. Imagine that sax and cornet in the same room. B.B. King was claimed, perhaps apocryphally, to have jammed with the boys' quintet on one occasion. This was all in the late forties, fifties maybe.

By Joe Billy's time the club was barely scraping by, Tully and his ill-tempered wife running the place by themselves. Problem was that rock 'n' roll was seducing younger audiences away from jazz and blues. Most of the performers drifting into Tully's were old men who no longer regarded themselves as professional musicians. They played for drinks and tips, or like Joe Billy came to chase women.

The veteran players only occasionally returned, their balding pates and graying hair wreathed in sweat and the smoke of cigarettes. Sometimes they'd let Joe Billy sit in, and he'd be keeping rhythm behind men with sobriquets like Blind John Davis or Pinetop Perkins. Pigmeat Jarret used to show up now and then. Nobody paid any attention to the kid on backup. But the night Joe Billy went behind that stage and unpacked his painted Gibson he acquired an instant audience—outraged, amused, intrigued—depending on the concupiscence of the beholder. Pigmeat spoke up first.

"Boy. Where you get that goddamn guitar?"

At first, only a few musicians sought him out. Only a couple of those actually surrendered their instruments to the painter's charge. But then as word of mouth spread news of Joe Billy's innovation, a coterie of Bohemians, serious musicians and the merely titillated began to provide something like a regular stream of demand. Even before I knew him, Joe Billy had worked on Gibsons and Martins worth more than a thousand dollars. He received acoustic guitars, electric guitars, double-necks and twelve-strings—exquisite canvasses for the conception of nudes variously innocent or salacious.

Joe Billy completed all of his illustrations at his mama's place on Pearl Street. Fanny was proud to own her own home, a white frame house that nestles, still, deep beneath a clutch of mimosa trees. She would remain beneath those lacy limbs on summer mornings, a glass of sweet tea sweating in her hand as she observed the endless passage of single, mostly unemployed men who strolled the broken sidewalk out front. Spying coyly from her shaded retreat like a demoiselle peeking from beneath a riot of pink parasols. Joe Billy would have remained in the shade of those trees himself, living rent-free and without responsibility, finding satisfaction and some profit in the transformation of guitars, had it not been for that mess with the church.

In 1963, The Mount Zion African Methodist Episcopal Church was situated on Fourth Avenue, only a few blocks from its contemporary location on Old Bainbridge Road. The architecture was unremarkable, two storeys of brick and hardwood vestured in Spanish moss. A pair of pilasters framed the double doors granting entry, the woodwork rough with dry rot. But there were lead-paned windows set into the east wall of the sanctuary that were by any standard distinguished, a morality play stained deeply into glass that each Easter fractured a rising sun's ordinary light into purple and green and gold reminders of the Passion and Resurrection. These were Mount Zion's pride and joy.

"The bed is way shorter than a man can stretch hisself on it!" The right Revered Willy Waintree used to bellow Isaiah's prophecies from his pinewood pulpit as if they were self-evident. "An' the covers is narrower than he can wrap hisself *in it*!"

Every Monday morning the Reverend selected a passage from his worn Bible. It was the church secretary's job to post those verses in wood-carved letters on a plywood sign that anchored just beside the single, splintered sidewalk leading from Fourth Avenue's steaming asphalt to Mount Zion's gospel shade. Admonitions from the Old Testament alternated weekly with replies from the New.

> *"For, behold, the Lord cometh out of his place to punish the inhabitants of the earth for their iniquity..."*
>
> ISAIAH 26:21

might be followed by:

> *"For God so loved the world, that he gave His only Begotten Son..."*
>
> JOHN 3:16

The scripture displayed on the moonless night of Joe Billy's pilgrimage was filled with revelation: *"Behold I come as a thief."* 2 PETER 3:10

It was rare these days to see the church unoccupied. A Florida judge had recently ordered desegregation of the county's all-white schools. This in Tallahassee, where public cafés, water fountains and toilets were still off-limits to black people. There were beatings in the wake of the judge's edict. Tires were slashed, windows broken. Mount Zion's faithful turned to their church in droves, initially seeking refuge, later with determination to resist, to demand. To "organize."

Not that any of this mattered to Joe Billy. Joseph William did not approach Mount Zion in stealth after midnight for any socially redeeming purpose. Weeks earlier Mama Fanny had been raising hell concerning an extra collection taken at church, the collection that came, she said, *after* the regular offering already destined for missionaries and air-conditioning and Vacation Bible School.

"Church gettin' itself all messed up in politics, I declare." Mama dipped a pork rind into her perspiring tea. "Talkin' 'bout some kinda march someplace. Got to raise three hundred dollah, just for bus fare! Mo' money than I make in half a year, and they sin that plate around asking *me* to put in my pennies. Like the widow in the pearble, tellin' me how righteous I am, giving all I got to Jesus! 'Shoot,' I tells 'em, 'Jesus rode a donkey,' I'm *keeping* my money."

Fanny reported the church's ad-hoc collection at two hundred and twenty-eight dollars, short of the needed fare, perhaps, but more money than Joe Billy could make in three months painting guitars. Just sitting there. Waiting to be claimed. And so buoyed by prophecy Joe Billy came to cash in, slipping after midnight from the cover of Mount Zion's splendid oaks and dashing across its lawn to reach the churchhouse steps.

His heart hammered in his chest like a child's—had he been spotted? Some other interloper lingered in the shadows across the street, a smudge in the gloom. Crazy Maggie, he realized, with some relief. Maggie was a crone known to everyone in the neighborhood, the original bag lady. She owned nothing but a shopping cart which she pushed day and night in a route which regularly circled Mount Zion. After a moment, not hearing her familiar caw, Joe Billy began to allow himself to believe he had reached the church unseen. Only then did he reach for a door, pulling its iron-worked handle.

Sweet Jesus, was ever a hinge so loud?

He stepped inside. There were no lights switched on at this hour to illuminate Mount Zion's ample nave, but a fulsome moon filtered through the church's famous stained windows, reminding Joe Billy of Jesus and Mary and the Tomb. Jesus and Golgotha. And Judas, of course, hung from the neck of a dogwood tree. Joe Billy jogged furtively down the sanctuary's wide aisle, lurched hard left at the pulpit, away from admonitions of glass. A selection of hymns was displayed in white letters on a large, varnished sign anchored above a doorway. "Pg 172: Just As I Am", or some variation.

The door below the lettered hymns opened onto a short hallway off which other doors accessed the choir's loft, the baptismal fount, and a storage room renamed for dignity's sake the Office of Church Secretary. The knob in Joe Billy's hand was brass and cool and did not turn. He applied a hammer and screwdriver to that flimsy obstruction—

Knock and it shall be opened unto you.

A short rummage later Joe Billy re-entered the church's somber interior with two hundred twenty-eight dollars and seventy-three cents in a velvet collection bag and was well down the aisle before he noticed on the eastern wall, a wavering, unsteady glow.

"Jesus!"

At first he had the notion that this was some apparition, a ghost, perhaps. Perhaps the Holy Ghost—Joe Billy was not entirely without superstition. But then he saw tongues of light licking up the stained glass windows from *outside*, a whole wall of light, growing. And then came the smell…

"FIRE!!"

Joe Billy bellowed at the top of his lungs and when he did he heard outside a muffled chorus of men, shouting, cursing.

"FIRE!" he yelled again, instinct overcoming any caution as he sprinted for the door. An explosion, then. Like a hand grenade, Joe Billy would later say. A WHOOOOOSH of fire, skirts of flame caught in an angry wind. Stained glass bursting in shards of shrapnel. Joe Billy picked himself off the floor and stumbled past rows of pews to stagger outside in a billow of black smoke, the church's collection bag plainly in hand.

"YOU!"

Some woman came off the sidewalk, running toward the burning church as if seeking death.

"YOU, BOY!"

Joe Billy thought at first it had to be Crazy Maggie, but there was no craziness in this woman, or fear, either. And then he recognized Mary Tully, Red Tully's fiery and born-again wife. She probably hadn't seen him on more than a hundred occasions at her husband's club.

"I KNOW YOU!"

She pointed a nailed finger and Joe Billy ran. He ran with his balls in his throat, down the line of oaks bounding the property on its fire side, through a thick hedge of ligustrum.

That's when he saw the truck.

It came tearing out from behind the sanctuary, a brand new '63 pickup sliding onto a street slick with dew. A Ford. Fire engine red. Rebel flag flying from a spring-loaded aerial. Spinner hubcaps. Spinner hubs on a truck. It ran the stop sign at Fourth Avenue, just ran straight through. Joe Billy would report seeing three men inside. Two or three. The cab was dark, the truck was hauling ass and so was Joe Billy. He could not even be certain that the driver was a white man.

"BURN BABY!!" Joe Billy was sure he heard that command coming from one of the pickup's confederates.

About that time a pair of boys sliced across Fourth on their bicycles. Joe Billy heard a truck's brakes lock on the damp pavement, saw the Ford swerve. More cursing then, as the black teenagers dumped their bikes and hurled abuse at the rampaging pickup. And then Maggie, Crazy Maggie, taking up the curse from the barricade of her grocery cart.

"You sons of bitches!"

Like the caw of a raven.

"I seen you sons of bitches!"

Dogs barking by then, porch lights spilling flimsy puddles of illumination all up and down the street and Joe Billy knew he was in trouble. Even if the boys hadn't seen him, or Crazy Maggie, Red Tully's wife surely had. The police would follow her accusing finger and even *if* between beatings he could get the cops to believe he hadn't dynamited Mount Zion's church, they'd know he stole their goddamned collection.

I don't know what I would have done. But Joe Billy King tucked his stolen purse beneath his arm like it was a football and he ran. He ran till there were sharp sticks scraping the inside of his lungs. He ran till his legs burned and cramped, and he kept on running. Straight to the heart of Frenchtown, to Mama Fanny.

She would know what to do.

Chapter two

A "Water Declared Unsatisfactory"—*The Clarion*

s Joe Billy painted guitars and robbed churches, I was raising my mama in Colored Town. Didn't matter whether you were black or white, everyone in Laureate called everything on the shady side of the railroad depot 'Colored Town'. Growing up I thought that Colored Town was a place name distinct and unique. Like Atlanta, say, or Montgomery, or New York.

Nigger Town was another appellation commonly used; I suppose I could have said I raised mama in Nigger Town. Or I could have simply declared that our family resided in The Quarters, a term reminiscent of slave quarters even though nobody in my community could point to the obvious shackles of that earlier enslavement. I cannot truthfully claim to have had a sense of enslavement in my own Colored Town, at least not in those early years, largely because I had no situation, other than a Pisgah view of white folks', by which to gauge my own.

I was not aware in 1963 that black men and women in Detroit or Pittsburgh could earn twenty dollars an hour for an eight-hour day. That daily wage would buy you three month's indenturement from anybody living in Colored Town. Not that you could depend on a month's work. Men and women in my community were employed according to the demands of the season, loading hay or throwing melons or working in the tobacco fields. Much of that labor was piecework. A penny a stick. A dollar a sled. A quarter a row. I wondered as a child whether those poor Israelites got paid by the brick. Seemed like a pyramid's worth of bricks could add up.

Children worked, too, of course. Black children and white children sweating side by side, and generally for the same precarious wage. I think any of us would have been astounded to know that you could find urban and suburban-dwelling youngsters who by 1963 washed cars when they felt like it, or received allowances for chores. These young people did not string tobacco or throw melons or crouch for hours pressing thorn-laced cuttings into the damp rooting beds of Mr. Thistle's nursery. No, sir. These other young people drove hot rods to sock hops. They played football or baseball or surfed golden waves, some of them, buying records by The Beach Boys or The Lettermen before heading off to college.

But not in Colored Town. Ours was a cul-de-sac isolated from the larger culture by a perimeter of unpaved streets. My concerns were mundane, day to day. I was seventeen years old, a big, rawboned girl with a Brillo pad of kinked hair, a flat face, unabashedly flared nostrils and lips. My job was to take care of Mama, make money, and keep water in the house. Schoolwork got factored somewhere in between.

I didn't mind the paying work; tobacco, melons, Mr. Thistle's nursery—it didn't matter. I didn't mind feeding Mama, or dressing her. Brushing her teeth. Wiping her clean. And Miss Chandler sparked a fire for learning in me that sustained a tolerance for the rote mnemonics that was my early education.

But I hated hauling water.

Hauling water was a daily chore I never ceased to grudge. You could see Laureate's water tower, a pregnant dome rising silver on steel stilts high above the live oak trees that separated The Quarters from 'City Park'. Graffiti yearly announced the most recent graduates, the white graduates, of Laureate High School. "LHS SNRS" was plainly visible, smeared over the tank's shining face like lipstick on a crazy woman.

For years white residents of Laureate had drawn tap water from that tower, a steady stream of clean water distributed through a grid of mains and copper lines to their homes and businesses and to the school. But there were no pipes crossing the tracks to Colored Town, which presented a problem. You had to have water—to drink, to cook, to bathe. But there was only one place in the Quarters to get your cup filled, and so twice a day, freezing rain or broiling sun, I pulled a pair of five-gallon pails over to Mr. Raymond Hatcher's front porch.

Mr. Raymond was a wiry, kindly old man. Retired from the railroad. Always dressed the same; long-sleeved shirt, white, with suspenders. Soft-shined, low-quarter shoes, black. Khaki trousers creased sharp as a knife. He had big knots on his face and skull, like carbuncles. He also had the only water well in Colored Town. There were probably forty families in our community of dog runs and out-houses, every one of us dependent on Mr. Raymond's largesse for our daily necessity. Mr. Raymond had a half-brother living with him, a loose and louche old man. Lester wanted Mr. Raymond to make people pay for the use of the pump.

"Why don' we charge? Just even a penny a bucket?"

But Mr. Raymond said no, that wouldn't be right, the water just happen' to be at their house like the water wells in the Bible where ever'body came and dipped and nobody got charge nuthin'.

"Damn fools, you ask me," Lester replied, but did not prevail.

There could be twenty or thirty women lined up by Mr. Raymond's porch, hardly ever a man or boy. Hauling water was distaff labor. It could make for a long wait, people taking turns on the long handle of his pump. First one to the pump, of course, was required to prime it. The pump would not bring water uncoaxed and it was funny how some women working that long handle, their hips rolling with the rhythm of sex, could get it to come right off, where others, laboring mightily, could bring up no more than air.

I was good at priming the pump.

Sometimes the pump would need fixing, the bellows, usually, leather valves that once torn or brittle would not allow a vacuum to be pulled in the pump's iron cylinder. Even with Sears, Roebuck and

Co. it took a week, sometimes two weeks, to get replacements, an intolerable state of affairs. So once every couple of years Mr. Raymond would send one of us young ones off to find or steal an inner tube so he could fashion a set of bellows for his pump.

He sent me one time. I had no idea where to find the suitable material so I crossed the tracks into Laureate and walked up to Mr. Charles Putnal's gas station. Mr. Charles, as I called him, was a white man who ran a Shell station there on Main Street. Maybe he'd know somethin' about pumps and tubes. I kept my head down as I found Main Street, a posture required of Negroes in town, and was pretending a fascination with the cracks in the sidewalk when a car prowled by that always frightened me. It was the Sheriff's car, a big Dodge with county insignia and lights and a big hoop antenna whipping back and forth.

The cruiser swung beneath the portico that offered the only shade at the Putnal station. Mr. Charles was changing a tire. I decided to wait for that job to be finished before I made a closer approach, trying the while not to imagine the Sheriff's billy club wrapping around my head.

Sheriff Collard Jackson, Collard Greens, Green-Man or more elliptically Hamhock, was a lawman we all assiduously avoided. He was rawboned and hard. His eyes, no more than a watery film sunk in a sinkhole, were usually masked behind a lens of cheaply framed sunglasses. He had a shock of white hair that ran like a skunk's tail down the side of his head, but he was not Cajun. He was just mean. Grandma Handsom held it on authority that Collard carried a snub-nosed revolver in his boot to augment the Smith & Wesson on his belt. But it was his nightstick, open and swinging like an extra dick from his hip, that was most used and feared. Collard Greens split skulls with that truncheon, and no man or woman, black or white, could find redress for his justice.

"What you want, Cilla?"

This from Mr. Charles. I just stood.

"Cat got your tongue, girl? What is it?"

"Need somethin' for Mr. Raymond's pump."

"Pump, hah."

Charles rolled to the balls of his feet tight and lithe as a gymnast. Disappeared inside his garage. I tried to avoid Sheriff Jackson's considered stare. Mr. Charles emerged after an eternity with a rust-red inner tube. Actually walked it over to me.

"Tell Mr. Raymond anytime, you hear?"

"Yes, sir."

"Whose girl are you anyway?"

"Corrie Jean's," the Sheriff answered.

I looked up, briefly, to meet the Sheriff's unbroken inspection. He chewed on something awfully hard for just a moment.

"Git your tube, girl. Git on."

I ran all the way back to Colored Town. The ground seemed to race beneath my feet. My heart was hammering in my chest by the time I reached Mr. Raymond's sweltering porch.

"Mr. Charles said anytime," I gasped.

I used to dream about a tub and endless quantities of water. All summer and through most of the school year, I was hotter than a June bride in a feather bed. The sun was hot. The sand was hot. I'd pad home from school or work sweating through my underthings. Then have to feed Mama her grits and cornbread sweating, comb her hair dripping sweat, sponge her off while blowing sweat off my brow.

Go to bed sweaty. Sleep in sweat. Wake up next morning rinded in salt. There wasn't enough Old Spice in the world to smother the perspiration of Colored Town and no water to bathe, and yet white folks complained because we smelled.

There were only two places where you could forget the heat, the sweat, and the slim feel of your wallet. One place was Mama's, a juke-joint way over in Suwannee County. The other place, and nearby, was Church. In both of these sanctuaries people looked forward to music. My mother played the piano at the Antioch Assembly of God, Fully Redeemed. And Corrie Jean could play *anything*—any tune, ditty, or composition. Religious, spiritual, popular, classical—it didn't matter. If Mama heard it, she could play it. "Plum perfect," folks used to marvel. "Note for note." That was Mama's gift, but it came at a terrible cost, for mother could not speak more than a dribble of anything that made any sense. She could not make sense of more than the most routine of outside stimuli. I cooked for her, cleaned her, and I'd always reply to whatever she said, however shocking.

"Fug me, fug me."

"Yes, Mama. Have some ice tea."

There was no doctor in Laureate to recognize autistic symptoms in any form, nor could we have afforded one if there was, and so Corrie Jean was labeled a retard, or, more kindly, "simple."

But there was nothing simple about her gift. Mother could play with absolute fidelity any music she heard, but she could not play anything unless it *was* first heard and that presented a problem because there just was not much music in Colored Town for Mama or anyone else to hear.

There had been no local AM broadcasts receivable in Lafayette County until 1962. FM transmission was twenty years away. White folks in Laureate mostly tuned in to WSM in Nashville—Hank Williams and Minnie Pearl. Maybe if the weather was right you could catch a scratch of Frank Sinatra or Doris Day. Even rock 'n' roll phenoms like Elvis Presley or Buddy Holly had to bounce off the ionosphere to reach northern Florida, and as for jazz? Or blues? I guarantee you there were GIs surviving the invasion of Normandy more familiar with Count Basie or Duke Ellington than any man, black or white, confined to radio in Lafayette County.

Mama was not bothered by that paucity of choice, of course. She didn't care what kind of music she heard or played. But the rest of us would rather be beat with sticks than listen to Minnie Pearl or The Grand Old Opry. We needed a wireless capable of receiving transmissions beamed far from Nashville. The sets available at the Western Auto were not adequate. Somebody said maybe Army surplus might have something we could afford. Somebody else said, no, we didn't have that kind of money, what we needed was a godsend, and you know—that's just about what we got.

Mr. Raymond was setting rat traps at Doc West's drugstore when he came across a radio, an old Philco '38–33, that must have been sitting unused for twenty years. The receiver operated from around 550 to 1700 kiloherz, which in those days were called kilo-cycles. It was called a tombstone set because its cheaply veneered cabinet was taller in dimension than wide. Thing must have had a half-dozen vacuum tubes; their filaments, glowing amber, looked like streetlights in a miniature city. It took a pair of six-volt batteries to juice the receiver's aging circuits, but once you did—Lord! You could pick up stations all the way to Canada.

If you had a good antenna.

Mr. Raymond could scrounge enough copper wire to ground the receiver onto the water pump on his front porch, but for the antenna he relied on the telephone company, cutting off what he needed from a spool of wire left untended behind the depot.

I got recruited to raise Mr. Raymond's aerial.

"Cilla, see can you shinny up that turkey oak, that fork up the top, thea. And take this here wire wit you."

Well, I could climb. And within a few minutes we folks in Colored Town had a dipole antenna mounted thirty feet high to the hardiest radio receiver in the county. Hardly a week went by after that feat that folks didn't gather 'round Mr. Raymond's overburdened porch, our water pulled, to snatch from the aether broadcasts origi-nating in New York or Cincinnati or Chicago. Sometimes we'd get Atlanta's WERD, though never for long, as that black-owned station was limited by statute to daylight transmission.

Mr. Raymond granted a much more generous license with his wireless receiver, allowing visitors to scan the vernier-styled tuner from afternoon to late night according to individual taste or caprice. Only two restrictions were imposed: First, we weren't allowed to tune in rock 'n' roll at any time; for that reason Chicago's WLS was generally off limits, as was Cincinnati's WSAI and New York's WABC. "Don't want ya'll messin'." Mr. Raymond's proscription needed no further specification. Secondly, you didn't get anywhere near Raymond's radio on Friday night, 'cause Friday was when Raymond and half the men in Colored Town gathered to hear the fights.

One Friday evening Mr. Raymond was trying to tune in a Chicago station for a Patterson fight, the classy older boxer defend-ing his heavyweight crown against the deadly hands of Sonny Liston.

The match was to be broadcast ringside from Comiskey Park, but Raymond could not get a signal off his tombstone receiver.

Nothing but static.

That's the way it is with amplitude-modulated transmission; sometimes it comes in clear as a bell, other times it's just noise. Mr. Raymond, normally a placid man, was having fits. Here he had looked forward all week to hearing his favorite boxer take on a reviled ex-convict in a crucially important match and all he could get was WSM and the Grand-Goddamned-Opry.

"Now, now," Preacher Dipps' corpulent wife tried to console him. "Forget about that radio. Have some ice cream."

Miss Mona had brought rock salt and a churn to make home-made ice cream. Somebody else had brought the vanilla extract, the peaches. Cream thick as molasses.

"Don't want no sweets," Mr. Raymond grumbled. "What I want is to hear my man fight."

Him bent over the radio, fooling with the tuner. Nothing in reward of that effort but the whistles and squawks of uncooperative carrier waves. Mr. Raymond seemed determined to sulk beside his Philco, but preacher's wife would not be denied.

"You need somethin' sweeten that temper," Mrs. Dipps declared, pulling a steel cylinder thick with ice cream from a wood keg filled with Morton's and melting ice.

"Nothing like a good churn."

She then grabbed the keg off the floor of the porch and dumped its salty slush to the ground beside Mr. Raymond's iron pump.

All of a sudden, clear as a bell—

"...Welcome to the Windy City where tonight Floyd Patterson is set to defend his title against... SOONNNNY JAAAAAIL-HOUSE LIIIISTON!!!"

Mr. Raymond jumped back like Moses from the burning bush.

"What happened? What'd you do?!"

"I din' do nuthin'." The preacher's wife was ironically skeptical of miracles in any guise.

"What'd you dump on my pump?"

"Just the leavings. Good Lord, Raymond, it ain't nuthin' but salt and water."

"Salt and water...? Why, sure!" Mr. Raymond slapped his lap with a meaty hand. "Miz Dipps, you can make ice cream at my house any Friday you likes."

The brine discarded from the churn's enclosing keg had, of course, boosted the effectiveness of the radio's antenna by improving its ground. From that night on, Mr. Raymond kept a blue-and-white bag of Morton's to sprinkle at the base of his pump and would not switch on his radio until buckets of water had soaked the sand around.

On fight nights boys were allowed to mingle in. These were my schoolmates, by 1963, juniors in high school. Johnny Boy Masters lived closest to me, only two houses down. Lonnie Hines, a shy, inarticulate boy, kept his desk behind mine at school. Lonnie had trouble reading, always getting things backwards. And then there were the class Romeos: Chicken Swamp Lewis and Pudding Reed, who were always feeling up whoever they could get next to. Chicken was lean as a chicken. Pudding had a large, strong frame, but never lost his baby fat. When he was little we called him Crisco, but then as he entered his teens somebody called him Pudding and that's what stuck. He was determined to earn himself a reputation. What they call a lady's man?

I'd be pumping water, or priming, bent over that long, iron handle and he'd come from behind.

"Keep you hands to youself, Puddin'."

"I ain' doin'!"

"Now, Pud'nin," Mr. Raymond would say. "Be a gennelmun."

I wasn't worried about the boys, but Mr. Lester was another matter. When I was little, Lester didn't pay me any attention at all; I was just the little bastard living with the retard. But coming through puberty I began to get heavy in the bosom. I was broadhipped, tall, with big shoulders. And that Brillo pad of hair. Lester started letting me know he was taking an interest.

"Ain' that girl growin'?" he'd say. Or, "Girl like that need a daddy. I be yo' daddy, Cilla? Yo' sugar daddy?"

He'd laugh, then, as if he didn't mean a thing by it. Nothing at all.

As I got older I began to get lots of looks from the men at Mr. Raymond's porch, until Friday nights became the occasion I most hated hauling water. Come fight-night I would dip my buckets and leave as quickly as I could manage. But the rest of the time the radio palliated my hated chore and I would crowd right up to that funereal cabinet with Mama where we could get in the mood with Glen Miller or Count Basie or Duke Ellington.

Those were magical nights, spent beside Mr. Raymond's receiver, inhaling the aroma of honeysuckle and magnolia trees, mixing that with the sizzle of lard and the smell of kerosene off somebody's stove. Mullet frying, or bacon, or chitlins. Somebody would bring out a mess of acre peas and we'd strip the shells as we listened to Perry Como catch a falling star or Fats Domino find a more intimate thrill. It was my first, best, and unsullied introduction to music.

There were limits, of course. I have mentioned that Mr. Raymond despised rock 'n' roll . And it was hard to make him linger on any of the classical pieces. One time I recall so well, he scrolled past WNYC and a kind of music completely unfamiliar to me. All I heard at first was a piano, then a swell of orchestra wove in, and then again the piano, taking up some theme. Then the orchestra. More instruments than I'd ever heard, some instruments I had *never* heard.

"What *is* that?" I can remember asking.

A structure as complex as jazz, but more deliberate and vastly instrumented with an execution so perfect, so powerful! My heart swelled up in my throat.

"Highbrow white." Mr. Raymond snorted and rolled the dial.

A solitary radio was our ear to the outside world, our censor not only for music, but for comedy, for drama. I heard "Gunsmoke" on the radio long before I ever saw it over cable-fed television. I heard Agnes Moorhead playing the bed-ridden Mrs. Stevenson in "Sorry, Wrong Number" while sipping iced-tea and gnawing sugarcane. I would tremble to broadcasts of "Green Lantern," or "The Shadow" (What Evil Lurks in the Hearts of Men?) And I have laughed at the antics of Kingfish and Sapphire never contemplating the insult implied in that black-face humor. But occasionally a jarring note would intrude. Once in a while, tuning in Orson Welles or Glenn Miller, Mr. Raymond would pause over a news broadcast. Politics would gain our attention for a fleeting moment. Kennedy and Nixon. The Communist Threat. Cuba. It may help in present crisis to recall that our country has been threatened before with nuclear weapons placed a boat ride from Key West.

And sometimes you'd hear other things, terrible reports from Birmingham or Mississippi. Confused claims involving water hoses and dogs. Lynchings. I remember my first inkling that trouble was close to home. It was early May. Mr. Raymond was tuned in to WSB in Atlanta and we caught the tail end of some local deejay reading off the UPI teletype.

"...reports today confirm that the Federal Bureau of Investigation has launched an investigation into yet another church burning, an alleged arson, that took place this past Sunday in Tallahassee...."

"Tallahassee? Is that *our* Tallahassee, Mr. Raymond?"

"Don' worry child."

He rolled the dial.

"It ain't nuthin' to do with Colored Town."

The several aromas of supper hung palpably in the air as I left Mr. Raymond's that evening. I was alone and would therefore have to haul the water back home by myself, but I didn't mind. I had recently taken (by which I mean stolen) a pull-wagon from behind the grocery store. A Radio Flyer, appropriately. I figured whoever left a good wagon unattended must not need it very much. It was ideal for hauling water. Without the wagon I doubt I would have taken the short detour which took me past the railroad station.

It was about ten o'clock. A full moon beamed silver through a pair of dogwoods that, I believe I have mentioned, bent toward each other like old ladies kissing to form a white-blossomed arbor over the dock where the L.O.P. & G dieseled to a noisy stop.

Railroads meant escape, I knew that. But for me the passenger car and the locomotive meant escape *to* some place not even imagined. For Joe Billy it would mean escape from a place all too familiar.

I liked to watch the people getting off, observe their appearance, their behavior, and then invent a story for them. She's got a baby, running from her rich mama to see some buck in Madison County. He's an insurance salesman. A politician, a movie star. You can be anything once you ride those gleaming rails.

So that's what I was doing that night, just making up stories, standing there with my water and wagon, observing a black porter helping some white lady with a portmanteau that I imagined held a million dollars. Couple of black men got off next, in suits. They couldn't have been local, but before I had a chance to make something up for that odd pair, Joe Billy bounded off the train.

I do mean bounded. Boy had springs in his legs. Those tight jeans. Jar of grease in his hair. A high forehead and narrow eyes. I had never seen Sammy Davis Jr. at that point in my life or my fantasies would have leaped to that suggestion on the spot.

He had a cardboard suitcase in one hand and a guitar case in the other. He saw me looking.

Time to leave. I leaned on my wagon.

"Hey, baby."

Time to leave for *sure*.

"Aw, honey, come on. Wait up."

I didn't wait up. But I have to admit I didn't make a big effort to outrun him. What chance would I have had, anyway, in sand ruts with a toy wagon and ten gallons of water?

"I don't know you," I said when he caught up. Before he could say a thing.

"That's fine by me, I ain't looking for recognition."

"Good, then why don't you just get you narrow ass back on that train and move on."

"I'm here to see relatives."

Relatives. Kinfolk? That was different.

"You got kin here?"

"Hatchers", he replied. "Lester Hatcher."

"That's Mr. Raymond's brother."

"Half-brother," Joe Billy corrected, which was good because it gave me confidence he really was connected, in some miraculous way, to Colored Town.

I stopped pulling my water.

"My name Cilla Handsom. My mama's Corrie Jean and before you hear stories my daddy got killed in one o' them wars. Now, I'm gon' be nice to you. See how long it take you to make fun of me."

"I ain' made no fun, sister."

"I ain' you sister. Now, Mr. Raymond, he's real nice. Lester is a bad man. A whorehoppin', straight-razor totin' son of a bitch. You can tell him I said so."

"I find his house I will."

"Good. Maybe keep his hands off my behind."

"How I find it?"

"My behind?"

"The house. Mr. Lester's house."

"House don' belong to Lester. Belong to Mr. Raymond, who let his half-ass brother live there out of the kindness of his large heart and let us get his water, too, and listen to his radio. You come here to harm Mr. Raymond?"

"No, ma'am," he declared, suddenly formal.

"Thass good. Cause they ain't but about two nice people in Colored Town and if somethin' happen to Mr. Raymond, 'bout half of them be gone."

"I endeavor to be careful. Now, please, ma'am? Where he live?"

"Go past the station," I pointed unnecessarily. "First road to the right, you take it, down three, four houses. Don' count Mr. Leon's smokehouse as a house. Only houses with porches count as houses—"

"Houses with porches."

"Thass right. Or either count Mr. Leon's smokehouse, which ain' no house, really, but count it anyway, you go down *five* houses and right there on the right hand side is Mr. Raymond's."

"What makes his house different than any of these others?"

"Got a pump by the front porch. You hurry they be a radio there, too. But don' go tell Mr. Raymond what to play on his radio. He nice, but he particular."

"'Preciate that warning."

"You welcome."

With that I leaned back into my chore, the wagon's hard, narrow tires pulling sand from the unlighted street.

"Whass your name again?"

He called to my back.

"Cilla." Even though my heart fluttered I did not turn my head. "Priscilla, really. Priscilla Handsom."

"You are definitely handsome, Miss Priscilla. And nice to boot."

My ears burned. My heart started jumpin'. The load I lugged seemed suddenly lighter in my hand. I worked up the courage to risk a reply. I stopped hauling my load and actually turned around with all intention to graciously respond to the first complement I could ever remember receiving in my life—

He was gone. Vanished.

"All aboard!"

Did he get back on the train? Lord, did I say something to drive that boy away?!

"All aboooooard!"

Then I saw him, beneath that wanton moon, angling across the street in the direction of Mr. Raymond's home. So it was true. He was here. He was *staying* here! I sloshed water all the way home that night. Lay straight as a ruler in my cot for I don't know how long. Mama there beside me on her mattress on the floor. I used to wonder what Mama dreamed, but that night I had better things to do. I had dreams of my own. Wonderful railroad dreams. I dreamed of a foreign traveler, a man of mystery who pauses on a dangerous journey, taken with a handsome princess who remains hidden, waiting for him to claim her from her mansion deep in the heart of Colored Town. I dreamed deeply, wafted to Neverland on a concatenation of honeysuckle and magnolia. And dogwood.

Chapter three

"Town Gives Up Plans to Enlarge
Limits."—*The Clarion*

I f you were a white man in the sixties, in Laureate, you chewed
your fat at Monk Folsom's Auto Repair. Pretending concern over a
brake job or the adjustment of your carburetor, you'd sink into a
bench-seat salvaged from some Plymouth or Studebaker, and in time
you'd know everything going on in the county.

Who was favored. Who wasn't. What it was going to cost.

The Lord only can divine how Monk's became the ground for
nutcutting in Lafayette County. His was certainly not a comfortable
place. The shop itself was an open bay facing the world and Highway 27. No air-conditioning, just a couple of industrial fans droning
inside an unshaded metal shed that rusted in a pasture bordering the
white folks' school.

Personality could not have been the draw; Monk Folsom had
the charisma of celery. About the same build as celery, too, long and
slender and translucent. There was room for at least three fingers
between his jeans and his waist. Charles Putnal used to say Monk
was so skinny you could shine a light on his back and watch his heart

beat. That exaggeration was about the norm for the discussions that pattered back and forth in Folsom's shop.

But Monk had two talents not common anywhere. First of all, even Charles declared that Monk was truly a genius with anything mechanical. Mr. Raymond said if you gave Monk a pair of pliers he'd fix Cape Canaveral. I did not at the time know what Cape Canaveral was, but I gathered it must be a challenge for pliers.

The second, rare quality that Monk possessed was that he *never* repeated anything that he heard. Never. You could tell the man you'd thrown a rod, lost a transmission and by the way you'd just killed your wife and fed her to the hogs and Monk would carry it all to the grave. He was like those eunuchs who watched over Persian satraps, their tongues cut out along with their balls.

However originated, a small court gathered virtually every morning in Folsom's steamy shop. You'd see farmers and tradesmen. Ben Wilburn, the high-strung principal of Laureate's thoroughly segregated school, was a regular at Monk's. And so was State Representative Latrelle Putnal. Mr. Latrelle was Mr. Charles Putnal's uncle, but you never saw Latrelle in his nephew's place. Not even to buy gas. But Latrelle Putnal was an habitué at Monk's, the archetype of a pussel-gutted and completely unreliable politician, that forehead bulging out from his face like an overhang on some fleshy cliff. Always had himself a Rotary pin stuck into a tie stained with gravy. Across from Representative Putnal you'd frequently see Sheriff Jackson, rawboned and hard and, unlike nearly anybody else in Monk's shop, gainfully employed. That shock of white hair templing along his head. But even with his badge and revolver Collard was not the majordomo in attendance.

There is always a pecking order in any community and in Lafayette County even the sheriff could not top Garner Hewitt.

Garner was a wealthy man, properly diversified. He'd got a half-million dollars from the government *not* to milk his cows. He got fifty or sixty thousand dollars in federal subsidies every year for tobacco. And the county had just given him, cost-free, enough seedlings to plant three hundred acres of slash pine on pastureland that the government was already paying him not to use. 'Course, Garner would be the first to tell you he hated welfare.

He was a large man, but not hard, not like the sheriff. He dressed in seersucker slacks that flapped around wingtip shoes. A florid complexion. Receding hairline. A strawberry-sized birthmark below one eye gave the constant impression that Garner had just emerged from a fistfight, but anybody knowing the man understood that fists were not among Mr. Hewitt's chosen weapons. Not his own, that is.

He had two sons. Cody, a junior at Laureate High School and Garner's youngest boy, could have hailed from Southern California. Cody was a teenager blessed with unblemished skin and a wonderful, well-toned physique. Blue eyes. Mop of hair that was white without the tease of peroxide. J.T. Hewitt was Cody's older brother, at twenty-six Garner's eldest son. J.T. was six feet six inches tall and had himself a reputation separate from the basketball court. Folks said that Garner Hewitt's oldest boy was beating on grown men before he'd even turned seventeen. For sure J.T. was a wifebeater. That is, before she left him. J.T. beat his help, too. Beat his damn dog. He wore cowboy shirts with the sleeves rolled up, an outsized Jimmy Dean. And J.T. had a trademark belt he was fond of wearing, ordered it from a catalog, a cowhide girdle adorned with the silver-embossed likeness of a rattlesnake. The buckle's tongue was also the serpent's.

About the only man in the county J.T. Hewitt didn't intimidate was Sheriff Jackson.

The alliance between the Hewitt family and the sheriff was well known and mutually beneficial. Garner Hewitt made it clear that Sheriff Jackson was his choice for Sheriff of Lafayette County. More than one man who had voiced interest in running against Collard found his tires sliced or his birddog poisoned. J.T. Hewitt was his daddy's enforcer. The quid pro quo, naturally, was that Sheriff Jackson looked out for Garner and his boys. There were thirteen complaints of assault directed at Garner's oldest son in one four-year period and not one of 'em got past Collard's desk.

'Course when it comes to politics muscle isn't much good without money. Fortunately for Garner Hewitt and for Sheriff Jackson, Lafayette County was a place where a modest investment could take you a long way. Mr. Hewitt used to brag that he'd got a man's vote for as little as a fifth of whiskey. Other times you might have to pick up a house payment, or buy a farmer his fertilizer. Garner bankrolled Collard in each of his three successful campaigns, sometimes buying off whole families. We are speaking of white families, of course. Negroes could not vote.

Garner Hewitt gave freely to his freckled electorate, yes, he did, but what he gave with one hand he could take with the other. A man might get a badly needed loan from Miss Pearl at the bank only to have it canceled when he made the mistake of telling his neighbors he was considering a change in his vote.

Garner owned Sheriff Collard Jackson just as surely as he owned his truck, his farm, and, before the government paid him off, his dairy. Mr. Hewitt also owned the Clerk of Court, the Supervisor of Elections, half the School Board, and the Tax Assessor. Everybody knew this, of course. However, alliances based on avarice and intimidation are never stable. A strain inconsequential to an even-handed relationship can become intolerable when raised between a lord and his vassal and Garner Hewitt had of late been pretty heavy-handed in reminding whoever was listening that *he* was the kingmaker in Lafayette County.

"No man comes to lasting prosperity except by me." Garner loved to bastardize Scripture. And then he added, "That includes Sheriff 'Collard Greens' Jackson."

It didn't matter that Garner was drunk in deer camp with his entourage when he made that statement, and it did not help that the sheriff found a fresh hind of venison waiting for him in the Safe-Way locker afterwards. The damage was done. Garner had slighted his servant publicly.

In 1963, Collard Jackson was only a year away from re-election. Those years there'd be a primary in the spring and, if need be, a runoff in November. Sheriff Jackson was already gearing up for the run in '64 that would give him his fourth term in office. He had no illusions about how he'd won his first three elections. He knew that his tenure in office had not been gained because of the electorate's affection. Collard Jackson was a practical man; he knew which side of his bread was buttered and he knew who buttered it. But Garner

Hewitt had jammed a spear into the sheriff's side. Garner had tossed his insult spitefully, unnecessarily, and before some of the very men loitering now in Monk Folsom's shop, and Sheriff Jackson was not about to let it stand.

The sheriff bided his time, but when the opportunity came, he took advantage, and I was there to see it. I was with Mama in the back of Mr. Frank Thistle's truck. Mr. Frank owned the nursery where Mama and I worked. He was stopping by Monk's for the ostensible purpose of settling a debt over a brake job or change of oil or some other weighty matter. As we pulled up to the shop I saw, I don't know, at least twenty men, all seated on the rigged lounges of car seats or stools of one kind or another. There were cars and trucks stacked at odd angles in various states of disrepair. Monk was working on an engine slung like a slaughtered hog in a system of hoists and pulleys.

Mama and I naturally remained on the hard bed of Mr. Frank's pickup, as invisible as bartenders to the white men gathered in the open bay of Monk's shop. We were huddled there, knees to our chests, when Sheriff Collard Jackson came rolling up in that Dodge cruiser, the big hoop antenna waving back and forth like a fishing pole. The cop-car shifted weight as Collard got out; Mama kind of stiffened up as he strolled past.

"Fug me, fug me!"

"Mama, hush."

Sheriff didn't act like he noticed. Just passed a hand along the rim of his Stetson and stepped into the open bay of Monk's shop. This was in May, a good six months since Garner Hewitt had shot his mouth off to his hunting buddies regarding Collard's subordinate status. What gave Collard his opportunity was that Cody Hewitt, Garner's unblemished seventeen-year old son, had got himself pulled over by the sheriff in Taylor County. Seems the bright-yellow road signs posted along the S-curves leading to Perry were just too much temptation for the young marksman. Cody got through half a box of birdshot before the county sheriff pulled him over.

But, after all, Collard Jackson got along famously with Taylor County's sheriff. Rumor was that the two men shared a run to Lake

City twice a year for whores and whiskey. Hard to see how you could get much closer than that. So Garner Hewitt had every reason to expect that Sheriff Jackson would make sure the charges filed against his son Cody would be dropped.

Collard wouldn't do it. And not only did the sheriff refuse to use any influence in Taylor County for Cody's benefit, Collard also made damn sure that he informed the boy's daddy of that fact right in front of God and everybody attending the morning roll call at Monk Folsom's Auto Repair.

"What's that you sayin'?" At first Mr. Hewitt could not comprehend, or did not want to comprehend, what everybody else who was present understood perfectly.

"Cain't help with that business with Cody, Garner. Just out of my hands is all."

"Out of your hands? The hell you mean?"

"About what I said, I reckon."

All of a sudden there wasn't a wrench being turned. Every man in the shop was looking at his feet. Mr. Hewitt kept a pleasant smile plastered across his dampened face. "Maybe we need to talk in private."

"Private, public. Won't change anything."

I saw the sheriff rest a gnarly hand on the knob of his nightstick. Garner Hewitt saw it, too.

"You eat some beans or somethin' this mawning, Collard?"

"Greens more likely," somebody quipped, but there was nobody laughing.

"Best advice I can give you, Garner, is tell your boy he wants to shoot signs, go down to Hatch Bend or someplace I can keep an eye on him."

"Big difference between 'can't' and 'won't', sheriff. We need to be clear."

"Fair enough," Collard allowed. "How 'bout this? I wouldn't do it even if I could."

J.T. Hewitt shuffled past his daddy like a mannequin jerked on a stiff string. Six and a half feet of mean.

"You don't wanta come over here, son," and there was not a tremor in Collard's voice.

"Gentlemen, let's settle down, now. 'Fore somebody gets their feelings hurt." State Representative Putnal twisting his Rotary pin in his tie.

"Monk," Mr. Hewitt's voice was flat. "You 'bout finished with my truck?"

"She's ready to roll."

"I 'spect I better move along." Garner Hewitt hauled his loose weight up from the rude couch. "Come on, J.T. Let's see how them pines is going in."

"Judge Blackmond'll be hearing the case," Collard remarked as Mr. Hewitt and his tree-sized son stalked off. "You get Cody a good lawyer, first offense, he oughta do all right."

"I won't forget your help, Sheriff," Garner snarled, and shoved his firstborn aside as he waddled out the shop's chain-raised door.

Collard would have been within his rights to ticket Garner the way he squalled his vehicle out onto the street. Brand new Goodyears burning rubber all the way through the town's one red light.

Principal Wilburn cleared his throat. "Nice looking truck."

"It is, it is." Latrelle Putnal tried to encourage the educator's attempt to diffuse the recent tension.

"What did Garner bring it in for, Monk?"

"Air condition. Bad compressor."

"I swear," Wilburn offered lamely. "Man's better off raising down a window."

"He is, he is." Latrelle would second any motion. "Still. It's a good-looking vehicle."

I turned from my own vantage point to look down the street. It *was* an awful nice vehicle, a Ford F-100 waxed up and red. A rebel flag displayed prominently from the cab's rear window, right in front of the gun rack.

"I don't like the hubs," Collard declared, and on that I had to agree.

Spinner hubcaps just do not look right on a pickup.

Mama and I worked at Mr. Thistle's nursery that Saturday at the rooting beds. I spent the whole day sticking cuttings of elaeagnus into a damp bed of peat and loamy soil, thinking about nothing but Joe Billy.

"You definitely are handsome, Miss Priscilla."

Nobody had ever called me handsome. Or *nice*, for that matter. I began to rehearse the details of his appearance. Processed hair, greased back. Narrow head, high forehead. Deep, piercing eyes. Could he play the guitar, I wondered? When would I see him? Or where?! Would it be at school? I didn't know. He could have been twenty years old, for all I could tell, impressed as I was by Joe Billy's sophistication. Even a sixteen year-old could drop out of school if he wanted.

Joe Billy said he was going to Lester's. Did that mean Lester was expecting him? Or Mr. Raymond? Was Joe Billy just visiting, or would he be staying with the two old bachelors? I had to find out. Could not *wait* to find out.

It was the first time in a long time, I can tell you, that I looked forward to hauling water.

Had to get home, first. Might as well tell you about my house, I guess. And my dog. The house, first. Don't know who built it, or when. We didn't rent it. We didn't exactly own it, either. Whatever claim we enjoyed was established I suppose in usufruct. It was identical to almost every other residence in Colored Town. A shack and porch were fashioned of rough cut cypress and pine, mounted a yard high on loblolly stumps above a grassless yard frequently runneled by rain. A tin roof. There were only two rooms inside and no ceiling, just a span of rough, pine eaves. A kerosene lantern hanged on the tenacula of a ten-penny nail driven through one of those timbers. I was so tall, even at seventeen, that my head would brush its metal base.

Almost no furniture. A cot for me and an unsheeted mattress where mother slept. Grandma had a real bed and a small chest of drawers in the other room, across from the kitchen. Planks stretched between cement blocks provided more than ample shelving. We had two deerhide chairs that doubled for use in the kitchen or on the porch. We had a sink and slop bucket and out back was the privy shared each morning with a rat snake big as your arm.

We didn't have anything like a lawn, only white folks spend that kind of money. But we had dogwood trees, two beautiful dogwoods. And crowding all around were riots of plant life native to northern Florida. There was French Mulberry, and Lady Lupine with its white shaggy hairs. We had bread-straw and scorpion-tale and frog-fruit. Goldenrod and dog fennel. Honeysuckle, of course. A wild and completely untamed tangle of vines and stems and blossoms presented an ever changing landscape for our back porch view. There was always something to catch your eye and what you didn't see you would surely smell.

The atmosphere between the Gulf of Mexico and the Suwannee River, always heavy with moisture, was a natural caravan for the transport of odor. Mornings in May could be particularly redolent, a honeysuckle's sweet aroma competing with pennyroyal or wisteria. Can you identity the smell of carrots that is Queen Anne's Lace? Add to that the smell of damp earth. Of decaying wood.

Coming home from work that evening I could smell a country ham, slaughtered locally, smoked and cured with plenty of fat hanging on the rind. Cooking somewhere.

Not at our house. Ours was a supper of grits and red-eye gravy. Milk was hard to keep without an icebox so we usually drank coffee or sometimes a homemade tea. The Pennyroyal makes a nicely minted tea and normally I would put off hauling water to sip from a Ball jar of grandma's homemade. Not that evening. That evening I was eager to be off.

"They a house on fire?"

"We need water," I sailed off the porch. "HARD ON!"

You could hear him coming, claws scratch-scratch-scratching on the pine planked floor. Seconds later a bull-chested mutt halfway between a bulldog and a Republican shot out my screenless window.

"Well, come on."

He turned his head askew, as if I had slapped his nose and turned him sideways.

"We're gone to GET WATER. WATER, Hard On."

'Hard On' was not so much a sobriquet as a truncation of an earlier name. While still a puppy and nameless, Puddin' Reed's little sister poured some honey in my dog's starboard ear. I wasn't there to see it happen, but later that night I could see my animal worrying that ear, worrying and worrying it.

I thought maybe he was hungry so I soaked some cornbread in clabber and gave it to him. Put him in a box to sleep. Middle of the night that puppy starts to yell. Started raising hell. So I went over to see what was the fuss and that's when I saw the ants. They were in his ear. In and out of his ear, actually. They had smelled the honey and burrowed clear down inside the poor thing's inner ear.

I got grandma and we washed out the ear with hydrogen per-oxide. Got the honey out with the ants but the ear got infected any-way. Pretty soon the poor mutt was falling down like a drunk. He could not stand erect. Couldn't look straight at anything, either; he'd try and you could see his eyes jerk horizontally, fast forward, slow back, in the presentation distinctive of nystagmus. Within a day or two those symptoms passed. My dog survived, but lost his hearing on the side of the infected ear. Hence the constant inclination of his puzzled snout.

"Got a name for him, at least," Grandma declared after that trial. "We'll call him Hard of Hearing."

But Hard of Hearing got to be a mouthful when you were in a hurry. It was only a matter of time before Puddin' or Chickenswamp or somebody came up with "Hard On."

"Where you at, Hard On? Whutchu doin', Hard On?"

That's how my dog got his name. But there was only one name interested me that evening; I just hoped he would be at his newly adopted home.

"Be back inna while," I called out, and hauled the Red Flyer with its unfilled pails toward Mr. Raymond's. I arrived with my dog earlier than usual. I didn't see Joe Billy. Didn't see Lester for that mat-ter, which normally would have been a blessing. I could have asked Mr. Raymond where his new boarder was keeping himself, but there were people all around and if anybody heard me asking after a boy I'd never hear the end of it.

"Cilla, you sweet on somebody?"

"Who you sweet on, Cilla?"

"Hey, but is they sweet on *you*?"

So I didn't say anything. I waited for Sunday and looked in vain for Joe Billy to attend church. I was slow giving mother her prompts that morning, which earned me a stern admonition from Preacher, but I didn't care. I went back to Mr. Raymond's porch again that evening with my Radio Flyer wagon and pails, and this time found Lester ruling the porch from his rocking chair. Still no sign of Joe Billy. Where was he? Gone? Dead? There were perhaps half a dozen women still milling around but I *had* to know. Finally my turn came to handle the pump.

"Hello, Sugar Baby."

"Mr. Lester." I pulled my water. "How you doin'?"

That was a mistake because I *never* inquired after Lester's health.

"I'm steady by jerks," he replied after a moment. "How 'bout you?"

"I'm fine," I said. "Hope I gave good directions to your visitor."

"Visitor?"

"I believe so. New fellah? Came in on the railroad? Said he was kin to you."

"Awww…" Lester settled back in his hickory rocker. "He's just dog kin."

"Stayin' with you and Mr. Raymond?"

Lester scowled. "I tole' him he can sleep on the back porch 'till he get his own place."

So he *was* staying. I kept my eyes on the pump.

"Well, that's good of ya'll, Mr. Lester. That's a help, surely."

"Help to *him*," Lester grunted, and I went home heartened by his unwilling intelligence but wondering whether it was much help. After all, there were only two places I could expect to regularly see

Joe Billy—at work or at school. So unless Joe Billy developed a sudden urge to either raise shrubbery or join the junior class our paths would not cross on any kind of predictable basis.

I was telling myself all the way home that I should not be disappointed. I had got my hopes up on the basis of a fairytale and should have known better.

"Come on, Hard On."

I got home wanting to cry, but I didn't have time. Grandma was pacing on the porch.

"Your mama. Havin' one o' her fits."

You could never tell when it would happen, or why. Some unseen agent or influence would set her off. The only exorcism we ever tried made things worse.

"Put up the water," I said, and went inside.

She was in our bedroom, on the mattress on the floor. Grandma hung back, wringing her shift.

"I too old for this chore!"

"I've got her, grandma."

"Raise a chile, you get ole, she suppose to take kere o' *you*!"

"I said I got her."

"Me here an ole woman raisin' *two* chirren, Lawd!"

"Go on, grandma. There's water, make some tea. I'll take care of Mama."

Corrie Jean was on the mattress on all-fours, in estrus. Hunching like a dog. When Mama was like that you had to be careful. It was like she was in a waking nightmare, or something, and if you came in on her like that and you touched her in any way, she was likely to turn on you, striking out with hands that, unless at a piano, were curled like talons.

"FUG ME, FUG ME!"

"Mama, it's Cilla."

"FUG ME FUG ME!!"

"Mama, Cilla's here. Cilla's right here."

I took up a pillow and slowly crouched so she could see me.

"Remember our song, Mama?"

She didn't respond.

"Our song, Mama. Remember?"

"Song…"

She was panting like a bitch in heat.

"Song…"

"It's *me*, Mama. Cilla. Remember our song?"

"Song, song," she sing-songed in reply.

"Sing with me, Mama. Mama? Sing. Come on, now—'Double your pleasure'…Come on, now…'Double your pleasure…'"

"Doubleyourfun," mother's head bobbed recognition.

"That's right," I encouraged. "Let's sing it together, Mama. Mama and Cilla singing."

She raised her head.

"Sing Cilla?"

"Sure, Mama. 'Double your pleasure/Double your fun/With DoubleMint, DoubleMint, DoubleMint Gum…'"

Her head bobbed in time.

"Double your pleasure, Double your fun…"

"That's right, Mama. 'With DoubleMint, DoubleMint, DoubleMint Gum…'"

Double your pleasure. Double your fun. Over and over. It didn't always work. I still don't know exactly why it *ever* worked. But something about that simple jingle for chewing gum was, on merciful occasion, a magical mantra for my mother.

We sang it over and over. Sang it till the words slurred in my mouth. But I could feel her begin to relax. See the taloned hands uncurl. Her eyes, wide with some terror, were low in their lids. Now I could coax her off her hands and knees.

"Here, Mama."

I got her to sit. I decided it wasn't worth the effort to get her into night-things. She'd just have to sleep in her clothes.

But now, I knew we would be fine. Once I got her this far, I could put down the pillow, hold her to me. Put her back to me. Her head next to my own. I could feel my mother's warmth on my new and heavy breasts. She would relax, then. Yes, I could feel her muscles go loose and long. And then a long, melancholy sigh. We just sat there, rocking back and forth.

Once, long ago, after a fit much like this one, she became lucid. It wasn't for long. Just moments, really.

"Cilla!"

I was so startled, I had almost dropped her.

"Mama? Is that you?"

"Isn't it bedtime, baby?"

"Yes, Mama. Yes, it is!"

"Then you best get to sleep."

There were only a handful of occasions in my life where mother ever directly addressed me, or even seemed to recognize me. Those moments always came when I was worst prepared to receive them. When I was tired. When I was bone-weary and unresponsive, they came. With no warning or preamble. Out of the blue.

I hadn't known what to do. What to say. I didn't know how long we had. I just held her close to me. Close!

"Why don' you sleep with mama, baby?" she said. Perfectly lucid.

"Oh, Mama! Can I?"

"Jussss tonight," she said, and then the awful affliction returned. A glaze passed over my mother's eyes. She lay slack as burlap once more in my arms and had not spoken to me since.

She was calm, now. Whatever it was that triggered the awful, recurring terror had run its course. I kissed Corrie Jean on lips wet with drool.

"Night night, Mama."

A small chore, then, to straighten her legs on the mattress, put the pillow, caseless, beneath her head. Smooth her hair. She had wonderful hair, have I mentioned? Soft, not like mine. I then pulled the one sheet over my mama before crawling into my own sheetless bed. I was hungry and had not cleaned myself and I was dead, weary, tired, but I could not expect a restful night's sleep. Mama would wake once, at least, I knew, before the rooster crowed. Maybe twice. And I would comfort her.

There would be no railroad dreams this evening.

Chapter four

"Hog Cholera Alert for County"—*The Clarion*

M y country 'tis of thee, sweet land of liberty. Of thee I sing," flowed in a beautifully chalked hand across Miss Chandler's blackboard. Miss Eunice Chandler was my teacher at Kerbo School, Colored Town's only schoolhouse. Mr. Raymond said the cypress timbers in those rooms were a hundred years old, and had been milled by a black man at Fort McKoon. I don't know about that. I had visited Fort McKoon, that flinty shelf stretching across the Suwannee and saw no sign of a sawmill. But I could see that my schoolhouse was very old, its beams notched Roman fashion and stacked in walls to rival Fort Ticonderoga. Kerbo School was built to last, but with no conveniences. No electricity. No restrooms. Even the blackboards were add-ons.

Grades one through twelve matriculated two grades to a room. Miss Chandler started her junior and senior class most every morning with something related to language or reading, usually something learned rote and drilled in class. It almost always started on the board.

"Miss Priscilla, are you with us?"

"Yes, Miss Chandler."

I was not. I was thinking about the boy at the train depot.

"I'd appreciate your interest."

"Yes, ma'am."

That was just like Miss Chandler, to ask. Now if it was the school principal, Miss Hattie, teaching there wouldn't be any asking. You didn't inspect your thoughts in Miss Hattie's class, or doze off, or betray any hint of inattention or fatigue, else that old sparrow of a woman would wrap a phone book 'round your head. Miss Chandler was as big as Miss Hattie was tiny. She was built heavy in the haunches, like a bear. Her jowls hung with flesh, like a basset hound. Her eyebrows were thick and not level on her forehead. Her nostrils flared wide as a heifer's.

"Ugly done got hisself a name, boys," Pudding said when first he saw Miss Chandler.

But of course neither Pudding, or anyone else, said anything about Miss Chandler's face *to* her face.

"Miss Cilla," she was surprisingly light on her feet for such a big woman.

"Yes, ma'am," I roused myself.

"To the board, please."

I didn't want to get up. I was in my period and had no napkins. I had no rags, either. The sanitary napkins I'd slipped inside my shirt at Mr. Land's SafeWay were so much easier I'd got used to them and forgot to boil rags and so now I'd run out all I had were some strips of linen and moss. I was petrified I would shame myself. That somebody would see.

"I have to get up, Miss Chandler?"

She took one look.

"You may remain seated, Miss Cilla."

"Yes, ma'am," I sighed relief.

"Let's all direct our attention to the board, please. 'My Country Tis Of Thee.' Cilla, why don't you start with 'Of thee I sing.'"

"Yes, ma'am."

"First off, is this a sentence or a phrase?"

"It's a sentence. Just like 'I sing of thee'."

"Good. So the word 'sing' is what part of speech?"

"Must be a verb."

"That's correct. Does it take an object?"

"No, ma'am."

"Which makes it?"

"Intransitive."

"Right again. And as a verb it has no person, case, number or gender. What about the 'I' in this sentence, Mr. Reed?"

"I's tired," Pudding cracked, and Chicken Swamp guffawed.

"Maybe you need to run see Miss Hattie. See if she can wake you up."

"No, ma'am."

Pudding was suddenly straight in his desk.

"All right, then." Miss Chandler put us to work parsing sentences and turned her attention to the seniors sitting an arm's length away.

Juniors and seniors and everyone else did most of our work at our desks, in class, because Kerbo had no textbooks for students to take home. If I had homework in mathematics, I had to copy the problems at school. And how can you study history or biology, or write a report, without books and without a library? What do you do?

We drilled. We memorized. We improvised. And this was not altogether a bad thing. Miss Hattie, to give her credit, forced us early to commit works of literature to memory. I had not even held a complete novel in my hand by my junior year, but I could recognize long passages from *Pilgrim's Progress*, or *The Deerslayer* or *Huckleberry Finn*. I could recite entire poems by Longfellow, "Under a spreading chestnut tree the village smithy stands...." Or from Tennyson's *Ulysses*:

> ...for my purpose holds
> To sail beyond the sunset, and the baths
> Of all the western stars, until I die.

We took the same approach to every subject, memorizing multiplication tables, for instance, names of states, presidents. By my junior year I could figure interest on any bank loan, could compute the area under a triangle or the volume of a cone. The New England states came as trippingly to the tongue as Genesis, Exodus, Leviticus, Numbers and Deuteronomy.

The law of the land had long held that segregated schools were inherently unequal, which was undoubtedly true, but as a junior in high school I had little sense of that deficit. You don't miss Bunsen burners in a place where there is no science lab, electricity, or indoor plumbing. The only thing I coveted from the white school was their piano. Kerbo had no piano, or any other instrument. I used to imagine what it would be like to come in at noon or recess and just sit down with a sheet of music at a piano, all by yourself. Play anything you like.

Mr. Raymond said the courts were trying to shut down Kerbo School. "Alla colored children gone be sent to the white school," he told us, with unconcealed disapproval. But Mr. Raymond also talked about hurricanes and communists and all sorts of things and nothing ever happened. Which was fine by me. I had no great urge to leave my neighborhood school. But then one morning Shirley Lee Lewis had caught me just as Miss Hattie was ringing us in off the playground.

"You know Miss Chandler going over to the white school?"

"Miss Chandler? Who tole you that?"

"Daddy say. Say in the paper the court gonna make us all go over."

"But Shirley Lee, don' white folks run the courts?"

"Surely."

"Then, girl, rest assured we ain' gone nowhere."

There were only about a hundred children at Kerbo, from the very first grades through seniors in high school. Why couldn't we just stay where we were? Why couldn't we remain in our own, lamplit rooms? With our own teachers?

"Miss Chandler," I burst out.

I had interrupted her but Miss Chandler remained composed. She just turned that big head like an owl until my face was all in hers.

"Why they want to shut down our school?"

A dead quiet ran through the classroom and I could tell I was not the only one who had heard the news. Miss Chandler folded the book she was holding in her lap.

"A lot of very powerful people don't want our school shut down at all."

"Then we can stay?"

"It's not settled," Miss Chandler replied. "And it won't affect our seniors. But you juniors need to prepare for the possibility of integration."

"Innagration?"

"When black students and whites share a school it's integrated."

"They gonna mix us up? Why?"

"You deserve a better education than you can get here," Miss Chandler answered simply. "You need to move on."

"I don't want to move on."

"That's understandable. Kerbo is familiar to you, Cilla. Familiar to all of you. I've heard Reverend Dipps remark that the Devil's been so long in Hell he's got comfortable. Even Hell can get familiar. But there are opportunities away from here, away from Laureate, that will pass you by if you stay comfortable."

The class fell silent. I could see Miss Chandler picking her words very carefully.

"Did you know that President Roosevelt built the school in Laureate? Yes, he did. He built it with tax money collected from everybody, black and white. So you remember it's not *their* school over yonder. It's not *theirs*. It's *our* school.

"Now, I'm glad you brought this up, Miss Cilla. And come Civics class we can visit here again. But remember what the Good Book says—leave the day's troubles unto itself."

You couldn't argue with the Good Book, I supposed. Nor Miss Chandler.

But I wondered what I would do in the white folks' school if I was bleeding and had no napkins? Would they let me go out at noon beneath some water oak and gather moss for myself? Would they let me cut strips of gingham from my dress for ties? To bundle a napkin?

Come lunchtime Pudding and Chicken Swamp had every boy on the yard recruited for baseball. The boys had no field, of course, no bats or gloves or balls, but that circumstance did not seem to dampen their enthusiasm. A broomstick served for a bat. You didn't need a glove, everybody played barehanded. Balls were trickier. What was required was something roughly spherical, tough and resilient. The heads of dolls were favored. Baby dolls, in particular, being larger, were preferred. Those bloated white faces. Sightless eyes. The boys would rip the head off a doll, pull the hair, and go to town. Chicken Swamp was famous for the curve he could put on one of these improvised baseballs. He was out there, now, fondling the stitches of his jerry-rigged ball, getting ready to deliver a blue-eyed strike.

Pudding was at bat, his slender slugger weaving like a cobra.

"Come own, Pudding! Put one outta here!"

Younger children cheered their elders about a makeshift diamond. Bare feet running to bases of burlap sacks.

"Come own!" Pudding challenged the pitcher. "Lessee some smoke!"

Chicken Swamp reared back and fired. The thwaaaaaack of a hard stick rang over a rude playground and, yep, there went a Kimmy or Baby or Sophie sailing for center field.

About that time Miss Hattie came quick-marching out the single door of our fort-like school.

"Miss Cilla."

"Yes, ma'am," I pulled awkwardly erect to jog alongside the school's principal.

"I want you and Pudding to the office. Got a chore needs doing."

I swear that woman could walk faster than I could run.

"Yes, ma'am...me and...Pudding."

"'Pudding and I.' Meet me side of the yard. We'll be taking Mr. Raymond's truck."

At about that point a gaggle of eager outfielders crossed our path, little Sarah Brock in ragged pursuit.

"Miss Hattie, Miss Hattie! Them boys got my baaaaby doll!"

"Sarah Brock hush that nonsense."

Kerbo School's principal never broke stride.

"Girl with any sense knows to leave her valuables at home."

Within minutes Pudding and I were on the grounds of the school that Miss Chandler insisted did not belong to white folks. There were two wings to the main building. Grades one through six kept one wing. The other wing was designated for high school, which in those days meant grades seven through twelve. These two wings were linked in a single building that looked like a bomb shelter, a one-storey monolith of concrete shaped like a giant "H", the exterior walls punctuated by heavy, jalousied windows.

As we approached I could see rows of yellow buses in a chain-linked enclosure off to one side of a playground generously shaded with yellowheart pine. The football stadium peeked into view. There was a cafeteria back there, somewhere, and a gymnasium and a band hall, all connected to the main building by shaded breezeways. I sat in the back of Mr. Raymond's truck with no clue as to why we had been transported to this alien place.

Turned out we were there to haul books.

The school's aging janitor, a colored man, was our envoy. Mr. Herman directed us to the breezeway outside the band room where dozens of textbooks used up by white students were crated for donation to Kerbo School. The books were in various states of disrepair. Some were completely ripped from their spines. All were marked or defaced inside. Nearly all had pages missing.

"Just load 'em up," Miss Hattie commanded. "We'll cull 'em later."

I wondered briefly why white people were giving books to a school destined for extinction, but I knew better than to voice that question. Miss Hattie was already fussing over our labor, directing Pudding and I to unpack every box of books so that she could conduct a strict inventory. Four seventh grade math books. One book, Driver's Education. Fifteen, no make that sixteen history books, eleventh grade. Twelve geometry books.

And so on.

It was lunchtime. There were no teachers or students in sight.

Nobody in the band hall, either, which was disappointing. I would have liked to hear the band practice. Especially close-up. The only reason I attended football games was to hear the Marching Saints' halftime performance. I would stand with Chicken Swamp and Pudding and Shirley inside the roped-off area where Negroes were allowed, wishing that I had my mother's gift so that I could play by ear the marches and arrangements floating to me on the Friday-night air.

When we had loaded our second-hand charity to Miss Hattie's satisfaction, she announced that she was required to check with the office before leaving.

"I won't be a minute," our principal declared tersely. "You two just stay with Mr. Herman by the truck."

She tottered down the shaded walk toward the main building whose ponderous rear doors, I noted, were open to receive whatever breeze was available. I waited for Miss Hattie to disappear through those twin portals before I slipped off the truck's tailgate. "Mr. Herman, I need a restroom."

The old man seemed nonplussed.

"They ain't nuthin' fuh you here."

"They's a chinaberry tree 'round to the back of the band hall. That'll do."

"Reckon it'll have to," he replied.

I was familiar with the chinaberry tree and its location, of course. It stood between the Shaw's watermelon field and the fire-door of the band hall which I hoped to find open. Public schools, particularly rural public schools, were nowhere near as concerned with security as schools are nowadays. Part of that had to do with air conditioning. You couldn't stand to shut the windows anywhere once the weather warmed. The hallway doors were almost always open. Teachers routinely opened classroom doors to take advantage of any moving air.

So I was not surprised when I rounded the corner to see the band hall's rear door propped open with a Coca-Cola bottle. I took a quick glance at the field behind me. Nothing but the rising waft of Bahia grass heating in the noonday sun. I strode quickly to the inviting entry, and stepped inside the band hall.

The hall itself was layered in shallow terraces, like an amphitheater. I stepped through the rear door and into what I would later learn was the percussion section. Snare drums and cymbals and other instruments unfamiliar to me were arranged like lily pads at the highest level of the theater. Moving through that section I jostled a music stand and a drumstick fell onto a snare drum. It sounded like the shot of a pistol and I cringed—could the janitor hear? Or Pudding?

I had to make a quick decision what I was going to take and get *out*. I saw a trombone left carelessly beside a folding chair. A clarinet, first one I'd seen up close. The tuba stood massively on its stand, hard to sneak that one out. Other instruments were visible but locked behind a cage of heavy-gauged wire. Didn't matter—I couldn't take anything larger than I could stuff in my blouse or under my skirt. So what would that be?

I wended my way quickly through silent stands of music to reach a corridor outside. One step around the corner and there it was, the director's office—'James M. Pellicore'. Had a nameplate cut out of the same colored brass as the trombone. I nudged the door with my foot. It opened without a squeak and I knew I'd hit a goldmine.

The director's cramped niche was junked with sheet music. There must have been a hundred folders stuffed in crates on the floor or lying loose on the director's roll-top desk. Books of music all over. One composition was taped to the wall with cryptic directions for a variety of gridiron choreography.

"South Pacific," I mouthed silently.

An upright piano crowded beside the roll-top desk. A folio stuffed with sheet music was opened for inspection. I perused the exposed and topmost sheet. God from Zion, how many instruments were scored here? I leaned over the piano and sighted the first half-dozen measures, then scanned them once more and my head began to fill with sound, a pattern nagging and familiar.

Yes! This was it! This was the exact same piece of music that had been cut short those weeks ago on Mr. Raymond's radio. The snatch of music lodged in my memory spread before me now in full, eternally captured in bars and measures and notes, reproducible at will.

"Mow Zart." I tried sounding out the composer's name.

And the title?

Concerto in D Minor.

I pulled the folio from its stand and scanned the contents to find completely unfamiliar names—Chopin, Haydn, Mendelssohn. But I knew this was no ragtime. I scanned my trove of titles like a miser, completely absorbed in my good fortune, when the bell rang and I almost shit myself. This was no schoolyard bell, you understand; this was an electrically hammered clarion. A bank alarm. I jammed the folder of music inside my blouse, bolted out of the Director's office.

And came face to face with Cody Hewitt.

I didn't recognize Cody at first, in my panic. For one thing I'd never seen him up close. For another he was dressed good enough for church, not in the familiar jeans, T-shirt or football pads. Most importantly, my startled flight had put me eye-to-eye with Garner's youngest son, a position so close as to blind recognition. Never, never would I of my own accord dare raise my head to look into a white boy's eyes, but that was exactly where I was now.

"The hell you doin' in here?"

A girl hung on his shoulder. Her hair dribbled down her shoulders like tallow off a candle. I stood there like a deer caught in headlights for a split second. Then I lunged for the door.

He caught me. I kicked and fought, but he had a fullback's arms tight around my waist. The girl started screaming. I don't know how many people started pouring in and I didn't care. I kept clawing, kicking. Somebody ripped the sheet music from my hand and then my head snapped to one side and stars floated before my eyes. When my vision cleared all I could see was Miss Hattie Briar. Standing over me, her face pulled tight as if with wires.

"Git up," her voice came like the hiss of a snake.

"Git up and get in the truck."

I pulled myself off the floor.

"What's that?" the tallow-haired girl pointed, and next thing I knew Miss Hattie had her hands inside my top and I saw my stolen sheets torn and scattered over the floor.

My music! My Mozart!

"*This* what you doin' in heah?!"

In anger my principal's speech became colloquial.

"I... I just found it."

She backhanded me, a hard, vicious slap, and once more I was seeing stars. I could hear the white girl's startled gasp. Others, too. I could sense their forms, their voices. But only indistinctly. I wondered if this was what it was like for Mama, this nimbosity of perception. But then things cleared. Cody swam back into my vision broad-shouldered and golden-haired, a pair of welts raising red and parallel across an otherwise unblemished face.

"Goddamn nigger scratched me," he said, like it was a boast.

Miss Hattie snatched me up like a pullet.

"Get your sow's butt into the truck." Her voice was now garbled, as if received distantly over a radio, but I discerned clearly the fury, the shame.

"And Pudding, gather up those papers."

The ride home seemed a journey to execution. I knew what to expect. Miss Hattie never glanced back at me, ramrod straight in the cab of Mr. Raymond's truck, that gentle man mystified by her obdurate fury and getting no explanation. Pudding held onto his knees, barely acknowledging my presence over our ragged load of textbooks. I had never seen Pudding Reed at a loss for words; his silence was a fearful portent of what I was to shortly endure.

"She hits you, you cry. Cry like a baby, or she won't stop."

"She'll stop when she's ready."

Pudding considered that a moment.

"And don' let go that door," was his final advice.

We got to school, I knew where to go. There is a doorless portal that leads from the corner room Miss Hattie calls her office to the wide, breezy hall outside. That's where we got our whippings. We called them whippings because Miss Hattie rarely used a paddle.

She used a switch. Persons never chastised with a switch may not appreciate the difference between that implement and a paddle. Well, a switch is flexible, for one thing. You get hit on your back, it can wrap clear around. There are different kinds of switches. You could use a mulberry or a persimmon branch and trim it to the purpose. But the most feared switches came, as Miss Hattie well knew, from peach tress. The whole length of that flexible branch is knotted with junctures intended for blossoms and blooms and branches of new life. But trimmed, those notches bite like teeth on a saw.

When you were little there was a line to stand on, and you had to stand still while Miss Hattie switched your legs. If you moved, if you got off that line, she just started over. You got older, you stood inside the doorway, you reached up and grabbed the lintel. Shoulder blades opened up your back when you did that. Stretched the skin. Didn't bother the boys too much, as they mostly wore work shirts. But for me in my gingham dress the assigned posture was dramatic. I would be as exposed for flaying as any shanghaied sailor.

I had stolen, surely, which was an awful offense. But it was not the sin of theft that moved Miss Hattie to her present fury.

"People in that school think we're ignorant anyway," she hissed, trimming a switch that looked as long as she was tall. "White folks see a colored child they think he's got lice. See a Negro anywhere, think he can't read or reason. See any black skin, think it filthy. So what do you do? I say WHAT DO YOU DO?"

"I don't know, ma'am." Genuine tears were pressed from my eyes.

She shoved the ripped sheets of music in my face.

"THIS! You just go on over there and show those white folks everything they already want to see in a Negro. What me and Miss Chandler and *every* teacher here are laboring with Jesus to *keep hid*!

"You shamed us, today, Cilla Handsom. And you make me ashamed. Over *this*? Now. You know what to do."

My palms came damply to press the lintel. I waited stretched out and exposed for what seemed forever. Where would the first blow come? The calves? My feet? Across my back. You couldn't flinch. Could *not* take your hands off that lintel or Miss Hattie would just start all over. That had been the point of Pudding's final admonition.

I heard someone weeping frightened in the hall, might have been Shirley Lee.

"YOU WANT TO TAKE HER PLACE?"

A cry strangled in some frightened throat. It was not normal for any student to witness another's corporal punishment. Normally it was just you and Miss Hattie, there would not even be another teacher present. But Kerbo's principal declared that my behavior had betrayed us all, every child and teacher at our school, and so my class-mates had been made to leave their desks and come into the hall to see my punishment. Punishment, yes, and example.

They were all trying to look away from me, Shirley Lee, Pud-ding, Chicken—all of them. All the seniors, too. Something was moving deeply across Miss Chandler's broad face.

"Miss Hattie..." she began, but it had already started.

I kept my hands on that lintel. I told myself I would not squall. I stood and gnawed on my nigger lips till my back was wet. Eventually somebody cried out. Begged even, I heard her. Then I felt something warm between my legs, gushing. Miss Chandler's voice hailed from some distance and it ended. I slid down the door's ancient frame, grateful to find the waiting floor, shameless in a mixing of blood.

Chapter five

"White IQ vs. Negro IQ" by
Jon J. Synon—*The Clarion*

I was sent home from the whipping, my back and legs cut to the pattern of shoelaces. People on their porches interrupted their daily chores or indolence to point, to stare. I was dizzy, the sun baking my bare head, and crying out freshly as sweat seeped into my open wounds, that added duress offering some distraction if not relief from the failure of my mossy napkin. Menstrual blood had ruined my skirt, run down my thighs, and Miss Hattie would not allow a wash.

"Git you butt home," was her unquestioned command.

I ran from the school, stopping only in our rude playground to snatch up the burlap bag that had been second base. I held that sackcloth in a sarong about my waist, hoping to hide my shame. But the burlap was insufficient armor for a gauntlet of porches and prying eyes.

"Look like Corrie Jean's girl got herself a whupping good-fashion!" Miss Dollie Lamb whooped delight.

"Got some other embarrassment, too!" Lester contributed from the deep recline of his brother's porch. I could see Lester's hands working beneath the bulge of his trousers. "Ain' she a woman for sho?"

My face was hot. I felt sick to my stomach. The cramps. I stumbled, fell, got up and ran again. The gentle breeze generated by my running scoured my back anew, but I would not stop. Neighbors stared or jeered or chortled. That is how we treat the disgraced in Colored Town.

My dog was the only creature showing me comfort. Meeting me at the boundary of our yard. Whining.

"Grandmama!"

Grandmother Handsom made some kind of liniment. From the blossoms of a dogwood, she said. She said when Jesus died on a dogwood cross he made sure it would never be used to hurt anyone, ever again.

And I thought that must be true because I had never seen anybody cut a switch from a dogwood tree.

"Go lay down," grandma said.

I took Mama's mattress. It was easier. A fresh breeze, normally welcome, drifted like sandpaper over the wounds that crisscrossed my back.

"Oh, Lord!"

I slept anyway. I don't know whether it was the effect of the liniment or my ordeal or simple exhaustion, but I slept till way past sundown. I woke and saw mother there before me.

"Mama!"

A child's instinct, I suppose, to sit up and reach for one's mother.

"OH!"

The wounds on my back opened to fresh perspiration.

"Oh, Mama!"

She put her hands out to me, both of them. She knew, then, that I was injured? She was offering comfort?

"It's all right, mama. I'll be fine."

But then Corrie Jean pulled her tin cup from beneath her mattress.

"Wawa," she said.

Water.

And I realized that she was not reaching for me at all.

"Grandma?!" I called weakly but got no answer.

So there I was, alone in the house, with my mother. And no water.

"Wawa! Wawa!" Corrie Jean waved her tin cup.

"PUT THAT DAMN THING DOWN!"

I slapped the cup away. Mother scurried from me like a field mouse from a cat. Huddled in the corner.

I did not move to console or comfort her.

"Wawa?" a whimper came from the corner.

How could I be expected to get water? To go once more in front of my neighbors? In front of Mr. Raymond? Or Lester?

"GET IT YOU OWNSELF," I screamed and mother trembled like a leaf in a bad wind.

"LEAVE ME ALONE!" I begged and put my head down.

About that time the six-thirty feeder hooted into the station. You could hear the whistle climbing. A couple of short toots from the engineer, then that long, whippoorwill salutation. I'd have give anything to be on a train that moment, any train headed anywhere, as long as it was out of Colored Town. I closed my eyes. The steaming whistle suffocated in the spiced and heavy air.

"....Cilla?"

That the Lord called Samuel: and he answered.

Here am I.

And he ran unto Eli, and said, Here am I; for thou calledst me.

And he said, I called not.

"...Cilla?"

Here am I.

I called not, my daughter, lie down again.

"Cilla Handsom!"

A voice. But you can ignore voices in a dream, grandmama said.

"Cilla, wake up!"

Speak, Lord; for thy servant heareth.

"Wake up!"

The mattress beneath my face was damp. So now I was drooling, too. Just like my mother. Mother? Where was she? I raised my head. There. Banished to the corner of our pine-box room, curled fetal and snoring. Something stabbed at my heart.

"Cilla, you up yet, girl?"

I knew that voice—Joe Billy! But where?

"At you window," he whispered hoarsely.

I turned and there he was, framed in the open sill and backlit like a movie star by a rising moon.

"I'm not decent," my voice slurred with recent slumber.

"I heard," he replied solemnly. "You want, I'll grab me a stake and drive it through that bitch's vampire heart."

A laugh bubbled up from some place I didn't even recognize and I realized I was smiling. "What's a vampire?"

"You don' know?"

"What if I don't?" I replied with some defiance.

"Thass better."

A mouth filled with teeth in that narrow face, those half-dollar eyes catching the moon like saucers. Hair processed straight and combed back.

"Come on out," he peered into my room.

"I cain't come out," I said. "I got to clean and get somethin' fresh to wear, and we all out of water."

"Not no more you ain't."

His head disappeared. I heard a curse, a grunt, and then Joe Billy hefted a silver pail of water onto my open sill.

"What have you gone and done?" I asked amazed.

"Heard you were untoward, thought I'd haul some water," he said modestly. "Got a barrel for you, too. Fifty gallon's worth. I figure we clean it up, fill it, save you-all some trips."

It was an act so generous and unexpected that I could not find words to thank him.

"A 'thank you' will do," he supplied.

"You a mind-reader?"

"You an open book," he returned.

"Gimme that water."

I rose stiffly, crossed to the windowsill and hefted the slopping pail into my room.

"How long it take you to clean up?"

"Another month?" I quipped, and he practically doubled up laughing.

"Thass good, Cilla. Thass real good. But I cain't wait no month."

"You wait right there," I told him. "And shush! 'Fore you wake somebody."

"How long you gonna be?"

"I'll be out when I'm out."

I sponged off on the back porch, slipped some underthings off the line, a clean shift. Time I got back out to the front of the house, Joe Billy had Hard On sitting in his lap like he'd known him forever.

"You spoil my dog."

"He need attention."

"*You* need attention. You a crazy boy."

"Crazy 'bout you."

"Don't make fun."

"I'm not makin' nuthin'."

"Everybody in this town laughin' at me."

He paused a moment. "Not everybody."

I turned to the shadows. "Whatchu want here, anyway? Not figurin' on some poontang, are you? 'Cause niggers don' like no jelly roll once it's bleedin'."

"Now, thass nasty talk."

"Yes, it is."

"That how you usually talk? Well? Is it?"

"...No."

He pulled Hard On gently off his lap.

"Are you a grown man?" I asked. "A boy? How old are you?"

"Old enough to be on my own."

"Man on his own have to work. You working?"

"Got myself a business."

"Hauling water?"

63

"I illustrate guitars."

"Kind of business is that?"

"Can be pretty damn good," he said. "Wanta see? I'll show you."

"Show me where? You livin' on a back porch!"

"Not no more," he beamed. "Got my own place. Take you there sometime. What about tomorrow? Right after school?"

"You in some kind of trouble. Aren't you, Joe Billy?"

"We all in trouble, Cilla. Some of us just better at it than others."

I can see, you can see, he can see. We can see, you can see, they can see.... Our penciled paeans to grammar were interrupted the very next morning with the arrival of a new student at Kerbo School. Joe Billy introduced himself awkwardly as Joseph William King to Miss Chandler, saying his family situation had changed and that he'd be a resident of Laureate for the foreseeable future.

Pudding snickered when Joe Billy said, "Laureate".

"You in Colored Town, fool."

"What was that, Peter?"

That got an open laugh. Everbody knew Pudding hated Miss Chandler using his given name.

Miss Chandler turned again to her newest student. "Where are you from, Joseph William?"

"Valdosta, born and raised," Joe Billy replied with a glance to me. "Valdosta, Georgia."

"Well, welcome to Kerbo School," Miss Chandler smiled. "Now, somebody sharpen Joseph a pencil. We're going to be working on some drills."

I would have welcomed the arrival of any new student that morning, anything or anyone to deflect attention that otherwise would have been given me. Joe Billy, unfortunately, became the immediate target of the petty intimidations invariably inflicted on newcomers. By recess there was a fight. Then a paddling. Joe Billy was no big kind of thing. He would appear to be an easy target. But he returned from Principal Briar's office with no apparent injury. Chicken

Swamp, on the other hand, slinked in rubbing his ass with one hand and cradling his nuts with the other. Miss Chandler called the class's attention to this latter predicament, pointing out that holding your privates was not polite behavior. Miss Chandler was a genius at using bad examples to good purpose.

I assiduously avoided any contact with my new classmate, plowing ahead through the day in a blur, intransitive verbs and the capitol of Vermont mere distractions, now, a prelude to the end of the day and my first invite-you with a boy.

"Meet me by the water tower." Joe Billy had slipped me the note at lunch time. "After school."

I first ran home to check on mama. She was fed and clean and Grandma was settled.

"Where you goin'?" Grandma asked when I skipped out the door.

"Mr. Raymond's," I lied.

I waited for Joe Billy beneath the white people's water tower. We had not set up a specific time for our rendezvous, I realized, and immediately began to fret that this was a snooker, a tar baby, and that I would be waiting forever beneath the water tower's crazy scrawl of graffiti. I had the greatest urge to pee, but was afraid if I left to relieve myself it would be at the very interval when Joe Billy chose to arrive.

I was also afraid to be alone. Town Park was not safe for any person with skin darker than fresh milk. I was not supposed to be here. The town's park was off-limits to Negroes, a reservation where white boys and their pale-skinned consorts could neck in anonymity. It was also a place for young toughs to race their trucks or drink or fight. I had no desire to be present for any of those entertainments.

Night began to fall. Spanish moss, welcomed in daylight for its shade, fell now in a dark and minatory shroud and I felt a tightness in my chest.

"Cilla?"

His voice floated from behind a massive water oak.

"Where you been?!"

"I'm sorry. Really. I should of tole' you to wait for dark."

He reached out to take my arm and I pulled away.

"You been out here since school?"

"Just about."

"Let me make it up to you. Here. I brought you somethin'."

I eyed him with new suspicion. "Whatchu brought me?"

He reached inside his shirt and pulled out what I took to be a sheet from our local paper, *The Clarion*.

"I get all the news I need at Mr. Raymond's."

"Don't judge no gift by its cover."

He unfolded the paper. What I expected to see was some kind of print arranged in columns to frame the usually indecipherable black and whites photos purporting to represent a board meeting or ball game or bigmouth bass.

"Go on, take it."

I lifted the folder from its cloaking paper. Opened it.

"My good Lord!!"

Right there in my hands was the folder filled with sheet music that I had stolen from James M. Pellicore's disheveled office. The torn sheets inside were scotch-taped to a decent repair, their riven staffs carefully realigned to perfect measure. I had been restored to Mozart, to Ellington and God knew who-all else!

"Where in the world—?!"

"I took 'em," he replied simply. "After that business at recess, me and Chicken was waitin' in the office for Miss Hattie to come paddle us, which she did. A paddle, not a switch. Anyway, I seen the music I know *you* must of took just sittin' there on the bitch's desk. Just out there in the open.

"Soon's she's done with me ole' Briar Patch turns her attention to Chickenswamp and while they's both occupied..." His teeth glowed like pearls. "I swiped it. Pulled it right out the trashcan. Right by her desk!"

"You *are* crazy," I responded in unqualified admiration.

"Fool, for sure," he allowed. "Now come on. I got a place I want you to see."

I don't think he actually took my hand. I just recall us striding across the tracks into Laureate, just like we owned the town with no fear, no doubt, no worry.

"Joe Billy, do you *know* where we at?"

"Sure I do."

Laureate's dozen stores stretched in bricked facades on either side of Main Street, a single avenue of commerce. There were no apartments, here. No houses. I could see the SafeWay, the offices for the *Clarion*. There was a moviehouse had shut down for lack of business. A gaudy marquis still wilted in a fractured window, "The Blob". I had not seen that picture.

Churches, always "First" something or other, First Methodist, First Baptist—extended uniformly white spires to bracket the town's one traffic light on each point of the compass. The courthouse occupied the center of town, of course. Its bronze-handed clock was in constant repair. There was a good bit of traffic which made me nervous, families coming to town for groceries. Teenagers cruised up and down their drag in hotrods and sedans that cost more than any house in our part of town. I thought I saw a passing jalopy slow down, a tow-headed passenger glancing back.

"We'll be all right." Joe Billy spoke to my yet unvoiced fear.

Black people just did not go for walks in Laureate. You were downtown, you'd better have a reason. You'd better be getting groceries, or kerosene, or of course you could be running errands for any white man. But just to go for a stroll? *Einen spaziergang?* We didn't do that.

In small towns most everybody gets recognized by his car or truck. I saw Mr. Thistle's vehicle—a decal for his nursery made that Chevy truck distinctive. I saw the Lands' Cadillac, the Henderson's bright green Fairlane. They didn't seem to notice me, not that I could tell. Then I saw Collard Jackson's cruiser, far ahead, pulled up to the town's only lighted intersection.

"I see him."

My heart was racing as if I'd run a mile. But nobody stopped us. Nobody said anything. We traveled nearly the length of the town, almost to its solitary traffic light, without a single catcall or challenge.

I found myself actually beginning to relax when up ahead I saw Cody Hewitt's bright-red pickup run the light.

"Shit my eyes."

Joe Billy pulled up short as though jerked on a leash.

"What's wrong? Joe Billy?"

"You know that truck?"

"Me an' everybody else," I replied. "Belongs to Cody Hewitt. That's the boy caught me in the band hall. You know Cody?"

"I don't know nobody," he jerked me hard into the alley.

"Joe Billy—?"

A flash of red dragging down Main Street.

Hubcaps spinning like one of those chariots in *Ben Hur*.

"It's all right," Joe Billy pulled me down the alley between the Western Auto and the drugstore. "Come on. I'll show you my place."

Mr. Raymond often recalled that during World War II the fate of men and boys got decided with slips of paper and a shoebox in the Masonic Lodge over Doc West's drugstore. Doc West's surviving son moved the old two-storey pharmacy so that he could build his own store on Main Street. It was still an old-fashioned drugstore with cheap sunglasses and a comic book section and a counter for ice-cream or sodas or burgers. Of course in 1963 you couldn't get any of those things, not even a glass of water, unless you were white.

Joe Billy and I emerged from the alley at the rear of the modern pharmacy to find the ruins of the original nestled in a grove of wild dogwood out back.

"Where we goin'?"

"Upstairs."

"I ain't goin' up there. They was *Masons* up there."

"Don't be country."

You entered Joe Billy's lodge by an exterior and rail-less stairway. A padlocked door offered security; Joe Billy urged me through, his palm in the small of my back.

It felt good there, that pressure in the curve of my spine.

"Downstairs is nasty. But here? Well. See fuh yourself."

The door closed and I could not see a thing. I mean not a *thing*. That room was darker than the inside of a cow.

"Joe Billy—!"

"Hold your britches," he said and I heard the snick of a switch, that distinctive snap of plastic and metal, and then—

"Lord!"

I visored my eyes with my hands against the glare of a lamp big as a headlight. Once accustomed to that singular torch I was able to survey a room as sparely appointed as a monk's cell. He had one small table and a straight back chair. A hotplate propped nearby on a milk can. There was a sink. A shelf above supported a jelly-jar glass. Welch's, it was. Grape. A single coffee cup drained upside-down alongside a wind-up alarm clock. Tick-tock, tick-tock. The only other possessions lay side-by-side in their cases on a pinewood floor.

"Those your guitars?"

"One of 'em," he said. "Other one I got to get back to Tal-lahassee."

A crate, hotplate and crockery, two cased guitars.

"Whass wrong? You don' like my apartment?"

"Joe Billy—"

There was vital information that needed to be conveyed here, but I could not find the words to do it.

"What is it?" he asked defiantly.

"Joe Billy, you cain't live here."

"Why not?"

"'Cause this ain' Colored Town."

"Sure as hell ain't. And it's mine. Thirty dollah a month. You can ask Doc West."

Was it possible there were arrangements for domiciles that I had not considered?

"They's a bathroom in that closet, right over there. Inside plumbing. And you know what? I got running water."

"Water? Anytime you want?"

"Any old time."

"Lord have mercy—!" To be alone? In your own room? All by yourself with light and water! No rat snakes or outhouse! "Joe Billy...how'd you do this?!"

"I am one amazing nigger, no doubt."

"But where you gonna get thirty dollars every month?"

"I got my business."

"You keep tellin' me."

"And now you get to see."

I saw a burst of bright, bold colors the moment he opened the guitar's case. At first I did not see a particular form in the pattern of line and color on the body of the guitar, but then—

"It's a woman!"

"You like her?"

The mouth dominated. The sound hole of the guitar was framed by lips as lush as Marilyn Monroe's and layered like flowers or labia in a psychedelic lavender. Only the barest suggestion of a nose or chin; you were drawn to the lips. Then I realized that the apparently random tendrils streaming over the woman's face were hair, wild blonde locks whipped by some unseen wind past those outrageously exaggerated lips and mouth.

"Can I hold it?"

"Go ahead."

I cradled the instrument as gently as a baby.

"How come the strings doubled up?"

"It's a twelve-string guitar. You can get richer harmonies with more strings. I cain't. But good players can."

He pulled over the second guitar case and pulled out a six-string Gibson. I saw the raven-haired harlot painted along its length.

"This here insterment was my daddy's. Mine, now."

He ran through a short progression of chords, pausing now and then to pick on a single string, up and down the neck, adjusting the tuning pegs according to a fair ear.

"Look like you know what you're doing."

"Some. Know this one? 'Summer time...'"

He picked those steel strings and the whole room filled up with sound. A rich, full tone. I would not at the time have known what tone color meant, or timbre, but I bet if you'd had a dozen six-strings playing the same song I could have picked out Joe Billy's blindfolded.

"...And the livin' is easy/Fish are jumpin'/And the cotton is high..."

"You wouldn't make our choir," I chuckled, and he smiled, pleased as pie.

We just had ourselves a good time. Joe Billy loved playing blues, but he listened just as much to jazz and swing. He loved B.B. King. Loved Satchmo's early horn. Loved singers of all styles, Jimmy Rushing, Eddie Jefferson, even Sinatra. Liked the ladies, too. It was Joe Billy who introduced me to Billie Holiday and Lee Wiley and Carmen McRae.

After a while he settled his guitar.

"If I had me some music written for the piano, could you play it? I mean, without hearing it first?"

"I'd have to work at it. Mama's the player, really. Not me."

He regarded me a moment.

"But you can read music?"

"Well, surely."

"Who taught you?"

"I don' know, I'd just kind of sit by mama while she play and look at the score. It just made sense."

"So you taught yourself?"

"Sometimes I'd get help. Revival one time this lady helped me."

"Point is—you can look at those beats and notes and measures and hear them in your head?"

"Anybody can," I waved him off.

"I can't," he said.

"You?" I did not believe him.

"I cain't read off no sheet," he shook his head. "I look at those black dots—I don' hear a thing. And here you sight-read?"

"Not well."

"But you read it, you know how it sounds?"

"Most of the time," I allowed.

"Here, then," he tossed the folder of music into my lap. "Find something. Make some music."

"I got no instrument."

"You got a voice box."

"There no words on this kind of music, Joe Billy."

"I know that. Make the sounds."

"Let me look."

The music familiar to me from Colored Town, the hymnals in our church, big band, swing, blues, even the jazz to which I had been exposed were outhouses compared to the cathedrals raised here. Haydn, Wagner, Tchaikovsky, Mozart—*these* were a different species of construction altogether, buttresses of sound and harmony, bridges of variegated instrumentation, sheet after sheet.

I saw a piece of Chopin I might have tried if I had a piano and just half of eternity to practice. But then I spotted something in that folder so ordinary as to seem entirely out of place. A simple piece.

"Whoa, mister," I sat up. "Here's one I can do."

"Whose is it?" Joe Billy leaned forward to see.

"I cain't say the name."

"Ludwig..." Joe Billy attempted. "Beat-Oven."

"'Ode to Joy'," I read the title supplied, confident that I could render its mute notation into sound, if not proper English.

A work of genius, Dr. Weintraub would later tell me, almost always consists in taking something very complex and making it simple. Well, you couldn't get much simpler than the music before me that evening in Joe Billy's apartment. There were no sharps or flats to begin with; you didn't even need the black keys. Key of C-Major, simple as pie. I scanned the staffed lines. Thirty-two measures, one slur after another, four-four time. This had to be the most elemental piece in my pilfered anthology.

"You know how to sing a scale?" I asked. "Like from choir?"

"You mean, 'Do Re Mi Fa So La Ti Do'?"

"That's it," I nodded and sat tall. "So here we go. 'Ode to Joy'."

Beginning on the note of "E", *mezzo forte.*

"Mi-Mi-Fa-So/

So-Fa-Mi-Re/
Do-Do-Re-Mi/
Miii-ReRe/

"Mi-Mi-Fa-So/
So-Fa-Mi-Re/
Do-Do-Re-Mi/
Reee-DoDo…"

Moving then to two hands and *mezzo piano*. But since I could only sing one note at a time, I held with the melody.

"Re-Re-Mi-Do/
Re-Fa-Mi-Do/
Re-Fa-Mi-Re/
Do-Re-Sooo/

"Mi-Mi-Fa-So/
So-Fa-Mi-Re/
Do-Do-Re-Mi/
Reee-DoDo/"

I was completely unaware that Beethoven never wrote a part for the piano in his Ninth Symphony. I had never heard the Ninth, after all, or any other symphony. I would later learn that the excerpt I rehearsed for Joe Billy was taken from a beginner's lesson book. It was only a thread of the Master's cloth extricated to lead some neophyte to the warp and woof of a much larger and grandiose pattern. Only a sample, a sip.

Something to prime the pump.

But it was enough. An ode to joy came alive in my voice and in my heart, and once it began I could not stop nor rest until it was finished. And when it was finally complete, when I finished my pure sung paean, the sheet music trembled as if alive in my hands. Joe Billy just sat there, his eyes wide and bright. The clock at his hotplate ticking like a metronome.

Tick-tock, tick-tock.

Joe Billy cleared his throat.

"Guess I better get you home."

The rail-less stairway returned our trembling weight to earth. From there we jogged along back streets in a zigzag toward Colored Town. There were dogs along that route with which to contend, but a hound's pursuit was preferable to what threatened on Main Street. Finally we reached Mr. Land's fenced-in yard and the bed of silver tracks that raised behind. We skirted that wired periphery, scrambled up the railroad's graveled bed, and only then relaxed, walking parallel lines of steel in perfect equanimity.

No conversation, at first. The moon was well up. The air was fecund with the day's stolen nectars. Joe Billy strolled along, deep in some unspoken rumination.

"Cilla," he finally broke the silence, "you need to be on a piano playing. You need to be practicin'. All the time."

"Tell you what," I replied, "I'll just pull out my upright from behind our outhouse an' get started."

"They's a piano at the church."

"Play anything but gospel on Reverend Dipps' piano, I'll be gettin' me another whipping."

"We was in Tallahassee, I could put you behind a piano anytime you wanted," he declared.

"But we ain't in Tallahassee," I said wearily. "And while we're at it, *you* didn't say you was from Tallahassee, neither. In school? You said you was from Valdosta. Why you need to lie about that?"

"Didn't kill nobody, if that's what you're worried about."

"Not 'till you mentioned it."

"*You* lied 'bout your daddy."

I felt blood rising in my cheeks.

"You tole' me your daddy was in the war," he pressed on doggedly. "Lester say nobody even know who you daddy is."

"Mama had me. That's all the information I need."

"Your mama, she kind of simple?"

"I don't know. Most times I don' think she knows."

Gravel showed white through the creosoted picket of crossties.

I tried to measure my step exactly to the ties. Joe Billy was hitting mostly gravel; you could hear his lace-ups—crunch-crunch, crunch-crunch.

"Grandma tole me when Mama got pregnant ever'body got theirself concerned 'cause they din' know how mama could even survive havin' a baby, much less take care of it once it was born. Soooo...they took Mama over to Dowling Park, to this midwife there. She nursed her and took care of her. Grandma stayed away, mostly, what I gather.

"But soon as I was out and preacher knew me and Mama was awright, he 'tole Grandmama it was time to come get us, and she did. She drove out with Mr. Raymond in his truck and brought us back to the house. We been there, the three of us, ever since. I don' know who my daddy is."

We crunched along together beneath a swelling moon.

"How old are you, Cilla?"

"Seventeen." I did not meet his eye. "Be eighteen come Halloween."

"I was born the week after," he offered.

"Scary notion," I said and we both snorted laughter.

"Maybe your birthday I get you a piano," he proposed. "Maybe I buy you a baby grand."

"Baby grand, yeah," I smiled. "Now that would punch the ticket."

Chapter six

"The Negroes' Blueprint for Civil War," by Dr. George S. Benson—*The Clarion*

Of course I knew I would be getting no piano, of any kind. There was only one piano in Colored Town, a battered Chickering regarded by Reverend Dipps as his private property. Occasionally I would slip into the church after school, risking eternal torment for twenty minutes of Duke Ellington or Scott Joplin. After my whipping I was banned from so much as touching the Reverend's piano for any purpose except to key the meager measures necessary for the stimulation of my mother's flawless and Gospel performance. As at Mr. Raymond's, my place at church was to prime the pump, and it was driving me crazy.

"I got to have me a piano."

Joe Billy gnawed a toothpick.

"Gonna hafta take you someplace, then. Or rob the church."

We had become an item, Joe Billy and I. All it took was a public rendezvous. I was to meet Joe Billy at Mr. Raymond's directly after Sunday service. Come the appointed hour, I dashed in my church things straight from benediction to that familiar front porch where Joe Billy waited with my Radio Flyer wagon, my dog and water buckets.

"Thought we'd fill that barrel up," he smiled as I arrived.

There were a few snickers among the women.

"Cilla got herself a boyfren."

"YA'LL GOT A PROBLEM WITH THAT?"

Joe Billy's challenge rang like a first sergeant's over a parade field and the women fell silent. Lester had been drinking. Usually the old coot tried to hide it, but on this afternoon you could see the brown-wrapped bottle sticking up between his overalled legs like an erection.

"Got you somethin' to squeeze, nephew?"

Taking up where the women left off. Joe Billy stopped, turned. Then he raised his hand and extended his finger like a pistol toward the old man.

"I ain't on your back porch no more, Uncle. And this here girl is now and hereafter out from under your inspection."

"You cain't talk to me like that!" Lester's eyes bulged in their dark sockets.

"'Pears to me he just did," Mr. Raymond's reply was sharp enough to cut another crease in his always-creased khakis.

Lester went mute and everybody around that porch knew that whatever gossip people wanted to make about Joe Billy and me would *not* take place around Mr. Raymond's porch. Joe Billy set himself up then and there as my advocate, my champion. I was convinced he was my only defender, my only friend.

It took me a long time to recognize there were others.

Two weeks after my public lashing I was still cleaning the privy behind Kerbo School. Miss Hattie had assigned latrine duty as an ongoing humiliation and mandated that the duty be performed at the end of the day. This normally would have created a problem for me, or at least a serious inconvenience, since my habit was to haul water as soon after school as I could. But Joe Billy's fifty-gallon reservoir relieved the necessity for daily trips to Mr. Raymond's pump, thank God, so Miss Hattie's punishment was not as onerous as I'm sure she intended.

Not that cleaning a shithouse can ever be an easy chore. First thing, was to knock down the spider webs and chase out whatever arachnids or scorpions had taken up residence. No snakes, praise the Lord. I never saw a snake at Kerbo, but there was always a stench. Sometimes the little ones made it worse when they made a mess of their business and I'd have to mop up. Except I didn't have a mop; newspaper served that utility, along with its other purpose. I used plain old ammonia for cleanser, scrubbing every square inch of that outhouse to ensure scalded lungs if not sanitation. I was finished with the hard part that Wednesday and was tearing more paper when Miss Chandler came waddling up.

"You about finished here, Miss Cilla?"

"Yes, ma'am."

"See me before you go."

"Yes, ma'am," I said and immediately became anxious. What else had I done? Whom had I newly shamed?

Miss Chandler, I believe I have mentioned, was as big as she was ugly. She couldn't begin to accommodate her wide buttocks on the small chairs intended for our narrow behinds and the school certainly could not afford specialized furniture so Miss Chandler brought to school a chair of her own: a wide, wing-backed antique. She told us that this well-crafted accommodation was a Chippendale, which we understood as 'Chip and Dale', the animated rodents familiar to us from the picture-show, so we renamed Miss Chandler's only concession to comfort The Chipmunk Chair and for weeks snickered just about every time she sat in it.

Miss Chandler was deposited now in the Chipmunk Chair, but I was not snickering.

"Yes, ma'am?"

She looked up from a pile of conjugations.

"Cilla, come in. Sit."

I stood looking at the floor.

"I didn't bring you here to punish you, Cilla. Take a seat."

She waited for me to settle into a hard-backed chair.

"I want to talk about your future, Cilla."

"Future, ma'am?"

"What happens tomorrow, Cilla. And the day after that."

"I be done with the restrooms by the end of the week," I offered.

"I'm not talking about punishment, Cilla. I'm talking about accomplishment. I want you to think about what you can accomplish after you leave Kerbo School."

"I got another year before I think about that. Don't I?"

The flesh on her jowls sagged like a basset hound's. "No, Cilla. This fall we'll be in the consolidated school in Laureate."

My heart hammered. "I cain't go to no white school, Miss Chandler!"

"Yes, you can."

"I'm not ready."

"Cilla, you're more than ready. You're a lot smarter than you think you are. And you have gifts you underestimate."

"Kind of gifts?"

"You read music, don't you?"

"Yes, ma'am," I confirmed, unsure how that could be construed as a gift.

"And the piano. You enjoy playing?"

"But I need practice. Joe Billy say I could be really good if I can practice."

"Joe Billy, yes. He's a musician of sorts himself, what I understand. The guitar?"

"He play *good*," I spoke up.

"Plays 'well'. So you think highly of Joe Billy?"

"Yes, ma'am," I looked at my lap.

"He speaks well of you, too."

My head came straight up.

"Joe Billy talk to you about *me*?"

"He stayed after school to tell me that you read music, that you taught yourself to read, and that you needed a piano and instructor. He pretty well laid it out, just like that."

"Don't be mad with him, Miss Chandler."

"I'm not mad with Joe Billy at all, Cilla. I admire anyone who takes time to help a friend, especially when that particular friend isn't exactly Miss Popular. And believe me, Cilla, I know something about what it means *not* to be popular."

That was the first time, I think, that I ever looked a teacher in the eye. And when I looked Miss Chandler in the eye, funny thing, I wasn't thinking anything about ugly at all.

"Can you teach me to play the piano, Miss Chandler?"

"No. But I know someone who can."

"Who?"

"Mr. James M. Pellicore. You know Mr. Pellicore?"

"He's the band director. I took his music."

"He is. You did. That is correct."

"What's he want teaching me?"

"First and foremost, Mr. Pellicore is a teacher. He teaches children black, white, green—doesn't matter. I'm not saying he's perfect, and I'm *not* saying you should ever plan to profit by theft, but Mr. Pellicore was intrigued that of all the pieces in his office you could have taken, you took a folder of classical music."

"It's the kind of music angels make," I said. "That's what Joe Billy say."

"What Joe Billy 'says'. I see. Well. At any rate Mr. Pellicore will be your teacher in the fall. We'll start right away, though. And all through the summer."

"All summer? On the piano?"

"Yes. You'll use the piano in the Band Hall."

"In the white school?"

"It's not a school for whites, Cilla. It's for everybody."

"Yes, ma'am."

"Now, there is one requirement in all this that you have to understand."

She meant payment of some kind. I knew this wasn't going to come free and clear.

"Yes, ma'am." I was more wary in this reply.

"Mr. Pellicore needs a horn in his band, a French horn. His lead horn graduates in a few weeks. The only other French horn behind him has quit band altogether. Mr. Pellicore won't have his Saints marching *anywhere* without a French horn."

"I never played any kind of horn."

"You can learn. Anyone who teaches herself to read music can master a horn. So you'll pay Mr. Pellicore back for piano and music lessons by learning the French horn for the high school band."

The band! That choreographed display of brass and wind and percussion. The uniforms, red and white and shiny. But then I realized that if I were on that lime-lined field I would have to march. I'd be exposed, the only black girl on the field, and a thief, caught in a crosshair of chalk.

"I don't know, Miss Chandler."

She leaned forward, that large woman, the flanges on her Chip and Dale spreading like the wings of angels.

"Listen to me, child. You are as good and as smart as any white child on the other side of these railroad tracks. You are gifted in music, probably also in mathematics. What you don't have, on *this* side of the railroad line, is an opportunity to use those talents.

"There aren't that many opportunities get presented to black people anytime or anyplace, but especially *here*, and especially to black women. So you have got to learn to take every single hand that reaches out to you, Cilla Handsom, black or white. And once you've got that hand you have got to find a way to pull yourself out of here. Pull yourself *out* and go on to something better."

A whole host of improbable scenarios jumbled for priority in my head. Me at a piano? In a white school? With a band and a horn?!

All those saints marching in.

I cleared my throat.

"Would you help me write Mr. Pellicore a letter, Miss Chandler? I want to tell him 'yes' and thank him and I want to make sure it's got good grammar."

I have never seen a face of any kind light up with such joy as did my teacher's in that moment.

"A letter, yes. That is a classy thing to do, Miss Cilla. *That* is the way to take an opportunity."

When I got home I found a grocery bag waiting on my cot, an ordinary brown paper bag.

"Miz Chandler came by," was grandmother's only explanation. "Lord, that woman homely."

I approached that bag the way most children sneak up on presents beneath a Yuletide tree. I opened it. Looked inside. First thing I saw was six bars of Ivory soap. Right below those scented bars were four rolls of toilet paper. The rest of the bag was boxed with Kotex, enough napkins on my regular period to last the year.

"What kinda teacher brings a mess like that?" Grandma scowled.

"She got me piano lessons, too," I reported with pride. "With Mr. Pellicore. At the school in Laureate."

"Ain' no school in Laureate—you mean the white school?"

"Miss Chandler say, says, it's everybody's school."

Grandmother spit between the floorboards of my room.

"Be careful, girl. Talk like that gone get us in trouble."

Trouble lingered continually, never far from Colored Town. For as long as anybody could remember, the Ku Klux Klan had conducted meetings right on the county line at Taylor's tavern. That hoochhouse of timbers and tin had been the scene of more than one atrocity seeded by race-hate. There had been crosses burned at Taylor's since the twenties, those midnight celebrations duplicated through modern times and spreading to Dixie County and Suwannee County. Even so, by the early sixties the KKK was a diminished organization. It wasn't that an enlightened citizenry disapproved of the Klan's outrages, so much as they did not want to be actively associated with its membership. A certain odor attached.

Even bigots have a sense of class. Or think they do. So white folks wanting to identify with the goals of the Grand Lizard but chary of acquiring the aroma associated with that membership simply formed another organization. 'The Council' was a euphemism for 'The White Citizen's Council', a clan whose nosegayed members enjoyed about the same status in the community as members of the Elks or Lions or Rotary Club. Organizations not transparently associated with reptiles or rednecks.

Or tar-covered crosses.

The Council met respectably across the street from Laureate's only bank, in Betty's Café, the only eatery in town. You could get grits and eggs and bacon at Betty's. Coffee and cane syrup. An enormous plate-glass window in the main dining area gave an unobstructed view of the bank and Highway 27, but a side room thoughtfully bricked into the original clapboard structure also provided a private retreat, segregated, appropriately, from the café's other diners.

On a good night, "The Council" could count on perhaps a dozen of its exclusively white members to attend its business. However, in the wake of *State of Florida v. Lafayette County School Board* so many people piled into her café that Betty had to move the Council's meeting from its private room to the main dining area. I was in the kitchen that evening, being rewarded with a drumstick and iced tea for skinning mullet on Betty's back porch, the porch where colored people were served. The kitchen looked out to the dining area through a large service bay, a good vantage from which to observe the Council's goings-on.

It started out with an invocation. Then Principal Ben Wilburn led the Pledge of Allegiance. One nation. Under God. Minutes came next, followed by some quasi-parliamentary wrangling. Old business, somebody called it, and somebody else said, no, it wasn't. People were mad, I could tell that, but had no notion what had stirred their anger until Garner Hewitt took the floor.

"We don't do something we're going to have nigras in our school this coming fall." Garner Hewitt summed up the new business nicely.

Representative Latrelle Putnal then straightened his silk tie and pin before rising to explain, or justify, the defeat of the School Board's court-side assault.

"...long and short of it is, we got sold out. The governor pulled out his support and the circuit court has ordered us to integrate."

But giving an order, Mr. Hewitt pointed out, was not the same as enforcing it.

"What you have in mind specifically, Garner?"

This from Mr. Land, owner of the SafeWay grocery and second only to Garner in property and cash.

"What I have in mind," Garner took over the floor from Rep. Putnal, "is for white people to stand arm-in-arm before the school-house doors and make clear to every colored child, and their families, that they are not welcome in our school. The court says they *can* go to Laureate Consolidated. Nothing says we have to *make* 'em go."

"Gonna take more than a protest to keep them niggers outta our school," came a voice I could not locate. "They's a couple of agitators at Kerbo, what I hear. And they's teachers tellin' those kids they *got* to go to Laureate. They *got* to!"

Garner Hewitt waited until it was quiet enough to hear the squeak of his shoes before he responded.

"Last thing any of us needs, white or colored, is outsiders telling us what to do with our children. But it's easy to manipulate a Negro; we all know that. Which is why we, as members and associates of this Council, must unite *right now* to make our views known. Make 'em known…and make 'em stick."

Ben Wilburn coughed into his Coca-Cola.

"Not talking about anything illegal here, are we, Garner?"

"I wouldn't think so," Garner closed a lid slyly over his birth-marked eye. "But that's for the sheriff to decide, way I see it. Sheriff's got responsibility for enforcing the law in the county. If he don't arrest, there ain't a crime, way I see it. It's the sheriff's call."

"But-is-the-sheriff-on-our-side?"

Monk Folsom raised that question as though reading off a cue-card.

"I must confess to the Council that this is the one area troubles me," Garner offered that condemnation like an apology. "I'm not sure where Sheriff Jackson's loyalties are. Not sure he understands the social and economic implications that will surely follow if we start mixing blood in our schools.

"Little black boys with little white girls. Young bucks with teenagers. It's too much to put young people in a situation like that and not expect something sooner or later to happen. I don't have to tell ya'll this. You know I'm right."

"If the sheriff won't back us it won't matter that we're right." This from Ira Gardner, owner and editor of *The Clarion*. Ira pushed a pair of thick-framed glasses deep into a thicket of silver hair. "Without Collard's backing, or at least assent, it is possible that in the normal exercise of our duly constituted right to assemble, *some* incident might transpire, almost certainly *will* transpire, that could put a right-thinking citizen in a dubious light with the law. *Could* put him, that is, depending on the stance of our sheriff."

Garner nodded in somber concession to Ira's assessment.

"We hafta make sure Collard's with us," somebody offered from the back of the room.

"Or get a new sheriff," Garner amended. "Get a new sheriff."

The white citizens convened at Betty's Café would not have been happy to know that as they debated Collard Jackson's intentions, a colored girl was already taking steps, however timorously, to attend Laureate's all-white school. It was my first time inside that enormous building. The long, wide, cool hall. Three or four sets of doors opening onto a campus shaded with pine trees. Mr. Pellicore met me and Miss Chandler in the lobby outside Principal Ben Wilburn's office.

I could see the principal through his open door, staring out at the colored teacher and her student. Mr. Wilburn wore those glasses you used to often see, the flat lenses set in heavy black frames, that seemed likely to slide off a pug nose bright enough to guide Santa's sleigh. Hair always neatly combed. Miss Chandler turned my attention to the director of the Marching Saints.

"Cilla, meet your director."

"James Pellicah, Mizz Hanesome. Chawmed."

Even if you'd never set foot in Laureate in your life you would have to know that James Montrose Pellicore was not a native to the region. I could only understand about half of what came out of his mouth.

"Mr. Pellicore will be different than anyone you've met," Miss Chandler warned me ahead of time. "He may strike you as impatient. Maybe even rude. He has some ways that are odd."

I'm sure she meant well, telling me this.

"Cam along," Pellicore bundled us away in a hurry.

On personal appearance: Our band director was one of those

gentlemen who every morning wakes up to arrange a few wisps of hair on a skull trying its best to go decently bald. He wore a long-sleeved shirt white as chalk and starched stiff as a board, with pinstripe pants too big in the waist and worn beltless which didn't matter because he always, and I mean always, had a pair of argyle suspenders holding up those out-of-place britches. I don't think the man took those things off to shit.

He had short legs. Even so I had trouble keeping up. Miss Chandler didn't even try, so by the time we reached the band hall Mr. Pellicore and I found ourselves with some moments unaccompanied.

"Why'd you take the folio?" he asked, with absolutely no preamble or introduction.

"You mean the music?"

"Of course I mean the music, that's what you took wasn't it?"

"Yessuh."

"'Sir'. Try the 'r'. Then why? Why classical compositions? Why not something popular? Big band? Or march?"

I swallowed. "I heard some of Mr. Mozart on Mr. Raymond's radio."

"Over the radio."

"Yes, *sir*. Then I saw the music in your folder."

"The same piece? You're sure of that?"

"Yes, sir."

"Hmph. Interesting," he muttered, and rested his head on his chest.

About that time Miss Chandler caught up.

"I believe you know the way," Pellicore said to me, and pulled a metal door open. He opened the band hall's door, but did not go through. He just stood there, in the breech, off to one side.

"Well, come on, Miss Handsom," Pellicore barked.

"You in the way," I shot back.

"Cilla," Miss Chandler puffed from behind me. "Mister Pellicore is holding the door for us. It's a courtesy. Something a gentleman does for ladies."

Pellicore brightened, the lines across his forehead immediately smoothing. "I have been described in a number of ways since my exile to this Godforbidden place," he said. "But that, my lady, is the first time anyone has called me a gentleman. Come in, ladies, please."

All of a sudden he was treating us like we were precious. Shooed us into his office like a hen behind her chicks. It was just as I remembered it, a mess. Papers strewn, pictures aslant. A hieroglyphics inscribed with magic marker ran off its board and onto the wall.

"Coffee, Mizz Chandluh?" he asked. I saw a percolator hiding behind a mess of Manilla folders.

"Yes, please."

He took out a handkerchief to wipe out a mug salvaged from behind his desk, chatting the whole time. Where had Miss Chandler attended college? Howard, she answered and he seemed real impressed. Asked her if she still had friends there. Scattered, she said and asked him if he finished his graduate work at Yale. Pellicore seemed amazed that Miss Chandler was familiar with Yale.

"We're going to be colleagues," she responded modestly. "I want to know as much about you as I can, within the limits of privacy."

"Yale *is* wonderful," Pellicore beamed. "Almost as fine a place, I'm sure, as Howard University."

Then the two of them laughed like they were sharing some private joke. For a while I was just happy to sit out of the way.

That was not to last long.

"Miss Handsom, here are the terms. I teach you the piano. You give me a French horn. That's the arrangement. Any questions?"

How could there be?

"Fine, then. Miss Chandler, thank you so much for coming. A pleasure."

By which Miss Chandler knew she was dismissed. Leaving me alone with this crazy Yankee music man. He jumped right in.

"We have a lot to do over this summer. Two instruments, God! If I didn't need a French horn so badly I would never consider this. And I must warn you—the horn is why you're here. I will help you a half hour each session with your piano. Your teacher says you can read music. We'll see. But understand that the balance of the time you're here you'll be fulfilling *my need* and what I need is a French horn for the Marching Saints. Are you ready to be a Marching Saint, Miss Handsom?"

"Don't think I'm ready for sainthood yet," I replied.

He wasn't amused. "You know what a mouthpiece is, Miss Handsom?"

No segues or transitions. That was his way.

"A mouthpiece," he snapped. "You've seen them?"

"For a trumpet," I affirmed without a note of sass. "But only at a distance."

"I don't need a trumpet." He reached into his pocket, pulled out a piece smaller than the cork on a syrup bottle.

"This is the mouthpiece for a French horn."

He handed it to me.

"What I do with it?"

"See whether you can spit."

The brass mouthpiece for the French horn felt natural to my wide lips, which was a surprise. Pellicore (he would not be called by any other name or title) demonstrated the technique of "blowing" through the mouthpiece. He called it spitting, which was misleading. It's more like buzzing, really. Buzz like a bee.

Once I demonstrated I could keep up a consistent buzz through the mouthpiece, Pellicore gave me an actual French horn, the first one I had seen close up. It looked like a sea shell.

"It'll be heavy," he said, but it wasn't. Not to me, anyway. Certainly not as heavy as hay or melons. And there were only four rotary valves, not the eighty-eight ivoried tongs of a piano.

Four valves against eighty-eight hammers? How difficult could this instrument possibly be?

I would shortly learn.

"Let's start with a small confusion, gets to many neophytes, the phenomenon of transposing instruments."

"Transposing—?"

"Instruments, yes. Like the French horn. You see, when you're at the piano and you play a C, what note do you hear?"

Was this a trick question?'

"A C?" I obliged tentatively.

"Bravo," he approved. "But if you play the note C on the French Horn you will not hear a C."

"I won't?"

"No. Assuming you've got an ear for pitch at all, when you play C on your French horn what you will actually hear is F."

"I hear a F?"

"An' F. Yes. And the reason for that is that instruments are built in different keys. Trumpets, for example, are in the key of B-flat. Alto sax in E-flat. The French horn is in F. I'll demonstrate."

He took my horn, but not before removing my mouthpiece. He replaced it with another piece, a clean mouthpiece, from off the piano.

"Listen," he commanded. "I shall play the C indicated by the staff here. Tell me what note you hear."

Sure enough, that F-note came across clear as a bugle.

"I hear it!" I was as delighted as if I had witnessed magic.

"Sure you're not just agreeing with your teacher?"

"Sir?"

He lowered the horn to the floor and, keeping his hands concealed by the girth of his trunk, reached back for the piano.

"You say you recognized the F on the horn?"

"Yessuh. Sir."

"Then do you hear this C?"

He hit a key on the piano and right away I was confused.

"That was a C?"

"For you to decide, Miss Handsom. Here. I'll play it again."

He keyed the ivory once again and this time I was sure.

"That wasn't a C," I declared.

"What was it, then?"

"That's an F-sharp."

His brow knitted a little as he continued to keep the keyboard concealed from view. Like a gambler protecting a hand of cards.

"What about these notes?" he said finally, and keyed a chord.

"E, C-sharp, B-flat, an' D." I replied without hesitation.

It seemed at the time a trivial demonstration. You either had pitch or you didn't. But Mr. Pellicore didn't seem too happy.

"I do somethin' wrong?" I asked.

"No, no," he said. "That was satisfactory. Satisfactory. But a good ear isn't enough to make a serious musician."

"No, sir," I said, chastened.

He took out the horn's mouthpiece.

"This will be your horn," he handed it over. And then he had me demonstrate a simple *Do Re Mi* in C which sounded like F. Then we talked about the different keys, and different notes within keys. Did you know you can get fifteen notes out of a French horn without depressing a single valve? Try that on a piano.

We went on to scales. I had several varieties of scales from my years around church pianos, but had never heard them named—diatonic, chromatic, major and minor, pentatonic, wholetone.

"These are your warm ups." Pellicore shoved a folder across his rolling desk. "You do these before you do anything else."

Then he talked about chords and scale degrees.

"Scale degrees can be used to name chords," Pellicore informed me. "For instance, a dominant chord is built on the fifth degree of a scale."

He talked about a minor chord, then, and then a Neapolitan sixth ("A major chord, in first inversion, built on the lowered second degree of the scale..."). Some of it I could follow, the rest of the time he might as well have been singing scat.

Scales and chords and Napoleon!!

Was I ever going to play anything?

But finally, his pedantry well demonstrated, Pellicore came down to earth and shuffled a sheet of music off the floor.

"Seen this before?" he settled the music onto a three-legged stand.

"Three Blind Mice," I read the title.

"Didn't ask for a title."

"Know the words. I never seen the music."

"'Have' never seen. Good. That means you'll be playing by sight. Well, go on. Play."

First time out on the French horn I managed to blind the mice without butchering them, which pleased my new teacher.

"Right, fine. That's all I need to hear for the time being. Let's see what you can do on the piano."

He swiveled his roll-around chair to the upright, sweeping sheets of music and Coke cans to the floor with total disregard for the mess ensuing.

"Take the bench, Mizz Han'som, we don't have all day."

I placed the French horn in its case, visions of farmers' wives and carving knives gaining prominence.

"The piano. Quickly, please. Chop-chop."

Well, all right, an axe would do as well as a knife, but I hustled on over. Pellicore slapped a sheet of music before me that had nothing to do with blind mice or any other grim tale. It took me a moment, in fact, to realize that I had seen this music, or at least a variation of it, before.

"That's 'Ode to Joy'!" I exclaimed.

"For the vulgar. It's actually a portion of the final movement of Beethoven's Ninth Symphony."

I scanned the score.

"It's different. Different than the 'Ode' *I* got."

"That you stole," Pellicore corrected.

"Yes, suh."

"Si*rrr*. If you talk like a field hand, Miss Handsom, people will treat you like a field hand. Enunciate the 'r'."

I was much too fascinated with the architecture arranged in measured harmony before me to worry about anything so mundane as elocution.

"Lord a'mighty."

"It's similar to scores you've already seen." Pellicore seemed pleased with the effect he had wrought. "Except, of course, that *this* is Beethoven's. We start with the flute on top, here. And work down to the string basses here at the bottom."

"But where's the piano?"

"There isn't one. There is a horn. There. You see?"

"Yes, sir."

"Play it."

I sat for a moment. Trying to get my time.

"What key?" he queried as I bent to retake my wind instrument.

"D Major," I replied, and buzzing into my stingy mouthpiece, worked through a few measures.

He frowned, "That's enough. Tell me, Miss Handsom, can you hear this in your head? Without an instrument? As you read? Can you imagine even a single cello, or violin, or clarinet or flute following this? How about all together?"

"I can hear some," I answered cautiously.

"Some?"

"A lot, then."

"Can you, now?" he slipped his hands inside those patterned suspenders. "Difficult, even for an experienced conductor to hold a symphony in his head, but here you are, a colored girl barely able to work through the scales and yet at a glance you say you can hear this music, this orchestra of magnificent music? In your head?"

"I don't know all the instruments," I qualified. "But what I know I hear pretty good."

"'What you know'—!" he shook his head. "Miss Handsom let me begin your education by informing you that you don't know squat. You hear me? You cannot sight-read as well as the sorriest church organist. You are barely competent on the piano and until tonight you never heard a French horn."

Not true, I *had* heard. Every Friday during football season I heard the French horn and the trombones and the flute—I heard every instrument in Pellicore's band! I even went home, sometimes, and wrote down the music. I used grocery bags, from the SafeWay, that parchment serving as the vellum for my own re-constructed compositions.

Something was stinging my eyes.

"You are the student, here, Miss Handsom. Don't forget it."

"Yes, suh—sir."

"Now take that horn."

He slapped another piece of music on the stand. It was tame compared to Beethoven's work, I discerned immediately. Not a lot of range. Regular as a metronome.

"What's this?" I asked.

"How you earn your piano lessons," he snapped. "'Oklahoma' will be our half-time feature for the first game of the season. We have ten games. You'll need to master this and nine other pieces. Plus 'Saints', of course. We always march out on 'Saints."

"But...when will I get to play Beethoven?"

"When you're ready. When I say you're ready. For now, you'll be with me here, practicing. Every night, Monday through Thursday. It will get old, I warn you. It will get hard. And sooner or later we have to get you on the field to march."

With that he spun his chair around, rolled across the floor away from the piano and into the dock of his cluttered desk. There was no formal dismissal. No, "We're done for the day." I was expected to realize on my own that the lesson was ended, that I had been dismissed and that my director was not interested in odes to joy or hope or ambition or anything else.

I was already out of Pellicore's office when I heard his parting words.

"Close the door behind you, Miss Handsom."

His back turned to me.

"And make sure it's locked. We don't want anything valuable to leave the band hall."

Chapter seven

"Court Orders Integration of
County School"—*The Clarion*

I skirted downtown Laureate on the way home from my first
formal piano lesson. Dusk had fallen by the time I left the band hall,
red streaks of what looked like fire coming up from behind the sil-
houettes of pines to lick the bottoms of clouds stacked like anvils. I
suppose I knew my path would take me by Joe Billy's lodging. I pen-
etrated the girdle of dogwoods easily enough, but it was not possible
looking up to that windowless retreat to know whether Joe Billy was
inside. I took the stairs two at a time, that fragile scaffolding swaying
as if with the weight of silent Masons.

"'Body home?" I rapped the postern of his feeble door. "Joe
Billy, you here?"

I imagined I heard someone inside, some shift of weight or
response. But it seemed to take forever before the door opened.

"Cilla, look at you! Whatchu up to, girl?"

"Practicin' at piano." I hesitated before stepping into his apartment. A sharp, pungent aroma stopped me at the doorway. I saw a
bench sagging with paints and lacquers and varnish, their vapors
pushing like a finger to the back of my palate.

"You painting guitars?" I asked.

"Started one."

"Best leave the door open," I told him. "Fumes are bad for your head."

"You prob'ly right," he said, peeking warily outside. "Or maybe work downstairs, there's plenty ventilation down there. Come on. Git in here."

A deliciously sinful invitation. To enter a dwelling inhabited by a single, young man, no adults or grandparents or half-uncles to chaperone or deceive. Just by yourself with one other.

"Tell me what it is." He plopped himself on the floor and I provided an edited version of my first lesson with Pellicore. Joe Billy let me go on and on. How fine it was. How much better I was going to play. All about scores and orchestral arrangements and the thrills of marching band and "Oklahoma".

"How's your teacher?" he finally asked.

"Just fine."

He nodded. "You got a talent, Cilla. You don't need to apologize for it."

"I'm just learning."

"Still—you got a talent. Don't go hiding under no bushel."

"I'm gonna take what he'll give me. And I do like the horn; I'm surprised, but I do. Playin' winds is like running. You get done, you got your music, but your heart and lungs, they're in it, too. It's like everything on you is making music."

"You a crazy colored girl." He ran a comb through his hair, past his temple and down a ducktail.

"You a fool." I ducked my head so he wouldn't see I was blushing, but when I came up there he was.

"Cilla—"

"What?"

He kissed me. It was a pretty timid effort at first, but then I started feeling real warm and I kissed him, and then we were down on the hardwood floor together, stretched out like cats, sucking tongue, his hands all over my scabbed back, that lace of wounds still healing. Not embarrassed, not hesitant.

Something between my legs got wet. I think I let down the top of my shift. He sat over me amazed.

"Cilla, you got the finest breasts inna world."

I knew I was blushing, then, but I didn't care.

He got something out of his pants pocket. I didn't look right at him, at first.

"I don't want no baby put in," I said.

"No, that's what this is," he said.

"Used one ever?"

"Sure, I have."

"Have you?"

"No."

"It's all right," I said.

I just assumed that my city boy had made time with lots of girls, but it turned out Joe Billy needed guidance about as much as I did.

"Can you help me?" he freely asked at one point.

I slipped on the condom.

"Thank you."

Then I leaned back, wrapped my legs over his hips and raised up off the small of my wide back. He was plenty long enough by then and hard as a dime and I guided him in.

"Cilla...Cilla!"

We'd have sex several times after that, on several occasions. But that was the first time. We lay like spoons afterward. I could see his guitar lying with us, on the floor.

"She got a nice belly."

"Who got?" he stirred.

"Girl on your guitar. What is she? 'Gyptian? Jezebel?"

Joe Billy followed the curve of my body with his hand, his smooth hand, starting at my shoulder, down the curve of my back, my hip, my leg.

"Maybe next guitar I do'll be you," he said.

"Be a dirty guitar sure enough then."

We both laughed at that. Virgin, no longer, but still innocent. We were shy getting dressed; I think I made him turn away. He had some milk yet unspoiled that was cooling in a block of ice in the sink. We had some of that. By that time it was well dark. Joe Billy walked me home, skirting the downtown, following the safety of the railroad tracks, wary of dogs and white

Next morning I was at Mr. Raymond's working the pump when Preacher Dipps comes trotting up the street like lickety split. I froze. Last person on the Lord's earth I wanted to see on the lee of losing my virginity was our hellfire and brimstone minister. But Preacher Dipps took no notice of me, instead stomping right up onto Mr. Raymond's porch waving an as-yet-unripped copy of *The Clarion*.

"You seen the paper this mawnin', Brother Raymond?"

"I have," Mr. Raymond might have been confirming the arrival of a train.

"They closin' down Kerbo! They shuttin' our school!"

"Looks like."

"What about our children? What's gone happen?"

Mr. Raymond inspected the crease of his khaki trousers in reply. Our preacher noticed me, finally, attached as if welded to the iron handle of the pump.

"Lawd Jesus," he declared and stumbled off the porch.

It would be wrong to assume that black people in all areas of the South unanimously welcomed integration. Many, perhaps most parents in Colored Town were not happy to see their children cross the tracks to Laureate. Many were loathe to give up the school that had for generations defined our community.

Most of all, no one wanted trouble.

The Friday following *The Clarion*'s headline, Miss Hattie Briar led the pledge of allegiance for the last day of the school year, the very last day for Kerbo School. Our teachers had, in the midst of many distractions, attempted to prepare their students for what I believe were called STEP tests. These were tests designed to evaluate progress in skills related to reading and mathematics. The County School Board had redundantly directed Kerbo School to assess all its students "in anticipation of the coming integration" of white and black students.

It seemed an insult to be so ordered; Kerbo students were routinely administered the STEP and Iowa tests. I had taken a STEP,

I'm certain, every year since the ninth grade. Then, as now, black students fared worse on these tests than whites. The courts had long seen that segregated schools for coloreds were inherently disadvantaged, but interestingly many people in my community either resisted that assessment or ignored it.

From my remove as an adult I can honestly say that Kerbo School's students were well-funded in what later came to be called the "basics" of education. But come test-time you had to know more than the basics to do well. For instance, I was rarely intimidated by questions related to mathematics or geography. But I was consistently flummoxed by questions related to vocabulary and reading.

I knew quite well what a shell was, for example; Lord knows, we had pecan shells and acorn shells right on our back porch. But if I got asked something like "An oar is to a shell as a propeller is to a/an: a)Rocket b)Automobile c)Airplane d)None of the above," my personal experience of a shell's possibilities made me hesitate to commit to the obvious answer. Pudding was stumped outright.

"What's a 'oar'?" he asked Miss Chandler.

"I can't help you, Pudding. Just do the best you can."

Math was pretty straightforward, though some of the algebra I had simply never seen. Same thing for trigonometry. There were questions related to set theory and slide rules that may as well have been written for somebody on Mars. Chicken and Pudding were lost after the first hour. Shirley Lee and Lonnie kept looking over my shoulder until Miss Chandler's stern warning waved them off. We were all distracted, naturally, both by the news that our school was to be closed and the fears associated with the coming integration. Still, we tried. By early afternoon, that STEP was finished.

"Pencils down. After I collect your tests you want to clean out your desks." Then came the ritual command. "Class will prepare for Final Assembly."

We all groaned. Every student at Kerbo hated final assembly. It was formal, uncomfortable, unnecessary and the only thing standing between you, the door, and summertime. This particular assembly would stand out, however; the last assembly of any kind at Kerbo School.

We gathered in the yard, of course. There was no auditorium. Grades one through twelve simply filed out onto our rough playground, at which point Miss Hattie led us in a prayer before reading a statement mandated by Principal Ben Wilburn and the Lafayette County School Board.

"'All grades from first grade through twelfth will be bussed to the Lafayette County Consolidated School beginning in the fall semester'," Miss Chandler read from the provided text. "'Teachers at Kerbo will be assigned duties as appropriate at LCCS. Students from Kerbo will be required to wear…'" Miss Hattie paused over her text, frowning. She smoothed the paper she was reading. Then she continued. "'Students from Kerbo will be required to wear shoes to class every day. Appropriate hygiene will be observed.'"

Hygiene would be observed.

The letter went on to specify procedures for registration and so on. But that business about shoes and hygiene was what stuck.

The required reading completed, Principal Hattie Briar offered her own terse remarks to the final assembly of her students.

"This will be the last time we gather at Kerbo School. But we move on to other assemblies of students and teachers, and other challenges. Do not be afraid. Be proud of Kerbo, and when you go next year to your new school, just remember that you are as good as anybody over there. You are just as smart. Just as valuable. And I am confident you are well prepared to participate.

"But you will have an extra burden. There will be extra eyes looking at each and every one of you. Do not do anything that will embarrass me or your teachers or parents. Do not do *anything* that might in any way bring shame to your community."

Looked like Miss Hattie was glaring straight at me. I glanced to Miss Chandler for reassurance, but her eyes were closed, her lips moving.

"All right, then," Miss Hattie concluded briskly. "You have received your report cards. Your grades are duly recorded. Students of Kerbo, you are dismissed."

The summer following the closing of Kerbo School did not begin auspiciously. Summers brought long hours of work in miserable weather and in filth. Mother and I had regular days at the nursery, of course; Fridays and Saturdays were hired out to Mr. Thistle. Strung tobacco for the Hendersons most other days, standing eight or ten hours a day accepting the poisoned, tarred leaves of tobacco from tired handers, children mostly, three to five leaves in a hand, thirty hands to a stick, thirty sticks to a tier, ten tiers to a barn. Nine hundred, a thousand sticks to fill a barn and sometimes with four stringers we'd fill two barns in a day. For five dollars a day.

When my day labor was done, I'd go home from the nursery or tobacco barn and sponge off with the luxury of barreled water, then scrub Mama clean, finally to snatch a hoecake and sausage on the run for the band hall and music lessons. I was studying piano and French horn side by side, graduating in the latter instrument from "Oklahoma" to "Singing in the Rain," to "The Impossible Dream."

Piano was coming along. I was sight-reading with more confidence. Pellicore was very good, if terse, in describing notations or progressions unfamiliar to me. I was well past scales and idiot-music and was pestering Pellicore for sheet music to match the tunes I'd only heard on Mr. Raymond's radio. Jazz and big-band, mostly. Duke Ellington. Glen Miller. John Coltrane.

"Nope." Pellicore denied that last request peremptorily. "It's impossible to put Coltrane on paper."

So Coltrane would have to wait. But classical music and swing starting jumping off the sheet and playing in my head. I *could* hear Beethoven's music or Ellington's. In fact, anything I could read I could hear. I educated my ear for classical instrumentation on Pellicore's substantial collection of LPs, reveling in the interplay of strings and winds, the cello and alto sax, a violin and oboe.

It was very interesting for me to see how differently instruments could be orchestrated, how Ellington, as an example, broke with conventional notions of organization when he integrated different *kinds* of instruments—brass and woodwinds and so on—into single, seamless units, creating a wholly new synthesis of sound and breaking the rigid lines that kept, say, cellos separate from trumpets.

I guess you could say that (in more than one respect) The Duke desegregated music.

The extent to which Pellicore tolerated my extracurricular explorations directly related to how well I satisfied *his* needs. I was doing well with the French horn, actually enjoyed it. I had vaulted that obstacle. But then I had to learn to march.

"You're no good to me if you can't execute on the field, Hand-som."

So every lesson concluded with Pellicore marching me in the martial sense of the word from the band hall to the football field, where I would be drilled like a Marine on a parade ground.

Left face, right face, about face.

Dress right, dress left, dress up.

The commands all ran together in my head. There were other adaptations that also did not come easy. It's one thing to play your instrument seated on a stable chair from music situated on a stand, quite another to perform that tune on the metered hoof with a half-secured score of music bobbing up and down on the lyre affixed to your brass.

I was so bad I had Pellicore wishing he had hair to pull.

"God damn it, girl, can you walk and chew gum at the same time?!"

I decided that I had enjoyed about as much of music and Pellicore as I could stand. I needed to get away from that chalked field, away from my director, away from any demanding thought or labor. "Please God...!" I left the specifics open to His pleasure, and on the following Saturday my prayer was answered.

It was late August, the weekend before the commencement of my senior year, a rare weekend—by which I mean a weekend completely free of labor. I was on the porch early that morning, seated alongside Hard On and Mama as I pored over the Sears catalog. Mama was fascinated by it. I wondered if she imagined that all those models displayed on its pages were actually small people. She kept pulling the thick volume from me and onto her own lap, rubbing her hands over the Young Adults Section, smiling at the displays of slacks and lingerie, the inflections in her voicebox rising and falling with exactly the same pitch and cadence as do young girls' when confiding to their dolls. Those dolls, that is, not already decapitated by eager boys needing baseballs.

I was trying to calculate how far my summer earnings would go toward buying the shoes and clothes I badly needed for the coming integrated school year. I was late to mail-order and worried I'd have to find a ride to Gainesville or Live Oak to shop. I had my Sunday things, of course, for my first day, but I didn't know if Sunday dress was appropriate for my first day in the white school.

That worry aside, it was a fine weekend. We were having a high-ol' time, for the Handsom family, Grandma shelling peas, me and Mama with the catalog, Hard On with his snout buried in my warm lap. About that time I heard a car pull up.

It wasn't unusual to hear a car or truck pull *by*, but nobody pulled *up* to our house, not even Mr. Thistle.

"Who that?" Grandmother noticed it right away.

"I'll go see," I said, extricating myself from mother, dog, and catalog.

Hard On followed me off the porch and out front and what did I see idling before my house but Joe Billy behind the wheel of a two-toned, '56 Ford.

"Joe Bee," I said severely. "I thought I tole' you 'bout stealin' them cars."

The smile on that boy's face like to have split his skull. "Ain't nuthin' stole here," he slid out proudly. "Bought her this morning. HEY, DOG!"

Hard On had his leg hiked and was pissing on a tire.

"Hard On, git off!" I tried not to laugh and failed.

It had once been a beautiful machine, white top over robin red panels, a fiery Ford Fairlane with the big v-8. A pretty hot vehicle for 1956, but by 1963 it was definitely pre-owned.

"Only one owner 'fore me," Joe Billy bragged, but I was way ahead of him.

"Ever'body know that's Spence MacGrue's car," I said.

Older folks in Colored Town insisted that Spence MacGrue was once a man of means. Owned his own timber mill, that yarn went.

Others had Spence flying fighter planes in the war. Some apocrypha claimed MacGrue was a mathematical prodigy. You know how it is. If you don't have a history, you invent one.

People got to have a story.

"How much you pay for this thing?"

"Repairs." Joe Billy said this with great self-importance. "Transmission needed work. Tires and brakes."

"Got air condition?"

"Right here." Joe Billy reached back to roll down a window.

"You in danger of turnin' country, Joe Billy, I do believe."

"Guess we better get to the city, then."

"Who's we?"

"You and me, baby."

"I'm'a just up and go? Leave Mama and Grandma?"

"For the day, yep. And well into the night."

"What city we gone to?"

"Jacksonville. City by the sea."

"I see you. Whatchu doin' in Jacksonville?"

Joe Billy jerked a thumb in the direction of the trunk.

"Got some merchandise."

"You mean a guitar."

"Couple of guitars. For some real musicians, Cilla. Blues-men. Jazz. A genuine nightclub. You should bring your sheet music. They might let you play."

"So this here is an educational opportunity, is that it, Joe Billy?"

"Like a field trip," he agreed, grinning to the promontory of his ears.

I considered a moment.

"Wait right here," I said. "I be right back."

Chapter eight

I have been on the road for most of my professional life, but I can honestly say that no journey or concert or cruise was more exhilarating than that first road trip with Joe Billy King. I had never been an hour away from my home in any direction, had never transgressed the county line. We went sailing past the Hal W. Adams Bridge at sixty miles an hour, then on to Live Oak and onto the interstate still under construction. I'd never seen a road so broad and so long in my life.

"Like a heat wave/ Burnin' in my heart..."—*Martha and the Vandellas*

Four lanes of traffic. And a median between?!

"You could put a field of tobacco in there and still have room for peanuts," I declared, and Joe Billy shook his head.

"Take the girl out of the country, but you cain't take the country out the girl."

"You country as I am, Joe Billy."

"Maybe," he allowed. "But at least I'm ashamed of it."

I pointed to the dash. "That a radio?"

"Yes, ma'am."

It took nearly four hours to reach J-ville and in that time I heard more pop tunes from more groups than I'd heard in my entire life. The Beatles were just reaching the charts. The Beach Boys were surfing U.S.A. I rolled into Jacksonville on Martha and the Vandellas wailing "Heat Wave" like I'd known the song all my life.

Ten minutes later we were lost. Joe Billy pulled over at a gas station. A black man tended the pump, a glowing cigarette lipping from his mouth.

"You wantin' Manuel's Tap Room? That'd be down on the jookin' side of town. Yeah. You want Ashley Street. Yeah. Broad and Jefferson and Davis, they all cross Ashley. Yeah. You'll see the Roosevelt Theater down there pretty close. The Strand."

"Anyplace to eat?"

"Roosevelt Grill. Yeah."

"Thank you."

"Be seven fifty."

I had never seen the civil face of a city before, much less its jazzy, violent, sensual heart. I was not sophisticated enough to see the pimps and hustlers trailing knots of shore-leave sailors, the brown bags wrapped in the fists of alcoholics. The boarded windows and jacked-up cars. All I saw from the comfort of Joe Billy's newly acquired coupé was a huge, mingling bustle of people and clothes and aromas as exotic as Egypt.

I had never seen such Negroes, these black men and women who walked, strolled, and swaggered with such insolent nonchalance. And nobody dropped his head, not even to white people.

"There it is." Joe Billy tapped the brakes.

"Hmm? What?"

"Manuel's. Up there." Joe Billy shoved his arm out the driver's window to indicate a storefront squeezed between two other businesses. The place looked more like a shoe store than a nightclub. I almost missed the signage:—Manuel's Tap Room—

We parked beneath a billboard advertising whiskey. A blonde woman reclined on a chaise lounge, an ink-black gown draped over white, white skin. She had a deep cleavage, generously revealed, and the tumbler of Seagrams in her hand promised a lot more than a nightcap.

"Don't forget your music." Joe Billy hustled his cased guitars from the Ford's back seat.

We pushed through a narrow door that did not immediately open out into the club's interior but into a cramped lobby where a bouncer kept the cash drawer. A monster blocked our way to the den's inner regions. I had never heard of bouncers or doormen, and this gatekeeper was the biggest man I'd ever seen. Pudding's daddy was a big man; I saw Mr. Reed lift a Farmall tractor one time. Lifted it, held it by the drawbar—with one hand—and spun a tire with the other. Did you know if you lift a tractor and spin a tire in a particular direction that the tire on the other side will rotate in the opposite direction?

This man didn't look as hard as Pudding's papa, but he was a head taller. Had on loose slacks and a tee-shirt cut low at the neck. Little curls of hair on a dark chest worthy of a sumo wrestler. He had a single key mated to a shoelace that wrapped onto a wrist thick as a fence post. A brace of keys hung from some kind of leather contraption on his belt. Made me wonder how many doors this place had.

"Chu wont?"

"Here to see Ruben," Joe Billy replied.

"He 'spectin'?"

"He's expecting me, yeah."

"Way chere."

So we waited. Few minutes later the bouncer comes back sucking a Coke floated up top with a handful of peanuts.

"Chu wont?"

Just like he'd never seen us.

"Here to see Ruben," Joe Billy repeated, without the least hint of impatience or exasperation.

"Thass right, thass right," the big man nodded as if confirming Joe Billy's intention.

"Come own back."

Turned out we were only twelve feet from the club proper, the area defended by the bouncer being a mere bottleneck to the interior. It had the smell of a nightclub; of stale beer, cheap cologne and cigarettes. It was dark inside, and cool. There were palm trees fading in amber pots. Fans churning at odd intervals from the ceiling. A teak bar ranged along one wall, its brass foot rail dragging a floor of cheap mexican tile.

The stage was raised low at the far end of the club, distant from the bar, overlooking a small empire of tables and chairs. There were two pianos onstage. An upright Baldwin was unremarkable, but the Steinway was a beauty, black as coal, hardglossed, a truly grand instrument with a sounding board big as a wing on a plane.

The grand was situated so that its ivory keys faced the still-depleted room. A man lounging on the bench that served the piano swung a microphone on its long arm to the lobe of his ear. He was about my height, just a smidgeon under six feet, tall even for a man in those days. He was pretty sloppy in that setting, a white shirt rolled up at the arms and stuffed into unbelted slacks. A slouched felt hat. Laces spilling, untied, off his shoes.

He had a cigar. I followed the smoke as it curled in gentle tight tendrils only to disperse in the heat generated by a spotlight hot and high in the rafters above.

"He the one want your guitars?" I nudged Joe Billy.

"No, that's Alex McBride. He's headlinin' at the club."

I didn't know what it meant to headline, but the headliner must have heard us enter his domain.

"Is this the guitar man?" Alex McBride turned on his bench to greet Joe Billy.

"Yes, sir. Is Ruben here?"

"Dressing room. Why don' you go on back? Tiny, can you take 'im?"

"On me," the misnamed bouncer detoured offstage to a side exit and Joe Billy followed, leaving me alone with Alex McBride.

He ignored me, at first. Just returned to his piano. He was a tall slender man, took off his hat long enough to run his hand through hair that was processed, like Joe Billy's, pomaded and combed back. With the advantage of broadened exposure I now see a strong resemblance between Alex McBride and Nat King Cole, though at the time, having never seen an image of Cole, I could not make that comparison.

McBride was working something out on the piano that teased me. It was probably no more than a dozen measures, played over and over, but never played the same way twice, which was irritating for me. I had heard this music before, or had seen it, I was sure. But what I was hearing did not match up with this man's rendition. It wasn't quite the same.

The hell was he playing?

"'Rocks in My Bed'."

It came out of my mouth as soon as it lodged in my head. Those slender, dark fingers stopped over the keys. McBride peered mildly over his shoulder.

"What was that, sugar?"

"'Scuse me. What you were playing? Duke Ellington's song? 'Rocks in My Bed'."

"It's an easy listen," McBride smiled.

"I 'spose. Never heard it, yet."

"Never heard?"

"Not till just now. With you."

"You never heard it, sugar, how'd you know what it was?"

"I saw the music."

"Saw it?"

"The sheet music. Once or twice. Not the whole thing." I hesitated. "You aren't playin' it right."

The smoke from his cigar scattered to the ceiling.

"What's that you're carryin'?" He nodded brusquely to the folder tucked in my armpit.

"Just some music."

"Ah hah. Why own't you come on up here?"

I backed away.

"Come on, sugar, it's all right."

He dragged leisurely on his cigar as I approached. "How old are you?"

"Seventeen."

"How *tall* are you?"

"Six feet, more or less."

"I'd guess more," he said.

He rose from the bench as I clumsily mounted the stage, and he remained standing for me.

"You play the piano?"

"Yes, sir."

"Call me Alex. Why own't you take a seat here?"

A seat at a real piano? At a real nightclub? With a headliner?

"Oh, I don't know."

"It's a piano, sugar. Same as any other."

He seated me graciously at the bench beside that grand, grand piano.

"Tall girl with long fingers. How big a reach you got?"

"I don' know," I blushed. "Enough, I guess."

He chuckled, the cigar wagging in the corner of his mouth, and nodded at my folder of music.

"You got 'Rocks in My Bed' in there?"

"No, sir, I only seen that a couple of times. At Mr. Pellicore's."

"Pellicore?"

"He's teaching me French horn and helping some with piano."

"He a good teacher?"

"He's the band director for the white school. We got to go there next year? I have to march in the band or he won't take time for lessons."

"He won't, won't he?"

The tip of the cigar glowed a ruby red.

"I catch your name, sugar?"

"Cilla Handsom."

"Cilla, does your teacher know you can sight-read?"

"He's got an idea. He don't, doesn't, believe I can hear the music, though. In my head? He say it take years to do that. Like a conductor, or somethin'."

"Or something," Alex agreed. "Tell you what, why don't we work us in a lesson right here?"

"With you? Now?"

"Ain' no big thang. Why don't you play me somethin' out your folder? Anything you like."

"How about *Ode to Joy?*"

"Didn't know they was a piano in there."

"I put one in. Sort of."

In fact, ever since I learned that there was no part for the piano in the Master's original, I had begun reducing his score to accommodate that instrument, sometimes finding it in the flute, sometimes with the strings or another instrument, playing the melody with my right hand, working out the harmonies as I sifted through Beethoven's densely orchestrated composition.

"You wrote a piano for the Ninth?"

"Just a little."

I slipped a sheaf of hand-staffed pages from behind the school-purchased original. My hands trembled.

"Butterflies are awright," Alex crooned. "Long as you know all they is is butterflies."

That got me to laugh. "Sorry."

"It's fine, sugar doll. Now play."

I had worked hard to come up with a performance that I could duplicate, something that I could play over and over, each iteration faithful to the last. Precise. Exact. Perfect as a metronome.

Just like Mama.

Mi-Mi-Fa-So/So-Fa-Mi-Re/Do-Do-Re-Mi/Mii-ReRe/

I couldn't have played for long, certainly not through the entire movement, but when I stopped I was sweating as if I'd been stringing tobacco. "That's all I got so far."

Alex smiled. By that I mean his cheeks pinched—he never displayed his teeth when he smiled.

"I'd say that was 'bout perfect."

Perfect? Nobody had ever told me I was perfect at anything. Except maybe Joe Billy when we were in his apartment. I had never received such praise. I was elated.

"Perfect," he nodded again. "No variation. Just like you got it on your paper, there."

It didn't sound quite so complimentary the second time around.

"Tell you what, doll, you stay at this piano."

McBride popped up from our shared bench to take the upright's nearby.

"Now what I want you to do is play four measures at a time. Just four. Then let me play those same measures, can you do that?"

"But you can't see my music," I objected.

"Long as you can," he assured me. "Now, you ready? One, two, three...."

Once again, I performed my handwritten piece as if on a metronome. But this time there was another piano in accompaniment and another interpretation. Everything I rendered on my piano Alex repeated, but not verbatim. He varied my own faithful reproduction, tweaking it, teasing it, ornamenting it with no apparent respect for my score or the original.

It was disconcerting at first. Then irritating. Sometimes he'd vary the key, sometimes he'd take my piece to a whole different chord or harmony. He wandered all over the tempo. And the melody—how could anyone tamper with Beethoven's melody?

I frowned visibly at one variation.

"Didn't work," Alex agreed, without losing a beat. "Just keep playing."

We went through the whole thing, I playing my modified ode, Alex complementing with variations based on progressions from blues and jazz.

It was a jarring experience. But then my own performance began to reach that wonderful place of what I call focused-inattention, the place non-musicians erroneously describe as "automatic", where I seemed to be observing my own performance, the keys and muscle-memory in perfect coordination and when that happened the music I heard in my head—

Was brand new. It was powerful. It was compelling. The harmonies and progressions of chords in Alex's performance, those liberties that initially seemed inchoate, began to build in layers, to comment upon, to reflect the progressions laid down before.

I realized, then, that Alex McBride was one of those very rare musicians who really could hear the music, hear *all* the music, hear past the melody to the possibilities of chord and harmony beneath to make something new, something different.

And to hear it in his head.

"That's enough," McBride concluded, with a rake down the keyboard.

I turned to him mute, discouraged.

"What was that?"

"Chord progressions."

"Mr. Pellicore told me about chords."

"Yeah, but all he's got you doin' is readin' side to side."

"Side to side?"

"Left to right. The melody. That's okay if all you want is to play like it's wrote. Hear one thing at a time. But if you want to hear *all* the music? Every instrument off the score? You need to learn to read up an' down 'cause *that's* how the harmonies are arranged. That's how you hear chord progressions, which is what I do. Which you *got* to do if you gonna jam."

"Can you help me hear them?"

"Sugar doll. I can do better than that. Come own set by me. Let's do the 'Boogie Woogie'."

Next thing I know I'm sitting beside Alex McBride following chord progressions off the old standard. Every now and then we'd stop and he'd coach me, always patiently.

"Hear that last one? That's a very simple chord progression, one-four-five-one. Now you do it."

Almost immediately I began to hear a whole range of sound and harmony that had until that moment been hidden from me. It was like waking up a week after Christmas and finding more presents under the tree.

"All right, let's see how much you learned." Alex stopped the boogie and launched into another piece. "Now what was that about?"

"I heard the major chord, heard the dominant. You started in C, then swapped to the key of G."

"You got it, sugar doll. You cookin'."

But I was shaking my head. "I'll never be good as you."

"They's plenty better than me."

"Hard to believe that."

"Well, you better believe it. And when you get as good as I am, and you will, you *really* better believe it or you'll go stale. You'll get sloppy. You'll get where you don't give a damn about anything except what you've already done and that, sugar, is the killer for a performer.

"What we just did? Keeps me sharp. I wasn't even thinkin' 'bout no Beethoven 'till you brought him in here, but now I own a piece of that man. It'll change the way I play tonight and the next night and the night after that. I'll see possibilities for things I already thought was iron-clad worked out in whole different ways.

"See, they ain't no 'right' music or no 'right' way, but there are rules. Trick is knowing the rules well enough to make 'em work for you."

"But when you march you can't vary anything," I objected. "You have to do the same thing over and over, that's what Mr. Pellicore says."

"You ain' gonna be marching all your life, are you? Well, are you?"

"I hope not."

"No hoping to it. You either are or you ain't. That band director sound like a prick to me, but that don't give you license to use him for an excuse. Tell you somethin', sugar doll, you don't know what you can do. You got no idea how far you can go.

"You gonna find Pellicores and pimps wherever you at in this business. You don' have to love the man. Take what you can from him. Do what he tell you. Just don't get to thinkin' it's Gospel. You ever hear any Mozart?"

"Oh, yes! But just on the radio."

"B'lieve I can improve on that. Hang on."

McBride got up from the upright's bench. Opened it. A litter of music was tossed carelessly inside. He propped his cigar on the upright before fishing all the way to the bottom.

"Here you are."

The blues man pulled out the worn jacket of a long-playing record.

"Mozart," he said. "There's a sonata for the piano on here, a couple of concertos, some opera—a bunch of stuff. Now, what I own't you to do is wear this record *out*. See what makes Mozart a different cat than Beethoven. See how he'll start something that look simple, and then how it change, how he varies it, mixes it up.

"Listen to him a bunch, 'till you get a feel, then go get some Ellington and Satchmo and Miles Davis and B.B. King and *listen* to what they doin'. Get they records, steal 'em if you have to, and play 'em over and over and compare 'em back and forth.

"You know what it means when a musician says somebody 'got time'?"

"No." I shook my head.

"Somebody got time it means they got a natural feel for music. You either got time or you ain't, but if you can take what Mozart teach you, and Beethoven? And put it together with Miles Davis or B.B. King or the Beatles? You on your way to making music gonna blow folks out they seat."

I stayed for most of an hour, I guess, listening to Alex work the ivory. He showed me some footwork, too. "Why I like my shoes untied," he explained as he worked the pedals. "I get a better feel." Then Joe Billy came out with the group's bass player, that would be Ruben. Alex got a kick out of Ruben's dirty guitar, the sound hole a leering cunt in the one, an innocent navel in the other.

It was getting close to showtime by then. The bartenders started rolling in fresh kegs. You could see the club's regulars drifting in, taking their favored tables. Alex's group drifted in one by one. He had a clarinet player, a trumpet and bass. Drum set.

"Boys, this here is Miss Cilla Handsom. Real serious musician. And tall."

I felt real grownup, being introduced that way. Being teased. One of the girls brought out a camera.

"Buck gets you a picture with Alex McBride."

"Cilla, get in there," Joe Billy pulled a dollar from his wallet. A bulb flashed, I 'bout went blind, and the girl said they'd mail it and they did and that's how I got my picture taken with Alex McBride.

"Thank you," I gathered my long-playing album as I left.

"You welcome, sugar doll. Come back."

"I will," I said.

But I never did.

Joe Billy and I headed home from Jacksonville dually enriched. It was late. We were virtually the only car on the road, that evening, all other traffic being commercial, big eighteen-wheel trailers, cattle trucks and refrigerated rigs. Trucks hauling watermelons or other produce. The sun settled on the road ahead like a BB centered in a rifle's sight. We held onto 690 AM as long as we could, gradually losing that signal as we drove the interminable alley of pine trees shouldering the highway from Jacksonville to Live Oak. I felt a pang when the aether went to static, as though I'd lost a recent friend.

"I wish Mr. Raymond liked rock 'n' roll ," I lamented.

"Owna get me my own radio," Joe Billy promised over the wind that coursed cool and humid through the opened windows of our Fairlane. "Gone put up an antennae taller than a tree."

I held Mozart's symphony close to my generous chest. Careful not to bend the long-playing vinyl in its worn jacket.

"Be nice if I could play my Motes Art."

"Get youself a record player."

"I cain't buy no record player."

"Who say anything 'bout *you* buyin'?"

I turned to him.

"Whatchu talking?"

"We can stop in Live Oak. I know a place."

"Oh, Joe Billy! You sure?"

"Baby," him smiling like Sammy Davis, "I got money burnin' a hole in my pocket."

We spent that night in The Lodge making love on a mattress

with clean sheets. Clean at first, anyway. We only had the one record, but any sonata by Mozart will get you a long way.

We were becoming more bold in our lovemaking. Except for oral sex.

"Long as I'm strong in the hips, I be weak in the lips," Joe Billy couched that reticence in humor. I didn't mind, particularly. I had not experienced the kind of orgasm, at that point, that Joe Billy took for granted. In fact, my satisfaction came mostly with bringing JayBee to climax, and it was convenient, sometimes, depending on how I felt, to bring that ejaculation quickly.

"Cilla, Cilla…." He arched like a gymnast when I brought him with my hand or with my mouth. We didn't need a condom when we were like that, which is one reason I'm sure he locked up so fast.

I loved the feel of his butt in those moments, how it tightened, his back and shoulders. More like a girl than a boy, really. He would come like a gorge. We took to keeping a towel or something handy.

I never saw why it was that much different than kissing.

"You do have a dirty mouth…" He moaned after one such experiment. "Praise Jesus."

I was perfectly satisfied to satisfy my man. Why wouldn't I be? To that point, I had never experienced anything else.

But the night Joe Billy bought me my record player I had a different experience with my lover. I don't know if it was the excitement of the trip to Jacksonville, or the attention I got at Manuel's, or the precious gifts bestowed in that jazz-joint, I don't know, but from the first brush of his fingertips against the underside of my thighs, even before he touched me inside, before I guided him in, I felt something building up like wanting to pee, but better. It got better as we went. Better—

"Cilla?"

"Keep it…keep it."

I could feel myself letting go. The walls of my uterus jerked in short spasms that got longer, more urgent. I wanted to paw myself, grind my genitalia with pumice!

"Keep it coming!"

I wrapped my legs around him when I came and almost broke his ribs. That was the first time I experienced a climax, the first time, too, that I understood how a woman is different in love than a man, how our orgasm can be as powerful and potent as any ejaculation. It was an intoxicating revelation. A liberating discovery.

But I could not stay to revel in it.

Chapter nine

"Negroes Bussed To White
School"—*The Clarion*

The next day Joe Billy and I and every other school-aged child
in Colored Town were bussed across the tracks into Laureate. Miss
Chandler met us as we boarded our buses, tall and massive, the singular presentation of her basset-hound face a comfort now.

"Miss Cilla, you all right?"

"Fine, Miz Chandler."

"You look tired."

"Yes, ma'am." I didn't even bother to lie, still warm with the
memory of my first real passion.

"You'll be on Mr. Raymond's bus."

We had three aging Blue Bird buses to transport ninety-five
black children, grade schoolers through seniors all mixed up.

"The drivers will bring you right to the front door." Miss
Chandler mounted each Blue Bird to brief us. "There may be some
people there."

"Kinda people?" Pudding was already scared to death with
rumor.

"No kind of people to worry about," Miss Chandler replied

firmly. "Do not look at them. Do not reply to them. Ignore whatever you hear. Remember that I and Miss Hattie and all the other teachers at the school will be there to meet you and take you to your classrooms.

"Now is everybody here? Count noses. I think we're all here. This is Bus Number Three. Mr. Raymond's your driver. You all know him. I will see you at school."

Miss Chandler stepped down from the bus. The doors slapped shut. I had never heard that sound before, the peculiar flimsy slap of a school bus door.

Mr. Raymond peered up into the broad rearview mirror mounted above his head.

"ALL ABOARD!"

That got a giggle. I could see the smaller children loosen up a little, could see, even in the rearview mirror, Mr. Raymond's calm, professional smile.

"Yawl stay in your seats," came the gentle command. "We'll be there in less than five minutes."

The transmission swapped cogs and the buses lurched out of Colored Town in a stolid caravan. An unnatural quiet fell over our bus. Pudding and Chicken Swamp, normally irrepressible, perched mute in their seats. I noticed that Chicken Swamp had gotten a belt for his always-too-loose trousers. And socks for his brogans. Pudding had taken his rooster-comb out of his hair and stuck it in his pocket. Nobody wanted to stand out.

"What's gonna happen?" I looked down to see Shirley Lee squeezing the blood out of my hand.

I turned with her fear to find Joe Billy.

"We're gonna be all right," Joe Billy announced loudly, calmly. "Just do what Miss Chandler tole' us. Don' look. Don' listen. Now, Pudding, Chicken—"

"Yeah?"

"Let's pair up the older children with the little ones."

That took some organization, pairing up names back and forth. Mr. Raymond glanced up to his mirror, but did not interrupt. I took the Sykes twins under my wing together. I knew they would not want to be paired off from each other.

"It'll be us three," I told them. "We get off, ya'll just stick with me."

"Everybody hold hands off the bus." Joe Billy just took natural command. "Just get off, look straight ahead. We'll all be fine."

"I need to pee," a tiny voice broke in, on the edge of panic.

"So do I, baby," Joe Billy turned to reassure Pudding's little sister. "But I know they got a restroom in that school."

He looked back at me. "It won't be long."

The bus shuddered again as Mr. Raymond swapped cogs to pull past the courthouse, past the white-steepled churches and through the red light. You could see the entry to the school just ahead, the school-zone marked in broad fading stripes across the street.

"COURTHOUSE, CHURCHHOUSE, OUTHOUSE STRAIGHT AHEAD," Mr. Raymond sang out, but the scene before us strangled that stretch for humor.

A gauntlet was gathered at Lafayette County Consolidated School. Garner Hewitt and the Citizen's Council had organized a call for "peaceful protest" that had brought a hundred white folks to the thick-strawed yard where the buses stopped to debark their children. White people lined up in phalanxes five deep on either side of the narrow sidewalk spanning the gap between the bus and the wide doors granting entrance to the school. That twenty yards of cement looked like a mile.

Garner was there himself to lead his minions, the flesh around his eye purple with the mark of birth, like he'd just got out of a fight. Working ringside in those seersucker slacks, those wingtipped shoes. Both of Garner's sons were there. J.T. patrolled up and down the line, his rattlesnake belt winking silver. Cody pulled up in his fire-red Ford, blatantly ignoring the court's restriction of his license.

The Council were passing out signs and placards to augment the hastily-scrawled cards wielded like clubs along the line that now pressed against the sides of the school buses bringing Kerbo's children to their new school. "KERBO NOT WELCOME," was the first and tamest expression of sentiment that I saw. "WHITE SCHOOL ONLY!" read another. There were other signs citing scripture from Leviticus or Ecclesiastes or one of those books ripe for interpretation.

Most remarks required no interpreter.

"NIGGER GO HOME!" a white woman screamed, and a volley of eggs were launched at our bus.

The little ones in our bus began to cry, to scream. Mr. Raymond pulled to a halt but kept his hand firmly on the bus door's long pull.

"NIGGERS GO HOME!" I thought it was J.T. Hewitt starting the chant that picked up quickly.

"NIGGERS GO HOME, NIGGERS GO HOME!"

"Mr. Raymond—?!" a panicking child gripped the back of my seat.

I looked down and saw urine pooling on the floorboard.

"I GOT TO PEE!"

"KEEP YOUR SEATS!" Joe Billy's command got Mr. Raymond's attention.

"What you sayin', boy? We're here."

"Mr. Raymond. Nobody's getting out just yet. Just stay in your seats."

Another volley of eggs splattered on the bus. One egg sailed through an open window and caught Pudding right up side the head.

"GOOD 'UN, CODY!" I heard a commendation.

The line of teachers began to waver. The slender alley giving us a causeway to the school was close to collapse. Then I saw Principal Wilburn nod over to Garner Hewitt.

"Jesus, Joe Billy, they gonna rush the bus!" I said, and a surge of white faces confirmed that tender prophecy. But then I heard the angry growl of a siren.

It's amazing how people react to a siren and a police car.

Garner and his citizens hesitated with the cruiser's approach. The teachers stiffened.

"LOCK HANDS," I heard Miss Chandler command and I'll

be damned if white teachers on both sides didn't take her hand. The cruiser cut a path right through the middle of the mob, right up to the sidewalk. The door opened. Only one lawman, familiar to us all, got out.

The Sheriff of Lafayette County strolled straight over to Garner Hewitt. An angry murmur was stalled. Collard Jackson stepped directly into that breach.

"Ain't you got nuthin' better to do, Garner?"

He spoke loudly enough to have been heard across the football field.

"Just a peaceful protest, Sheriff." Garner's nasal reply was weak by comparison. "Just exercisin' our rights."

"Exercise," Collard chuckled. "Garner, you ain't exercised anything but your lip since Christ was a corporal."

I thought surely then the crowd would turn on him, that Garner and the rest would simply overwhelm the county's sheriff. But Collard knew what dog was leading that pack. And Garner, pressed close on all sides by the mob he created, could not disguise the fear he felt when face to face with Sheriff Jackson.

Collard Jackson placed one hand on his revolver, propped a foot up on the bumper of our bus and looked around calmly. Staring them down.

"Harvey Land, the hell you doin' here, you got a store to run! Thurman. Randall. Surprised you boys could get talked into a stunt like this."

The Sheriff turned, then, to Principal Ben Wilburn.

"Ben, that a watch on your wrist? What about it?"

"Ahmmm. Yes, Sheriff."

"Give it here. Come on."

Wilburn extended his wristwatch to Collard gingerly, his arm stretching like a stick.

"Thank you, sir."

Collard took it casually with one hand. And with the other he took out his firearm.

"FIVE MINUTES!" The sudden thunder in his voice surprised us all.

"FIVE MINUTES THERE BETTER NOT BE ANY-BODY ON THIS PROPERTY THAT AIN'T A STUDENT OR TEACHER. THERE BETTER NOT BE ANYBODY HERE AFTERWARDS, NEITHER. NOT TODAY. NOT TOMOR-ROW."

"You got no right, Sheriff," Garner growled.

Collard stepped over to Garner briefly, inclined his head to the chairman's hairy ear and Mr. Hewitt disappeared beneath the broad rim of the sheriff's hat. A short conversation was overheard by Ben Wilburn and Garner's eldest. It went something like this:

"You burnt any churches I oughta know about, Garner? Or more likely J.T.? Or how 'bout Cody?"

Garner's head jerked out from the blind of Collard's Stetson. "The hell you talkin' about?"

"Got a call from Tallahassee, is all. Something about a vehicle fleeing the scene. Red pickup, Ford. Partial plates. Spinner hubs."

"Bullshit."

"No. They didn't say anything about bullshit, Garner. Just a church, some dynamite. And then the truck."

Even from the bus you could tell Garner was apoplectic.

"Are you fucking with me, Collard?!"

"Stay here four and a half more minutes," Collard assured him, "and I'll make damn sure you find out."

Garner's head snatched back. Collard consulted his watch. "FOUR MINUTES."

Time to fish or cut bait.

"Daddy?" J.T. shoved over to intercept his father.

"Go on back to the house."

"Go *back*?"

"You heard me goddamn it!"

J.T. followed his father out of the pack like a whipped pup. With their chairman gone the remaining citizens shifted uneasily, wavering in their purpose.

"THREE AND A HALF MINUTES," Collard announced loudly.

That did it. People dispersed like oil poured on water, tossing their signs, their eggs. One or two of Garner's crew shouted defiant curses, although only once safely distant from Collard's truncheon. The Sheriff did not reply to those minor iniquities, did not budge until the last second of the last minute was run from the Principal's cheap watch.

Jackson then returned the Principal's timepiece.

"Ben—"

"Yes, Sheriff?"

"I better not have to do your job for you again."

Principal Wilburn stood mute as Collard Jackson pulled away in his police car. Miss Chandler bustled forward. Those great hips, that fold of face.

"Let's get these children to their rooms."

The white teachers stepped forward in the vacuum created by their principal's voided command to follow Miss Chandler's. I was stunned, even in the turmoil of that moment, to see white people follow a black woman's direction.

"PAIR UP!"

Joe Billy's was the voice of command in our bus. "Older ones with little ones. Don't forget to hold hands."

I found the Sykes twins.

"We gonna be all right?" They shivered in unison like they'd been out in the cold.

"'Course we are, babies," I reassured them. "Can't you see Miss Chandler? And the Sheriff? They ain' gonna let nuthin' bad happen to nobody."

The first day went by in a blur. We had names and room numbers to remember. Where the restroom was. Cafeteria was easy, you just followed the crowd. And of course I knew all about the band hall. I didn't know anything about homeroom, though. Homeroom for me and Shirley Lee and Joe Billy fell under the domain of Myron Putnal, a distant relation to Latrelle, our distinguished representative at the State Legislature. Myron resembled a politician himself, specifically,

Abraham Lincoln. In fact if you took Honest Abe, cut about three feet off his legs and left him his beard, he'd be the spitting image of our homeroom teacher.

A distinguishing characteristic of our integration with Laureate's student body was that we newcomers already knew many of the white students. In fact, one of the worst trials for me that first day of integration came from the cold shoulders I endured from white girls with whom I was very familiar. Take Sherry Pridgeon, for instance. Sherry was acknowledged to be the prettiest girl in the county. Every male past puberty at Laureate High School had, I'm sure, dreamed of getting in Sherry's pants or beneath her bra. I used to love stringing tobacco beside Sherry. She had a pile of gorevan hair that cascaded over suntanned shoulders wide as a weightlifter's to a flatiron belly. Her legs looked to be as long as mine, even though she was a head shorter.

I liked to watch the muscles of her abdomen work as she leaned over her stringhorse, snatching hands of tobacco faster than we could pull them from the sled, each bundle of leaves looped and tied, hand after hand, stick after stick, a strand of twine feeding from a ball secreted in a blouse damp with sweat. The easy sway of her hips and belly. As sexy to me as a rock star.

Sherry asked me after one particularly long day in the sun if I'd put some Solarcaine on her back, at which point I instantly became the envy of all boys present, my hands freely wandering a torso they could not approach, the long spine tan with exposure, the lotion cool and white ejaculating onto that bared skin, the moan of contact, her rump finally beneath my hands, my dark hands, black hands.

White boys holding themselves.

We used to chatter over our labor like sorority sisters. We'd talk about anything: boys, grownups, picture shows. Sherry loved the drive-in, could capture accents and repeat dialogue word-perfect, Jimmy Stewart and Sandra Dee, or Bogart and Bacall, or Marlon Brando. She was the Corrie Jean of movies. Most of the filmed narratives familiar to me were gained from Sherry Pridgeon's re-enactments. I must have heard *On The Waterfront* a dozen times before I ever saw it.

"I coulda been a contendah—!"

Of course, there was segregation, even at a tobacco barn. We did not drink water from the same cup. We did not take meals at the same table. We did not use the same restroom, which in my case meant that I had no restroom to use at all. But we did talk. We exchanged harmless anecdotes and intimacies. We were warm at the Henderson's barn in a way unrelated to the climate.

So it was natural, for me, entering a new homeroom and seeing my summertime companion to offer some small pleasantry, to say hello. To smile. To meet her wide jade-colored eyes. In fact, Sherry Pridgeon's were the only eyes I made an effort to meet that first day of class. I looked straight at her.

"'Lo, Sherry."

She didn't even turn her head. Just looked past me as though I were not present. As though I were truly invisible.

"Sherry P...?"

The protest on my lips died with the bruise on my heart. She would not acknowledge me. Would not meet my eye. The easy congress I had come to take for granted was replaced by this icy distance. I wanted to shout at that injustice, to say, "Here I am! Here I am! Look at me!" but I did not. Instead I replied to her indifference with feigned nonchalance of my own.

I refused any but the most necessary of communications. I kept my eyes averted from any kind of contact with Sherry or any other white classmate. The ugly gauntlet that greeted our arrival would have been trauma enough for my first day at LHS. But the ostracism imposed on me by students whom I knew well and with whom I had imagined some kind of mutual regard scratched like sandspurs over my heart.

There were only seven of us from Kerbo in that senior homeroom: Lonnie Hines and Shirley Lee Lewis, Pudding and Chicken Swamp and Johnny Boy and Joe Billy and I. Seven black students. Thirty-three whites. The Kerbo students took pretty much the same classes during the day, except for Chicken and Johnny Boy who were not, as polite speech put it, 'prepared' for an algebra course.

I didn't think I was prepared for algebra, either; I had never heard the word. But Miss Chandler assured me that the course would not be over my head.

"Your test scores indicate you have a gift for mathematics, Cilla."

"But won't the white students be a leg up? Haven't they got courses before this? To get ready?"

"It's not a big jump from fractions and geometry to algebra," my teacher assured me. "Even word problems are algebraic in function. If you run into a snag, I'll be here to help out."

"How 'bout Joe Billy? He's signed up, too."

"That boy," Miss Chandler shook her head. "We'll have to go on faith."

I wasn't faithful enough to be reassured, but in the event faith was not needed. I was not embarrassed in homeroom. The gaps in my education were not explored or revealed. In fact, Myron Putnal did not call me to the board at all. Fact was, he never called on any student with suspicious skin, not even if we raised our hands. Our teacher did, however, let us know exactly what place we would have in his class.

The first day, for instance, we began our introduction to algebra with something like this chalked on the board:

$25 < 100\ a < b$

"What is an inequality?" Mr. Putnal inquired breezily, before he even reached his desk. Before he even took roll.

"An inequality, what is it? What things can we say are unequal?"

"Niggers and whites," Cody muttered, and snickers rippled through the class.

Mr. Putnal appeared not to have heard a thing.

The contrast between Myron's class and Miss Chandler's English and Lit. could not have been more striking.

"I would begin by introducing myself," Miss Chandler waited until we were all seated, "but that would presume that we all don't know each other and that would be dishonest, wouldn't it? I know Miss Bonnie Hart, for instance, and Miss Bonnie knows me. Ya'll might not know that Miss Bonnie's father helped me move my furniture when I first came to Laureate. Loaned me his truck. Helped me get my things. I shall never forget that kindness.

"Now it's a fact that Miss Hart and her father live on one side of the tracks, and I on the other. But that does not mean we don't know each other.

"We all know each other, don't we? One way or the other. For instance, I know that even though Mr. Simms and Mr. Reed have until this year attended different schools, they have cropped Ed Henderson's tobacco side by side for—how many years, Mr. Simms?"

"Since I was ten," Terrell Simms allowed.

"Yes," Miss Chandler nodded. "Since you were children. So let's not start off the year pretending we're strangers."

She let that sink in a moment.

"All right, then, let's get started." Miss Chandler reached for the glasses that hung by a string of pearls about her round neck. "What I need ya'll to do now is to get a piece of chalk, and take a place at the blackboard."

"Go to the board?" Cody Hewitt asked, as if that were the most absurd notion in the world.

"You have problems finding it, Mr. Hewitt, I'm sure I can help you out."

The nervous laughter that broke then was at Cody's expense, a situation to which he was not accustomed.

Miss Chandler addressed each student by name as we passed her desk. Cody sat in a huddle with the class jocks. Barlow "Cutter" Land was Harold Land's son, a poor relation of the Lands who owned the SafeWay grocery. Terrell Simms was second only to Cody in status at the high school, a fullback destined for Florida State. Dean "Digger" Folsom was Monk Folsom's nephew. Dean's mother taught fourth grade at the school. Theirs was the only family in the county split by divorce. People excused it by saying Dean's daddy was just plain crazy and it was clear to me looking at Digger that the apples in that family did not fall far from the tree.

"To the board, class. Everyone," Miss Chandler repeated herself calmly.

There was some jostling, then, black students and white necessarily in close contact. Elbows and shoulders brushing. Side by side. Lonnie trailed me (as he used to do at Kerbo) to the board. Bonnie

Hart cut ahead of us, squeezing out a space between Cody and another white boy. Everyone saw that maneuver, of course. I took the other board, winding up with Lonnie hard on my right hand but nobody at the board to my left.

"We have spaces remaining at the board," Miss Chandler observed.

Sally O'Steen slipped in beside me shyly. She was a big-boned kind of girl, what some would call a dishwater blonde, and others, unkindly, trailer trash, even though at that time there were no trailers to speak of in Lafayette County.

"Chalk?" Sally offered.

"Thank you." She pressed a piece into my hand. Her nails, I noticed, were dirty.

"We all have a place?" Miss Chandler breezily inquired. "Yes, I believe we do. So let's start with grammar. Conjugate for me, please, the verb 'see'."

Black hands rose in virtual unison from the board's dusty tray. Black hands scratching chalk on the unfamiliar board.

I see, you see, he sees.
We see, you see, they see.

The white students stood nervously, limed stubs impotent in their hands. One or two giggled at their predicament. Sally's fair face flushed pink as roses.

"Mr. Hewitt."

I saw Cody scowl. "What?"

"That is not how you address a teacher, Mr. Hewitt. I am 'Miss Chandler'."

"What, Miss Chandler?"

"I don't see you conjugating."

"Conugatin'!" he guffawed. "Who does *that*?"

"Educated people." Miss Chandler smiled sweetly and there was genuine laughter in the classroom.

Miss Chandler turned to the board. "Miss Handsom, what is the simple past conjugation of the verb, 'see', singular and plural?"

"Yes, ma'am," I responded from the ritual of a thousand drills. "The simple past for the verb 'see', singular and plural, is: I saw, you saw, he saw. We saw, you saw, they saw."

"Thank you. Now the point here, class, is not simply to be educated about grammar. It is to demonstrate that we all have things to learn from each other. Miss Handsom and Mr. Reed and the students new to your classroom have much to learn from you. But you, Mr. Hewitt, and all the rest of you, have much to learn as well from your new classmates. And from me.

"So before we get to Shakespeare and Macbeth we are going to use this first six week period to review the basics of grammar—"

Groans erupted around the room. Miss Chandler smiled good-naturedly.

"You can thank me when you take your SATs. For now, you need to return to your desks and get out your Little Browns. We'll start with Chapter One."

Miss Chandler's third-period class was a respite from a morning bloated with apprehension. My stomach was growling before eleven o'clock and that distress had little to do with hunger. The integration that had begun with the bus ride from hell had continued to produce one gut-wrenching experience after another. I had barely caught my breath in Miss Chandler's class, seemed like, when the jarring intrusion of the bell forced me from that safe haven to Fourth Period and Band.

I was petrified that I was going to make a fool of myself. I had never sat with *anyone* making music unless you counted Mr. Pellicore or Alex McBride. I had certainly never performed "Oklahoma" with forty other musicians, and even if my performance was sterling there was no guarantee I'd be welcomed into the company of the Marching Saints. There had never been a colored girl in their band. Wouldn't I be seen as an interloper? An embarrassment?

And then, of course, I wore the added brand of thief. Not just a nigger girl, but the nigger who stole music from Mr. Pellicore's office. I had already endured a beating in Kerbo for that offense. Would there be some fresh humiliation to be endured here?

With the bell I was gathered like a leaf in a torrent of students pressing down the breezeway toward the band hall and gymnasium. Many of the youngsters negotiating that passage were freshmen and sophomores, students with whose names I was unfamiliar. I allowed myself to be carried along in that current of milling students to reach the band hall's double doors. Gushing through with the press of that eager crowd.

Hoping to remain invisible.

"Miss Handsom." Mr. Pellicore appeared.

"Yes, suh."

"'Sir.' In my office, please."

The other students coursed by with barely averted glances. Bonnie Hart was already inside, I noted briefly, her skirt riding up her legs as she uncased her beautiful clarinet. There was no music in the hall, only noise, a slaughter of melody perpetrated by a racket of instruments each bawling for attention like dying calves in a hailstorm. But when Mr. Pellicore closed the door of his office, that reassuring din was suddenly dimmed.

"Miss Handsom, I can't find your horn."

"Sir? My horn?"

"Your instrument, Cilla. The French horn. Did you take it home, by any chance? Get the janitor or someone to let you in?"

"No, sir," I shook my head.

He ran his pampered hands through what was left of his hair. "It's gone. Somebody took it. Sometime today, I think."

Today?

"I've got in the habit of locking the door recently," Pellicore continued. "Got in that habit since...well, you know since when."

Yes, I did.

"But today I was working on your horn, right here in the office. One of the valves was sticking. I was cleaning it when Mr. Wilburn called. Had to run down to the office; couldn't have been gone fifteen minutes! So I left the door out back open. It gets so damn hot in here."

"Yes, sir, it do. Does."

"Yes. And worse I left my own office unlocked. As I say—ten, fifteen minutes. Anyway when I got back I saw your horn gone."

He hooked his thumbs beneath argyle suspenders.

"I am sorry to ask you this, Cilla, but where were you third period this morning?"

"Miss Chandler's room!" I replied too eagerly. "English!"

"You were there all period?"

"Yes, sir," I pumped my head. "You can axe, ask her."

"Thank God," he sighed with obvious relief. "I will ask Miss Chandler, of course. Just so I can vouch for you myself."

"Vouch?" I was unfamiliar with the word.

"Take your side," he nodded. "I don't want anyone accusing you of something you didn't do, Cilla. I can be pretty self-serving, but I hope I would never falsely accuse any student of something so serious."

I could not remember any adult taking my side in any dispute and here was this man, a white man offering to—what a marvelous word—vouch for me. But without an instrument what was I supposed to do?

He released the hold on his suspenders. "Just find your seat and follow along. This afternoon I want you on the field. Instrument or no, you need practice marching."

"Yes, sir."

"After class you and I will see Mr. Wilburn." Pellicore was back to all-business. "Somebody's got to tell him about the damn horn."

I left Mr. Pellicore's office to encounter a raucous hall gone suddenly quiet. Every student was seated, instruments propped and ready. I felt as though I were exposed to a hive of pale eyes.

"Everyone," the director took his podium oblivious to my reception. "Cilla Handsom has been working hard this summer to take our French horn. Who will direct Miss Handsom to her chair?"

"It's my turn, Mr. Pellicore."

A voice piped up whose face I could not at first find. But then she rose from her seat, this tiny freshman, slender as a reed, still in cornsilk ponytails, a flautist. I thought I knew everybody in the county but this nymph was unfamiliar.

"Right here," she offered what appeared to be a genuine smile. "Just one row up from the clarinets."

"Thank you," I mumbled and was threading my way past the reeds to reach the brass when this little twig of a thing intercepted me.

"No, no. I'll take you."

"Take me?"

"To your chair. It's traditional," she bobbed her head. "Every newcomer to our band gets taken to her chair, first time around. And then *that* person shows the next rookie to *his* chair. I am the youngest member of the band, see. Just started last year with the flute. So I get to take you to your chair."

"Get" to take you—not, "have" to take you, or "supposed" to take you.

"What's your name?" she asked.

"My name is, is Cilla."

"I'm Juanita Land."

I knew the name and as her palm slid inside mine I realized that this was the daughter of the Land whose grocery I regularly plundered.

"Watch your step."

My chair was situated with the other brass, a simple foldout before a tripod of music. But mine. My very own. A trombone player seated a row above offered a weak and congenitally lopsided grin.

"Cilla."

I recovered enough from Juanita's introduction to acknowledge Rodney Morgan's. I didn't really know Rodney all that well, but I had spent two summers on a stringhorse with his sister. Mandy Morgan on one side. Sherry Pridgeon on the other.

Thousand sticks a day.

"Rodney. I din' know you played anything."

"We're not so sure ourselves," an acne-scarred percussionist leaned over his drums—

Ba-da-boom.

"But we heard you were hell on the French horn."

134

I looked hard for sarcasm but found none.

"I don' know," I replied with caution. "I only had the summer to practice."

"Pretty damn amazing summer, what I hear."

He stowed his sticks and stuck out a hand.

"Jerry Fowler. Rock and roll."

Chuckles rippled round the band hall; I realized then that this was a place where I might actually be able to relax, to let down my guard. Here were faces willing to give me the benefit of the doubt, even knowing my tainted history. Here were people who, in however qualified a way, valued talent.

"Very well, ladies and gentlemen," Pellicore rapped a music stand with a pencil-thin wand. "Tradition is served. Now pick up our feature, please. We've only two weeks left before our first game."

The rest of that class went by in a blur. But it was a pleasant blur. I actually enjoyed "Oklahoma" for the first time in my life. The bell came too soon.

"Bye, Cilla." Juanita bounced up. "Hope you find your horn."

"Thank you."

The trombones and drummer left with similar expressions of goodwill. Most of the girls said something, though Bonnie Hart once again snubbed me.

"Don't feel too special," Rodney Morgan made an effort to blunt that edge. "Bonnie's on the outs with everybody one time or the other. Even Juanita."

"Juanita Land?"

"Bonnie's got the notion Juanita's interested in Cody Hewitt, which she ain't. Now, he *has* got an eye on her. As much for the money as all the rest."

The notion that money could be a more stimulating inducement than sex was at the time a foreign notion. But I deferred to his opinion—

"I see."

—and made for the door cheered by the thought that white folks' gossip was as banal as any in Colored Town.

135

"Not so quickly, Miss Handsom."

Pellicore speared his baton like a matador into a block of styrofoam.

"We have an appointment."

Chapter ten

"Turnout Good for Football
Team"—*The Clarion*

suppose everybody figured I was in trouble, hitched to Pellicore's train on the way to the principal's office. Miss Hattie Briar surely made that assumption.

"Lord," she said. "Already?"

Mr. Pellicore herded me brusquely down the hall and into the anteroom outside the principal's office.

"Take a seat," he told me, leaning over to the school's secretary. "Miss Gertie, will you tell Mr. Wilburn I need just a moment?"

"He's inside with Miss Chandler," Gertie replied, over a typewriter and a triplicate of forms.

I looked and sure enough, there through his opened door I could see Miss Chandler standing before our principal at his pinneat desk.

"Just a moment," Pellicore assured Gertie, and without waiting for permission, stepped past her blockade and into Wilburn's office.

Miss Chandler paused with the bandleader's intrusion. I could see the three of them, Pellicore, Wilburn and Miss Chandler routed to a new conversation. I was reading body language the way a mute would read lips. Miss Chandler's large head turreting to find Pellicore as he bulled into Mr. Wilburn's office. Gimballing, then, to find me outside. Then back to the band director, him now leaning on Wilburn's barren desk. Like a Neanderthal, on the knuckles of his hands. Principal Wilburn rocking like Whistler's mother in his high-backed chair, hands raking repeatedly over a hairless skull.

A truncated, uneven consultation ensued. Principal to band director to teacher. Back and forth. Miss Chandler breaking off abruptly, dismissing her boss's strident summons with a casual wave of her large hand.

"Miss Handsom," my old teacher addressed me the moment she cleared the membrane of Wilburn's office.

"Yes, ma'am."

"Is there anything you can tell me about this morning that might help us find your horn?"

"Not right off."

"Cilla," she settled beside me privately. "Were you threatened? Were there any remarks?"

"Cody said 'nigger' in home room."

"He said what?"

"Said niggers were unequal to whites. We were talking about algebra."

"Clearly you were not. What did Mr. Putnal say? Was Cody punished?"

"No, ma'am. Nothing. Nobody said nothing."

I don't know if God or simple inspiration turned Miss Chandler's eyes out the window at that moment. It was lunchtime, I recall. I was again aware of my stomach. Out through Gertie's wide and open window you could see a line of cars and trucks, mostly students', nestled beneath a shade of pine trees.

Cody was out there, throwing a tarpaulin over the bed of the shiny, red truck he was unlicensed to drive.

"Excuse me," Miss Chandler startled me, she got up so fast.

"Mr. Pellicore?"

Pellicore turned from Ben Wilburn's desk.

"Miss Chandler?"

"Can you come with me? Quickly?"

I left my seat for the window. Presently I saw Ben Wilburn following my old teacher toward the line of shaded vehicles, huffing protest every step of the way.

"We can't just go looking at every vehicle in the yard!"

"Won't be looking in every vehicle," Miss Chandler assured him, and made a bead straight for Cody's truck.

From my vantage point I saw the principal overtake her in short, jerky steps.

"You cannot go in that truck, Miss Chandler."

"Not going in."

"I forbid it."

She turned on him, a big woman whipping around tail to snout, like a sow defending a litter.

"You *forbid*, Mr. Wilburn? Stolen property at your school and you forbid a search of this vehicle? Very well, I'll call the sheriff."

Wilburn's hands fluttered at his waist. "No, don't do that. You can't do that."

"Yes, I can. So can Mr. Pellicore."

"Pellicore!"

The principal appealed to the band director for help that would not come.

"What's the problem, Ben? There's probably nothing in there anyway."

About that time Cody saw the teachers and Wilburn converging on his truck.

"Hey," he started over at a jog that turned to a sprint. "YOU CAIN'T TOUCH MY TRUCK!"

"That's Garner's son, isn't it?" Miss Chandler observed coolly slipping the knot that secured Cody's tarp.

It was the band director who actually pulled the tarpaulin back. There were two bales of hay beneath that rude cover. A spare tire. Some lumber. And one French horn.

"I'll be damned," Pellicore leaned over to retrieve the school's property.

Ben Wilburn looked ready to choke.

"HEY!" Cody skidded to a halt on the caliche drive.

"Any idea where this came from Mr. Hewitt?" Miss Chandler's sarcasm would have chilled ice.

"Who said you could go in my truck?!"

"Be quiet, Cody."

This from the principal.

"You let her go in my truck. I saw!"

"Quiet!" Wilburn snarled and you could see the gums above his teeth.

"You should call the sheriff, Ben," Pellicore huffed.

"No need. You've got your horn."

"Got our thief, too," Miss Chandler observed.

"I'll make sure my daddy knows about this," Cody bowed up to Miss Chandler. "Breakin' in my truck!"

"I intend to tell your father myself," she assured him. "I'm sure the chairman of our school board would want to be informed of stolen property. Especially when it is recovered."

"I'll make the calls, Miss Chandler, thank you," Wilburn's open hand snaked out to take Cody's arm. "Young man, you go to the office. Wait for me there. Go on."

By now the entire schoolyard of juniors and seniors, black students and white, were fully engaged. Only moments before Cody had been bragging to his teammates that there wouldn't be any nigger playing horns in the band. Now here he was slinking off to the office. Wilburn turned around to face the gathering students.

"Nothing more to see here. Go on. Get about your business. I said, get on!"

The yard of students turned sullenly to obey, leaving Pellicore and Miss Chandler with their principal.

"What do you plan to do?" Miss Chandler inquired.

"Do?"

"For punishment. It's a serious theft."

"You're one to talk about thieves, Miss Chandler."

"If you'd consent to have Master Hewitt punished in the same manner as that Miss Handsom endured, I'd be pleased to administer it myself."

"You stay out of this!"

"Do I have to remind you who *found* the instrument, Mr. Wilburn? Now, I know that there are political considerations for you, here. I know who runs the school board. What I don't know, but suspect, is that some effort is being coordinated to intimidate black students at this school."

"That's outrageous."

"Not an ounce of conviction in your voice, Ben," Miss Chandler called the principal by his given name.

"Watch what you're saying, Eunice."

"*You* watch. Watch good, 'cause I will not stand by and see any student, black or white, made the scapegoat for bigotry."

"This wasn't bigotry!"

"Of course it was," she retorted. "Unless you're fool enough to believe Cody Hewitt's got a sudden urge for music."

With that Miss Chandler bustled off. Mr. Pellicore followed, laden down with brass. Ben Wilburn took up the rear, following Miss Chandler like a rooster after a hen, jerking along with those truncated steps.

I returned to my seat in the anteroom just as the bell rang. Doors burst open from the playground. Teenagers rushed in from the drama outside.

"What's happenin'?" Joe Billy caught me in the hall.

"Tell you later," I said. I did not want to be late for Biology.

The afternoon seemed to move in slow motion. I was ravenously hungry through fifth period, sixth. Seventh period was nominally free but Pellicore expected band members to prepare for practice after school. My instrument was stored in its summertime location. I got it out. Went through a scale tentatively. The valves were a little sluggish at first, but I stuck with my scales and within minutes she was blowing free as ever.

Juanita skipped up, a virtual Pan trailing her flute.

"Cilla! Got your horn back!"

"Miss Chandler found it."

"Good. Mr. Pellicore asked me to walk you through the routines this afternoon."

"Routine?"

"For half-time."

"I don't know 'em so good," I confessed.

"Rodney said you tramped around all summer, up and down the field. Right by yourself."

"Naw, I had Mr. Pellicore."

"Like I said—right by yourself."

Took me a moment to realize she was kidding. I felt something tugging the corner of my mouth.

"That's better," Juanita approved. "I don't want our French horn looking like she plays dirges for a living."

I didn't know what a dirge was but I made a note to find out.

"Now come on." Those ponytails danced irrepressibly as puppies. "We've got work to do."

Our band rarely got to practice on the football field. Most of the time we rehearsed on a rutted boundary chalked off between the football stadium and Shaw's watermelon field. From those wavering demarcations I could see Cody Hewitt and Cutter Land dressed out in pads, running drills opposite Digger Folsom and Terrell Simms. The roped-off area reserved for Colored Town was the only buffer between our field and the team's. I had never been outside that rope.

Pellicore got us out on our field around four. It was a hundred and three degrees, the air thick enough to cut. We stayed on the field from four to half-past six. Dress right, dress left. Diagonals. About face. I tried not to screw up as the band formed its basic formation, L-H-S. The covered wagon was harder. Pellicore wanted a wagon as emblematic of "Oklahoma" but the wheels were a problem. Any band will tell you circles are the hardest thing to get right in formation. Everyone but me was in shorts. There was no shade. I don't know how white people stood such heat. And Pellicore was in a foul mood.

"Dress and cover, people! That line is crooked as a black snake!"

I began to see stars in my eyes.

"I want some energy people—OOOOOOOOklahoma!"

Halfway through the Sooner State I had grass in my face. My instrument stared at me, a brass Cyclops.

"Back up everybody," a shrill voice filtered through a bale of cotton.

"Cilla, are you all right?"

Juanita's elfin face was prominent among those leaning over me.

"I didn't eat," I said.

"You just stay still."

I thought that was a good idea.

With some water and an ice compress I was able to stand, though with a splitting headache. Pellicore didn't lose a beat during the whole episode. Neither did the band. Neither did anyone on the football field. Save for Juanita, everyone just kept marching. I wondered if this was what it was like to be a soldier, looking up from your wounds to see your mates marching into maws of shot and grape to the trill of pipes and the snare of drums, their advance marked out, as with chalk, in perfectly dressed lines.

I wished many times going to school that I could hide behind some martial formation. There was always a provocation of some sort. Between classes was worst, in the halls, all those fists and elbows. And slurs, of course. The things people said. The big thing was, you never wanted to be alone, or isolated. Black students stayed bunched like bovine, seeking security in numbers and in the open. Many of the rules already internalized for behavior downtown applied double at school.

Don't look anybody in the eye, especially in that long hallway.

Keep your head down.

Stay out of the way.

It didn't take long to figure out what tables at the cafeteria were reserved for jocks, which for the fall semester meant the football team.

And there were other rules that you picked up on the fly. Despite official policy, for instance, we did not drink from the water fountain. You wanted water you cupped your hands under the spigot in the restroom. We did not raise our hands in class. We did not laugh or speak boisterously. We did not buy ice-cream or drinks from the little store Mr. Butch ran within sight of the playground. We knew how to keep our place, even in crowded and uncolored quarters. Everybody in Colored Town knew.

Everybody except Joe Billy.

From the first day, Joe Billy walked the halls and raised his hand in class and asked questions just like he'd been in white schools all his life. In particular, Joe Billy refused to defer to Cody Hewitt, whether at the water fountain or in the locker room. And then there was that issue with the football team. Before integration Joe Billy, Chicken Swamp, Pudding, Lonnie and Johnny Boy would meet the Saturday morning following every Friday-night game to re-enact on our rude yard every play they could recall from the white boy's game. I'd see my friends at that pitiful reconstruction, calling out signals that had no real meaning, spiraling a Del Monte juice can for ten, twenty, thirty yards and an imagined first down, or touchdown. This was where black students were supposed to dream their gridiron dreams. These were the friendly fields on which they were expected to stay.

Joe Billy wasn't in school a week before that policy got challenged. It happened on a Friday. Joe Billy was standing in the lunch line waiting to get served. Cody cut in front.

"Whoa, there, sir," Joe Billy spoke to Cody with the formality expected of an adult. "I believe they a few folks in line ahead of you."

"Football team gets to cut, Sambo."

Sambo?

You could see hairs rise like ridgebacks on both sides of the color line, everyone poised for Joe Billy's reply. Which came with remarkable aplomb.

"Team gets to cut line? Really?"

"Anybody with balls to play."

"Well, I be damn, I didn't expect that."

"Bet you didn't," Cody moved to take a tray.

Joe Billy stepped in smoothly to take back his place.

"The hell you doin', nigger?"

Everybody heard it; the students, the ladies in hairnets behind the counter. Soup spoons and ladles halted in medias res, and for a moment the cafeteria was as frozen in time as a snapshot.

But Joe Billy still did not rise to Cody's bait. "You said the team gets to cut."

"What I said, Kingfish."

"Well, guess what?" And then Joe Billy stepped right into Cody's face. "This morning I saw Coach Newton. I joined the *damn* team."

Cody went scarlet. "The fuck you did."

"Watch your language, Cody Hewitt." A woman behind the counter not offended by racism and inured to threats of eternal torment felt compelled to protest any reference to fornication.

"I joined the team, Cody," JayBee was no longer smiling. "Me, Chicken, and Pudding. Three Negroes come to play in your *fucking redneck* conference."

That offense to gridiron reputation gave Cody all the justification he needed to swing. Fortunately, for everyone, our biology teacher was there to intervene.

"Mr. Hewitt, I would not act on that impulse if I were you."

Carter Buchanan was forty years old when I knew him, a long-standing member of our faculty. Miss Chandler called him Brother Carter in deference to the fact that he preached part-time at a local Baptist church. There was Indian somewhere in the man's blood, you could tell. He had high, almost feminine cheekbones. A burnished complexion. Face cracked like a creek bed. It was startling to see the blue eyes that never blinked in that permanently seamed and ocher countenance. His hair didn't age like other men's, running black as coal well into old age, and he wore it long, very long, down below his collar. This at a time when crewcut and flat-tops were still the fashion.

He had a bad heart, people said, as if this were a character fault rather than a medical condition. And he had the reputation for being a soft man. Everyone knew Carter had been discharged from service during 'The War', by which they meant World War II. Didn't have the stomach for it, people said, and I suppose there was some truth in that because without doubt there were things that Carter Buchanan would not stomach.

We all saw that long-haired preacher march Master Cody and Joe Billy out of the cafeteria and across the hall to Mr. Wilburn's office, Cody loudly proclaiming the whole time that *nobody* was giving him a licking for standing up to a colored boy.

"A man can't serve two masters, Ben." Mr. Carter was reported to have anticipated his principal's objections as he gathered the wide paddle hung by a loop of rawhide on the ornate knob of Mr. Wilburn's door.

"Tell Garner I stole the initiative if you like. If you must."

Only moments passed before those of us left behind in the cafeteria heard something like shots from a rifle in the hall.

PAM-PAM-PAM.

Then a pause. Then another report—

PAM-PAM-PAM!

Directly afterward Cody trailed Joe Billy back to the cafeteria. Settling into their widely separated seats both boys were observed shifting cheeks.

Chapter eleven

"Kerbo Student in Marching
Band"—*The Clarion*

A couple of days after the boys got their bottoms warmed, Mr. Folsom paused at my desk and, with a curious inflection, said, "You've been called to the principal's office." That was it. No explanation. No reassurance. I went in fear and trembling to The Office, imagining myriad crimes of which I might be accused. Imagining, too, the report of the principal's wide board on my ample bottom. But I had not been brought to be punished. There was only a note, handed to me by the principal's secretary in a sealed envelope, labeled "Confidential for Miss Handsom."

I opened it. Inside, on ruled paper, was a note from Miss Chandler.

"Come to my classroom fifth period. Imperative," was scrawled the urgent if enigmatic command.

Why in the world hadn't Miss Chandler put her name on the envelope? Why couldn't she have just passed me the note herself? Or passed it along by the hand of my homeroom teacher? What in the world merited such discretion? I rushed to finish lunch quickly,

clenching my note like a passport as I traversed the hall to find Miss
Chandler sunk into the Chip-and-Dale chair only recently integrated
into her classroom furnishings.

"Cilla! Come in," Miss Chandler rose heavily.

"Yes, ma'am."

"I have some good news, Cilla. Exceptional news! Extraordi-
narily exceptional considering your circumstances."

I wasn't sure what she meant by circumstances. Would that
refer to my performance in Myron Putnal's algebra class? Carter
Buchanan's Biology? Miss Chandler's English? What about P.E., History or Pellicore?

"No, no," Miss Chandler's jowls wattled like a turkey's. "Talkin'
about your tests scores, first of all. The STEP test? That you took at
Kerbo School?"

The STEP, yes. At our old school. Already Kerbo had acquired
the distance of Troy. Miss Chandler shuffled a leaf of papers off her
desk.

"I have your scores, Cilla."

"Did I do bad?"

"No. On the contrary, you did quite well. You scored in the
seventieth percentile in language skills, which is remarkable, I would
argue, considering. And in math skills, Cilla, you are ranked in the
eighty-fifth percentile of students taking this test. That is a terrific
score. Pushes you into the seventy-ninth percentile overall."

But what did that mean? What good would it do me?

"I've been talking on the phone with Dr. Clarence Ransom,
he's a professor in the School of Music at Florida State. I've told
him about your situation. Cilla, if you can demonstrate as much
competency with your French horn as you did on the STEP and finish your academic year with decent grades, I believe you can earn a
top-notch scholarship."

"Scholarship?"

"To college, Cilla. Florida State University."

"How much of a scholarship?"

"With a job on campus I think it would amount to a full ride.
But your horn has to be good. You have to be able to perform."

"Would I have to march?"

"No. The scholarship isn't attached to the marching band at all. It's offered through the School of Music."

"Music? You can study music in college?"

"You most certainly can."

The prospect was so alien, so overwhelming, that at first I could not digest it. I almost missed the remainder of Miss Chandler's excited brief.

"...they want a recording. Something you perform on your instrument. Mr. Pellicore has agreed to arrange that. You listening, Cilla?"

It was a lot to hear.

"Dr. Ransom doesn't expect perfection. But the scholarship is performance-based. We need to do well enough to get his attention."

"His attention?"

"I'm hoping you can be invited for an audition, Cilla. A formal audition. This is just the first step."

To study music? Without marching? It seemed too good to be true.

"But, Cilla, you can't look too far ahead. You still have obligations to Mr. Pellicore. You can't quit the Marching Saints."

"Oh, Lord."

"You *can't*. You accepted Mr. Pellicore's quid pro quo and you're going to keep your part of that commitment. It's the proper thing to do, not just for you, but on behalf of the next Negro coming behind you."

The next Negro? I don't suppose I realized until that moment that I was at the center of several 'firsts'. I was the first black student of any gender to play in the high school band. The first to march on a field that still flew a Confederate flag in its end zone. Friday night would also be the first time I marched before a real audience. The first time any Negro ever marched with the Laureate's virgin saints.

"Cilla. Cilla, are you hearing me?"

I roused myself. "Yes, ma'am."

"This is a tremendous opportunity, an exceptional opportunity."

Tremendous? I didn't know whether to shout or hide.

"But, Cilla—and this is very important—we can't go bragging about this. The word will get out, but not from you, do you understand?"

"I wouldn't never brag, Miss Chandler."

"It goes beyond the issue of comportment, child. Lots of students in this school would resent anyone getting this kind of opportunity. Much less a Negro. *And* a girl. So you don't talk about scholarships or colleges to anyone."

"No, ma'am."

"Something else. Keep a record of your grades. Keep every quiz, every test, every piece of homework. Just take 'em home and put 'em in a box. I want to make sure, come semester's end, that you get what you earned."

That I earned? "My grades? Can they take them away?"

"Not if we keep everything in the light, Cilla. And I aim to keep a very bright light. That is my job. Your job is to study hard, practice your instrument, and keep your commitments. Don't give *anybody* an excuse to pull you down. Remember that a full ride to college is now a real possibility. Stay humble, stay prayerful. Keep your eye on the ball."

First thing I did on leaving Miss Chandler, of course, was to corral Joe Billy in the hall and give him the news.

"College, can you 'magine?! And I wouldn't have to march! Whatchu think?"

"Beats hell out of stringing tobacco," Joe Billy agreed, but not with enthusiasm.

"Joe Billy, aint, aren't you excited for me?"

"I am, Cilla. It's just—"

"Just what?"

"We got kicked off the team. Me and Pudding and Chicken."

"Off the football team?"

"They fired Coach Newton, too."

"Who? Who did?"

"The hell you think? Garner Hewitt watn't about to have niggers playing on the same field as his blond-headed boy."

"Joe Billy. But—? Does that mean you cain't be excited for me?"

"I'm 'cited. Just ain't showin' is all."

The bell rang. Joe Billy seemed disinclined to elaborate regarding his enthusiasm for my opportunity.

"See you this afternoon, then," I said.

He shook his head. "Got to make a run to Jacksonville. 'Nother Jimmy wantin' hisself a guitar."

"When you back? When I see you?"

The press of students filling the hall pushed him downstream.

"Sometime."

And before I could reply he slid sideways along the wall and down the hall. A lump started crowding out the glad place that had been in my heart, in my stomach.

"Hell with you, then!" I called out to the startled aspect of students nearby. "To hell with you, Joe Billy!"

I didn't see Joe Billy the remainder of that week, not at school or in his lofty apartment. I was pressed with obligations of tests and homework at the time, and had other distractions at home. Corrie Jean had acquired some kind of croup. I was up two, sometimes three times a night, rubbing liniment on her chest.

"Fug me," Mama crooned gratefully.

Come Friday morning I was dog tired. By Friday afternoon I was nervous as a long-tailed cat in a room full of rocking chairs. That night, I knew, a thousand people would be watching me, seeking in my performance evidence for conclusions already reached or justified. Waiting for that nigger girl to go marching on their field.

"Settle down, Cilla," Pellicore jerked me to earth sometime around fourth period before addressing the rest of the band.

"Remember to check your uniforms early. Go over your instruments, your music. Check with your section leaders if you have questions."

"When you want us to be back here, Mr. Pellicore?"

"*In* the hall by six o'clock."

We got out of school around three-thirty. Grandma and Mama would not have supper before six. I decided to remain in the band hall. Juanita brought me a soda and banana and a tuna fish sandwich. We shared a meal quietly.

"You'll do fine," she patted me on the arm. "Just follow the trombones. And if you make a mistake, don't worry about it. Everybody does. Just don't stop. Get back and pick it up."

I would hear that advice many times in my career, and would freely give it to other nervous musicians.

"You make a mistake, don't stop. Keep going."

I remember performing with an opera orchestra in Milan in the late seventies for a performance of *The Marriage of Figaro*. I was not a featured player, then, but I was at principal on my instrument. Act IV of that opera can be a challenge, Mozart's music tumbling from one number to another in keeping with the activity on stage, revelations, switched identities, a piercing of disguise, an apology. It is a pall-mall piece of storytelling in music, an operatic denouement of Beaumarchais' play.

You miss a measure as I did in that kind of run and you can throw off an entire orchestra. But the only thing you can do is keep playing. The singers can't stop, the conductor can't stop, the musicians absolutely cannot stop, but the audience can stop, can be lurched to a halt dead in their seats which is the last thing in the world you want them to be.

So you just keep going. You pick it up as though you never missed a beat. But on this one occasion I paused, I tried to correct a mistake, God knows why. I knew better. And so at the end of the performance the conductor cornered me in the pit.

"YOU LOST AN ENTIRE MEASURE!"

"Yes. Sorry."

"WHO THE HELL MADE YOU FIRST CHAIR?!"

I stared at him coldly.

"Probably the same asshole made you conductor."

Before I left the house I called my agent and told her to get me another orchestra. In life as well as in art you learn quickly that when you make a mistake the worst thing you can do is stop.

Juanita Land and I had the band hall to ourselves and I was a bundle of nerves. I seem always to either have too much time on my hands or too little. That day I had roughly two hours to kill between the end of school and preparations for my first, momentous appearance on a high school football field. Two hours to kill and no idea what to do with myself.

After our short meal Juanita had a suggestion.

"Let's take a look at your uniform."

Earlier that week we had been given our uniforms; red wool with white leather epaulets and trim, Prussian hats with fake horse-hair plumes and genuine leather visors that Pellicore had us shine with shoe polish. They were stored, all the band's uniforms, in a classroom just off the auditorium. It was a nice smelling room, a mixture of leather and mothballs and wool. Damp and cool, too, like a basement.

The band's uniforms hung on hangers from a long steel pipe that ran sagging at intervals the length of the room. A litter of harnesses, instrument cases and spare parts crowded the floor.

"Here's yours," Juanita had to get on tiptoe to reach my accoutrement.

I had the largest jacket on the rack except Rodney's, who was nearly three inches taller than six feet. I already knew that the trousers fit me perfectly, plenty of room, fire-engine red with a gray, Confederate stripe straight down the side. The jacket was all right, too, except in the arms. I felt like a yokel with half my forearm sticking out to reach my two-toned hands. Felt like a vaudeville player. In blackface.

"Got mine," Juanita sang out, fishing her own uniform off the jerry-rigged rack. She paused a moment to fuss over her jacket's brass buttons, bright as dimes with Brasso, the set of the collar. A very masculine collar.

"What do you think?"

"Looks nice," I replied.

"Think I'll try it on," Juanita declared. "Watch the door."

But before I could take a step to bar that entrance her T-shirt came up over her head and there she was tiny and white and naked from the waist up. No bra. Her breasts were perfectly firm and small as pears. The chill in the cloakroom had her nipples hard.

"Cold in here!" she shivered coyly, and something still unfamiliar lurched in my loins. A contraction. A flutter.

"How do I look?"

"Fine," I said through thick lips.

"Well, then," suddenly she was all brisk and ponytails. "Let's be sure we put these back where we found 'em or Pellicore will have a hissy."

It wasn't too long afterward that other students started dropping in. Pretty soon the band hall was a mayhem of teenagers scrambling to find their ensembles of uniform and instrument and music. Pellicore arrived to center the maelstrom that from then on I would find churning every Friday. It took what seemed to me a completely unorganized hour for the band to get uniforms and instruments and music and line up section by section beside the chinaberry out back. Section leaders strolled through the gathered ranks in military inspection. Rodney tapped me briefly on the shoulder.

"Chinstrap, Cilla."

"Oops."

I snugged my chinstrap secure. Glanced over to Juanita. She was already in posture with her flute, straight and serene as an elf. Jade eyes caged straight ahead.

We marched to snares toward the bleachers. Ralph-stepped up to our assigned places on those aluminum tiers. The air was so sharp, that evening. A concession stand situated along a Gulf-born breeze wafted aromas of popcorn and hotdogs. The field, just cut, was heavy with evening dew. That special smell of cut grass. That Friday night smell. Even the bleachers' metal seats were damp with humidity.

I wished Joe Billy could be in the stands, to see me. He was installed with Chicken Swamp and Pudding in the colored section. The rope that delineated the formal pen into which black spectators were herded had been taken down, but even Joe Billy could be influenced by local mores to keep his appointed place. Miss Chandler, however, rejected any such restriction. I was amazed to see my

Kerbo teacher fixed like a boulder in the midst of the bleachers, her gaze, it seemed to me, fixed on the ostracized students at the end of the field.

I felt like a fly on a plate. In a few minutes I would be the only person of color on the Hornets' white-lined field. It would be I—not Pudding, not Chicken, nor Joe Billy—who would be the first black student that whites would see in uniform. Was that a cause for resentment among my classmates? Or jealousy? Was Joe Billy jealous of my sudden achievement, or the opportunity at Florida State?

These concerns and others already in play threatened to disrupt the concentration I would need to do my business, tempting my eyes to stray from the monotonous music Pellicore required. It was simple music; nevertheless I was worried I would screw up, that with the first step onto the field I would freeze. And then our director stood up with his baton.

"Instruments!"

The brass of my horn crushing into my ribs.

"Fight Song. One. Two. One, two, three…"

A percussion of wind and brass split the summer air, the heaving air. LHS's students accompanied our rousing fight-song with homegrown lyrics.

"You bring the whiskey, I'll bring the rye/ We'll get together at Lafayette High/ Send the seventh graders out for gin/ And don't let a sober eighth-grader in…"

That innocent and trivial variation was followed by other antics, other rituals and I began to relax. I felt secure on the sidelines, in the band. There was no marching required here.

Kickoff came and I found myself cheering as if I had been in this high school forever.

"AIN'T THIS GREAT?" Rodney Morgan offered a genuine grin.

I nodded. "YES!"

Before any time at all had passed Cody Hewitt had quarterbacked the LHS Hornets to one first down, two interceptions and a two-touchdown deficit. Not auspicious for an athlete looking for a ride at Florida State.

And then it was halftime.

"PLACES!"

Our drum major and section leaders scrambling off the stands.

"PLACES, PEOPLE!"

My lungs started to heave like I'd swum the river. I rushed to find my spot of ground in a blind panic.

Dress and cover.

"First impressions, people!" Mr. Pellicore strutted before us like Napoleon. "I want those instruments snapped up on the beat. Step out with a full stride, brisk tempo, full and confident. "Miss Handsom—!"

Pellicore's fading dome suddenly thrust into my face.

"Yes, sir!"

"Find your ground! Keep your mind on your business!"

"Yes, sir."

"Remember follow your section leader and if you make a mistake—"

"Don't stop, yes, sir, I won't."

"All right, then. Here we go. Drum Major!"

I felt scrambled like a chicken with his head cut off. I needed to find Rodney Morgan.

"HERE, CILLA!"

I heard laughter from the stands. There were people looking, I knew, as I scrambled to my choreographed location. That big, awkward black girl in a redcoat uniform. I found my place finally, but my knees began to lock. About that time a sharp elbow got jammed into the cage of my ribs.

"Flex your knees," Juanita commanded. "Flex 'em."

"I'm scared!" I wailed as I tried to comply.

"Everybody's scared. But you are not alone out here, Cilla. We are a band. All of us. Just follow Rodney."

Her ponytail tossed with the bob of her head.

"Here we go," our section leader hefted his trombone.

Then the rap, rap, rap of a snare drum.

A public-address system cursed with feedback echoed over the field. A garland of girls twirled batons out front, like slave women sent to precede the arrival of royalty. I dressed and covered on my section leader. The chalk lines gridding the field had already compromised the shine of my black leather shoes. I located the Drum Major centered before us, our general on the field. Ryan Tunney was our major domo, our metronome, the brother of the man who would later bury Joe Billy.

He raised his silver staff.

Three quick blasts on a silver whistle.

We were on the field.

Ball players talk about how scared they are until that first hit, that first contact with an opposing player. You endure that initial jarring collision, players will say, and generally things settle down. Marching in a band is similar. It's a rack of nerves until you get on the field, until you make that first beat, execute that first left or right face. Then a thousand separate gears go into play requiring such coordination and concentration that you don't have time to be scared.

We only had three formations to choreograph. I found my spot in the "H" of LHS, that was easy enough. Pellicore placed me at the hub of a wheel for the "Oklahoma" feature. No problem with dress and cover from there. I was, however, slightly out of step on the final march of saints—

"Cilla. On me," Rodney commanded loudly and I recovered.

When the Saints/Go Marching In/Oh, when the Saints go marching in...

Then we peeled off the field in compact ranks and that was it, my first performance before a large and hostile audience. I retired from the field with my eyes searching the bleachers for Miss Chandler.

"We're not done yet, people," Pellicore herded us to our sideline seats. "Keep moving."

We were filtering off the gridiron and milling toward our seats in the bleachers when the players of both teams galloped out of their lockers. I was still on the sideline trailing the trombones and trumpets when Cody Hewitt stepped directly into my path.

His uniform was damp and stained from a halftime of troubles, a handsome, angry surfer-boy in pads and helmet. I could not avoid him; I was crowded by other band members within the length of his arms.

"Bitch," he challenged me.

I think it was only at that moment I fully realized that there would always be a Cody Hewitt in my life, and people like him. That for those people nothing I accomplished would count for shit. No trophy would ever come untarnished. Miss Chandler came down from her seat in the bleachers afterwards.

"What did he say to you?"

"Who?"

"You know who."

"Nothing."

"Don't listen to that boy, Cilla," she seized my arm. "You looked wonderful out there. You did us proud!"

"I did?"

"Yes. Now go on. Enjoy yourself. Have some fun."

For a moment I thought I actually could enjoy myself. After all, you can't find better camaraderie at any football game than among members of a band. Those kids were funny and fun-loving. They were smart and sassy and obnoxious. But they were not colored. It quickly became apparent that my white companions had plans for the night that could not include me, boys and girls drifting off in twos and threes to some destination communicated as if by telepathy.

Rodney did bring me a coke before he left with his girlfriend. That was nice. And Juanita squealed over and over how well I'd done. How proud she was of me. I didn't feel abandoned by them, nor even by the other departing Saints. It was my Kerbo companions who deserted me that night. Who did not come to me in the stands or at the end of the game to tell me how perfectly I hubbed my wheel on the football field. How well I played "Oklahoma".

"You need a ride home, Cilla?" Juanita asked when we'd hung our uniforms.

"Yes," I admitted. "Please. If you don' mind."

I had already gotten into her truck when I saw Joe Billy's two-toned '56 pull up, Joe Billy himself slumped low, in the posture now associated with gang-bangers. Pudding and Chicken crowded in the back seat.

"'S'matter, Cilla? Too good for yo friends?"

"Got that kind of attitude you ain' no frenna mine," I snapped back.

Give Pudding credit for intervening. "Cilla, he din' mean nuthin'."

"Sure he did."

"Naw, he din'. He proud of you, girl. We all proud. You looked good out there."

"You did, Cilla," this from Chicken. "Now, come on and go wit us."

"'Wit' you where?"

"Live Oak. Mama's Store. Man there playin's got one of Joe Billy's guitars."

"Guitar?" Juanita perked up. "JayBee plays the guitar?"

"You're welcome to come," Joe Billy offered politely, though all of us knew Mr. Land's daughter could not possibly accept.

"No, thank you," Juanita tossed her ponytail over her shoulder. "Got somebody I'm 'sposed to meet. Says he's got plans."

Juanita winked at me. "Can't imagine what."

I waved goodbye to Mr. Land's daughter before dropping into the seat made available beside Joe Billy.

"I'm gonna have me some friends, Joe Billy," I declared without a hint of deference.

He ran his hand over the arc of the steering wheel.

"He knows, Cilla," Pudding said. "It's just hard, is all."

Things loosened up on the way to Mama's. Chicken Swamp started things off with a six-pack.

"I'm gone dance tonight!" he yelled, spraying beer all over the back seat.

And, of course we had music.

"Put on the radio," Chicken yelled. "Let's hear some rock and got-damn roll!"

It's over thirty miles to Live Oak. We had a run of Dionne Warwick and The Beatles and the Mamas and Papas so that by the time we got to Mama's everybody had held everybody's hand, everybody had walked on by, and we were all looking forward to dancing in the street, which, of course, was why we were going to Live Oak in the first place. You see, you couldn't dance, at least not legally, inside Laureate's city limits. Dancing of any kind was forbidden first of all by canon—

Do you know why Baptists never fuck standing up? the tired joke went.

No, why?

'Cause somebody might think they're dancing.

—and then by statute. The Laureate City Council initiated the statute, kowtowing to local clergy shortly after Elvis Presley thrust his pelvis on *The Ed Sullivan Show*. They passed an ordinance that made it illegal to "simulate sexual gyration" inside the city limits.

Mama Snipes was free from canonic, statutory and most sexual repressions. Mama had a jukebox inside what was actually a garage that looked out onto the parking lot of an old Texaco gas station. The garage and attached house was what Mama called her store, one of the few places black teens could get a coke or hamburger and dance.

In the bay, where the lifts used to be, was where you danced. Mama would just roll up those big doors, put on a fan and some music and let it rock. There were maybe twenty couples dancing at Mama's when we pulled up that evening, with as many singles milling around. A live band was setting up beside a pair of Fender amps, but the Wurlitzer was filled with quarters. I could hear Little Anthony.

"Come on, now," JayBee pocketed the keys. "Let's see can you dance."

Dancing is a lot easier than marching, especially with a little beer to go along. Maybe some weed. It was the first time I smelled marijuana. Smelled like dry weeds burning.

"Want some?" Joe Billy cupped a joint in his hand.

"Is it like cigarettes?"

"Naw. Makes you feel light. Goofy. Take a hit. Hard. Hold it."

I tried and when I did it felt like somebody shoved a poker

down my throat. Seconds later I was coughing like a coal miner. And then a kind of fog seemed to clear.

"Daaaaammmmn."

Joe Billy grinned. "Yeah."

Let me go on record to say that Joe Billy was one outa-sight dancer. He could twist, he could frug, he could Bosa the goddamned Nova. He could alligator, jerk, or shimmy and he could mash your sweet, sweet potatoes all night long.

I gave myself up to the music and alcohol and grass. Let the cool evening air wash over. "I don't give a shit if syrup goes to a dollar a sop," I declared.

Spreading my arms to heaven as if I were in a revival. Joe Billy sliding inside. I leaned on him heavily, content to follow along or be dragged.

Then I began to notice the other couples dancing.

There was this one girl, in particular, a black girl near us, who had a narrow waist, like Juanita's, a white haltertop over tight jeans. Processed hair, all straight and nice. When she moved I could see the muscles in her back working. See her hair spilling down that long, long spine.

She looked like a gypsy out there. Like Jezebel. Like one of those sirens my boyfriend put on his guitars. I was dancing with Joe Billy, but I could not take my eyes off the anonymous siren alongside. I began to move my legs the way she moved. And my hips. My pelvis.

Let you backbooooone slip.

My shirt began to stick to my skin and I was hot. I was hot, Mama. I gathered up my top and tied it off in a knot.

"Lawd God O'Mighty!"

Someone shouted.

"Look at that tall girl dance!"

It wasn't too long before Joe Billy was telling Pudding and Chicken they were going to have to find their own ride home.

"For somebody never danced before, you sure let the dogs out," Joe Billy declared as he let me in his car.

All trace of color bled from the scenery on our way back to Laureate. A full moon fluttered in and out of autumn clouds to paint the road in a chiaroscuro of light and shadow.

"That girl next to us? At Mama's?" Joe Billy broke the silence. "The one with the top?"

"Mmm hmm," I could see her still.

"Her boyfriend checking you out."

"Her boyfriend?"

That was unexpected.

"Checkin' *me* out?"w"Thought I's gone have to kick his butt," Joe Billy assured me and slipped a hand off the steering wheel.

"Be nice, now," I said. "Be nice."

"Oh, I will," he promised.

I coupled with Joe Billy once again that night in his rude loft. But I had Mama's and the cloakroom between my legs, that black, nubile dancer, and Juanita.

Chapter twelve

"...Monk Folsom has declared he will oppose Collard Jackson for the office of County Sheriff. Mr. Folsom will run as a Republican in that race..."—*The Clarion*, Sept. 17, 1963

By the third week in September, Collard Jackson's political future looked dim. By that time, everybody knew that Garner Hewitt had shifted his formidable weight to back Monk Folsom for sheriff. It was easy for Garner to dump Collard Jackson. In the twisted logic of that time and place, a lawman who broke up a mob intent on assaulting children was not a man you could count on. The word coming out of Monk's Auto Shop was that Sheriff Jackson had metamorphosed into a "nigger-loving lackey" beholden to "outside agitators."

"Ain't nobody gone believe that tripe," Mr. Raymond dismissed the strategy early on. "Collard Jackson? A friend to colored folk? Man got to be a fool to believe that."

But the frictions erupting between black students and whites confirmed for bigoted voters that integration was a mistake and that those nigras wouldn't be so uppity 'cept they thought the sheriff was in their corner. More tolerant voices were divided in opinion, those who believed Collard was not responsible for conflicts that were

163

inevitable splitting with those who believed he greatly exacerbated the situation.

"If the vote was taken today," Garner crowed to his boys, "Collard would lose three to one."

Miss Chandler refused to let her students dwell on the turmoil roiling our community. We were in the middle of *The Scarlet Letter* and were not allowed to stray from discussions of Hawthorne and Hester. The tensions arising from integration were omnipresent, of course. But the local race for sheriff was not engaged. Questions related to the Sheriff's affinities or future were nowhere assigned.

In fact, a kind of doldrums fell over our small campus. September bled into October without a single fight or serious provocation. An early autumn chill gave way to a late Indian summer, a heat that in northern Florida pours over your skin like heated syrup. It is sticky. It is inescapable. Sweat stings your eyes and sticks to you in places you cannot politely scratch; your groin, your armpits, the wedge of your ass. It is a resurgence of humidity that makes you indolent and irascible.

At least it came late. Boys donning short-sleeved madras shirts and girls retrenched in cotton blouses were thinking ahead to Homecoming Week and Lake Butler while little ones looked forward to Halloween, all in an interregnum characterized by what in comparison to the first weeks of the semester seemed a balmy truce between the races.

In that false eddy I prepared for my audition at Florida State. Dr. Ransom had already received a tape recording that captured samples of my horn. Mr. Pellicore made the tape on his reel-to-reel and sent it by mail. It featured "Oklahoma" and other football-related fare.

"We'll be going up Thursday the fourteenth." Miss Chandler brought the news to me in Mr. Pellicore's presence. "There will be two faculty waiting, including Dr. Ransom."

"Waiting for what?"

"Your recital."

"Recital?"

"Certainly, Cilla. They want to hear you play."

"But what? What will I play?"

"The French horn, girl. One of the pieces you play at halftime will do. Anything familiar."

"I want to play more than 'Oklahoma'," I responded stubbornly. "And I want to play the piano, too, not just my horn."

"You play your horn and you play it safe," Pellicore admonished. "They're not looking for a symphony, Cilla. And don't forget Lake Butler."

The Lake Butler Bulldogs were our conference nemesis. The entire student body was engaged in the construction of floats and paraphernalia associated with the traditional parade that would flatter the team and fire up the hometown crowd. The field behind Monk's Auto Repair was stacked with flatbed trailers and littered with crepe paper and bunting and styrofoam. These constructions took enormous quantities of time and effort. Students spent hours stuffing tissue paper into the trailers' chickenwire skirts. A small army of carpenters had invaded the school shop, turning out simulacra of Hornets and Bulldogs and goalposts.

A kind of carnival atmosphere reigned in the school that absolutely amazed me and my Kerbo classmates.

"Miss Hattie would of done whipped every one of these people," Chicken declared, and he was right.

Normal rules of behavior were suspended. There were pep rallies on a daily basis and gags in the hall. Boys painted their pale faces. Cheerleaders went to class in their short skirts. I saw Bonnie Hart in the hall with Cody, her tongue halfway down his throat. Schoolwork was ignored. You could cut class.

You could kiss off studies.

You could get away with murder.

But for me the big game could not have come at a more inconvenient time. Mr. Pellicore, to start with, assigned the band new music in anticipation of the home team's crusade against the reigning conference champion. I was certain that a halftime performance of "The Impossible Dream" would bring hoots of derision but was overruled.

"The Impossible Dream" demanded a new and elaborate choreography that had to be mastered, this at a time when I was preparing for my crucial recital in Tallahassee. I was also taking two days a week to bone up on reading and English skills in preparation for something called the SAT. I had work at school, work at band, work at home.

Without Miss Chandler's help, and Joe Billy's, I could not have done it. Every day after band practice Joe Billy drove me straight, and I mean straight, to Miss Chandler's front porch, where she would coach me through the day's homework, prepare me for quizzes and prep me for the Boards. Then she'd make me eat. That didn't take much encouragement. I had pork chops and blackeyed peas five nights a week, the best week of eating I'd ever had in my life.

With schoolwork completed and food in my stomach I trotted straight from Miss Chandler's to Kerbo School where I daily prepared for the recital that would determine my future. I loved retreating inside my old school. The building offered a fortress against the outside world, a sanctuary for my labors, a retreat immune to all distraction.

It felt good to be within the embrace of those cypress walls, inside the penumbra of familiar smells and memories. I had my horn; Pellicore allowed me to take my cased instrument home for these extracurricular sessions. I would give the Florida faculty a full performance of "Oklahoma" in martial regularity, unvaried from the sheet music Pellicore would provide. A metronomic performance I would render, note following note like Mama would play.

"Oklahoma" was safe.

But there was something riskier in the wind. I was writing music of my own that I wanted somebody to hear, music for strings and winds and keyboards. I started by working out variations of original scores, pieces for the piano, mostly, of Mozart and a reduction of the Ninth for the piano. It was in my grandmother's shack and singlehanded that I began my career as a composer.

For the first time I was doing something that had begun with Alex McBride in Jacksonville; I was allowing myself to experiment, to make mistakes, to alter the music on the sheet. It had started with

Beethoven's ode, just variations on chords and harmonies already penned by a distant composer. I began to jot down sounds in my own head. They were just small riffs at first, a pleasant shift in chord or mood or rhythm. I'd jot them down on scraps of paper at first, but that got too unwieldy, so I got grocery bags from the SafeWay, a grand expanse of paper, and scored my compositions by hand on that rough parchment, trying out small beads of sound at first, then looking for a bracelet to mount them, a theme, a hook, a melody. I'm not sure I even realized that I was composing original music.

I had no instrument. I wrote my music by the light of a kerosene lantern, nodding to an imagined score in my mind's ear. I'd stay up hours into the night, long after Grandma was asleep, long after Corrie Jean had begun her recurrent inchoate dreams. Sometimes the sun would rise and there'd be Hard On curled at my feet, a half-deaf dog witness to the dawn of my music.

My basic notion was to take a classical piece and vary it with riffs I had culled from Joe Billy's cache of blues and jazz and popular records. I penciled my compositions on the backs of grocery bags saved from SafeWay. Miss Chandler saw my work, but had no idea that these scribblings were intended for Dr. Ransom and his colleagues in Tallahassee. I was told to play it safe. I was warned. But I remembered Jacksonville and Alex McBride and I just decided to swing for the fences.

As it turned out, so did Miss Chandler.

The selection of the supervisor of elections for Lafayette County ran on the same schedule as that for the sheriff, but Jim Hicks had been unchallenged for so many years that lots of folks probably thought he was appointed to his position. For years Jim had been charged with certifying candidates and electoral results in county-run contests and for years he had routinely denied black citizens the right to vote.

Jim Crow provided the legal basis for that discrimination. Poll taxes were common. Registration required street addresses that, in Colored Town, could not be provided. Other tools for disenfranchisement were more subtle. Take literacy tests, for instance. You had to read to vote and you had to read to Mr. Hicks' satisfaction. Mr. Jim kept a Bible handy, or sometimes a newspaper, to evaluate the occasional colored citizen intrepid enough to seek registration. All applicants of African American descent returned from those examinations unqualified to vote.

Lyndon Baines Johnson would later railroad legislation through congress to sweep away the last vestiges of what had long been an evisceration of civil rights. But in 1963 there was no local presence to challenge the supervisor of elections. Had not been since Reconstruction. So Mr. Hicks must have been astounded when one October day, around noon, Miss Eunice Chandler placed her purse on the marble counter that dominated the lobby outside his office.

"You need anything?"

It was Jim's sister, Wanda, who handled the routine queries and applications. Wanda Hicks proudly pronounced herself an evangelical Christian. Not just a Christian, mind you, but an evangelical Christian. It seems Jim's spinster sister had discovered the special potency of that label long before the modern majority did.

She had a broad, untroubled visage. Wore an unadorned one-piece dress belted with a muslin sash at her thick waist. She kept her hair dishwater blonde and held back so tightly it pulled at the corner of her eyes.

Mandarin eyes in a hard-shelled face.

"Yes, please." Miss Chandler's loose and folded countenance would have rippled like a walrus with the smile I know she presented. "I'd like to register to vote."

"…Vote?"

Wanda was truly unsure what she had heard. Surely this ugly large black woman was looking to get a driver's license, or perhaps welfare?

Miss Chandler abided Wanda's confusion without comment, and nodded, gazing at the nameplate set in a block of hardwood atop the counter.

"You're here to vote?"

"To register," Miss Chandler amended sweetly. "I am here to register to vote in Lafayette County."

A frown deepened below Wanda's Mandarin eyes. "Just one

moment." Jim's sister left her post at the counter to step through the open door of his office. "Jim?"

"What is it?"

A muffled consultation had the supervisor reaching for his Bible. Mr. Hicks emerged from his office with a smirk that quickly faded when he recognized the black woman looming at the counter.

"That a Bible, Mr. Hicks? I wasn't aware I had to be sworn in."

"Miss Eunice—"

"Miss Chandler," she interrupted, sweet as pie. "Eunice is my given name. I'll get right to the point; I am here to register. Want to make sure I'm in time for the May primary."

"Uhmmmm," Hicks laid the useless Bible aside. "Uhm. Law says you got to wait sixty days, Miss Chandler."

"The law says? May I see it?"

"See...?"

"The law, Mr. Hicks. The statute, in particular, related to a sixty-day wait."

"Now, Miss Eunice, Miss Chandler, I don't think I'm required to clerk the law for you. You want to see Judge Blackmond, or the Sheriff, you're welcome."

"Mr. Hicks, I have already seen Judge Blackmond."

"You...you have?"

"Yes, I have. And there is no mandatory waiting period beyond your authority. All that's required is that I produce identification, which I have with me. A birth certificate—"

"Could take a while to verify that, Miss Chandler."

Wanda smirked. It was a point of fact that it always took an inordinate length of time to verify the circumstances of any black person's birth.

"I also have a letter from the supervisor of elections in Leon County. Harold Sykes, you know Harold? Tommy's uncle. Anyway, Harold was kind enough to save you some trouble, you and me. See here? He's already verified the birth certificate and related information. Had it notarized, wasn't that thoughtful? I have a Florida driver's license, too, if you need it..." She plopped the license along with the offending letter onto the marble counter. "...and my transcript from Howard University, along with state certification for secondary education. Do you need me to read from your Bible?"

"No, ma'am," Jim was no longer smiling. "No, I don't think we'll bother with the Bible."

"Excellent," Miss Chandler beamed goodwill. "Then if you'll just kindly lay out the paperwork, I believe I can be registered in time to get back for lunch."

"I'm afraid that won't be possible, Miss Chandler."

"'Afraid'?"

"I cannot verify these documents," Jim declared coldly. "You're welcome to apply again in the spring, if you like."

"I do not like," Miss Chandler declared, and Wanda began to experience something like pulmonary distress.

"Miss Chandler, are we gonna have a problem here?" Jim seemed to be looking forward to that prospect.

"You definitely will have," Miss Chandler assured him. "There are laws, Mr. Hicks, that you are not above."

"I don't see anybody with a gun to my head."

"Call the sheriff," Miss Chandler suggested. "I believe he's equipped."

"Wanda."

"Ah hah?"

"Call the sheriff, please. Get him over here. Use my phone."

By the time Collard walked up the stairs from his office to Hicks', everybody in the courthouse knew that one of them nigger teachers was backtalkin' to the supervisor of elections.

Collard would have had no trouble facing a shootout or a fist-fight. Crosses and burned churches were mere aggravations. But he had his hat in his hands that noon by Jim Hicks' office.

"Miss Chandler," he began. "I believe it's best we leave."

"As soon as the Supervisor discharges his sworn duty, Sheriff, I'll be free to go."

"She can go anytime," Hicks snarled. "I done told her she can't register."

Miss Chandler turned the sheriff's attention to the documents on the corner. "One of those is from Judge Blackmond, Sheriff."

"Judge don't rule my office." Hicks became more bellicose in Collard's presence.

"The judge will be glad to hear that," Miss Chandler responded calmly. "In fact, if you'll put it in writing, I'd be glad to take it to him."

"You go do anything you want."

"And then I shall inform the FBI."

"Ain't got nuthin' to do with me."

"And then the governor, then the State Attorney General—"

"Miss Chandler—" Collard tried to interject.

"And then finally I will go to the Attorney General of the United States. I believe Robert Kennedy takes a dim view of local officials who use their office to deny African American citizens the right to vote."

"Get her out of here, Collard," Jim Hicks ordered the sheriff—which was a big mistake.

Collard just stood there a moment. Then he put his hat back on his head. Ran a scarred finger round to test the brim.

"The fuck you think I am, Jim? Your house nigger?"

"Well, I—" Hicks was taken aback. "Well, Sheriff, I just assumed—"

"'Assume' is right. Makes an 'ass' outa 'u' and 'me'. Mostly you, Jim."

"Sorry, Sheriff. Didn't mean to tell you how to do your job."

"'Assuming' you got the goddamnedest idea what my job is."

"Of course. Of course."

"So now in the discharge of *my* duties, Mr. Supervisor, I order you to serve this woman the papers she needs to register to vote."

"Lord Jesus!"

Expressed in local vernacular—Wanda like to have fainted.

"What? You cain't do that, Sheriff."

"Don't make me come around that counter, Jim. You already pissed me off. Now *get the god-damn paperwork!*"

Hicks turned, pale, to his sister. "Well? You heard the man."

"I'll need a hundred, Mr. Hicks."

This from Miss Chandler.

"WHAT?"

"Well, what did you imagine, Mr. Supervisor? That I was the only Negro born or literate in Colored Town?"

Jim's silent appeal to Collard Jackson went unheeded.

"You can tell Garner they's more people gonna wipe their ass with those things than register," the sheriff waved him off. "It ain't no more than a fart in a whirlwind. Just give the woman what she wants."

Miss Chandler left with a heavy box of registration forms propped on her hip. But it was one thing to tote a box of paper across the tracks to Colored Town, quite another to rally a frightened and feeble population to actually vote. All the legislation in the world would not accomplish that task. Bobby Kennedy and LBJ and Martin Luther King put together could not get that job done.

Even with but a single radio and a half-ass newspaper we all knew what had followed registrations in Mississippi, in Alabama. Hell, there had been lynchings of civil rights workers as close as Taylor County. What protection could colored people expect in Laureate? There would be no angels guarding Jim Hicks' voting booths, no salvation sent from above. If we did this thing we would have to bear the lash on our own, we told ourselves. And what did we have to gain? What good could possibly come of such folly? These were the opinions that held sway on Mr. Raymond's front porch, mouthed by mostly unemployed men.

And so when word came back to the quarters of Miss Chandler's audacity there was no cheering, there was no rush of support. To the contrary, Miss Chandler's initiative quickly divided our community right down the middle.

"We go up to that town wantin' the vote, Garner and all them white men gonna pound our heads," Pudding echoed sentiments heard at home. "She should stick to the classroom, keep outta politics."

I agreed with Pudding, for reasons totally selfish. Here I was trying to keep out of sight, after all, trying to keep a low profile just as Miss Chandler had told me to do, so that I could get on with my life, and now here Miss Chandler was going out and bringing all this attention. Me trying to grab a foothold in the dark, and she goes out and grabs the limelight. How was this going to help me go to college? How was this going to help me get out of Colored Town?

Some voices praised Miss Chandler's courage. Others acknowledged her courage, but decried any attempt to organize voters. And some people were downright angry at Miss Chandler. Miss Hattie Briar was vocal in her disapproval.

"Colored people? Voting? You think we been injured so far, just get in the white man's politics! Lord. Might as well shoot ourselves in the foot. Or the head."

Comments even more pointed came from the men.

Somebody oughta tell that woman mind her own damn business.

We don' need no agitatin'.

Or, this one—

She watn't so damn ugly she'd be married, yeah. Would'n have time be messin' with no election.

Chapter thirteen

T"cbs Stirs The Race Pot," by
Jon J. Synon—*The Clarion*

he false summer that had settled so close to our Homecoming
Week was banished by a cold front that by the time of my recital had
brought a hard freeze to Colored Town. It was easy to forget that the
first relief from summer's hell later exacted the winter's. Nevertheless,
and however shortsighted, I welcomed the hard frost that came on the
day of my Tallahassee audition, the freezing combinant of atmosphere
that placed an icy lace on the Queen Anne crowding our outhouse,
that crowned the tall floreted heads of Joe-Pye weed with delicate
crystals of frozen dew and drove the rat snake to warmer lairs.

The night before, while a norther howled its bitter lamentation, I put out my clothes before the sputter of our kerosene heater.
The clothes would singe the hair on my legs come morning, but that
was preferable to slipping from Mama's warm flank into garments
stiff with cold. I only had one coat for winter, a field jacket got from
the Salvation Army in Lake City. Grandma gave me a scarf for my
head.

Next morning I danced on tiptoes to our kitchen and shim-
mied into my things. I had a substantial breakfast; bacon and extra

biscuits and mayhaw jelly. I then made sure Mama was up and had food before making one last dash to our privet, washing my hands afterward with cold water and Comet. Time then to brave the brisk wind for the short walk that took me to my Yellowbird bus.

I lugged my French horn in a fist exposed to the elements, the horn's cardboard case banging my leg with each step. I had music stowed inside. The prescribed performances, of course. A safe selection. But I had the other material I'd prepared surreptitiously whose purpose I still concealed from Miss Chandler. I flexed my fingers. I would not be sticking tissue into floats or gluing one-by-twos into make-believe goal posts today. This was the day when I would finally perform for real professors at a real college.

The bus rolled past West's Drugstore and my thoughts shifted to Joe Billy. He had been absent from school the entire week; somebody even said he was quitting. The Ford was gone from its usual place behind the upstairs loft; I figured he was off selling guitars. I hoped he'd be back for my birthday. We would both soon be eighteen. I turned on Halloween. His birthday was the week after. But even though I thought about my boyfriend, I can't say I missed Joe Billy enough to pine. I told myself that I had important business only a bus ride away. I could not afford to be distracted, was what I said.

I could not afford to anticipate any future further away than Florida State.

The bus dropped me off at school where I found Miss Chandler waiting. She was dressed nice. A kind of taffeta dress with lots of fabric on the shoulders fell below her calves. She had a hat fit for a revival.

"Morning Miss Cilla," she beamed.

I put a hand on my stomach. "I feel funny."

Miss Chandler took my instrument. "It's just butterflies."

"Yes, ma'am," I replied, glad to hear it wasn't buzzards.

We took a Greyhound to Tallahassee. A bus ride is different than a car or truck; it rolls on its long axis like a rocking chair, only more ponderously. The engines labors behind you. The *cadende* of a massive transmission rises and falls. It was soothing to hear.

The landscape was soothing, too, the frost fallen from the previous night thrown like some magnificent, sparkling cloak to follow the topography in gentle undulations on either side of the highway. Copses of hickory and oak and pecan trees stuck like buttons onto that fabric. Fence lines running like seams or zippers. A rising sun plotted to diminish my imagined garment. Roadside ditches steamed like cauldrons. The frozen precipitation clinging to lily pads and cattails melted away like drying tears. It wasn't like the drive to Jacksonville at all. Even in winter I saw a much wider variety of plant life on our route to Tallahassee than I had driving to J-ville. Thickets of crepe myrtle still in bloom competed with mimosa and oak and hickory trees. Topiaries of kudzu vines draped in fantastic profundity over the metal skeletons of power lines.

"Look here, Cilla."

A forest had been burned for new ground, every tree cut to expose the rich and torn earth beneath, their stumps cleared and piled, every vine and bramble ripped by the roots and pyred—except for the dogwood trees. Every dogwood had been spared. Those trees, sown wild, were distributed stochastically about the riven ground, scattered survivors standing between smoldering piles of stumps and vine.

It would be a nuisance, come planting time, to have to steer your plough or harrow around those dogwood trees, to break the uniform rows of your corn or peanuts or tobacco in deference to a wild tree. But someone was willing to put up with that aggravation, all for the sake of a pearl-white blossom. I had never seen anything quite like that before—labor consciously hampered for a love of beauty.

It took about two hours to reach Tallahassee. We disembarked from the bus and immediately piled into a cab, my first.

"One-thirty-two North Copeland," Miss Chandler directed the driver and I heard the meter tick.

Even the homes in the slums of Tallahassee were nicer than anything in Colored Town, but as we moved away from the bus station and toward the university I saw vistas of architecture that promised comforts and space I had never even imagined. Quaint frame houses gave way to sprawling brick homes. Front porches became

Colonial facades. There were other changes in the landscape, too. At some point, probably along Tennessee Street, I realized I was not seeing any black people.

"Here's our turnoff," Miss Chandler prompted the driver and I saw him frown at the unprompted instruction.

"Cilla, don't forget your horn."

We got out of the cab on Copeland and approached the university's music building on an angled sidewalk, dodging the traffic of students who seemed headed either for fires or funerals, racing like horses or else slow as snails. I saw no mode of perambulation between those extremes. They looked older than students ought to look, more sophisticated. And all white. I saw no Negroes in that throng and found my eyes drawn to my feet on the sidewalk.

"Nuh uh," Miss Chandler chided. "You're as good as anyone here, Miss Cilla. You be proud."

I lifted my head to follow my teacher to a building I would have described as a castle. The Kuersteiner Music Building is still one of the most elegant pieces of architecture on Florida State's campus, its arched, almost Gothic entry flanked by heavy-paned windows framed in brick and hardwood. The foyer before Kuersteiner's oaken doors reminded me of a throne, broad stone arms thrust out to either side of wide-slabbed steps. On the right hand side of that royal portal were two magnificent specimens of palm tree. I recognized hedges of japonica and pittosporum.

"Looks nice, doesn't it?" Miss Chandler prompted.

I shifted my cardboard case to my other hand.

"What say we go on inside?"

We passed from a layer of icy air into an interior cozy as a boot.

"Lord!" I exclaimed. "It's warm!"

"And come summer they've got air-conditioning, too," Miss Chandler supplied.

Air-conditioning? For an entire building? It did not seem possible. Unfortunately, I would later be disappointed to learn that Kuersteiner's were the only centrally cooled classrooms on Florida State's steaming campus.

We passed a long marble bench on our way into the Music Building's cavelike interior. It had the smell of a seldom-used closet, but I didn't mind. It was warm, but not the least bit damp. The walls, cool as lime. Polished tiles of marble, clean and cool. Made you want to walk barefoot. And I liked the doors that punched regular intervals into the hall. They were heavy, oaken and well worn.

Students were dashing to unknown destinations in an apparent rush to make some class or another, but I heard no bell. Then I saw something that made me reach out with my free hand to take Miss Chandler's ample arm.

"Cilla?"

"Over there!"

He strolled in spit-polished shoes near a stairway, a white man in a tan uniform, a handgun holstered prominently.

"That's campus police, I imagine." Miss Chandler extricated herself from my panicked clutch. "Just for security. He won't bother you. Now, where is our room? Remind me."

"Two Oh Nine," I replied.

"Right," Miss Chandler reaffirmed our destination. "That means it will be room number nine on the second floor."

I hung on her hip like a calf as we skirted the guard to find the stairs. Turning up the generous stairwell I almost ran into a student gliding down. She was African American, tall, as I, dressed in a simple black pleated skirt with a white blouse. She had a sweater slung over her shoulders like a movie star. Her hair was straight but did not look processed. Her skin looked like coffee mixed with cream, and just as smooth.

I felt crude in her presence, out of place, but if she sensed my discomfort she didn't show it. In fact she didn't appear to have noticed that Miss Chandler and I were the only black people, besides her, in the building. Not even a glance to acknowledge us on her leisurely glissade down the stairs. I looked back briefly, looking at the figure beneath her blouse, her skirt, and was astounded to see the holstered lawman defer to her line of travel. She had not altered her path to accommodate the armed white man at the bottom of the stairs, had not even acknowledged his presence, and I was intimidated by her confidence, her sophistication. How had I ever talked myself into believing I could walk with people like these?

"Cilla?"

"Yes, ma'am, coming."

"Just keep your mind on your music."

We were right about on time or about two minutes late, depending on whose watch you used. The recital was set up in an ordinary classroom. Ordinary for a music school, that is. There was a piano, an upright Baldwin, set before rows of seats that ascended in gentle terraces to form part of a circle. A man whom I took to be in his thirties looked up when we entered the room. He seemed preoccupied, grinding a ballpoint pen over a letter in his lap as though intending to shred it. There were glasses stuck in the thatch of unruly hair above his forehead.

He wore the same button-down shirts and slacks that were ubiquitous on campus. And penny loafers. Running shoes were not yet the assigned footwear for students at university. "Dr. Ransom—" Miss Chandler stepped forward to offer her hand.

He looked at the pale underside of her palm for a moment as if he wasn't sure what to do.

"Hullo," he stuck the pen in his mouth to free his hand. A rich, southern accent. What I later found to be a true gullah accent.

"Actually, Dr. Ransom has been detained." The apology seemed perfunctory. "I'm, ah, Jeremy Highsmith. Ah, Dr. Ransom's assistant. And I am to begin the, ah...what is this? Early recruitment. Yes. Assessment for early recruitment for—

"Handsom," Miss Chandler replied with stern civility. "Miss Priscilla Handsom."

"Right. So hi, Priscilla."

I did not know how to reply.

"I see, well. Why don't you get out your instrument?"

"A moment, Cilla."

I stood like a tree.

"Mr. Highsmith..."

"Yes?"

"Our appointment is with Dr. Ransom. In our conversation I was told there would be at least two faculty in attendance—"

"We are *so* unorganized—"

"Then you need to *get* organized, Mr. Highsmith."

He quit scribbling on the letter in his lap. He pulled the glasses from his thatch of hair.

"Excuse me?"

"You need to recheck your schedule and alert Dr. Ransom that Miss Eunice Chandler and Miss Cilla Handsom are waiting for him. As arranged."

I saw his larynx travel once to clear the frog from his throat.

"Why don't I go do that?" he agreed. "Excuse me."

He stuck his pen behind his ear and bustled from the room.

"Don't worry," Miss Chandler anticipated my question. "He'll be back."

About five minutes passed.

"I need to pee."

The restroom was bland and institutional, not unlike the loos I would later see in hospitals, in prisons. I rushed to a stall and threw up. Then I relieved myself and cleaned up. I had never experimented with hot and cold water taps, so elected to remain with the cold. The soap came out of what looked like a milk carton, pink and fluid and viscous as molasses. I washed my hands and splashed water on my face. When I raised my head from the sink I saw myself in the mirror. A broad face, black as mud. Bulging lips. Protuberant brow. Deepset eyes. I turned up the collar on my field jacket, ran a hand uselessly through the wire of my hair.

I hoped I didn't look too country.

I got back to Miss Chandler just ahead of Master Highsmith. He returned with two other people in tow. The woman I liked right off the bat. She was a pale thing, pale as a sheet, in a wool suit and black shoes. Her hair was the color of straw. Her hands looked like tallow. You couldn't get much whiter than this woman. But there was something about the way she walked in. She just took a bee-line straight through the door, straight as a string, and looked right at me with eyes blue as buttons and smiled hello. Some people can do that. They don't have to say a thing; they can just smile and you know they're saying hello.

"You two ladies are the only two people on this campus who know how to keep an appointment. I'm Dr. Weintraub."

"Hello, Doctor," Miss Chandler immediately accepted her offered hand.

"And this must be Cilla."

Dr. Weintraub stuck out her hand. I took it tentatively. She kept it a moment.

"I really am sorry we're late. Auditions are hard enough without adding uncertainty."

"It's all right," I swallowed. "I had Miss Chandler."

"Yes. A formidable accomplishment in itself, I imagine."

The man stepped forward in a more measured, uncertain way. He was dressed in a wrinkled suit. Shirt, no tie. And his shoes, I noticed, were unlaced.

"I am Dr. Ransom, Miss Handsom. It was really entirely our fault. We had you down for another time..." He glared pointedly at his graduate assistant. "I would dearly love to blame someone else, but in the end the responsibility is mine. Please accept my apology, both of you ladies."

"Your shoes are untied," was my reply.

That caught him offguard. "My shoes? Why, yes. I suppose they are."

"I saw a man this summer? In Jacksonsville? His name is Alex McBride; he 'tole me he always unties his shoes. Said it makes for a better feel on the pedals."

"Not sure I can use that excuse."

"Then you need to be careful," I admonished. "You could get tangled up an' fall down."

Dr. Weintraub laughed at that. I could tell it was genuine, not brittle or jaded. Certainly not sarcastic. Her laughter was gentle as the rain.

"Well," Dr. Ransom regarded his lace-ups a moment. "If introductions are complete I suppose we should get started. I understand you are interested in the marching band, Miss Handsom?"

I took a deep breath.

"No, sir."

"Cilla—" a hint of alarm rippled in my teacher's face.

"It's all right," Dr. Weintraub raised her hand. "Cilla, would you like to clarify what you mean for us?"

"I mean that I am not interested in marching," I replied. "Miss Chandler, she said the scholarship didn't have nuthin' to do with the marching band."

"Does not have anything to do with it, that's correct. I think Dr. Ransom is probably working off your band director's recommendation. Mister…?"

"Pellicore," Miss Chandler inserted.

"Mr. Pellicore, yes. His recommendation seemed to imply you could be an asset to the university's Marching Chiefs."

"I march if I have to. I'll march or hoe weeds or anything you tell me. But I have other things that I am interest' in."

Dr. Ransom tapped his thumbnail onto the enamel of his teeth. Like a tiny snare drum. Tap. Tap.

"What do you have prepared for the horn?" he asked finally.

"What Mr. Pellicore told me," I replied.

"And that would be?"

"'Oklahoma' and 'The Impossible Dream.'"

"Those are good to start."

"Yes, sir." I tried to think about that girl on the stairwell. "But it ain't all."

"I see. Well. What else do you have for us, then?"

"I have a chunk of 'The Marriage of Figaro' by Mr. Mozart. From Act IV, I can play that. An' I have some of Mr. Beethoven's Ninth Symphony, I can play. From the last movement?"

"The 'Ode to Joy'?" Dr. Weintraub asked, and I wished Mr. Pellicore had been there to hear it.

"Yes, ma'am. And I made a part for the piano, too."

"You made a part?" Dr. Weintraub arched a pale brow.

"Yes, ma'am. I had it pretty well worked out, but then Mr. Mac-Bride, he plays *real* good, he gave me some ideas, so I been workin' on some very-ations."

"Variations? For Beethoven?"

"Yes, ma'am."

Master Highsmith did not bother to hide a smirk. But like Miss Hattie says, you might as well hang for dogs as cats.

"And then I have just one other thing."

Dr. Ransom seemed intent on an inspection of his errant laces. "And that would be?"

I fumbled open my case to retrieve the music. "It's kind of jazz," I supplied.

"'Kind of'?"

"Something I wrote myself," I ploughed ahead. "The beginnings of something, anyway. I call it 'The Dirty Guitar'. I just have it for the piano. Haven't worked out the horn, yet."

"May I see the score, please?"

I gave it to him.

"And you have your reduction? Your piano, Cilla. For 'Ode to Joy'?"

So I handed him that.

"Lord, Lord," Miss Chandler seemed more astounded than distressed.

Dr. Ransom passed my sheeted scores after what seemed an impossibly casual inspection to his colleague. Dr. Weintraub brushed a straw of hair from her face as she scanned my penciled notation.

"Your teacher tells us you are an autodidact."

"Auto…?"

"Self-taught. You taught yourself to read music, to compose."

I frowned. "Mostly, I guess. It just makes sense."

"So if I gave you something you had not seen before. Say, some other piece of Mozart. Or a pop tune. Or a hymn, say, do you think you could play it?"

"I could read it. I could hear it in my head. But I'm not like Mama; playing takes practice. Mr. Pellicore's helped me with the playing."

For a moment nobody said anything. Then Dr. Weintraub turned and looked straight at Dr. Ransom. Didn't say a thing. Just the look.

"Jeremy." Dr. Ransom nodded to his not-yet-graduated assistant. "Close the door on your way out, would you? And hold my calls. We are going to have ourselves a recital."

It took an hour. They wanted to hear everything *except* "Oklahoma" and "Impossible Dream." I played my reduction of "Ode to Joy" first, with variations. Then I switched to the horn for Mozart's famous marriage.

"The part where Figaro plays like he's making love to the Count's wife?" I explained the opera's storyline. "It's really Figaro's wife Susanna disguised as the Countess, and Figaro, he really knows it's Susanna, but he don't tell *her* that."

"Why doesn't he, Cilla? Why doesn't he tell her that he has pierced her disguise?"

"He's just jerking her chain, really," I perched on the edge of the bench. "See, the Countess, he been after Susanna and it drives old Figaro crazy, so now he just lettin' Susanna know how it feel— feels. Kind of put the shoe on the other foot. Just to make her jealous, a little."

"Jealous? Really? You mean he actually is not in love with the Countess at all?" Dr. Weintraub's eyes split into crow's feet when she smiled.

"Oh, no, ma'am," I assured her. "He loves Susanna to pieces. She loves him, too, once she gets over being mad. They make up and it's some nice music."

"Speaking of nice music, let's hear yours."

So I spread my "Dirty Guitar" on the piano's stand.

"May I?" Dr. Ransom joined me on the bench. "When you're ready."

I ran it through. It wasn't much, just a snatch, really.

"Let's do that again."

I played my score through once again, only this time he stopped me at different intervals.

"You might think about slowing the beat through these two measures…. Nice bridge, here…. And then substitute a dominant seventh, I think. Instead of a minor chord?"

"You think so?" I pursed my large lips.

"Well, you can try it."

"Yes, sir."

It was only two or three minutes of music. But everybody was tapping their feet. Dr. Ransom's laces never quit slapping his leather shoes. I ran the keyboard when I was finished, just like Jerry Lee Lewis.

"Bravo!" Dr. Weintraub pronounced, and everybody gave me a nice applause. It was the first time anybody actually put their hands together in appreciation of something I performed.

"Well, well," Dr. Ransom pushed away from the piano. "A confession, Miss Handsom—I don't really think anything I offered actually improved your music, and to be honest that wasn't my primary reason for suggesting changes. I just wanted to see how you'd react to a critique, whether you'd balk or give it a fair try."

"Did I do good?"

"You did fine. I was glad to see you were not afraid to try new things. I noticed a good bit of improvisation as you played, but that's all right. Your score keeps you on track with that solid melody. A good mix. Reminds me of Ellington."

I told him all about "Rocks in My Bed," and Mr. Raymond's radio and how I used to listen to The Duke and Satchmo and even some Bird and Coltrane, but he was complicated, Coltrane was. I had a lot to learn before I could follow a sax like that.

"Back to your original composition, Cilla," Dr. Weintraub pinned me with those blue eyes. "Exactly what is a 'dirty guitar'?"

"I, uh, I don't think Miss Chandler would want me to tell you," I stumbled, and was rewarded with chuckles all around.

"That's all right," Dr. Weintraub relented happily. "An artist is allowed her inspiration."

Had she called me an artist?

They had me run through a few more things on my horn and on the piano, scales and things like that. There was a discussion directed mostly at Miss Chandler, concerning test scores, grade point averages. Nothing, it seemed to me, that had anything to do with music.

Then it was over. We were finished. Almost finished, anyway. "Cilla, would you mind giving us a moment with your teacher?"

"Just step out to the hall, Cilla," Miss Chandler suggested, and I obeyed.

But I kept my ear close to the door. A verdict was coming, I had some sure sense of that, and I had no idea what it would be. The first snatches I could make out were not encouraging.

"...she'll be far behind most other students."

"I know," came Miss Chandler's voice. "I know that."

"There are almost no Negro students on campus, Miss Chandler. You know that. You understand?"

"What are you trying to tell me, Dr. Ransom? What is your decision?"

Then there was some back and forth I couldn't catch and then I heard Dr. Weintraub's clear, direct voice.

"...do not let her become distracted, Miss Chandler. Cilla's senior year will be crucial. But if she can graduate in good standing, with good grades and reasonable assessment, and if she is willing to stick with the French horn, I personally guarantee that I will find a way to bring Miss Handsom to this university."

"Hallelujah!" I heard Miss Chandler's fervent response.

I whooped like an Indian. A pair of buttoned-down sophomores walking by must have thought they were looking at a crazy girl jumping up and down in the hall.

I don't even remember the ride home except that Miss Chandler suspended nearly every rule of formality. She kept calling me by my first name. Kept saying such nice things. Holding my hand like I was her sister.

"I never expected to hear anything like that in my life, Cilla!" She had a grin like to have split her face. "You were so good. Sooo...competent! I just never imagined. Never dared to imagine! Hallelujah!!"

Hallelujah, yes ma'am. And I guarantee if I'd known anything about Handel or his "Messiah", I'd have been singing "Hallelujah" all the way home.

We got back to school in time for band practice. Miss Chandler accompanied me to my director's office, to convey the good news. Mr. Pellicore was not overjoyed to hear that my audition had taken a path which he had not approved.

"Beg your pardon, are you saying that Cilla is not being considered for the marching band?"

"Actually, the scholarship Dr. Ransom and Dr. Weintraub hope to award will steer Cilla toward music theory."

"Music theory?"

"And composition, yes."

"So Miss Handsom will not—?"

"No, sir," Miss Chandler could not keep the pride out of her voice. "Cilla will not be marching at Florida State."

"But I wouldn't have got anything without you, Mr. Pellicore." I hoped to assuage a dangerously wounded pride. "That music you gave me? Those records and things, they helped. And the piano lessons? That's what did it. That's what made all the difference."

He frowned. "The law of unintended consequences applies, I suppose. But I hope you won't neglect responsibilities nearer to home. We have our Homecoming game tomorrow. Not to mention the parade."

"Oh, yes, sir, and I'll do good, Mr. Pellicore. I won't let you down."

His smile was brittle. "Of course not. Congratulations, Miss Chandler."

"Congratulations to you, too, Mr. Pellicore. Oh, and Dr. Ransom said to be sure and thank you for preparing Cilla and for thinking of Florida State."

"He did?"

He, in fact, had not.

"Well, then," Pellicore brightened. "That improves the odds for some other student's success, don't you think? A rising tide lifts all ships!"

"It does," Miss Chandler encouraged that interpretation. "It's good for everybody."

With a claim to that larger triumph, Mr. Pellicore was assuaged.

He even made an announcement before the gathered band that Miss Handsom had completed an audition which had concluded with the offer of a full scholarship to the School of Music at Florida State.

I was stunned when the entire band hall stood up to cheer. Everybody—except Bonnie Hart—came over to thump me on the back or shake my hand. Rodney Morgan led the whole trombone section over.

"Cilla. Cool," he pumped my hand.

Jerry came down from his drums to congratulate me. "First Saint ever to get a full ride to Florida State! Or any kind of college! Ever! Righteous."

Then Juanita Land came running up and crushed me in a bear hug, her small belly pressed into mine like a cup to a saucer. "I'm gonna tell *The Clarion*," she declared, tossing that fine ponytail. "'Bout time they had something nice to say in that paper."

But my small success was not to be covered in that week's paper. That week's *Clarion* was devoted, ink and quill, to Laureate's Homecoming Week, its ritual parade a prelude to the long-awaited contest between the LHS Hornets and the Lake Butler Bulldogs. The parade was always held the day of the game, a Friday. Bonnie Hart was elected Homecoming Queen that year. Cody Hewitt was her escort. Cody and Bonnie waved from a float skirted in pink Kleenex. I may have stuffed part of the chickenwire that bunted their trailer. There were five floats, one constructed by each class nine through twelve and one especially dedicated to veterans by the Future Farmers of America. A small convoy of convertibles followed the floats, then a fire truck. Mr. Pellicore's Marching Saints led the way.

The whole business was anticlimactic for me. I was required to march with the band, of course, exposed on the right flank as we stepped down Main Street. I tried to cage my eyes on my sheet music as I marched, but there were distractions impossible to ignore. Cutter Land and Digger Folsom jeered epithets from the curbside, their letterman's jackets in confederate colors, their hands pushed to their balls inside the pockets of their Levi jeans. I could hear the anger in their vulgar commentary, could feel it.

Black people had never been able to observe the parade from the street before, but that year was different. I saw Miss Chandler and Miss Hattie standing like bookends on either side of the black students who stood with white students along the street. I spotted Shirley Lee and Pudding and Chicken Swamp. Johnny Boy was not there that day. Lonnie Hine was, Lonnie waved. The little ones were there, too, those small black faces bright with hope. I hoped the children could not hear the filth coming from Cody's minions down the street.

Would have been marvelous, I guess, for those white boys to bring their special rage to purpose on the football field. But as predicted, the Lake Butler Bulldogs whipped our Hornets like they was a stepchild, adding insult to battery on the final play of the game when a second-string cornerback intercepted Cody Hewitt for an eighty-yard return. The evening's performance guaranteed that LHS would again fail to make the conference playoffs. It also scotched Cody Hewitt's chances at FSU or any other respectable school.

We performed "The Impossible Dream" at halftime and I could not wait for the nightmare to end. I came off the field as emotionally and physically exhausted as any padded player. I shucked my wool uniform, downed a quart of orange juice and a banana and secured my instrument, and emerged from the band hall to find Juanita Land and a score of Saints waiting.

"Go Cilla!" Juanita pulled me into that cohort for a round of extended congratulations. "Go Florida State!"

Cody Hewitt passed along the perimeter of that friendly band, shorn of armor, sullen and furious and resentful. If I did not gloat at the boy's public fall from grace, it was not because I was noble, but because I was terrified of jinxing my own chances for success.

I missed Joe Billy. I could gloat in private with JayBee. I wanted him to see me surrounded by admiring white people, to be caught in the penumbra of my small triumph. Sometimes wishes are granted.

"Is this my college girl?"

There he was. Big grin and tight jeans.

"Didn't think I'd miss your last gig, did you, girl?"

I let him take me in his car to our rude loft. We had not

coupled in weeks. He came almost as soon as he was inside, a quick ejaculation the consistency of shampoo and colored like pearls. He fell asleep quickly, as usual, and then I touched myself. It was sinfully arousing to masturbate beside a sleeping man. Like I was having an affair, somehow. Sneaking around. Which in a real sense, I was.

I got up after a while and did not wake Joe Billy. I had to get back to my own bed before sunrise or Grandma would know, if she didn't already, where I had spent the best part of the night.

I entered my bedroom through its shuttered window. Hard On was deaf to my entry. Corrie Jean was asleep, sucking wind through her inarticulate mouth. It was normally an aggravation for me, that constant sough, but that night I had longed for her familiar refrain, the rhythmic exchange of my mother's lungs in perfect time with the beat of her daughter's heart.

"I did good tonight, Mama." I slid like a spoon into the bowl of her withered flank. "You'd of been proud."

Chapter fourteen

I soon learned that my new fame did not extend to Colored Town. The Friday after Homecoming I was pumping water at Mr. Raymond's and nobody mentioned my yet-to-be-granted scholarship. It was Fight Night; the gathered men were there to cheer Joe Louis or Patterson or some other pugilist. No bastard child's accomplishment could compete with that spectacle. It was only minutes before the bell, Mr. Raymond was coaxing the tuner and I heard a name break through the static. Something about a man name of Medgar Evers.

"Negro Birth Rate Rising"—*The Clarion*

"Roll back on that, you don't mind, Mr. Raymond." Pudding's father made the request.

The story was being broadcast from WSAI in Cincinnati. I knew when Mr. Reed quit churning ice cream it had to be important.

"Cilla," Mr. Raymond reached over to pull the unfrozen paddles from their bucket of rock salt and ice.

"Yes, sir?"

"Dump this here bucket 'roud the ground of my antenna. Quick, girl, they's somethin' tryin' to come in."

I dumped the water and salt. Even with the improved ground,

the carrier howled. But intermittently through the aether you could make out a broadcast.

"…Attorney General Robert Kennedy issued a statement today saying that the Justice Department will conduct an independent investigation into the murder of civil rights worker Medgar Evers. Evers, the NAACP field secretary in Mississippi…"

"Mr. Raymond?"

"Hush, girl."

He leaned closer to the wireless's fabric-covered speaker, absorbing details that absent context were meaningless to me. I did not understand what was meant by "the NAACP" or "civil rights" and was distressed that my own recent triumph could so easily be eclipsed by any news from Mississippi.

The men were all huddled around the radio as I left, and no one was talking about the fights. I was leaning hard into my 'Flyer and its load of ten gallons of water when I saw the Sheriff's cruiser turn onto the unpaved street leading to my home. I didn't think much about it, at first. The Sheriff was known to pass through the quarters at will. Passed our house all the time. But at some point I realized he was coming for me.

I heard more than saw the Sheriff's undisguised approach. The tick of the radiator trying to cool that massive V-8.

"Hold up, girl."

His left arm loose on the door. I could see a Timex watch on his wrist. Could almost imagine I heard it tick, too.

"Dammit, girl, I said stop."

My wagon didn't roll an inch in that soft sand.

"Look at me."

I could see the film behind his eyes. I could see the blackheads lodged in the deep crevices of his pale, scarred face.

"You're Joe Billy's girl, ain't you?" he drawled. "Well, what about it?"

"Sometimes, maybe. Yes, sir."

"'Sir', now I like that. Almost like a white girl."

"Yes, sir."

"Get in the cruiser."

"Sir?"

"You heard me, get in."

"But my water?"

"Front seat," he commanded.

The seats were dark blue. Leather, it felt like. There was a cage between the front and back, a metal grille. There were two or three radios mounted up front. A shotgun was racked amidships. The interior panels of the doors were badly scratched, I noticed as I bent to enter, and there were craters in the windshield, like what you'd get if you got caught behind a truck hauling gravel.

We rolled out of Colored Town and my insides started to shake. The sheriff drove in silence until we reached the water tower.

"We're gonna have us a little talk. Quicker we get it done, quicker you'll get back home. Awright?"

"Yes, sir."

"I'll tell you straight out your boyfriend's got hisself into some serious trouble."

"Kine of trouble?"

"You don't know? Don't lie to me, girl."

"No, sir."

"Well. We'll see."

He took me to the jailhouse. I had never been inside the chain-link fences surrounding that fearful place. I had never been through the sallyport that protected its windowless keep, those double-locking doors that sealed tight as any airlock.

"Watch her," Jackson brusquely ordered a deputy. "Gimme the keys."

The floor was concrete, polished smooth, hard on your feet. The Sheriff rounded the duty desk on his way to a large gray door off to one side. We had all heard stories about what went on behind that closed door. Even white people knew. It was a metal portal, pierced by a tiny, rectangular pane of glass laced itself with some kind of wire or grating. There was a pad of numbered buttons alongside. Collard keyed it briefly. A buzz sounded sharp and loud with the sound of a bolt released.

"Be back in a minute," Collard nodded to his desk sergeant.

It seemed like an hour. It might have been an age, I don't know. My bladder was fit to burst.

"I need a restroom," I called over to the front desk.

"Hold it."

"I can't," I admitted, ashamed.

"Come own, then."

About the time I was relieved and roughly reseated, Collard Jackson herded Joe Billy back through that damned gray door.

My lover-boy was cut above one eye. His face was swollen. Looked to me like he was dragging a foot as well.

"Book him," Collard guided Joe Billy with an incongruently gentle hand to the desk.

"Charge?"

"Disturbing the peace. Resisting arrest."

A laugh wrenched out of Joe Billy's mouth. Blood trickled fresh out his nose and down his chest.

"Don't you bleed on my desk, boy," the desk sergeant growled.

"Give him some towels."

"He's messin' my desk, Sheriff!"

"I said git him some towels. You get him booked, I want him back in the tank and I don't want *anybody* in there with him, you clear on that?"

"No prisoners?"

"No prisoners, no law, no preacher—I want him in there by his goddamn self. Nobody sees him till I come back. Have you et, boy?"

"Sir?" Joe Billy cupped his braceleted hands beneath his nose.

"Gimme yer hands."

Collard released the handcuffs as he spoke again to the deputy. "Call Betty, have her bring him somethin' to eat. Bring a pitcher of tea, too."

"He'll be pissin' all night."

"Give him a bedpan. Go on. He won't drown in it. You won't drown yourself on me, now, will you, boy?"

Joe Billy shook his head. "Nossuh."

"How 'bout hanging? Do I need to pull yer sheets out?"

"There ain't no sheets," the Deputy supplied.

"Takes care of that, then."

I watched as Joe Billy was routed back through that gray door. A loud buzz. A bolt shot home. Collard waited for all that business to settle before he turned to me.

I saw the baton, loose on his leg. My heart sucked up into my throat.

"You saw your friend just now?"

"Yes, sir."

"You wanta help him? 'Cause if you don't I might have to pay him another visit."

"Don't do that, Sheriff! Don't!"

"You answer my questions, answer 'em straight, he'll be fine. You smoke?"

"Wha—? No. No, sir."

"I do." He produced a pack of Marlboros. Retrieved a Zippo lighter from his shirt pocket, raked it to life across his boot. "While back I got a visit from some fellahs work out of Washington, got themselves real concerned over a church burned in Tallahassee. You know anything about a church burning?"

"No, sir," I shook my head. "I ain't burn a church."

"Didn't think you did. What about Joe Billy?"

"He never said anything 'bout a church, no, sir."

"They tell me you got some smarts, girl. Be real smart to tell me what you know and tell me right goddamn now."

"I don't know anything about burning churches, Sheriff Jackson. I don't!"

"There was a truck seen near a church that somebody burned. New Ford. Red. Spinner hubcaps. Sound familiar?"

"That's Cody's truck."

"Joe Billy ever mention seeing Cody in Tallahassee?"

"No, sir."

"He ever tell you he stole money from the Mount Zion Church?"

"No, sir," I said. Replying less certainly, having been a thief myself.

"Appear a little unsure about that."

"Joe Billy don't have to steal, Sheriff. He's got money. Got himself a business!"

"Oh, yeah," Collard chuckled. "I saw." The smoke from his cigarette catching errant currents of air to mingle with the exhalation of his nostrils. His eyes on mine. I tried not to flinch. "You sleepin' with this boy?"

"Sir?"

"You get yourself knocked up you think they'll take you in that college? Think they'll give a shit?"

"Come to that, I'd get rid of it," I declared with sudden resolve.

"Just like a nigger," he grunted. "How old are you, anyway? When's your birthday?"

"My birthday?"

"There an echo in here?"

I felt my face flush. "I'll be eighteen this month," I picked up my head. "October the thirty-first."

"Right around the corner, then. Halloween."

"Yes, sir."

"Dowling Park, wasn't it? Place where your mama had you?"

"Yes, sir."

"Yeah," Collard nodded shortly. "I remember."

He took a final drag on his cigarette, dropped that coffin nail to the hard floor and ground it out beneath the heel of his well-buffed boot.

"Come on," he said. "Let's get you home."

It was my second trip in the sheriff's car. I was not as frightened, this time. But then I had not endured the session meted out to Joe Billy on the other side of Collard's gray door.

We passed beneath the water tower's swollen belly. Sheriff Jackson salvaged a toothpick from the cruiser's ashtray.

"You ever hear of a woman name of Meadows?" Barely glancing in my direction with that new line of interrogation. "Fanny Meadows. Ever hear that name?"

"No, sir, I know 'bout Joe Billy's mama, but her name's Fanny King."

"Is now," he confirmed. "But when she was married it was Fanny Meadows. Married old Clifford Meadows. Sorry son of a bitch if ever there was one."

"Joe Billy never said much about his daddy."

"Reckon not. Clifford left 'em when Joe Billy was little."

"Joe Billy told me," I nodded. "That's why he moved to Tallahassee. I just thought he was always a King."

"A king, yeah," Collard snorted. "That's what he is. King of fuckin' Colored Town."

I almost missed the derision, so amazed that our sheriff would bother himself to know the murky genealogies of colored people.

"Mr. Raymond is Fanny's great-uncle," Sheriff went on. "Before Fanny and Clifford ran off to Valdosta they used to work at the orphanage. In Dowling Park."

He glanced at me, then, to see if it was sinking in.

"Clifford worked the dairy. She was a midwife. When your mama got down the river, it was Fanny looked after her."

"Looked after?"

"What? You thought your mama had you all by herself?"

My own severely autistic mother was never able to supply any details regarding the first moments or weeks of my life. She could not talk about what it meant to be pregnant, to anticipate birth. She couldn't tell me whether I nursed on a nipple or from a bottle. Whether I was raised on cow's milk or goat's. Did I smile a lot? Was I a good napper? Grandmother never answered those questions, saying only that she was overburdened, that it had been too much, and that anyway my first weeks of life were molded in Dowling Park.

I wondered if Joe Billy knew? Surely not! I could not imagine Collard taking time from his interrogation to say, by the way, your mama saw the girl you're sleeping with way before you did.

Collard dropped me off by my wagon of water.

"Don't worry 'bout Joe Billy," came the unexpected solace. "I got a use for him."

I had to get back to Mr. Raymond, to let him know his

nephew-at-remove was jailed. It was late by the time I got back to the old porter's porch. The fights were already over. I was surprised to see that none of the men had left.

"Where you been, Cilla?" Mr. Raymond's voice floated over a battery of hostile eyes.

"I been at the jail," I replied directly. "Joe Billy's in jail."

"We know where he is."

"You get a look at him? How is he?" Chicken Swamp's father asked that question.

"He's beat up," I replied carefully. And then, "I was so scared!"

"Ain't talking 'bout you, girl."

It came with the sharp edge of reproof.

"We gone hafta get word to his mama," Lester scowled.

"Fanny King?" I rejoined.

"Mrs. King to you." Mr. Raymond put me in my place.

"Sheriff said Joe Billy would be all right," I volunteered. "He said he'd be fine."

"Use that stick on you, think you'd be fine?"

"Didn't have to use no stick on *her*, though, did he?" Mr. Reed observed sourly. "Got everything he needed without touching a hair on that brillo head."

I realized then that I had been skillfully interrogated myself, that Jackson had plied me for confirmation to questions whose answers he already knew.

"Ya'll can think what you want," tears welled in my eyes, "but Joe Billy didn't burn any church!"

"That boy," Lester shook his head. "I knew he was runnin' from somethin'."

"He didn't do anything!"

"Doin' plenty with you!" he sneered and the porch cawed laughter at my expense.

"Hush that nonsense!" Mr. Raymond spoke and silence fell like a shadow passing over the porch. The old porter stood from his deerhide rocker. "That boy saw something in Tallahassee likely to get us all in trouble and you-all laughin'?"

Heads bowed in contrition all around the porch before Mr. Raymond turned again to me.

"Now you set down and you tell me ever'thing that happen from the time Sheriff pick you up to the time he let you go. Word for word."

It was apparent to me now that Joe Billy's plight and Colored Town's hinged on some question more important than the discovery of my mama's midwife, so I sat for the next hour recalling every impression of the afternoon, reporting every question put to me by Sheriff Jackson and every scrap of idle talk I could recall that had anything to do with Joe Billy or Tallahassee or Cody's fire-red truck.

My own history would have to wait.

Chapter fifteen

"Monk Folsom Bids For
Sheriff"—*The Clarion*

My eighteenth birthday passed unremarkably. I did
not celebrate its passing with tricks or treats. Halloween was not celebrated in Colored Town. Preacher Dipps roundly condemned the
hallowed night as a Devil's holiday and in any event black parents
were not amused at the notion of their offspring running around in
white sheets offering threats for favors.

The biggest concern in Colored Town the last day of October
related to the many fears raised by Joe Billy's incarceration.

The Sheriff said he had a use for Joe Billy; whatever utility that
implied surely could not be good for Colored Town. But at least Halloween passed uneventfully. There were no crosses burned, no midnight rampages through our sandy streets. The night passed without
a window smashed or a mail box shotgunned from some speeding
vehicle. There were no incidents to report anywhere in the county, in
fact, unless you counted the usual misdemeanors at Leb's tavern.

But then came the first of November and the FBI.

Johnny Boy Masters saw the black car that parked behind the
sheriff's cruiser the morning after Halloween. He saw two men get

out, dressed in white shirts and dark-colored jackets and slacks and ties. Johnny Boy's mama was Wanda Hicks' maid, and that evening she repeated Wanda's excited blabber about a sit-down between the sheriff and federal agents.

Rumors circulated immediately that Joe Billy King had fingered Cody for the burning of the by-then-well-known Tallahassee church. Joe Billy, the *Clarion* reported indignantly, had been discounted as a suspect for that arson. The Federal Bureau of Investigation visited Sheriff Jackson to request a "preliminary interview with the Negro."

I got to see Joe Billy just once during his county tenancy. It was in early November, not even a week after my birthday on the thirty-first. I'd made a cake, however tardy. Actually Miss Chandler had as much to do with the cake as I had. She loaned me her stove and the fixings. Even gave me eighteen candles. Seven pink ones and eleven blue—we couldn't find enough of one color.

The sheriff met me at the jail, he and Thurman Shaw. Mr. Shaw was a local attorney just beginning to make his reputation. He still had himself some hair back then, just a shock of red, like a cock's comb, a bantam rooster of a man not three years out of law school. I walked to the jail from Colored Town, my church dress and flimsy jacket my only insulation against a cold, steady wind.

Mr. Thurman met me at the front desk.

"Don't you look nice," he said. The first compliment related to appearance I ever received from a white man.

So there I was, with an attorney and a sheriff, escorted in perfect safety and under no duress, burdened with nothing more offensive than a pound cake, but still I was scared of that gray door and petrified to contemplate the journey beyond, the untimed walk past those iron cages.

"Lookee here. Lookee that tall piece o' chocolate!"

Catcalls and jeers were my marching tune that day as I plied a strict, straight line down the middle of the passage that divided the cells on either side.

Joe Billy was standing by the time I got to his cell.

"Sorry for these other sons of bitches," were his first words.

The cut above his eye was not closed. It needed stitches. But his face was not swollen. And he didn't look to be favoring that foot.

"It's late for my birthday," I said stupidly. "And a few days early for yours. Kind of an in-between cake."

"I'll take it."

"You awright, JayBee?" I asked, glancing to the deputy who loitered within a shirtsleeve of our conversation.

"They ain't beat me again, if that's what you mean."

Thurman turned, then, to the standing deputy. I waited for that gaoler's retreat before I gave Joe Billy my lemon-flavored loaf. Had to turn it sideways to get it through the bars of his cell.

"They wouldn't let me bring a fork," I apologized.

Candles went in next, one by one, eighteen of them through the bars of his cell. Our fingers touched each time.

"No matches, neither," I cringed.

"'Long as you make a wish," he assured me and broke the cake on his lap like a melon.

"What's the Sheriff gone do with you, Joe Billy?"

"Let me go. Soon's I testify."

I was not sure exactly what constituted testimony.

"Mr. Shaw done cut me a deal," Joe Billy was almost cocky. "All I gotta do is tell what happen at the church."

"What did happen, Joe Billy?"

"I *saw Cody's truck.*"

"Oh, Lord!"

"I was inside when the dynamite went off. I come out, there's Cody's truck, haulin' ass. 'Burn baby!', I heard 'em yell it out the cab."

"Who was driving?"

"Think I was lookin'? I just stole damn near three hundred dollah. I was runnin' my ass. But the police, they got witnesses. Two brothers an' ole Crazy Maggie. Guess Cody near run them niggers over. Or maybe it was J.T."

"And when you told the Sheriff, he believed you?"

"Din *tell* the Sheriff anything. Not voluntary, anyhow. But by the time he got done with his baton, I was persuaded. He cut me some slack after that. Say if I help him out, he help me."

"Why the Sheriff wantin' to help you?"

"The Sheriff doesn't give a damn about Joe Billy," Thurman Shaw interrupted to reply. "Sheriff Jackson wants to keep his job. Anything he can hold over Garner Hewitt, he'll take. Even if it comes from a no-account nigger."

Next day, *The Tallahassee Democrat* quoted anonymous sources confirming that negotiations concluded between federal prosecutors and Attorney Thurman Shaw granted Joseph William King immunity from felony charges of grand theft in return for testimony related to the arson of the Mount Zion Church. The Democrat did not specify that Joe Billy's testimony would put Cody Hewitt's vehicle at the scene of the crime, but it didn't have to.

We all knew. Cody knew. Certainly Garner Hewitt knew.

The grand jury would not be convened before mid-January. Joe Billy was moved under federal supervision to his mother's residence in Tallahassee and Garner Hewitt raised all kinds of hell. He accused Collard Jackson of framing his sons for a crime they did not commit, that treachery accomplished, according to Garner, in retaliation for his support of Monk Folsom in the coming election.

In a county registering fewer than twelve hundred voters it didn't take a lot of gossip to tip the scales. Collard Jackson still had supporters in the county, from his family, from those who quietly hated Garner Hewitt, but that constituency was shrinking in relation to the percentage of white folks furious at their sheriff for colluding with niggers and federals to put a pair of white boys in jail. They called Collard nigger-lover, those voters of Lafayette County.

But what they really meant was that he did not hate enough.

By mid-November Joe Billy was back at his mama's shaded house in Tallahassee. Rumor was that charges related to burglary (and resisting arrest) had been dropped in return for what was loosely described as "cooperation with authorities." I can't say I made much effort to stay in touch with JayBee. I told myself I could not afford the time.

I was burning my candle at both ends, keeping my grades aloft in hostile classrooms while laboring to master my French horn. Three afternoons a week Miss Chandler drilled me mercilessly in preparation for the Scholastic Aptitude Test. The usual chores at home could not be slighted. Mama had not been able to shake her croup, which made things even more trying than usual. Even so I was composing music, sneaking off to Kerbo School with my brown grocery bags. Scoring my imagination in clefts and bars.

Citizens with broader interests or less crowded schedules were engaging the larger events of the day. President Kennedy, recovering confidence after the debacle at the Bay of Pigs, was challenging the Soviet Union on a broad front from Cuba to Berlin, mangling German and extricating missiles as the situation demanded. He challenged the nation to sacrifice, to excellence. He pledged to put a man on the moon. He was willing to pay any price, was President Kennedy. Bear any burden.

He'd even go to Dallas. If he had to.

But neither space travel nor nuclear war nor rumors involving sex, lies and Marilyn Monroe were topics generating appreciable heat in Lafayette County. As I studied and drilled to improve my understanding of set theory and the distinction between shells and rowboats the citizens of our county raged in Old Testament fury over Sheriff Jackson's treachery, and Joe Billy's, those righteous voices suggesting that one way to shut up Collard's witness was to stretch the nigger's neck on a rope.

One afternoon I was at school, with Miss Chandler poring through the paperwork required to apply for admittance to Florida State. Miss Chandler had insisted that I apply early. There were bundles of forms involved for a variety of offices, most in triplicates separated by carbon and all demanding accurate reply. If my Kerbo teacher had not been there to assist, I'm sure I'd have given up.

The other seniors were attending a mandatory School Assembly, some somnambulist from the Department of Public Safety urging students to use seatbelts. I completed the required formalities for Florida State before the program was concluded; Miss Chandler said rather than risk interrupting the invited speaker to our auditorium I should simply go on to the location of my next class and wait for the bell.

My next class was band. I thought I'd go down and get some solo time with my horn. Our football team was to play Greenville that night, an away game with antagonists the Hornets would entertain with a record worse than their own, but we still had our halftime theme to perform. I headed for the band hall. An icy wind sliced right through my olive green jacket as I negotiated the breezeway connecting the school proper to the band hall out back. I arrived at Pellicore's Hall chilled and alone.

I went into our modest amphitheater, set up my stand and music and broke out my horn. After a few scales I went right into our halftime theme. "I've Got Rhythm", the Gershwin standard. How many pop groups have copied that tune? But for a title dedicated to rhythm the piece was monotonous as a metronome. Nevertheless, I dutifully plugged along, following the score designated for my French Horn. Couldn't have been at it more than ten or fifteen minutes when I looked up and there was Cody Hewitt.

"What you doin' here?" I put down my instrument.

At first he didn't answer.

"You got no business at band, Cody. You know you don't."

"I wasn't there," he replied in *non sequitur*.

"'There'?"

His chin began to quiver. "I was not at that church!" Swear to God, I thought he was going to cry. "Nnn…neither was J.T." Cody stammered on.

"Joe Billy saw your truck," I edged off my seat.

"Joe Billy'd say anything to get out of jail!" Cody seemed to recover. "But I ain't havin' it, you hear me? YOU HEAR ME?!"

"What is goin' on here?"

Mr. Pellicore stepped into the band hall. Looked at Cody. At me.

"I am tired of this nonsense. You two. With me. Now."

I flanked Mr. Pellicore on one side, Cody trailed on the other as we cut a trough down the middle of the school's Olympian hall.

By the time we got to the Principal's lair I was convinced that I was somehow at fault, that somehow I had to be in the wrong for *something*. The door to Ben Wilburn's office was pulled open by Pellicore's pale hand and I saw our principal, motionless with his secretary and Miss Chandler, before, of all things, a television.

I had never seen a TV, not even in a storefront. It was startling to see that blizzard of black and white. Like a photograph, but with sound and a picture that moved. A middle-aged white man with soft jowls and owl eyes stared from a nearly round screen, his eyes bright behind thick, black glasses.

"Mr. Wilburn?"

The principal did not reply to my band leader's salutation, but I failed to register the significance of that lapse. I was preoccupied, juggling the warring effects of my recent assault with the intrigue sparked by space-age technology.

"Mr. Wilburn?" Mr. Pellicore asked more slowly, as if doubting the propriety of his intrusion, and that's when I realized that something was wrong. That my principal's response, my teacher's, the secretary's, were out of the ordinary. It seemed to take an effort for Miss Chandler to drag her eyes from the TV's wavering screen.

"It's the President. President Kennedy." She mopped her face with a wilted Kleenex. "He's been shot."

JFK's assassination eclipsed all other events of the day. Cody and I were ignored as the band's director joined the other adults hanging word for word on Walter Cronkite and the hard news from Texas. We were eventually and cursorily dismissed with the promise, not kept, that the band hall incident would be dealt with on the following Monday. The biggest issue pressing for a decision was whether to cancel the football game, our game away from home. Should the contest be called?

No, it was finally decided. Not even the death of a president could interfere with football. But there would be a prayer before kickoff. A moment of silence. Something appropriate to acknowledge the nation's loss.

I don't recall whether we lost, won, or tied. The bus ride back to Laureate gave no indication. It was quiet, not the usual pranks or teases. Sometimes somebody'd cry, a quiet cry. I walked home alone. Plodding onto my sandy street I heard the Live Oak train, but that far-off whistle held no promise of romance that evening, nor of escape. It was a raven's call, the night Jackie became a widow, a rip of fabric, a piercing of cold air offering an invitation as dark as a hearse.

I crawled into bed with Mama and held her close. "I applied to college today," I censored the day's events. "President Kennedy got shot."

Corrie Jean stirred with that last. She was warm beneath our flimsy blanket. I tucked in close. Closed my eyes.

"'Night, night."

The Thanksgiving following the President's assassination was subdued. I was surprised how personally the elders in my community took the death of Jack Kennedy. Everyone gathered around Mr. Raymond's porch to follow the broadcast of the President's funeral. Little John saluting his daddy.

People wept openly. The Sunday following, Corrie Jean played "Rock of Ages" as Preacher Dipps exhorted us to remember what a good man Kennedy was. What-all he did for black people.

The younger men were more divided in their opinion of JFK. Pudding's father, for instance, said that Jack Kennedy had been mostly talk.

"Now Bobby, he for real," Pudding's father averred. "You put Bobby in the White House, he gone do somethin' for the black man. You kin count on Bobby."

"No one is going to help us, unless we help ourselves." Miss Chandler challenged Pudding's daddy. "And by the way, Mr. Reed, have you registered to vote?"

As democrats in Washington pledged their allegiance to a vulgar Texan, Garner Hewitt was calling in favors in Lafayette County. Was unheard of for the county's leading democrat to be backing a republican for sheriff, but voters understood that Garner had been forced by the timing of primaries to adopt that tactic. Garner himself was confident that his constituents would not hold a titular affiliation against Monk Folsom, but he was not about to take chances.

The general plan was to get blocks of votes. Best way to do that was to organize around the white folks' churches. There were about as many churches in Lafayette County as there were outhouses and Garner Hewitt went to every single one, telling those congregations that if there was to be any hope of keeping their children unsullied and safe, Collard Jackson was going to have to be turned out of office. He'd invoke Jesus as his helper in that campaign and then walk right outside to bribe the deacons. Roofs always needed fixing. Pews, missionaries, air-conditioning—Brother Hewitt knew how to reward the stalwart, yes he did.

And he knew how to punish backsliders.

Miss Chandler's own campaign was quiet by comparison, but indefatigable. By the end of October she had registered half the eligible African Americans in Colored Town and by December was reaching with little assistance toward the isolated and rural population.

I did not care at the time which horse won the race for sheriff. Made no difference to me. I was focused on the single, narrow goal of getting admitted to Florida State University. I had grades to worry about. Final exams. Those were pressure enough. And then, of all things, the high school fouled up the standard application required to receive our college board exams.

The school board blamed Ben Wilburn for the screw up. Ben blamed the guidance counselor. Laureate High School had missed the first cycle of the SAT and, worse, had failed to reschedule. Miss Chandler rescued the situation, contacting somebody on the Board to authorize a special test for our senior class. Myron Putnal and Mr. Pellicore proctored the examination. The test took most of the day. I don't think I could have spelled "cat" by the time it was over.

"How'd you do?" Miss Chandler caught me in the hall.

"What is 'puerile'?" I asked.

"If that's the only thing stumped you," she smiled. "You did just fine."

Cody Hewitt kept his distance. In fact I never had two words with Cody or Cutter Land or Digger Folsom or any of that crew from Thanksgiving until well after Christmas. Part of the reason for that reticence was that Miss Chandler had me escorted every single minute of the day. She had students designated to be at my side between classes, at lunch, even on the bus.

The only person I spoke to with less frequently than Cody Hewitt was Joe Billy. It had been a month since I'd heard from my first-time lover. He had not written me, or sent word through Mr. Raymond, but I was not offended. Cannot truthfully say that I even missed him. I would be reminded of Joe Billy sometimes, surely. I never hauled water without a silent prayer of appreciation for the barrels that saved me so much labor. But I was not interested in Joe Billy sexually, at that point, and he certainly seemed to have lost interest in me. And at any rate, I was involved with another love, a passion that would claim all my time, all my energy.

I was writing music. Composition in one form or another now occupied virtually every free moment I could manage. I was making a systematic effort to hear the sounds in my head and write them down. And as I heard the music coming to be in my head, a completely unexpected gift came as if from Heaven to help me along.

I got a piano.

If you're going to seriously compose you need some kind of keyboard, and I acquired a piano virtually to myself. That Christmas surprise was made possible when Rev. Dipps bought a new Baldwin for our local church. At first Preacher wanted to keep both the old piano as well as the new, but Miss Chandler talked him into selling her the old Chickering. Paid him seventy-five dollars for that badly tuned upright and had it delivered to the "old school" at Kerbo.

"It's over there now," Miss Chandler had smiled to me. "You can play any time you like."

"But…how can I pay you back?"

"Make music," she replied.

The rude timbers of my old classroom at Kerbo School became my conservatory. I took my horn and the three precious books of music that were my frankincense and myrrh and hauled the lot to my old alma mater, where I reworked familiar pieces while fashioning new ones, scrawling my nascent compositions on grocery-bags anchored with soda bottles along the floor. For that span of days it seemed that my fingers could not keep up with the scores I could hear in my head. I'd rip through a score of measures and try them out on my piano, sometimes on my horn, the crude and dim interiors of my clandestine studio as liberating as a cathedral.

I had a visitor other than Miss Chandler once. I was working out the piano for a piece of music from an opera, *opera seria*, actually, Mozart's transcendent *Idomeneo*. Professor Weintraub had sent Miss Chandler that piece, minus the libretto, along with some other music and a list of things to read to "be prepared" for my first year at Florida State. When taking breaks from my music I was engaged by a paperback of *The Inferno*. I expected Dante's to be an alien work, and indeed the language was far from colloquial, something like a King James translation in its archaic structure and syntax. But the heart of the story was not foreign at all. The Leopard of Malice and Fraud and the Lion of Violence and Ambition, even the She-Wolf of Incontinence, as I presumed to understand incontinence, were completely familiar. I was actually reading the morning of my unexpected visit, trying to figure out exactly what the situation was between Dante's hell-bent traveler and Beatrice, who was, for me, a beguiling and sensual benefactress, more intriguing by far than her sniffling suitor.

"So there you are." It was Carter Buchanan, my science teacher. "May I come in?"

Took me a moment to realize a white man was asking my permission.

"If it's a bad time—"

"Yessir," I swallowed. "I mean, nossir. Come own in."

"Miss Chandler told me I'd find you here."

He stepped into the room, a luxury of raven hair falling loose over the collar of his denim shirt. He was attired in khaki trousers and a wool jacket cut out at the sleeves to become a vest. I saw a hunting knife sheathed inside a belt, I think it was of alligator hide. Not his usual attire, certainly.

And then I saw a tangle of hemlock in his hand.

"Don't worry," he winked. "We're not going to poison anyone."

"No, sir."

"Actually, I'm just here to let you know that if there's anything I can do to help over the next few months, please don't hesitate to ask."

I just sat there, with my book.

He kind of nodded, as if he understood it was not my place to reply.

"You have a talent and an ambition that are God-sent, Priscilla. And there are people around you, more than you know, white as well as black, who think it's very important we do everything we can to help you succeed." He nodded to the book in my hand. "That Dante?"

"Yes, sir."

"He knows a lot about Hell, doesn't he?"

"Seems to."

"But I wonder if he knew anything, really, of Heaven?"

Then he left. He just regarded the lethal bouquet in his hand a moment, and then stepped out, the heels of his departing brogans almost silent on the timbered floor of the hallway, and I wondered if I had just been delivered a sermon.

The New Year came with firecrackers and Roman candles. By that time Jack Ruby had shot Oswald and the Governor of Mississippi had exonerated his state of any culpability for that business with Mr. Edgars. The Cold War and Cuba kept the banjo strung pretty tight, though, and already MacNamara was playing dominoes with Lyndon Baines Johnson, but it did not affect me. I had insulated myself from outside influences, had found my fortress, my hideout and my life's work far from the paths of freedom riders, astronauts or vulgar politicians.

I had come to believe I might rise above county bigotries and quotidian concerns to reach the School of Music at Florida State. Even at eighteen years of age I had some half-formed notion of a career, a vocation. And I was about there, too. I had just about established an equilibrium in the balance of my responsibilities and was well on the road to seizing my prize when one Sunday I heard Mr. Raymond tell Preacher Dipps that the grand jury in Tallahassee had "failed to return."

Chapter sixteen

"Negroes' Testimony
Discounted"—*The Clarion*

The grand jury impaneled in Tallahassee declined to indict Cody Hewitt or his older brother for any crime and you couldn't find a deaf-mute in our county who did not have some reaction to that news. Some held the opinion that if Cody or his brother had been sent to trial, regardless of the verdict, Collard would have stood to regain some status among voters. Anybody who stood up to Garner Hewitt and got in a lick was someone to be respected, if not feared. But with the failure to indict, Garner Hewitt clearly emerged as the big dog in the fight.

"Siding with that nigger put the nail in Collard's coffin," Garner crowed to those gathered at Monk's Auto Shop.

As for Joe Billy, I guess he expected to be treated like a hero after surviving a beating, jail time and the hospitality of the FBI, but it did not happen. He got no thanks from the Bureau or the State Attorney for his grand jury testimony. He got no autograph from Bobby Kennedy or accolade from civil rights organizers. Hollywood did not call with plans for a Movie Of The Week. In fact, in 1964 there was no such thing as a movie-of-the-week.

It wasn't that Joseph William had shirked his duty; not only had he, JayBee, testified, he was believed. Jurors counseled to keep silent regarding their deliberations told reporters that the identification of Cody's truck at the scene was not contested; that it was the State's witnesses identifying its driver and passenger who were without credibility.

Mr. Raymond said asking a white jury to take the word of two nigger boys and a crazy woman just about guaranteed that the Hewitt brothers would never stand trial. That the State's failure could not be blamed on Joseph William's testimony did not, however, make him welcome in Colored Town. The adults on our side of town now agreed with Mr. Lester.

"That boy bring trouble on two legs."

This was the indictment Mr. Raymond relayed to Fanny King. "You tell Joe Billy he needs to stay with you awhile. We out of room down here."

Where Joe Billy couldn't get spit to polish a dime in Colored Town, Cody Hewitt couldn't open his wallet for a stick of gum. Couldn't open a damn door for himself. To say he was sympathetically received would be to betray understatement for prevarication. Cody Hewitt returned to the long hall of our school like Caesar fresh from Gaul. He was back on top and everybody knew it.

We black students certainly knew it; the slights and indignities that for months had lain dormant now returned with a vengeance. Pudding's textbooks went missing. We found them behind the gym, in a trash dumpster. Shirley Lee refused to dress out for gym, Bonnie Hart being the immediate cause, instigating in the locker room a daily barrage of taunts, ridicule, and provocation.

Faculty looked the other way as Kerbo students were shoved off benches, banished from whole regions of what was without irony called the playground. I avoided walking by myself. I didn't look anybody in the eye. It was only much later that I would read Ralph Ellison's magnificent work, but I must say in that day and in that place, I'd have given much to be truly invisible.

"Joe Billy was here, this wouldn' be happen," Chicken Swamp

complained as we Kerbo kids clustered in the cafeteria at our single table. "Joe Billy was here we wouldn't put up with this shit."

"Why you think you have to put up with it now?" I retorted.

"'Cause of Miss Chandler," Chicken replied.

"'Cause of you," Shirley Lee amended.

"Me?" I said. "What's this got to do with me?"

Not one of my classmates would meet my eye.

"Pudding, how do I get blamed for these crackers? I ain't the bigot here. *They* are."

"But we cain't do nuthin' *back*," Pudding snapped. "We cain't talk back, we cain't fight back. Miss Chandler say just wait out the semester. Wait! And why she say that, Cilla? Whatchu think?"

"I don't know," I lied.

"Is all for you," Shirley Lee grated. "Miss Chandler say we cain't do nuthin' might spoil Cilla's chances. Cilla's our trophy, she say. Our example. We all got to support Cilla. Well, I'm tired of it!" Shirley Lee slammed her plate into the cafeteria table. It sounded like the shot of a rifle, sudden, abrupt. All around us spoons and forks stopped in mid-air. "Next white girl crosses me," Pudding's sister announced broadly, "I'm gonna make her pay. You think all us niggers is Uncle Tom? You try me. Just try!"

She turned then and marched for the door.

"Miss Reed, take your plate and silver," Myron Putnal ordered to her back.

"Take it youself," she replied, and to the hoots and jeers of white students, she stalked out of the cafeteria.

I scanned my table. No one would look at me. No one spoke.

February bled into March. A hard frost gave way by degrees to the warming influence of the Gulf of Mexico. Joe Billy returned to Colored Town with the blossoming of the dogwood trees.

I was washing my mother's unruly hair on the planks of our porch when my old beau pulled up in his two-toned automobile.

"Well, look what the cat drug in."

"Cat!" Corrie Jean clapped her hands. "Cat, cat, cat!"

"What you doin' in Colored Town, Joe Billy?" I challenged as he piled out of his Fairlane.

"Got some business."

"Business, bull. You marked worse than Hester, JayBee."

"I gotta clean out my 'partment." Joe Billy did not inquire after Hester. "Doc West tire of my rent money, I guess. Got some clothes I need to get. Couple of guitars. I only be down a coupla days."

"Need any help?" I asked, as he reached the porch.

"Naw," he stepped up the porch. "Hello, Corrie Jean."

Mama reached out her hands like a child. He took them unembarrassed.

"You sure lookin' nice, today."

"Fug me," she crooned. "Fug me."

"Mama!"

"It's all right, Cilla."

I poured a final ladle of water through Corrie Jean's hair, wrapped it in a towel.

"You got a place to stay?"

"Car," he shrugged. "And a shade tree. Maybe you let me wash up here, I need to?"

"That'd be fine," I poured Mama's soiled water out to the yard. "Or I can make you a place on the porch."

He followed me inside. I settled Mama and put some water to boil. Found some coffee. Instant.

"How's things at school, Cilla?"

I shrugged. "Be better if you was there."

"I just be gettin' in trouble," he shook his head. "Get everybody else in trouble, too."

"And how life treatin' you, JayBee?"

"I'm paintin' guitars," he smiled broadly. "Sold three since the new year."

"Three guitars? Sold?"

"Cash in hand," he affirmed proudly. "Made myself over five hundred dollars."

"Five hundred dollars?! For real?"

"Money ain't hard, Cilla. I can always get money." He paused. "Wanta take a drive?"

Your life can turn on the most trivial of decisions.

To remain or to stay.

To drive or not to drive.

"Can we go by Betty's?" I asked. "I'm hungry."

Betty allowed black people to order food from the back porch of her café. The porch gave a nice view of Town Park and the water tower and the great oak trees. Everybody from the quarters knew to approach the café from the park-side, that is, from the rear of the café. Once there you could eat just like the white people. There was fried chicken and pilau and coleslaw and country ham. Also hamburgers and onion rings and Cokes. Sweet-tea, of course. Pies made of whatever berry or fruit was in season.

Spring was nascent that day. A bright sun warmed the air just enough for folks to be comfortable in a long-sleeved shirt. The sky was bright, bright blue which signified a dry atmosphere, a *rara avis* in North Florida during any season. The redbuds were in early bloom, those discreet scarlet blossoms scattered at random in the yard behind the café. There were crepe myrtles, too, showing plumb and lavender all around, and oak trees, their moss hanging from rough-barked limbs like the beards of druids.

No dogwoods. Not at Betty's.

"Sure is good."

Joe Billy was not complimenting the ambiance but a hamburger improved with cheese and bacon and green onions. He paused from that powerpack of cholesterol to slurp a six-ounce Coke topped with boiled peanuts. Followed with the onions.

"Hope you aren't planning to kiss me with that mouth," I warned him.

"Kissin' all you got in mind?"

"I am *way* past that."

We were in good spirits, easy with each other, like two old lovers got on in life.

About that time Pudding Reed rolled up in his daddy's seldom-running truck. "Well, look what the cat done drug in."

"Twice I heard that, awready," Joe Billy stood like a celebrity to pound fists in the ritual becoming fashionable in Negro fraternity.

Word raced back to Colored Town that its prodigal son was returned and within a half-hour the café's porch was packed like melons in a trailer. All of the Kerbo seniors were gathered, and scads of the younger kids. Even a few adults. There must have been fifty black people on that veranda, all come to see Joe Billy.

"Lordy, lordy," Betty exclaimed as she took orders for burgers and rings. "Is there some kind of feast goin' on back here?"

It was impossible to have any kind of private conversation. Everyone wanted to talk to JayBee, everyone was fascinated to hear him describe his experiences in Tallahassee, with the grand jury, the FBI. And of course he'd spent time in jail, an accomplishment always respected. But unlike some young men who loved talking about themselves, Joe Billy was also genuinely interested in listening. Wasn't too long before he turned the conversation.

"So Pudding, whass happenin'?"

Pudding and Chicken Swamp and Johnny Boy talked all over each other trying to get their soul brother's attention, plying JayBee with stories of high school—life in the classroom, life in the hall, life at the gym.

Life After Joe Billy, basically.

Lonnie Hines sat shyly, as usual, though even he was coaxed to contribute. "We helped build the Senior Float," he offered, and Joe Billy smiled.

"Then I bet it was the best damn float out there."

It was good to see JayBee among his friends, however briefly. Things just looked brighter when Joe Billy was around. He exuded a kind of optimism, a joy in life. Also that quick fuse. Ready to take a chance.

"You got to come back," Pudding urged.

"I am back, boy!"

"To school, Joe Billy. We need you, man."

"Last damn thing in the world you need is me and Cody Hewitt in the same place," JayBee demurred. "That wouldn' help anybody."

They must have gone on another twenty minutes like that. Swapping boasts and lies. Eventually Joe Billy noticed me nursing my sweet tea.

"Tell you what, boys," he ended the soiree abruptly. "Cilla and me got some catching up to do. We're gone take us a drive."

Joe Billy helped me into the car. "Feel like I din' pay you enough attention," he apologized.

"It's all right, Joe Billy," I said, and meant it. "They're glad to see you. We all are."

As we pulled away, he reached over to the car's radio.

"Put in some new speakers," he announced proudly and pretty soon we had Ray Charles to accompany our journey.

…Georgia…Georgia… The whooooole day through…

"He went to school in St. Augustine, Ray Charles. You know that?"

"No. Really?"

"Oh, yeah," Joe Billy draped a hand over the steering wheel, pleased with the breadth of his sophistication. I suppose if we had not been so satisfied with ourselves we'd have noticed the pickup following behind. Joe Billy turned left at the town's single light, putting us on the farm-to-market road that led past the Suwannee to Live Oak.

"What say we stop at the river?" Joe Billy stretched his legs. "Maybe work our way down to Fort McKoon?"

I hesitated. Fort McKoon was not a site often visited by black people. I never knew exactly why. All you could see were the hidden traces of buildings and shops and yards long overrun by poison oak and palmetto. It used to be the site of a lumber mill, I'd heard, a thriving concern. I heard, too, that Spence MacGrue used to own the place, but, again, there were lots of rumors about that old man. What did remain was a rot of lumber and vine situated along the flank of the Suwannee on a kind of anomaly, a shelf of flint that in low water reached ankle deep almost all the way across that untamed river.

"We can look for arrowheads."

For eons, Creeks and Seminoles had fashioned their spears and arrows from Fort McKoon's flinted bounty.

"I'm too full to be scouting for arrowheads, Joe Billy."

"S'awright," he obliged easily. "I'll do the scoutin'. You can just sit back and watch."

It was warm enough to roll down the windows of the car, which we did. I've mentioned the smells of my native region. The mingled aromas of a fecund spring rushed past. Even cowshit has an interesting smell at fifty miles an hour. I saw the cabled span of the Hal W. Adams Bridge far ahead.

We left the hard road just short of the bridge. Dionne Warwick was walkin' on by as we negotiated the sandy ruts that would, with many toils and snares, get us to Fort McKoon.

"Mama Fanny brought me down here one time," Joe Billy remarked. "To Fort McKoon."

"Don't get us lost."

"Just keep the river on your left hand," he shrugged. "Sooner or later you got to run into it."

We weren't on that dirt road long when I happened to catch a glimpse of a truck in our rear view mirror. There was nothing particularly alarming about seeing a vehicle along the river. People came to fish, to picnic. Wealthier people had houses and boats. And it wasn't like the truck stayed in sight. A half mile down that twisting road you couldn't see more than ten or twenty yards in any direction. There were walls of hardwood trees and undergrowth all around. Scrub oak and blackberry.

You couldn't hear anything, either. Could have been a vehicle ten feet behind and I'd never know it. We had the radio on, recall. The rumble of our own v-8 was amplified by Joe Billy's rusted muffler. The road itself diverted attention, those twin ruts offering a bone-jarring ride over a pan furrowed by rain and erosion.

"Hope we don't lose an axle." I was gripping the dashboard.

"We're almost there," Joe Billy promised, and almost immediately wheeled off that dirt road to enter a clearing hedged in palmettos.

"Here we are."

A sudden silence as he killed the engine. The chatter of a squirrel. Caw of a crow. Nothing more.

I couldn't even see the river, at first.

"See?" He pointed and I saw the Old Landing, the one that used to receive ships of timber and turpentine. The flint shelf stretching beyond. And the Suwannee, of course, waters running dark. The Ford was parked before a grid of decomposed timbers. It took me a moment to realize I was looking at the foundation of some purposefully constructed structure. Actually several structures.

"Used to be a busy place," Joe Billy reported. "They'd bring logs down the river. Square 'em off and cut 'em into lumber. Then ferry that dimension to the mouth of the Suwannee and load it onto these big-ass sailboats. Take that lumber all the way to Jacksonville with nothing but some wind an canvas and some drunk-ass sailors. Made a damn fortune, too, what I heard."

But whatever concern had thrived in years past was now thoroughly overtaken in a riot of brambles and undergrowth. The only thing left of interest or color inside the rotting foundations of the abandoned mill were yellow motes of camphorweed, and sensitive briar.

And dogwood trees.

There was a splendor of wild dogwoods raised in the ruins of Fort McKoon. They flourished in the clearing created by the mill's construction. Pearl-white blossoms framed against a hyacinth sky.

Chaste and perfect.

Joe Billy walked with me past that Christ-cursed arbor and toward the landing.

"See the water? Breaking over the flint?"

Whitecaps foaming over the submerged shelf.

We sat down, Joe Billy and I, pressing our backs against a water oak spreading massive roots into a bank of loam and clay. You could hear the brook of water over the ancient rock beyond. You could hear the calls of robins and the raucous reply of blue jays and squirrels. From somewhere on the river came the far off whine of an outboard engine. Some fisherman, probably. Or maybe a diver taking his tanks and fins to the caves at Mearson Springs.

It had been a long time since I'd idled by a tree. The sun warming. The somnolent effect of uncoordinated sound. A breeze.

Odors of damp earth and new life. Of wisteria and the blooms of dogwood trees.

"I'm sleepy."

"Lay down," Joe Billy accommodated. "Take a nap, you want to. I'm owna find me a arrowhead."

The last thing I remember seeing before drifting off to sleep was Joe Billy calf-deep over that flint shelf. That cyanine sky. The blooms of dogwood trees.

I woke up some time later. The sun was low on the rolling water. Too low.

"Joe Billy?" Where was he? I pulled up on an elbow lazily, turned west to gauge the set of the sun.

"Joe Billy?" I asked again. Some deep instinct told me to turn around.

There were three of them. Three sets of identically faded jeans. A pair of brogans. Pair of sneakers. I was seated, remember, so I saw their footwear first. The third one wore some kind of rubber overshoes. Something like you'd wear if you worked a dairy. They had masks. They were hoods, actually, just like for Halloween, shapeless sacks with holes that distorted their shapes, their sounds, their voices.

"Where's Joe Billy?" I croaked, and Rubber Foot cawed derision.

"You want Joe Billy? Well, come own. We'll take you to him!"

I am no small thing, but there were three of them. They got my arms, first, one on either side and pulled them back behind. I heard my shoulders pop in their sockets and I screamed.

"Go own," Rubber Foot urged. "Scream all you like. Scream 'till daylight if you wont to."

"JOE BILLYY!"

They had him spread not fifty yards away between a pair of dogwood trees. He was naked. Strung up like a deer you were getting ready to gut.

"JOE BILLYYYY!!"

He tried to reply, to give voice to outrage or fear or whatever meaningless comfort could be imagined, but a smear of duct tape secured the socks gagging his mouth. His arms were pulled out wide as if in an enthusiastic parody of some semaphored message, just pulled up and out, tied to the slender trunks of dogwood trees. His feet were similarly stretched and anchored just above the ground. His genitals were exposed and hanging. His penis shrunk inside its foreskin.

"Oh, God!"

They dragged me to a pair of trees facing him. I was fighting every step of the way. Terrified. Kicking wildly. My feet banging into roots and bottles and broken timber. They got me beneath the dogwoods' arbor.

"Turn her over."

Rubber Boot kicked me in the kidneys and I couldn't breathe. I had stars before my eyes. That's when they tied me up. A heavy rope cinched over my wrists, first one, then the other, each coil cutting deeply, deeply. I could not imagine bearing more pain. They threw one end of my leash over a branch and jerked me upright.

"Got us a college girl, boys."

A cackle of laughter.

"'College bound'!"

Then they took an ankle each and pulled. Like a wishbone.

I heard my pelvis pop and I screamed.

It took a while, even defenseless, to get me situated on the twin pillars of my dogwood trees. They wrestled one limb at a time to its separate tree. Then a cinch around my belly.

"One, two, three—"

Screaming again as they hoisted me off the ground.

"Git her clothes."

His fingernails, filthy, scratched sharply, stripping me of my blouse, my skirt and underthings.

"Whooooooeee, boys! She got lips all over!"

Joe Billy screaming through a gag of tape, thrashing in his wild-wood frame. The dogwoods shook with the violence of his objection, their blossoms loosed and tumbling gently like snowflakes to scent the earth stained with urine at his feet. The Hooded Men ignored him for the moment. They were recovering from the labor required for my crucifixion. Rubber Foot in particular labored to regain his breath. I could see his hood suck in with each respiration, like the gills of a fish.

"Damn nigger...put up a...fight...din' she?"

The voice was distorted, yes, by that hateful hood, and filtered through my own pain and panic. But I tried to place it. Tried to place it.

And then I saw his belt. It was a wide belt, inlaid with silver. The silver latch was familiar to me, familiar to anyone in the county. The head of a rattlesnake. That long, slender tongue.

"J.T.?!" I gasped and he punched me in the belly.

I didn't have air to scream. My whole body just cramped up like fingers in a fist. Those ropes cutting deep. I kicked in spasm a couple of times, as helpless as a moth. The only thing that didn't hurt were my fingers which I could no longer feel. He let me recover, so calculated was the cruelty.

And then I cried. I bawled. I prayed. I begged to Jesus for mercy.

"Please, don'! Please, Jesus!"

"Heard you could blow a horn, college girl? Well. We'll see."

"Please...please, Jesus!"

Snake Belt took me from behind and humped me like a dog.

"JESUS! JESUS!" he cawed.

Rubber Foot hooted laughter, and Sneaker, and I didn't care. I was past caring. My sobs heaved with the hammer of my heart. But eventually I had to stop, to breathe if for no other reason. They waited for that respite and then let me see the razor.

"We're gonna do him, first," Snake Belt promised. "And then for you? You muddy bitch? We got somethin' special."

It might have been two hours or two years later when Carter Buchanan docked his outboard at Fort McKoon's well-known landing. "I came looking for deer tongue grass," he would later tell investigators. "It was getting dark. I saw Joe Billy's car. Then I saw where something was dragged along the ground."

I was delirious when he found me, hemorrhaging from my crotch, my breasts. My lips, of course. Joe Billy was in a critical condition, unmanned, unconscious and bleeding. They say Carter's mother was some kind of medicine woman. I don't know. But I know he managed to staunch Joe Billy's hemorrhage. And I can remember him ministering to me, too. Coaxing something into my mouth.

Bitter. Like gall.

"Take it, Cilla," a voice directed me calmly, and I did.

"There, now."

Then water. That was welcome. Then there was nothing. Some vague sense of sky. Blue. I came to and tried to say something but only mush came out. You know you're in bad shape when you can't pronounce a scream.

"Wowz Zho Birry?"

(How is Joe Billy?)

"He's in surgery," Preacher Buchanan was there to answer.

His hand holding mine. I saw a wedding band.

"You're in a hospital, Priscilla."

"We're ready for her."

A calm, professional voice.

"Don' teh' GramMaaah!"

(Don't tell Grandma.)

"Pwease doan."

(Please don't)

The request sounded ridiculous, even to me.

"I doan wan nobye worryin."

I was fortunate Brother Carter favored water transport. I would not have survived the jarring, root-crossed ruts leading back out to the paved road. Joe Billy certainly would not have survived. Carter took us across the river in his flat-bottomed boat and moored on the far side, near Convict Springs, where he actually was forced to briefly leave us as he ran with that bad heart to fetch the Highway Patrol always loitering at the weigh station.

We were ambulanced to the hospital in a black and tan cruiser of the Florida State Highway Patrol. Apparently the car was later auctioned. Too much blood to be cleaned, was the official explanation. Our teacher stayed with us the whole time, which was why Carter was at my side at the Live Oak emergency room.

I remember being wheeled beneath a bright and enormous lamp. Freezing cold. Needles and masks. Somebody in a green smock leaning over.

"God in heaven..."

I heard the words.

"What kind of animal did this?"

Chapter seventeen

"Martin Luther King Gets
Nobel"—*The Clarion*

Joe Billy remained in the Live Oak Memorial Hospital for less than a week. I, on the other hand, required an extensive hospitalization, though not at the Live Oak facility. The reconstruction I required would be performed by a specialist affiliated with the medical school at the University of Florida in Gainesville. Carter Buchanan and Miss Chandler and even Mr. Pellicore lobbied to get me admitted to Shands. There was no Blue Cross for me, you see. No safety net. Fortunately, the university's hospital did admit Negroes for treatment.

My doctor was nice. He was from Senegal and was doing research involving plastic surgery. Discussing my case, he explained that the labia was normally a good site to take tissue for rebuilding the lips around the mouth, but that my genitalia were too mutilated to be salvaged for that purpose. But there were options, he assured me, and did his best to prepare me for the procedures that were to follow.

"It will not be easy," he warned me.

"Iss saw ride," I spread my hands on my clean white sheet. "Log as I gan blay mah hon."

But I couldn't play my horn.

I believe I have already made the point that you don't actually blow a horn. First thing you're given when you start a brass instrument is the mouthpiece. Instructors will typically give you the piece specific to your instrument, just the mouth, nothing else. If you can't lip that lump of brass, if you cannot excite in that vulva of metal the peculiar buzz familiar to any youngster starting out on the trombone or trumpet or the French horn, then you cannot sustain the vibration of air necessary for the controlled production of melodious sound.

Whether your ambition is to jam, swing, or sit first chair, it all starts with a purse of powerful lips. The lips of my mouth had been razored both laterally, left to right, and vertically. The nerves were severed in too many places to count which, with the resulting scar tissue, accounted for the problem with elocution.

But I wasn't concerned with oration. My future did not depend on that eluctation. It depended on my ability to make a mouthpiece buzz and I couldn't, not with all the surgery in the world. My hopes for college, for music, were taken away with the wizards' pass of a cruel wand.

"Day tug my hawn!" I wailed.

(They took my horn.)

I was sedated much of my first week in Gainesville and spent most of my recovery by myself. I honestly did not expect regular visits, from anyone. Even though the hospital where I would endure my several surgeries was little more than an hour south of Laureate that was a journey from Colored Town. Miss Chandler was good about sending notes of information and encouragement, but with school in session she could not do much more. Mother and Grandmother were barely able to take care of themselves; they never made the trip. Other folks were similarly strapped or occupied. They had their own concerns. So I was left alone in my hospital room for long periods of time, a circumstance initially welcomed which quickly became tiresome.

Distraction is hard to get in a hospital. My room had no television, a common diversion nowadays. I had no radio. No newspaper or magazines. My bed was situated beside a single window through which I could see storey after storey of twins to my own, metal-framed and recessed into walls of uniform brick. The only variable in that exterior was the steam rising in cotton tendrils from the hospital's boiler, strands of steam sundered in what Frost once called the capriciousness of summer air.

I did have water. At my bedstand was a splendid steel pitcher invariably replenished and ice cold. As the ice melted, beads of sweat would slide down that metal decanter's curved landscape. I would follow those stochastic meanderings with the focus of a shaman, guessing the destination of an individual blister of water. This was all I had to differentiate one moment from the next.

I was restive and bored, but even so became increasingly ambivalent about receiving visitors. After all, I knew, or imagined I knew, what I looked like. Even the carefully restrained reactions of doctors and nurses were hard to bear. I was not even sure I wanted Joe Billy to see me. I was spared that encounter, at least, when a day or two after my first surgery a nurse entered my room.

"You have a call."

She handed me a telephone and I experienced for the first time in my life the thrill of long-distance communication.

"Cilla. Iss me."

It wasn't the same voice. It was tired and distant. But I could hear him perfectly. Every word! Joe Billy, however, had a hard time understanding me. I had to articulate slowly, had to often repeat myself. And of course it was more difficult, talking by phone. I had supposed that Joe Billy was still in the Live Oak hospital and was stunned to hear that he was already released. "They just sewed me up, put me on the antibiotic, and sent my ass home."

I figured home was back to Fanny and Tallahassee, as far away from the Suwannee River and Colored Town as could be managed, but I was wrong.

"Mr. Raymond say I can stay with him," the voice on the line went on. "Mama ain' no nurse. Besides, Sheriff say it'd help him if I am close by. Has he come to see you, Cilla?"

"Woo?"

"The sheriff, has he talked to you?"

"I doan wan dalk do duh shaff. I gan' dalk!"

(I don't want to talk to the sheriff. I can't talk.)

"You got to try, Cilla. Please, baby. For both of us."

Sheriff Jackson arrived the very next day. He stooped slightly, unnecessarily, to enter my semi-private room. My Senegalese doctor insisted on being present. A nurse filled up my pitcher as Collard took off his wide, tan hat.

"Lo, Cilla."

There was a chair at the foot of my bed. Sheriff paused beside that obvious accommodation.

"May I sit down?"

He asked my permission.

"Yath thuh," I granted it and then to my astonishment he picked up the distant chair and walked it right up to my bedside.

Right by my bedstand and my pitcher of water.

He was studying that steel jug like it was a painting. Anything to keep from gazing at me, I suppose.

"'Saw ride," I gave him permission.

"Errbody loog ad id."

(Everybody looks at it.)

His eyes met mine, then. Gelid orbs out of place in the hard seams of that anthracite face. No pity there, but no aversion, either. I thought I must be imagining sympathy where there could be none. This, after all, was still the Sheriff of Lafayette County.

"Nurse says it might be easier for you to write."

I nodded. "Yath thuh."

"I got some paper and a pencil. Take your time. Joe Billy's already given me his statement, but you might have some additional information. Even something little could be a help."

"Hith bet," I said without hesitation.

"'Scuse me, what was that?"

I reached for the offered pencil, planted a legal pad on my knee and scrawled.

'J.T.'s belt. The one with the snake.'

And then I sketched it. The snake, how it was inlaid the length of that leather strap. Its silver tongue. Like J.T. himself.

That silver-tongued devil.

The muscles in Collard's jaws tightened like a vice as he accepted my penciled artwork.

"This is good," he said huskily. "Damn brave of you, Cilla, to have the presence of mind to remember anything."

"I gan do moah," I mouthed painfully and then to my utter and further surprise he reached out and he took my hand.

"Just write it. Write it all down." Then he gathered up his hat, nodding to the doctor. "I'll wait outside."

Collard rose and was past the foot of my bed when he stopped, rolling on the balls of his feet. There was no contact of eyes at that juncture, just a partial rotation of his head to let me know his words were meant specifically for my ears.

"I might not be sheriff after this May election, Miss Cilla, but don't you worry. One way or the other I will find the son of a bitch did this to you. One way or the other. And by God when I do, he will wish to hell he'd never seen a dogwood tree."

I had my first nightmare that evening. It would recur in identical detail through the years. A cross of dogwood, a crown of thorns in my brilloed hair. A rattlesnake coiled below, vicious, striking at will, its pearl fangs seeking my sex or my mouth.

I had my second visitor not too many nightmares later. I did not see a face, at first. I was inclined, even before my mutilation, to avert my eyes, a habit that had become compulsive. It was embarrassing for me, even painful, to risk face-to-face encounters with a physician or nurse or orderly unfamiliar with my circumstance, to absorb their shock or disgust. So I spent a lot of time looking at shoes.

You'd be surprised what you can discern by the manner in which a person shoes his feet. I knew right away, for instance, that my new visitor was not a nurse. Nurses tend to be a practical, no-nonsense lot, partial to some variety of industrial shoe, the kind of footwear you can get in a catalog. The newcomer entering my room had not got her shoes from any catalog. She was more elegantly appointed, a female in open, low-heeled footwear fashioned in an expensive leather the color of blood.

"Cilla? Can you look up at me?"

It was Dr. Weintraub. She held what looked like the case for a shotgun in her hand.

I pulled my sheet up to my chin.

"May I sit with you a moment?"

Seemed like everybody was asking my permission. I nodded.

"Eunice Chandler called to tell me what happened." Doctor Weintraub put the dimpled black case on the floor beside my bed and then, abjuring the chair, settled along the edge of my bed. Her thigh was full and warm.

"Miss Chandler asked me to convey her 'hello', by the way. Let you know everybody has you in their prayers." She delivered this last offhand, fishing as she spoke into the pocket of her smartly tailored jacket.

She was wearing a light wool skirt, pleated, same material as her jacket. Beneath the jacket was a cotton blouse that rose to what I would later know was a Mao collar. A very small cross hung to the swell of her breasts.

Jade eyes. Pale skin. Hair like straw.

"I gan blay my hon!" I blurted as though in confession and felt water run from my eyes.

"I know." She pulled a Kleenex from the nightstand beside my bed. "I'm surprised you have any tears left to cry."

"Me doo," I snorted.

Dr. Weintraub gave me a moment to settle down. Then she slapped the pillow beneath my head, puffed it up. "Better?"

I nodded. "Thag you."

"You're welcome. Now Cilla, I bring some good news. Very good news. But I want you to take it slowly; Dr. Hosni tells me that even good news can be a problem in the wake of what you've experienced. And I also bring a caveat, a condition. A challenge, really. So let me start by making sure you remember me."

I nodded my head.

"Dogdur Wine Troud."

"Close enough. And you remember our discussions about music? About the possibility of your coming to the University?"

I nodded again, "But I gan blay."

"One thing at a time, Cilla," she cautioned. "Now. First thing. We were never interested in you simply because you could play the French Horn. Don't misunderstand me; we were impressed with your horn. I couldn't believe you had been playing less than six months and had perfect pitch. But much more significant to Dr. Ransom and me was your overall sense of music, your intuitions regarding structure and form. Your ability to improvise. And to compose! I don't think you realize how rare that is. And finally your ability to conceptualize. To, in your words, 'hear the music in my head.' Miss Chandler says you were writing like a demon before school started?"

"Yeth ma'am. Bud nod now."

"Understandable. Y'know we have a policy at Florida State."

"Pawicy?"

"Policy, yes. We allow all abused and tortured students to take a break from original composition."

Until she winked I thought she was serious.

"We don't even bill them. So don't feel like you're slacking off, okay?"

I felt my lips pulling against the stitches. Dr. Weintraub patted my leg with her pale hand. "That's better. Now. Miss Chandler has mailed me some of your work. Some amazing stuff here, Cilla. And I have to say it's the best use of grocery bags I've recently seen."

I even laughed at that. It hurt. The stitches again.

"So let me start by saying that you have a scholarship for a freshman year to the Music Department at Florida State."

I put my hand over my heart.

A scholarship? Mine?! They didn't take it away?

"Here," Dr. Weintraub poured me a tall glass of water.

I slurped the offered beverage like a hog at a trough. She remained unperturbed. Just waited for me to finish.

"Thag you!" I nearly choked. "Thag you!"

"You earned it. By the way you scored thirteen hundred and twenty on your SAT exam, did you know?"

I shook my head.

"That puts you in the top ten percent of applicants to the entire university, so don't believe anyone who tries to say you got in the back door, Cilla. This is not a sympathy gift. You didn't squeak in. You earned this scholarship. More than earned it.

"Some details. Dr. Ransom has made me your advisor; normally you don't get an advisor until graduate school, but in your case we think it's imperative for you to have a faculty member in frequent contact right from your freshman year on."

"I gan dalk do you?"

"Yes, you can. Any time. Well. Anytime I'm not talking to someone else."

It was hard to believe. I was going to study music! Write music? Compose?!

"But there is a condition, Cilla." She seemed to read my mind. "Here's the deal: To keep your scholarship you must become competent in another instrument."

I didn't understand what she was saying.

"The Music Department requires graduates to be able to perform, even those studying theory or composition."

At that I dipped back into despair. The prospect of tackling another instrument, of any kind, was depressing beyond belief.

I had just lost my horn!

"Wy gan I juss study music?" I asked.

"It's a requirement," she was firm. "They'll give you a ride your freshman year. In light of circumstances. But after that you will need to demonstrate competency, and, Cilla, I mean college-level competency, in some instrument."

My head sank like a stone into my pillow. I turned to find the trail of tears on the side of my chilled and metal pitcher. The vagaries of boiled steam.

"I know it seems a lot right now," Dr. Weintraub's voice was distant. "But I will help you. Miss Chandler will help you."

"I guezz I gud blay biano." I slurred the words without enthusiasm.

"Play the piano? Why, yes, you might," she answered. "You might. You need to consider, though, that there are many more orchestral opportunities for winds than for the piano. That means more opportunities to perform. More avenues to find work after college, to build a career. So before you retreat to the piano, there's something I'd like you to see. Something I hope you'll want to keep. Cilla? Take a look. Please?"

She displayed what looked like a plug of whittling for my inspection.

"You know what this is?"

I did not.

"It's a reed. Double reed, actually. A particular reed for a particular sort of instrument. A very demanding instrument."

Very demanding?

"I know you like the feeling of a wind-driven instrument. You've told me. 'Like running', I believe you said. Well, I want you to think about converting from brass to reed, from the French horn to the bassoon."

A bassoon? It was not immediately familiar.

"A bassoon is a wind instrument, like your French horn. But not brass. It uses this reed to set up the vibration in its chamber."

"Buh I gan' mag win," I shook my head. "I gan wo!"

(But I can't make wind. I can't blow.)

"Oh, yes, you can," she contradicted. "See, you don't need to purse your lips to play the bassoon, Cilla. You do have to be a damned good musician. In fact, my best musicians are generally my bassoonists. And you have to get quick hands. The keywork is demanding, thirteen thumb keys alone. But you do not have to pucker your lips."

She gathered my hands from beneath my sheet, gently, as if retrieving ducklings.

"The bassoon is a natural for you, Cilla. You already have a brilliant sensitivity to music. You have enough piano to make playing a snap. The rest is practice."

Practice. At that moment the word carried the weight of anchors.

I made no reply.

She nodded to the case on the floor.

"This is my instrument. One of mine."

That revelation got my attention.

"You blay?"

She displayed her reed, that whittled plug of wood.

"Made of a special bamboo, you know. From France. You can always tell a bassoon player; we carry these damn things around like worry beads. And this—"

She dug back into her jacket pocket. Came out with some kind of cutter. Smaller than a pocketknife.

"It's called a reed knife," she informed me. "You use it to create a reed, which involves paring a blank to the particular demands of your mouth, your tongue. I keep a half-dozen going all the time. Gives me something to do when I'm in front of the TV."

She swiveled the nightstand around, and dropped the carved reed into my glass of water.

"Takes a while to soak. Ordinary water works fine."

"Bud I *gan' blay!*"

"So you've told me," she acknowledged, leaning down to heft her case from the floor. "But if you find the courage to try…"

She stood to lay the case beside me on my bed. A black, leather case. Brass keeps, two of them. The locks opened in syncopated time. Snap-snap. The leaves of the case spread on soundless hinges and there, snugged in velvet, were the most beautiful cylinders of wood I had ever seen. Hardwood. Maple.

"Let's start as the poet does with the naming of parts," Dr. Weintraub assembled her instrument. "We have the bocal, where the reed is fixed. Looks like a swan's neck, doesn't it? This one's from Germany, plated in silver. The bell, here, just as your horn. And then the various chambers, long joint, wing joint, boot joint. Seat strap. You sit on it. You see? So that the instrument doesn't have to touch the floor…"

As she spoke I realized that somewhere in the collection of operas and symphonies in Pellicore's office there had to be parts for bassoons. I probably had actually been exposed to this double-reed, if only on a record and buried beneath a symphony of strings and brass and other winds. I must have heard a bassoon. But I certainly had never seen one.

"And now shall I play you something?" Dr. Weintraub's offer was accompanied by a fully assembled bassoon.

I pushed my head into my pillow.

"Cilla," Dr. Hosni urged gently from the door. "Surely there's something? Anything."

"Nod Oagahoma," I returned.

Dr. Weintraub chuckled.

"Not "Oklahoma". Okay. That's a deal."

She paused a moment to pull over the chair. Her fingers ran over the keys absently as she fit the seat strap into its brass hook.

"Oh," she said. "I know."

And then without preamble she launched into Beethoven's Ninth Symphony, but not in scores familiar to me. Nothing, certainly, that I had ever heard performed.

"Weh—? Weh ah yo?"

(Where are you?)

Dr. Weintraub's paused with my badly elocuted question.

"The Fourth Movement," she moistened her lips. "About half-way through, at the beginning of the chorale. You get the strings, first, twenty-four bars of melody. And then when the melody repeats the bassoon comes on top of the strings to counter. Some really nice stuff. See what you think."

I *had* heard the bassoon before, as I said, but only briefly, on recordings, and never without the company of other instrumentation. The device in the doctor's hands offered a range and timbre I had not imagined, a primal invitation, a moan, a sigh, an exultation.

She filled the room with Beethoven, did my visiting professor. I could feel the music, see the score in my head. It was, after all, written on my heart. She played and played and I knew then, surely, why Dante's art would always fall short of Heaven's. My alien physician edged back into my room. The nurses, one by one, paused at their stations or lingered at the door, hanging on every stop and fret of that brief, ebullient concert.

When she finished a great pain began in my chest and burst through my lungs, my throat, my mouth. An awful cacophony.

"CILLA?"

Dr. Hosni rushed to my bed.

"CILLA, CALM DOWN."

"I GAN' BLAY!!" I bellowed. "I NEVAH BLAY OHGAN!"

Then there was the needle, the small burn in my vein. I saw Dr. Weintraub pale and white.

"Tag id away," I shoved the case off my bed.

(Take it away).

"I doan wan id."

Chapter eighteen

I "Negroes Found At Old Mill
Site"—*The Clarion*

was released from the hospital in Gainesville somewhere near
the middle of April. Reverend Dipps came to get me in a battered
station wagon. Windows down. No air conditioning. No radio,
either, which was a disappointment. Miss Chandler accompanied
the preacher. It was she who checked me out of the hospital. I saw
her sign a paper where it said, "Parent or Guardian." I hoped I didn't
need guarding.

Preacher Dipps loaded my things. On the way home I saw an
aging and stained copy of *The Clarion* wadded up on the floorboard.
The headline caught my eye: "Negroes Found at Old Mill Site."

It's an odd feeling, first time you read about yourself in the
paper. Even the headline felt offensive. "Negroes Found", for instance,
implied that Joe Billy and I had simply got ourselves lost. That was
it. A stroll along the river got those poor Negroes plumb dislocated.
Or perhaps the headline was meant to encourage the implication that
the Negroes were *discovered*, yes, found in a place where they were
not supposed to be. If you were where you weren't supposed to be,
you couldn't complain about what happened, could you? Knowing

your place, in this case, an injunction that was meant to be taken literally.

There was no hint in the headline that the foundling Negroes were assaulted or tortured or even inconvenienced. How about in the accompanying copy? I still have a clipping. Here is the sum total of what the local paper had to say about the horrific ordeal inflicted on Joe Billy and on me:

> ...Sheriff Jackson confirmed that two Negroes from Colored Town were found in suspicious circumstances near Fort McKoon. Joseph William King and Priscilla Handsom are reported to be in good condition...

Suspicious circumstances? Good condition?

"How you doin', Cilla?" Miss Chandler was checking on me from the front seat.

(Fine.) I replied.

I knew that's what I was expected to say. You couldn't say, "I feel terrible." You didn't lay that hardship on other people, not in Colored Town. Not until you got so old it was expected, like from Grandmother, in which case the complaints were a mantra so constant as to be safely ignored.

"Mizz Janduh?"

By which I meant, Miss Chandler.

"Wi din' Joe Bee gom ged me? Gan' he drive?"

(Why didn't Joe Billy come get me? Can't he drive?)

Miss Chandler did not immediately reply. Reverend Dipps hunched over the wheel of his vehicle, searching for any obstacle that could claim his attention.

"Mizz Janduh?"

"Joe Billy's having problems, Cilla," Miss Chandler answered finally. "You know...what they did to him."

"I zaw, Mizz Janduh! I wah *theah*."

"Yes, of course, you were," she said. "I'm sorry."

The Reverend shook his head. "Shame to see a boy so full of life done like that. 'Member how he used to love to socialize? Be on the porch with Mr. Raymond? Or with you youngsters at school? Always in the middle of everything."

He sighed heavily. "Not now."

We crossed the Suwannee at Brandford. An angry whine from down below got my attention. I looked out the window of Moses's automobile and saw a motorboat crease a coconut wake across water as brown as chocolate. The racket from the boat was what caught my ear. It was an engine, an outboard engine, and I remembered everything.

Dusk was falling by the time Preacher Dipps nosed his paneled wagon up to my shanty house. Grandma Handsom held a lamp on the back porch as Miss Chandler and Preacher brought my things.

"Whass dat?" Grandma pointed at the long, black leather case.

"It's a bassoon," Miss Chandler replied, and Granny sniffed.

"Look like a shotgun."

Then Granny stared at me. "C'mere."

She raised my chin. Held the lantern before my face. Dropped it, shaking her balding head. "Lawd, Lawd. I too old be nursin fuh two."

"Ah woan need nurdin," I promised.

Mother waited in the bedroom. She turned to me when I entered, vacuous and stupid and dull.

"Mahmah, izz me," I said as Miss Chandler arranged my things. I checked first to make sure she was clean. Grandmother hated wiping up after her daughter. I sort of looked on it like changing diapers. She was fine, on this occasion.

"Lemme gome yo air," I fumbled for a comb.

Mama sluffed over and I pulled a rake through the tangles of her dark, dark hair. I was preoccupied with that task as Miss Chandler entered with my suitcase.

"You going to be all right, Cilla?"

Her face had taken an ashen pallor. Like the leavings in the fireplace. "You all right?" my teacher asked again.

"Yeth, ma'am. Thag you, ma'am."

"Just get some rest." I did not know at first whether my teacher's advice was intended for me or for herself.

"Wad aboud sgool?"

"School can wait."

I was so tired myself I didn't even bother changing my clothes. I just crawled into my cot, pulled over my blanket.

"Naad, naad, Mama."

I meant to say, 'Night Night', of course, that simple preamble to slumber which was one of the few phrases that mother recognized, one of the few things to which she could respond.

So simple to say, even for an idiot. So easy to pronounce. I tried again.

"Naah, naaahhh…"

I could not shape the sounds, could not make them conform. I sounded like a retard, I knew.

Exactly like my mother.

I fell to sleep like a stone into a deep well and I dreamed. Or maybe it wasn't a dream at all. Maybe it was an hallucination conjured in that half-world between consciousness and slumber.

I was with my mother, in her company. But this was my mother as I had never before seen her. This was a woman polished and intelligent and cultured, dressed in a silver gown and seated with other swells in a place also without precedent, a vast auditorium. A theater, I realized. Carnegie Hall, perhaps, or maybe some European theater with chandeliers dropped from a cathedral ceiling and balconies fixed with gilded decoration and heavy, scarlet curtains.

She is beautiful, my mother. Her hair is naturally straight, and soft, almost like a white woman's. She is as tall as I am. I don't believe I had noticed that before, my mother's height. A regal carriage. She carries one of those small binoculars, opera glasses.

"Sit with me, Cilla."

We share a box. I, too, am gowned, the bodice deeply cut. I have a necklace, a small cross fashioned by some Basque artisan in Spanish silver. I like the feel of the chain around my neck, on my full breasts. My mother indicates a plushly stuffed accommodation. I take a seat beside her to overlook the chandeliered hall.

"Mother," I say and kiss her the way I imagine Ingrid Bergman would kiss her mother, the way I used to mime movies I had never seen.

A chaste gesture. One peck for each cheek.

"Pick a peck of pickled peppers." She smiles at me, warm and beautiful. Her voice is cultured, well-elocuted. The consonants break clean and crisp, like fresh celery.

The lights dim.

"Look," mother indicates with her glasses.

I follow her golden arm and see a tall African-American woman stride onto the boards. Wiry, undisciplined hair, I can make out that much. Not at all like mother's. She takes a seat at center stage beside a bulky, unfamiliar instrument. It could be a length of pipe. But bulged at the lips, on one extremity, like a blunderbuss. A swan's neck plated in silver and thinly attached.

No other player attends. No composer. No diva. She is by herself before the arena.

Alone.

"I can't play," I tell my mother.

She adjusts the lenses of her binoculars. "That is a beautiful woman onstage."

I do not have binoculars. I can tell that she is tall and black as ebony. The hair sprouts out like a sinner's halo. That is all I can see with unaided inspection.

"Cilla."

I turn back to my mother, but we are no longer in the box of a grand theater. We are at home. In our shack. But Mother is still beautiful, still grand, even in her simple cotton shift. She holds a comb in her hands instead of binoculars, but her words still break crisply.

"She sells seashells on the seaswept shore," Corrie Jean recites proudly and I throw myself into her arms.

"Mama!"

Her breasts are warm and I want to bury myself between them.

"I can't play," I confess again, but this time my own words have got back their edges. The consonants report as cleanly as acre peas shelled into the thin wall of a tin pan.

Tap, tap, tap.

"You will play, Cilla."

My mother speaks and I listen. I try not to covet her hair and I listen.

"Music is your heart, your soul, and you will play. You will become one of the most recognized performers in the world. People will wait in lines outside concert halls in foreign lands to hear you play. They will camp outside shopping malls to buy tickets for your concerts, to purchase recordings of your performances.

"Your scarred lips will make music more wonderful than anything anyone has ever heard," my mother promises me. "You will mix jazz and blues and classical compositions in ways no one anticipates. And after all that you will find that you are beautiful, as well. Just like your mother."

I did not want the dream to stop. I could see it getting away, the way dreams do. Like water receding from the stern of a speeding boat.

"Mama!" I protest and touch my mouth.

Then I wake. A febrile light filters into my pine-boarded room. I remember, now, that I have been discharged from hospital. That I am home. But there is something warm in my bed. It's Mama, of course, lying beside me. A puddle of drool collects, dampens her filthy pillow. I pull the blanket down to cover her feet and when I do, I see the brass hinges of the well-used case on the floor at the foot of our pallet.

The sun was barely risen as I slipped from beneath my blanket. Red sky in morning, sailor take warning. I barely took time to don jacket and sneakers before grabbing the hated case and slipping past Grandma and out the back door. I stumbled a distance from our modest home. Away from the sagging porch. Away from the outhouse and associated vipers.

I opened Dr. Weintraub's finely constructed case and with some clumsiness assembled the instrument inside. A fingering chart was tucked neatly beneath a pair of double reeds. I was completely untutored, of course. If there had not been some guide for my fingers and a pair of reeds pre-carved and ready for use, I would probably have just re-cased the bassoon and carried it back to the house. After all, I had only risen on the inspiration of a dream.

I handled the instrument, finally. The feel of the reed on my mouth was unfamiliar. A tentative effort produced no sound at all. I pressed the reed once more between my corrugated lips and blew until I saw stars before my eyes, and then, at the limit of my exhalation something came out of the bassoon's long, hardwood chamber that sounded like the baying of a scalded pig.

"Thit." I mauled that word easily enough and would probably have packed everything in right then and there had it not been for some unexpected encouragement.

"Don't stop," somebody said, and I turned around and it was Joe Billy.

"Don' stop," he raised his finger in warning. "Don' you even think about stoppin'."

His face appeared bloated, tumid. His eyes, always set narrowly, seemed squeezed now on either side, like pecans pressed between pouches of dough.

"Joe Birry."

"I wanta hear some music."

"Ah gan'."

"Yes, you can. You surely can. Try."

I fit the reed between my ruined lips and I tried again and got a perfect C. It floated in the heavy air like the song of whales.

"Sound good to me," Joe Billy declared.

If he had not been there to encourage me, to challenge me after my first, futile effort, I am convinced I would have laid the bassoon aside and never looked at a piece of music again. Not ever. Not for any reason.

But Joe Billy was there and that first successful note got followed, with some fits and starts, by another. Then I decided to play something simple. A nursery rhyme, perhaps.

"Try 'Three Blind Mice'," Joe Billy suggested.

Instead and out of some perversion I played the eight bars of a piece I hated.

OOOOOOOOOaklahoma!/

When the wind comes rushing down the plain!

Joe Billy chuckled and his swollen face seemed lighter. I played just a few measures more. Then I stopped. I laid the bassoon into its case and walked over to JayBee. We held each other like children do, our arms wrapped fully about, heads side by side, swaying mutely. The aromas of wild hyacinth and wisteria and camphorweed and vanilla plant pressed into our nostrils like gentle tissues. Scenting our tears.

We held each other for a long interval in that glade near my home. We didn't talk.

After a while we disengaged.

"Leth me go," I articulated carefully.

He shook his head and pointed at my still-open case.

"You got work to do."

"Ah dired."

"Tired ain't gonna get it done."

"Joe Birry!"

"Looking for slack from me, Cilla? You ain't gone get it. You got a chance here none of us has. Me or Pudding or Chicken or Shirley Lee. You cain't let what happen' pull you down. Pull *us* down. You got to practice."

It was a chore to gain a new facility, to overcome the frustrations inevitable when learning to master a new instrument. I would never have persevered but for Joe Billy. He was my coach, my cheerleader. He simply would not let me quit. Every moment not engaged with algebra or history or some similar regimen was devoted to the bassoon. Mr. Pellicore gave me what help he could, but I was mostly on my own. I was not an instant success at my instrument, my still-borrowed double-reeded wind. But at some point I began to like the way it felt in my hands, my mouth.

I practiced in a gentle shade surrounded by blossoms of scarlet and white, the fruit of redbuds and, yes, even of dogwood trees. I kept a jug of water close by in sober imitation of Omar Khayam, a jelly jar to soak my reeds, and a papyrus of grocery bags onto which I scribbled my original scores.

I was beginning to heal. It was still hard, even so, to leave the privacy of my shaded retreat for public scrutiny. It was especially embarrassing to register the reaction of my peers and teachers. To see the disgust in those eyes, or the fascination. To endure the whispered comments.

Worst of all, of course, I had to face Cody Hewitt. He was inescapable. I would be walking down the hall from second period to third and there he would be, in his bright letterman's jacket. I saw his truck every day when I came through the front door. I saw Cody and Cutter and Barlow and Digger in every chemistry class. At home room. My stomach would churn when I saw Cody. Had he been one of the cowled threesome who entertained me at Fort McKoon? Was he the Sneakers in that ugly coven?

Bubble, bubble, toil and trouble.

I inspected Cody's shoes to see if they matched those of any of my tormentors. The relief I experienced at discovering his footwear to be unfamiliar was mixed with anger, with anxiety, uncertainty, fear.

Would any perpetrator ever be discovered?

Was there any great impetus to find the men who butchered Joe Billy and me?

Almost five weeks had passed since Fort McKoon and Sheriff Jackson was nowhere nearer an arrest than when he started. The County Judge told Collard bluntly that he was not about to sign an arrest warrant for J.T. Hewitt based on the identification of a mailorder belt. The Klan was not about to finger one of its own. In the absence of other evidence or witnesses, the case simply stalled.

"They gonna let it drop, you watch," was Joe Billy's conclusion. "They don' give a tinker's damn."

Which was fine by me. I did not want to become the center of any further attention. I would give anything to be ignored. Joe Billy, however, felt very differently.

"Cut a man up and leave him, it ain't right!" Joe Billy shook his pinched head. "Ain't right just to give up on somebody been done like me. Sheriff, all he care about is his damn election."

I pointed out in response that if the Sheriff was not re-elected then there would be no hope at all for justice. Monk Folsom, certainly, was not about to investigate the Ku Klux Klan in Lafayette County.

"Then we're fucked for sure," Joe Billy replied bitterly. "'Cause Monk is damn sure gonna be the next sheriff."

That prognostication was accepted universally. If you'd spent the Saturday before the election in Punk McCray's barbershop the only disagreement you would have gleaned from the patter of patrons and gossips would be around the margin of Monk's victory.

"You couldn't get a bet on Collard Jackson," Cutter's daddy complained, "if you offered odds of a hundred to goddamn one."

That was on Saturday.

But Monday morning Miss Eunice Chandler emerged from West's Drugstore and marched straight across Main Street, past the courthouse to the County Jail.

"I'm here to see Sheriff Jackson," Miss Chandler informed the desk sergeant.

Pudding's father was there to record the event. He was being released from his cell after an overnight binge, a regular gig for Mr. Reed.

"I'm here to see the sheriff," Miss Chandler repeated.

"You'll have to wait."

"Is he in?"

"I said you'll have to wait."

"Tell Sheriff Jackson if he'd like to win his election he will see me now."

I would love to have been there to register what look of astonishment, incredulity or fury was kindled in the deputy with that retort.

"Wait here."

A few seconds later, according to Pudding's daddy, Collard came out.

"He looked wore out to me," Mr. Reed later declared when

reconstituting the scene for those gathered on Mr. Raymond's porch.

"He come right out from behind the desk and said, 'Miss Chandler, I know you're worried about this business with Cilla and Joe Billy, but...'"

"I'm not here about that," Miss Chandler interrupted smoothly.

"You're not?"

"No, Sheriff. I am here, as I explained to your deputy, to help you win this election."

The deputy wagged his head back and forth, like a hound trying to get rid of fleas.

"May we speak privately, Sheriff Jackson?"

And to the deputy's astonishment, and Mr. Reed's, Collard Jackson stepped to one side.

"My office," he said.

Thus ended Mr. Reed's contribution to the tale. But there were at least half a dozen other witnesses, black and white, to take up the narrative when within the hour Jim Hicks emerged from his courthouse office to find Sheriff Jackson, two deputies, two cardboard boxes, and Miss Eunice Chandler waiting.

The supervisor of elections was nonplussed.

"What-all is this, Sheriff."

"Little paperwork is all," Collard replied gruffly. "Some voters need their cards. Just want to make sure they get put in before tomorrow's election."

"You mean registered? By tomorrow?!" Mr. Hicks wrung his hands. "Sheriff, I can't do that."

"Let's set a minute, Jim."

It was not a request. Collard came around the counter to guide Mr. Hicks back to his office. The door closed. The walls trembled with the conversation that ensued. Jim emerged from his office whiter than the average sheet.

"Wanda," he barked, and slapped a slip of paper beside her. "Get this man on the line for me."

"Washington D.C.?" Wanda seemed to require a higher authority. "But, Jimmy, that's long distance."

"Just make the call," Hicks barked again and then, bam! slammed the door as he re-entered his office.

Wanda slowly dialed the number she'd been given. She used a rotary phone. All they had in those years. And there was no direct dialing, either. Click, click, click. You could hear the travel of that old phone's rotor.

"Long distance, please."

People began to drift in from other offices, from the hallway. From the County Clerk's office.

"Would ya'll quit lookin' at me?" Wanda complained, and then with the distinctive chirp of a connection segued smooth as pie—"Mr. Jim Hicks for Sydney Reiner...Mr. Hicks, yes. Supervisor of elections...pardon me...? He's expecting the call? Well, yes, certainly. I'll just transfer you...JIMMY!"

Wanda yelled through the closed door to her brother.

"IT'S THE DEPARTMENT OF JUSTICE."

I knew that Miss Chandler had been collecting black signatures on registration cards. What I did not know was that, rather than turn them in piecemeal, rather than alert the county to the growing potential for a vote of color, Miss Chandler had hidden her lights under a very large bushel. Kept a card up her sleeve, you might say.

Actually, a bunch of cards.

By the time Garner Hewitt knew what was down it was too late to do anything about it. With the Attorney General of the United States threatening an investigation of Jim Hicks' conduct, the supervisor of elections was forced to certify virtually every Negro in Lafayette County eligible for the following day's election. I should quickly say that it wasn't obvious how the new registrants would affect the outcome, if at all.

Black people had been beaten for trying to vote. We had been lynched. And just because you cast your ballot behind a curtain didn't mean it was secret; it was hard to keep secrets from Garner Hewitt. It was a time of fear and trembling and not even Miss Chandler could say with confidence how many people of color would cast a vote for Collard Jackson.

The next day, we all found out. On the fifth of May, a Tuesday, 1964, the white citizens of Lafayette County acquitted themselves well. The paper reported that of the thousand eighty-eight votes registered to Caucasians, over seventy percent made their mark at the polls. Seven hundred and eighty-three votes altogether, all from white people. Collard lost that constituency by a margin of three to one, gaining only 196 white votes from the 783 cast.

That was the white vote.

But Miss Chandler had made a deal with the devil in Lafayette County. Colored Town would deliver the vote to the incumbent sheriff. And in return?

"I just told him to enforce the law," Miss Chandler would insist when asked. "I asked for nothing special. No favors. Just that he enforce the law fairly. Without regard to race or color."

In return for assurances that he would uphold the law, Miss Chandler promised Collard Jackson that she would do her best to turn out the vote of the county's newly emancipated constituency and that she would urge every Negro voter to cast against Monk Folsom.

Turns out that the cardboard boxes Wanda Hicks was forced to accept held registrations for four hundred and thirteen African American citizens. Of that population, four hundred and three black women and men from all over the county made it to a voting booth. One hundred percent of those citizens cast for the democrats and Collard Jackson.

People remember dates for different reasons. The end of a war. Family tragedies. The assassination of a President. But the date that Colored Town still holds sacred is Tuesday, May 5th, 1964, because that was the day my people beat Garner Hewitt, Monk Folsom, and all their minions by the margin of just twelve votes.

"Twelve votes!" Preacher celebrated from the height of his makeshift pulpit. "Twelve! One for every disciple! Praise the Lord!"

Miss Chandler changed our town and county a lot more with her patient, stubborn campaign than I ever would with my music. Garner Hewitt woke the following Wednesday morning to taste the bile of defeat and to reflect that the Negroes he despised now made up more than a third of the vote in Lafayette County. May 5th, a Tuesday—that was the day my people were truly free. It broke Garner's hold. It ruined Monk. But it would also ruin Joe Billy, ultimately.

And, absent a great sacrifice, it would have ruined me.

Chapter nineteen

"Negroes Vote in Primary"—*The Clarion*

I could not afford to spend a lot of time celebrating my community's first political triumph and newfound strength. I was not, for example, present at the Wednesday prayer meeting when Collard Jackson in person came down the aisle to thank Miss Chandler and our congregation for giving him a victory that was by any account Providential.

"There's gonna be changes," the sheriff promised. "Gonna be some changes made."

It's not that I didn't care about the election. I was proud of Miss Chandler, proud that my community had gone to the polls, even though at eighteen I was too young to participate. But there were other things competing for my attention.

I had missed more than a month of school. There were weeks and weeks of homework and tests to make up: trigonometry, English literature, world history, biology, civics, and, of course, band. I had to make time for the bassoon. And beyond those immediate demands was a summer regimen that Dr. Weintraub mandated, readings in literature and philosophy and fine arts. A glance at that list told me there would be more to college than cosines and scarlet letters.

My physical condition was a great hindrance. The wounds to my crotch and lips were not completely healed, not to mention the scars on my psyche. I never felt I had enough time; there were only three weeks between the election and final exams. I completed the semester tapped out, terrified that I would not graduate.

Miss Chandler saw my grades before I did. I did not at first believe her report.

"You will graduate, Cilla," Miss Chandler was beaming. "And with distinction."

My standing in class necessarily suffered due to the absence caused by four weeks of hospitalization. Even so I graduated salutatorian of our class. Juanita Land was valedictorian. I don't think I would have been comfortable being on stage with any other classmate. Juanita was never afraid to look at me.

I got to see her backstage, out of her gown. That silk of hair swaying like a rope between slender shoulders. Down to the small of a well-toned back.

Mr. Land's daughter delivered the kind of valedictory address expected by her community. Articulated well her remarks, mated a heartfelt optimism to sparkling notions of choice and destiny. It was a clean, predictable world Juanita painted, a place where Guinevere never cheated and Lancelot never got hard.

I was not required to speak. It is traditional for the salutatorian's address to complement the address given by the valedictorian, but I was physically unable to elocute anything so demanding, and even if I had been able to speak I don't believe I could have delivered, at least not convincingly, the sorts of sentiments that seemed, coming from Juanita, entirely believable.

I could have been heroic, I suppose. I could have, for instance, performed 'The Impossible Dream', on the piano at least. Or I could have muddled through some sort of pithy expression of gratitude. But I didn't. With Joe Billy's help, I had begun to aspire to a wider audience. I wanted a different accolade in a different theater.

Someplace with boxes and curtains and chandeliers.

The formal dinner that traditionally followed graduation was held, as always, at Betty's Café. Pudding and Chicken and Shirley Lee were all excited about going. It was as close to a prom as we would ever come. I was reluctant to attend, for a variety of reasons, including the fact that I would be virtually the only attendee unaccompanied by a parent. But Juanita recruited Rodney and Jerry Fowler and a dozen other of my band hall stalwarts to insist that I be present.

"You can sit with us," Juanita proclaimed. "We'll be your family."

Tradition was broken when for the first time black students and their families mixed in the same space and time as whites. I was greeted by white folks I'd known all my life as if we had never met. I knew Juanita's parents, for instance. Had seen the Lands innumerable times at their SafeWay store. But we had never been introduced. Not socially.

Mrs. Land made a special effort to be nice.

"You've been through so much, Priscilla. And you've been such a good friend to Juanita."

"Ses ban gud do me."

(She's been good to me.) I honestly replied.

"You going on to college now?"

"Yeth ma'am."

"Music, is that correct? Florida State?"

"Go Seminoles!" Pudding chimed in, and with the levity that followed, you could almost believe there were no divides of any kind in our newly gathered commune.

Cody Hewitt attended, of course, his popularity only slightly diminished by his failure to get a football scholarship of any sort to any university. Plans were quietly announced that Cody would attend junior college in Lake City. I don't think they even had a football team. We circled each other in that dining room like twin suns tied by a mutual gravity, but determined nevertheless to remain distant in our forced orbit.

Garner and Florence Hewitt made a grand entrance. Garner could not afford to be absent at these public affairs, especially in the aftermath of his failure in the recent election. When I saw him, Cody's father was smiling broadly. Grabbing hands and slapping backs all over that café. I even saw him buttonhole Preacher Dipps.

Betty rang a cowbell to signify the serving of dinner, that sit-down meal spread over a dozen tables. I floated from pudding to pilau, listening in on the carefree give and take of my classmates, their flirts and teases mixed with apocrypha and memory, those last categories sometimes difficult to separate. For instance, it was surprisingly hard for our white classmates to believe that Pudding played baseball with heads ripped from the torsos of Barbie dolls, or to imagine Chicken spiraling passes with a juice can.

Easier to believe that Rodney Land put Kool Aid in the Boy's Room commodes—that solved a semester-long mystery. Or to hear squeaky-clean Juanita admit to smoking pot.

"But just once. To see what it was like."

One tote won't take you there, girlfriend.

As I already knew.

There were similar confessions of clandestine sin woven with expressions of hope, promise, and anxiety for The Future. I would have liked to take a more active role in that back and forth but was greatly inhibited by my impeded speech. I could not yet articulate well enough to be easily understood, especially above my classmates' boisterous conversations. Of course, there are persons to whom a salutatorian is obliged to speak on these occasions. Miss Chandler was my interlocutor for those duties, making sure I left my classmates at intervals to say something pleasant, if not always sincere, to my principal and to each of my instructors.

"Thag you Mister Pud'nal," I made my manners to the master of home room.

"Why…of course, Cilla." He would not look at me. "Good luck at Florida State."

I nodded a thank you, using the language of body rather than tongue. So many people approached to offer me congratulations, to express admiration, even. Some of these were my own people, neighbors, folks from church. Some, like Juanita's mother, were white people uniformly gracious in their congratulations and encouragement. It was, as Carter Buchanan would say, a pleasant span of moments, and yet I was prevented from fully enjoying them. It was hard for me to believe the accolades I'd received were deserved. Some deep pessimism warned that I was not really worth this kind of attention. From where did that dark voice originate? Why couldn't I make it go away? Why couldn't I believe that the praises I received on my graduation night were deserved?

I circulated under Miss Chandler's wing until my social obligations were fulfilled, returning to spend another hour or so with classmates. Then Miss Betty once again took up her cowbell. The tradition was for parents to dine with the graduating seniors and then, on the second bell, to leave. Normally board games or some such would be cursorily dispersed by chaperones as couples paired off to talk or smooch. This year, however, tradition would be violated a second time as amplifiers and speakers and crates of LPs were lugged in from Betty's back porch and the floor was cleared for our school's very first dance.

Did some stories come out of that sock hop! Chicken Swamp got an instant reputation as a rug-cutter, a regular James Brown. Pudding was more predictably dubbed "Chubby", for Chubby Checkers. There was some white soul on display, too. Juanita, for one, was reported to light fires all over the floor. Even the chaperones got funky; I would not have minded seeing that.

But I did not stay for the dance. I offered the excuse of seeking fresh air to exit the dance floor, drifting without challenge through the kitchen. I exited the café by the veranda and saw off to the side the orange-tipped glow of a cigarette.

Joe Billy stood up for me like a gentleman.

"Cilla. Don' you look somethin'?"

(Look nice yourself.)

His shirt was open at the collar, and short-sleeved, but he had added a nice blazer, very sharp, that complimented well-pressed slacks. His socks were white inside a pair of penny loafers. He was dressed as someone who wanted to attend an affair but was not invited.

(How long have you been here?) I made myself understood.

He shrugged. "How long are you gonna be here?"

I hesitated. I did not want to return to the dance. I would

be embarrassed to be approached with any invitation to go out on that wide floor. To be exposed. Not that I thought such an invitation was likely. I was convinced that whatever goods I had were well damaged.

"Ah juss wan go ohm," I said.

Joe Billy took a drag on his Marlboro. A flame fueled on tar and tobacco glowed quick and bright in an effluvium of oxygen.

"Go home? You mean right now?"

The smoke from his cigarette rose in sylvan tendrils to cling on the heavy air like grapevines, like vines winding in and out of each other, their vagaries reminding me of the steam rising from the boilers at the hospital.

"I wuz juzz leveng," I answered.

(I was just leaving.)

"How 'bout I drive you, then?" he asked. "Maybe just a quick stop at the park?"

Joe Billy opened the passenger door of his Fairlane and let me in. The engine coughed once or twice.

"Sorry," he said tightly. "Needs a tune."

But with a little encouragement the engine turned over, the transmission thudded gently to engage and we drove the short distance, probably no more than a hundred yards, that separated Betty's Café from Town Park and the pregnant swell of its silver tower. There was no moon that night and a canopy of oaks and moss blocked the stars. There were no street lights, of course, so when Joe Billy finally killed his headlights there was an immediate, almost claustrophobic sensation of darkness. The press of air against your face, like a velvet hand.

We were parked beneath the water tower. That landmark, at least, was visible, red lights placed at intervals on its towering legs. The scrawl of graffiti on the tank above. Like lipstick on a crazy woman. The ground beneath piled deep with the leavings of oak trees.

"Why you been avoidin' me?" Joe Billy asked.

Just like that. Out of nowhere.

I tried to form my lips with my thoughts in reply.

(What are you talking about?) I stalled.

"You know what I mean. They cut off my balls, girl, not my brain."

(You think you're the only one got hurt? Feels hurt? Feels like she got part of herself cut off that won't grow back?)

"I'm a man. Was a man."

(The hell has that got to do with anything?)

"It's different."

(Hell it is! You wanting somebody to hold your hand? Tell you how sorry she is you lost your balls?)

"You got no right to say that!"

(Hell, I don't! You said not to let anything drag me down, you remember? Well, I'm not. Not no Klansman. And not you, Joe Billy. You want pity, go back to Mama Fanny. Go back to Frenchtown!)

"You should'n say that, Cilla. You should'n!"

(Kiss my ass.)

"Say again?"

"Kith mah ath!"

He got it that time.

I jammed myself as far on my side of the car as I could, refusing to speak, to acknowledge him at all. But then I heard something like a croak on the far side of the bench seat and when I finally deigned to look I could see his shoulders shaking over the steering wheel.

(Oh, Jesus. Joe Billy—)

"Leave me be!"

He shoved me away, fumbling for the latch of his door.

(Where are you going?)

"Away from you!"

(Let me come.)

"NO! No, you sit right there."

(Joe Billy, I care about you. You know I do. You pulled me out of a pit, you know you did.)

"What about me?" he slobbered like an old man. "What about my pit?"

That was the heart of it. That was the thing.

(I'm sorry)

I slid across to the steering wheel.

(I see what you're saying, I do. And I am sorry. What can I tell you? I'm just a selfish bitch.)

"No!" he nearly stumbled, his shoes slick on the polished leaves.

(Just take a minute.) I urged. (Take some time. I'll wait. We'll talk as long as you want.)

He steadied himself on the side of a tree, then, a water oak. He reached into his pocket, I saw a pint come out.

(Joe Billy, don't!)

"Just stay in the car." He wiped his nose across the sleeve of his new blazer. Took a swig. "Give me a minute."

He then lurched around to the far side of the tree, and within seconds was invisible. A black man swallowed up in a black place.

I was tempted to follow, to coax him and bring him back, but did not.

He had told me to wait, for one thing. For another, I wasn't sure I could track him in the dark, certainly not without yelling and raising a ruckus. It was clear that he'd been drinking. He probably did need just a little time alone. To piss, maybe. Certainly, to recover his dignity, his composure.

Everyone needs privacy. If I learned nothing else at the hospital I did learn that. So I decided I would simply honor Joe Billy's request. I was fine in the car and I knew that as soon as he was composed he would return. I had no doubt about that. The keys were still in the ignition. I would just listen to the radio. That's what I would do. I would tune in KOMA or some other common-carried super station. Maybe catch the Wolf Man from the aether.

I slipped beneath the steering wheel, turned the key back hard. Then I switched on the radio. I listened to the circuits heat, saw the faint glow on the dial's rectangular face. I could not get Oklahoma City with clarity but The Temptations came in just fine on Jacksonville's Mighty 690. I was settling down to some Motown when through the open window I heard shoes shuffling over oak leaves.

(I'm glad you're back) I said, reaching over to turn down the volume.

"I heard the glad part."

The voice was familiar. But it was not Joe Billy's. I jerked away from the driver's side, seeing the torso of a man filling the open window. He was tall, that fact registered, his waist higher than the door's side panel. A country-western shirt tucked into a pair of jeans. And then there was the belt, the same belt I had seen before, its cheaply plated buckle shaped like the head of a snake.

"Yea Dee—?!"

A cigarette lowered into view, tracing a lazy, amber arc through the window's frame. That's all I could see at first, the torso, the cigarette, a pale, unhealthy hand. Then the cigarette dropped past the ledge of the door and out of sight, like a tiny aircraft plunging at a distance from heaven to earth. I heard a long, low chuckle. Then the smoker bent down and leaned in and I saw his face.

"Nigger bitch. You glad to see me?"

But it was not J.T. Hewitt.

He was tall, all right. And he was dark-haired. And he now sported the same mail-order belt made chic by Garner's oldest son. But he was not J.T. Hewitt. The door opened and I sat like a deer caught in headlights as Monk Folsom slid in on the driver's side of Joe Billy's well-used car.

"Come here."

That command broke the spell. To that point I had been charmed like a cat before a snake. Paralyzed. Immobile. But when he spoke the stench of whiskey jarred me from that catalepsy and I reared back and kicked as hard as I could. I kicked. I kicked again. But I got more of the steering wheel than I did of the Klansman who cut my lips at Fort McKoon.

He jerked the door open and grabbed my legs.

"I said come here, bitch."

The smell of rotgut on him. I screamed for Joe Billy and he laughed at my cotton-mouthed attempt.

"Don't go lookin' for help there."

Had he hurt him? I babbled. Had he hurt Joe Billy?

"Not much, he'll get over it. So will you."

I kicked again, but he was already between my knees.

(Not again. Oh, God.)

He slapped me once, hard across the face.

"Watn't for that goddamn nigger teacher I'd be sheriff! I could throw your ass in my cruiser and fuck you any way I want and not a goddamn thing you could do about it. You or your jungle bunny boyfriend!"

He was putrid.

"Goddamn nigger thief, if I'd of known he was in that Zion church I'd of burned his ass with the rest, I can tell you that. Burned him and a hundred other niggers in that goddamn churchhouse."

I jammed up against my own door and he smiled boozily.

"You thought it was Cody did that work? Or J.T.? Naw. Them boys is all talk. We just borrowed their truck, is all. Like I told Collard, it was in my shop. And we were doin' just fine 'till your boyfriend sees the truck. Even then we'd of been all right if he'd stayed in goddamn French Town. But, no, the little nigger comes running down here for Collard to pick up. Next thing you know we got the fucking FBI breathing down our necks.

"I should of killed that boy when I had him on the river. Killed you both."

His hand dipped into his pocket and when it came out I saw the moon sliding along a mother of pearl handle and I tried to scream.

There was air in my throat, waffling air, and nothing more.

He cackled.

"Naw, naw. I already cut what I wanted to cut on you! This here? Is just a reminder. So if you tell anybody anything, if you breathe a goddamn word to Collard, your preacher, your teacher. Your nut-less boyfriend. Anybody. You know what I'm'a gone do. Don't you? Sure you do. And it'll make our last little time look like somethin' to cherish."

He reached back to carefully place the razor on the dashboard, then snaked a filthy hand up my blouse.

"You think you're good as anybody, but you ain't. And there's plenty like me gone make sure you keep your place. We're strong, no mixed blood. And we're organized. I could die tomorrah, they'd be twenty taking my place. There—!"

He fondled my breasts. First one. Then the other.

"See this is all I want, this time," he promised me. "Maybe some other time we can do more. But this ain't so bad. Is it?"

Then he pinched a nipple. My knee came up in reflex, just snapped up and banged into the dash so hard the glove compartment spilled open. I cried out, tried to reach for my kneecap. He slapped my hand to the floorboard. Something cool, down there in the velvet dark. Something cool and hard that along with a crumpled wad of cellophane and a book of matches spilled with weight from the glove's shallow keep.

He let go my breast, finally. That drunk he probably couldn't get an erection. Could barely sit up on his own. Had to grab the steering wheel to accomplish that chore.

"You think going to college makes you white?" His breath was labored. "Think a education makes you anything but a polecat nigger? Shit!"

He retrieved his straight razor from the dashboard.

I let him get out of the car. In fact, I made sure he was out of the car with his back turned and his pearlhandled blade well pocketed before I slid across the seat, and throwing my feet to the ground, steadied my extended arms inside the car window's sheetmetal frame. The door hinge complained with that effort. Monk turned sloppily in mid-stride.

"The hell you doin', you muddy goddamn bitch?"

Were the last words Monk Folsom said before I yanked on the trigger of Joe Billy's revolver.

An explosion, then, a physical concussion inside the car. My ears rang like bells. He squawked like a chicken ten, maybe fifteen feet before me. Spun around, like a drunk man. I shot him again. Then as he was fully turned I pulled the trigger again and Monk fell face first and limp as a sack to the damp and mossy carpet. The gun smoked at the barrel. Like a cigarette. Or like steam writhing upward from an angry boiler.

The weapon dropped as if on its own accord from my hand and I retreated, screaming incomprehensibly, to the far side of the coupe's interior.

"HALB ME!!"

"CILLA!"

Joe Billy came staggering out of inky shadows.

"HALB ME!"

There was only the dome light of the car for illumination. But as Joe Billy pulled me from the front seat, I could see that his scalp was cut and bleeding.

"Cilla! Cilla, you all right?"

"I shod 'im! I shod 'im!"

There were dogs barking, I realized. They must have heard the firearm's discharge, because every backyard hound in Colored Town was baying for attention.

"You what?" Joe Billy's eyes went wide. "Shot who?!"

I bent over and threw up on the side of his car. Joe Billy looked out over the hood.

"My God, is that Monk Folsom?"

I threw up again.

"Jesus Christ!"

(I had to! He was on me! He said he would kill me if I talked. Kill you!)

I don't know how much of what I said Joe Billy understood, but it didn't take much conversation for him to interpret what had happened and to quickly learn that Monk was my rapist, was our cruel Inquisitor. And also the man who burned the Mount Zion church.

The dogs were raising hell, now. Barking all around.

"Jesus God," Joe Billy pressed a hand to his forehead.

(What are we going to do?)

"Just hold what you got," Joe Billy leaned on the car warily, as if it might suddenly jerk from beneath him.

"Give me a minute. Let me think. Where's the gun?"

"I drobbed id."

"Dropped it. Where?"

266

My pointed finger trembled like a wand, but with the help of the car's interior light Joe Billy found his revolver.

(We got to call the sheriff) I began to say over and over. (We got to call the sheriff).

"Yes, Cilla. We gonna get the sheriff here soon as we can," Joe Billy promised. "You wait here. I'm just goin' to Monk. Just be two seconds."

My knees buckled as Joe Billy approached Monk Folsom, Laureate's favorite mechanic still twitching on the ground like a chicken with his head chopped off. His fingers in particular, I remember, were fluttering like a butterfly's wings, like when you straightpin a butterfly to a piece of cardboard. Joe Billy edged up to Monk as if the fallen man were a landmine, nudging him with his shoe, first. Then a kick to the armpit. Nothing. The fingers quit their nervous dance.

(Is he dead?)

Joe Billy dropped to a knee without reply and keeping the revolver in one hand, rolled the body face-up. Then he fished Monk's razor from the pocket of those denim jeans. I watched as he wrapped Folsom's pliant hand about the blade's alabaster handle.

That work done, he pushed himself erect. Backed off a pace or two.

"You fucking bastard."

The handgun jumped in Joe Billy's hand. Another violent concussion into the heavy air. Monk's body jerked with the impact of a slug to his chest. I jumped like I been hit with a cattle prod.

"JOE BIRREE?!!"

"Be quiet, Cilla. Cilla, hush."

He returned to the car, his face going in and out of shadow as he dipped beneath the domed light into the interior, then up again.

(What did you do that for?!)

He displayed the handgun.

"So when they look at me they'll be powder burns on my hand and shirt. You shoot a gun they's got to be some burn. Sheriff's gonna wanna see that."

For a moment I did not comprehend his intention.

(But you didn't shoot him, Joe Billy! Didn't kill him, anyway. I did!)

"That's not our story," Joe Billy shook his head and I realized then, fully, what he had in mind.

(Oh, Lord. Oh, Lord.)

"It'll be all right. I can claim self defense same as you."

(You can't do this, Joe Billy. Joe Billy this isn't right! I can tell them. I can tell them it *was* self defense.)

"Drunk man shot by a Negro girl? With a round in his back? You ain't hit. You ain't cut. Or raped. Are you?"

I shook my head, "Nah."

"Well, what white jury's gonna let you skate on that ice, Cilla? You tell me."

(But you didn't do it)

"No, but at least I got a wound. And from behind, too."

I was wringing my hands like a washrag.

(But you didn't kill anybody. I did.)

Dogs were barking all around. Raising hell.

"We don' have much time," Joe Billy turned me around and pointed me in the direction of the train station.

"You go home. Just go home and don't let anybody see you. I'll be fine."

(No!) I dug in my heels. (I want to stay with you!)

"You stay now, you'll stay here the rest of your life."

His small hand crushed my arm.

"And what about college? What about music? What chance you gonna have if you stay by me now? 'Cause no way you gonna get by without a trial, Cilla. And it'll be a trial in Lafayette County, not Leon. It'll be a white jury. Monk's neighbors. His kin. What makes you think you'd ever git off? And even if you did what makes you think there'd be a scholarship left for you to take? Innocent or guilty, it won't matter. A white girl couldn't come out of this mess clean, let alone a nigger from Colored Town."

I saw a swatch of headlight cut through the mossy tops of the trees.

"Go on!" Joe Billy turned me toward the depot.

Then I heard the long whistle of the midnight train and thought again and differently of escape.

"Go home."

I heard Joe Billy behind me.

"Home, I said! And don't look back. Whatever you do, don't look back."

I ran away from Monk Folsom and Joe Billy like Lot's wife, away from the shroud of moss and the silver tower grinning like a crazy woman. But unlike the wavering woman of old I did not look back. I followed Joe Billy's command. I did what he told me.

What else was I to do?

I ran all the way home.

And I did not look back.

Chapter twenty

"County Population Decline
Grows"—*The Clarion*

J oe Billy drove straight from the water tower to the county jail
and turned himself in. Collard was over in Taylor County and
had to be raised by radio. In the interim, Monk's body was otherwise
discovered, Bonnie Hart and Cody looking for a good time in the
park finding something else.

I can't imagine the scene, Bonnie and Cody rushing back to
Betty's, telling everybody who'd listen they'd found a dead man. The
homecoming king and his queen did not know it was Monk, apparently, not right away. By the time Joe Billy convinced the deputy
uptown that a homicide had actually occurred, there were twenty
cars and forty teenagers cutting doughnuts around the water tower,
their headlights lashing the tower's legs and belly in fleeting, ephem-
eral beams.

Cody called his daddy from the café. Mr. Hewitt and his posse
arrived shortly thereafter at a crime scene already trampled. Thunder rolled as if to announce Garner's approach, a fork of lightning

and fat drops of water spattering from the heavens onto the bloody leaves below. A douche for any evidence clinging to the body, the ground. By the time Collard's deputy pulled up, a murder, a mess, and a mob were waiting.

"You got to find who did this!" Garner was bullying the lawman before he could get out of his marked car.

Lightning flashing in random frames of blue and white.

"Goddammit, Garner, look at ya'll, stompin' all over. Has this body been moved?!"

"What are we supposed to do? Wait for the sheriff?"

"Damn straight. That's exactly what you do. All of you. Now back up. Give me some room. Who found him?"

"Better question is who killed him," Garner's retort cut off Cody's reply. "'Cause whoever did is loose with a gun!"

"Just settle it down," the deputy replied, the rain now tapping like a snare drum on the brim of his hat. "You ain't in any danger. None of you."

"'Till we find out who did this we are!"

Then the deputy did something either really stupid or patently malicious. Whether in deference to Garner, or thinking to defuse the situation, or out of malice or stupidity, he informed the crowd that Monk's killer had already turned himself in at the jail, claiming self defense.

"So you got a man? In jail?!"

"Didn't say it was a man, Garner."

"Don't bullshit me. Is he white? Who is he?"

And the crowd took it up.

"Who is he?"

"Who is the son of a bitch?!"

"No, no," the deputy was by now retreating to his cruiser. "People! We don't even know if this was foul play. I don't know. You don't know. But what I do know is that none of ya'll are in any danger and that we have a suspect in custody. And Sheriff Jackson is on his way."

"The sheriff?" Garner snorted. "Well, mother hump I feel better already."

By the time Collard arrived in Laureate over a hundred people were gathered outside his jail, many of them with shotguns still dirty from deer season. The men were getting liquored up, bottles passed around, every swigging son of a bitch proclaiming undying loyalty to the county's favorite mechanic. Everyone calling for the name of Monk Folsom's killer.

Thunder and lightning. Mostly thunder, at first.

Collard had already radioed his desk sergeant to dispatch off-duty deputies to secure the crime scene and take charge of Monk's corpse. His main concern, he would later say, was not centered at the water tower, but on the streets around his own jail. The sheriff who owed his fourth term to Negroes drove into Laureate knowing that a lynch mob was brewing. He had to trip his cruiser's siren to clear a path, and lay down on the horn of his car to get inside the chain-link fence that secured the jail's perimeter.

Pudding's father was inside that night, inhabiting his usual cell, along with a couple of other drunks. And, of course, there were the deputies. From those disparate reports, it's possible to roughly reconstruct Collard's exchange with his deputies.

"Where you got him?" Collard asked first.

"Drunk tank."

"Good. Tell those folks outside to go home."

"We have."

"Then start cracking heads."

"Sheriff—there's a lot of heads out there."

According to Pudding, Collard showed no sense of alarm or pressure at all. He just paused a moment. "Call Sheriff Polk in Taylor County. Tell him to send every man he can spare. Call the Highway Patrol. Tell them the situation and arrange for an escort."

"Escort?"

"Just tell 'em we're gonna need to transport a prisoner, Ronald."

By that point the mob on the streets could be heard, even through the obstacle of the calaboose's concrete walls.

"Steady by jerks, gentlemen," Collard grabbed a shotgun off the rack. "This ain't no big thang."

Joe Billy had been thrown in the drunk tank, alone and left to imagine the worst from the signs around him—hostile deputies who
would not inform, and a mob outside. When Collard opened the
cell toting a shotgun, JayBee told me he expected to be executed
on the spot.

"What's this bullshit about self defense?" were the first words
out of Collard's mouth.

"He had a razor, Sheriff. Said he was gonna cut more than my
nuts!"

"Your nuts? Are you saying it was Monk Folsom strung you
up?"

"Yes, sir."

"And *he* told you so? He told you himself?"

"Yes, he did. You can see the razor. And he got a belt, too. Just
like J.T.'s. The snake and ever'thing."

"What's that on your head? Your scalp?"

Joe Billy tested the backside of his skull gently. "I 'magine it's
blood."

Collard grunted. "What I thought. Now git up."

"Suh?"

"Get off your ass. We're gettin' you out of here."

Collard was not about to wait on Taylor County's lawman or
the Highway Patrol's or anyone else's. What was later proven, what
the sheriff already suspected, was that he could not trust his deputies.
Someone on the inside, one of the deputies, telephoned every instruction Collard gave inside his jail to West's Drug Store, from where it
was relayed to Garner Hewitt. Garner knew Joe Billy was inside that
cell. It was no protest he had organized. It was a lynching.

Whatever deputies remained loyal to Sheriff Jackson must have
been as surprised as the mutineers when Joe Billy came out of the
tank handcuffed in Collard's custody.

"Sheriff?"

"My car in the sallyport? Ronald? What about it?"

"Yes, sir."

"All right, then, listen up. I am transporting the prisoner to

Suwannee County. Call Buddy Williams. Tell him to meet me at the bridge with an escort.

"I can make the bridge in five minutes from the fenceline. If I see a single goddamn headlight I will know that one of you pukes has told Garner and his men outside what I'm up to."

"No reason to say something like that, Sheriff. No reason!"

"I'll be lookin'. And I will tell Sheriff Williams to shoot any son-of-a-bitch tries to get between me and his jail. Is that clear?

"So if there is a Judas in this jailhouse, just wait five minutes. Then you can tell Garner anything you want because I'll be to the bridge before he can do anything about it. Nobody'll have to get hurt."

"What about the Highway Patrol, Sheriff? What about Sheriff Polk?"

Collard smiled. "If Garner and his boys want to mess with that bunch, they're welcome to it."

Collard did not even hit the siren or lights as he pulled slowly from the fenced protection of his jail. He deliberately turned on the dome lights so that the mob pressing close could see the car's interior, see the passenger cage in the back, that it was empty.

He actually stopped the car at one point, and rolled down his window in the rain to address Garner Hewitt.

"You need to tell your people to break this up, Garner."

"I don't have that authority, Sheriff."

"Tell 'em anyway."

And with that Sheriff Jackson drove off calmly, deliberately. He didn't even pick up speed after the red light. Joe Billy would have to stay in the locked trunk of that cruiser the full five minutes that it took to reach the Hal Adams Bridge. Once there he was transferred into the custody of the Suwannee County sheriff.

"How you want him booked, Collard?" Buddy Williams came out himself to ensure the safety of the transfer.

"Suspected manslaughter," Collard said after a pause. "He's claiming self defense."

"Don't they all?"

"Might be some truth in this one, Buddy. Just so you know."

"I'll be damned. You got a statement?"

"A start. I'll be over tomorrow for the rest. If you'll just watch him for me."

"Glad to oblige."

"I really appreciate this, Buddy."

"I know you do."

"May I have just a short word with the suspect?"

"Certainly. No hurry."

Joe Billy would recall the details of that harrowing escape many times over the next few weeks. But the thing I remember most vividly from his report, the thing *he* recalled acutely, were Collard's parting words on the bridge.

"All right, Joe Billy. Now you need to get some things straight."

"Yes, suh."

"'Cause once you cross *this* bridge there ain't no turning back."

"No, suh."

"So before we go to all that trouble I want you to tell me again—did you kill Monk Folsom?"

"Yessuh. In self defense."

Collard spat on the road.

"I don' believe it."

Joe Billy floundered.

"I... I did kill him, Sheriff. I did."

"You told me he had a razor."

"He did, Sheriff! You'll see!"

"Oh, I'm sure I will. I also see a gash along your skull. Dried blood. Wasn't scalping you with that razor was he, boy?"

"He...he hit me."

"You didn't say anything about him hitting back in the jail. You just said he threatened you with the razor. Words to that effect."

"Threaten, yes, Sheriff. Said he was the man cut my nuts and he was gone finish the job."

"Uh huh."

Collard leaned over. Joe Billy could hear the report of rain, the engorged drops splattering one by one on the broad brim of the Sheriff's hat.

"Now you listen to me, boy. Sheriff Williams is a good man. You don't need to be afraid. But you don't say a thing to him or anybody else about what happened tonight. You understand? Anybody asks, you just tell 'em I said wait for me."

"I got it, Sheriff."

"Tomorrow I'll be back with Thurman Shaw. He's an attorney. You better have a story makes sense and you better stick to it, every damn detail. Thurman's good. He'll walk you through it. You understand what I'm tellin' you to do? Well, do you?"

Joe Billy was so astounded at that point that he could not reply.

The sheriff paused to locate the other lawmen on the periphery of his vision. There was no one standing close. No one in earshot, anyway.

"Awright," Collard seemed satisfied. "One last thing. Word of advice. Whatever you say. Whatever yarn you come up with?"

"Yes, Sheriff?"

"Keep it simple." Collard turned away. "Simple is best. Juries hate to think."

Monk Folsom's homicide generated tensions exacerbated by the fury still felt by white citizens over losing an election to black votes. Garner Hewitt's supporters stirred that boiling pot, those white folk religiously incensed that a nigger who wasn't even local had shot one of their own, and furious with Sheriff Jackson for ferrying the suspect beyond the reach of their ropes.

Thurman Shaw urged the State's attorneys to drop all charges against his client, insisting that whatever forensic evidence was not washed away or trampled backed up a claim of self-defense.

"There is no *mens rea* here, gentlemen. Joe Billy was attacked. He used the force allowed by law. This boy should not be tried for any crime."

Thurman went on to point out that Monk's fingerprints were found on his razor blade. Fresh, even after a heavy rain.

Prosecutors replied that of course Folsom's prints were on the razor, he shaved with the damn thing every morning.

Did he shave under the water tower? Thurman countered. In black dark?

The State was not moved to dismiss and a grand jury comprised entirely of white citizens was swiftly impaneled. Mr. Shaw did everything he could to illicit sympathy for Joe Billy while painting Monk Folsom as a monster, but it was rough going. No member of the Klan was about to corroborate Joe Billy's claim that Monk burned churches and crucified Negroes. Joe Billy's castration could be objectively established, of course, but a grand jury convinced that Folsom was responsible for that terrible scission could not fail to see that it also gave the accused an excellent motive for murder.

In consultation with his attorney Joe Billy stuck to the script that Monk had bragged about castrating him and said he meant to finish the job.

"Those were Monk's words, 'finish the job'?"

Thurman jotting notes on a long, yellow pad.

"Yes, suh. Then he swiped at my head with his razor and I ducked over to the glove compartment for my gun. I don't know how many times I shot him, or where. I just kept pullin' the trigger."

"Okay, that's too much," Thurman coached his client shamelessly. "Keep it simple."

"He came at me with the razor. I shot him," Joe Billy rehearsed his reply. "How's that?"

I, of course, knew that the evening's events were not quite so simple, but I was never called before the grand jury. Nobody questioned my whereabouts that evening, which was not surprising. Half the town, after all, shook my hand at Betty's Café and no one saw me leave that graduation night, though Pudding knew I had skipped the dance.

"You should of boogied with us, Cilla."

"You'd ask a girl with a face like this?" I replied coyly.

"Sure, I would," he lowered his eyes.

"I was too tired to dance. I went home to my bed."

I tried to believe it was all right to lie. I was only following Joe Billy's strict instruction, wasn't I? And anyway my old beau was going to be fine. Told me so himself.

"Thurman say they ain't enough to make a trial," Joe Billy declared when I visited him in his Suwannee County cell. "He say the Grand Jury got to see it was just self-defense."

Thurman was wrong. On the last day of June, Joe Billy was indicted. A count for manslaughter was expected. A count for murder in the second degree was unsettling. But Joe Billy was indicted as well for first-degree murder. Homicide with premeditation. Which meant that if convicted Joseph William King would surely face the electric chair.

Summer brought equal parts heat, humidity, and despair. July passed like a bitch in labor before wilting into August and I was having trouble sleeping. I'd wake up sticky and hot, roused by the nearby lament of the train. That long call. I tried to convince myself that my insomnia could be given to God, that a sacrifice of restful slumber would deliver Joe Billy from the State of Florida, but I knew that in the end there was only one sacrifice sufficient to that task and so began to contemplate a tardy confession.

"Don' do it." Joe Billy stayed that impulse. "Thurman say he ain't afraid of no trial. He say they ain't got nuthin'."

My hands were tied. At any rate, that is how I chose to regard it, as if I had no volition of my own.

It helped to get out of town. Professor Weintraub brought me up to Florida State almost every week, which was a godsend. I would perch before my professor with my bassoon for an hour's practice, sometimes more. Then I would see a speech therapist, a graduate assistant engaged by Dr. Weintraub on my behalf. I was improving my articulation on my own, but the exercises helped. You could do them any time.

She sells seashells on the seashell shore.

Dr. Weintraub always took time after practice and therapy to show me around Florida State's verdant campus. She would engage me in small talk during those perambulations, or at least make the attempt. I was articulating almost well enough to have normal conversation, which was a blessing. But I was constantly censoring my own speech, terrified that some unguarded comment regarding Monk Folsom or murder would get me sacked from the School of Music.

Dr. Weintraub probed on one occasion. "Cilla, are you okay?"

"Tired, maybe, a liddle. Bud ahm all right."

I am all right/You are all right/He is all right

We are all right/You are all right/They are all right.

Joe Billy will be all right.

I parsed possibilities like verbs on the bus ride back to Laureate. It was not uncommon on my return to find Miss Chandler waiting.

"Hello, Cilla, honey."

She in a print dress by Mr. Land's SafeWay store. I remember on that occasion that my teacher took my instrument case as I stepped off the Greyhound.

"How's my college girl?"

"Fine, Miss Chandluh. Thag you."

She tucked her free arm into mine. "Why don't we detour by Betty's? Get ourselves a nice glass of ice tea?"

A tall glass frigid with ice cubes and sugar-sweet tea is the only sure antidote to August. We entered Betty's from the rear as was still required in ordinary time, and found a bench. The place was nearly deserted.

"Just two teas, please," Miss Chandler deposited my bassoon for me, inquiring as she did so about my sessions with Dr. Weintraub, the progress of my music.

"Are you composing?" she inquired mildly.

"Not much," I confessed.

"Why not?"

I didn't expect that question.

"I'm just tired." I repeated the excuse I had only hours earlier given my Tallahassee mentor.

"Is that all?" Miss Chandler stirred the ice in her tea.

What a temptation, then, to blurt my awful secret. Surely, Miss Chandler would hear me. Surely she would know what to do. And I wanted to tell her, I did. It would be a joy to cleanse my soul with a simple confession.

But could I bear the consequences?

Miss Chandler did not push or prod. She left me at my back porch with a cheerful benediction. I trudged wearily to the kitchen, hefted my instrument onto the table and got mother some supper. I washed the dishes, voided myself and bathed well afterward with a tub and soap and, praise the Lord, plenty of water. Then, making sure there were no immediate responsibilities unfulfilled, I left my home in the light of a vapored moon and walked to town.

I walked past Mr. Charles' gas station, past the closed theater and the drugstore, crossing Main Street to skirt the courthouse lawn. I could see then the air-conditioner recently replaced atop the jail's flat roof. There was a single door for the public, a metal door triple-hinged into a featureless concrete wall that looked over steps stenciled, "Slippery When Wet." I had never noticed that admonition. Goes to show how much you can miss when you keep your eyes on the ground.

I entered the jail and got the immediate attention of a deputy propped on raw elbows at the desk sergeant's formica counter.

"Whatchu want?" he challenged.

"See da...see thuh sheriff."

I kept my eyes trained on the concrete floor.

"Speak up, girl."

"See the sheriff."

"What's goin' on, Ronald?"

That coal-bin voice. I knew it was Sheriff Jackson, but I did not turn around. Or raise my eyes from the stained floor.

"You need to see me, girl?"

"Yes, sir."

"Come own, then."

Collard's office was accessed through a coded door on a hallway running on the side of the building opposite the cells. Joe Billy said you could see into the office most of the time, if you got past the desk sergeant and into that hallway. Sheriff Jackson apparently did not believe in closing his door.

People coming into the same place will notice different things. Coming into the sheriff's office, I was taken with the State Seal badly decoupaged on his government-issue desk. The Seal of the State of Florida features a woman standing erect in a confused iconography featuring among other errors the kind of native garb that might as well belong to Pocahontas as any Seminole. Wearing a headdress, too, which women of that tribe (or any other?) did not do. Perhaps she was a dyke, this Seminole princess or serving woman. Whatever she was.

Atop the seal I saw a quart jar filled with arrowheads (genuine) and the rattles of the familiar snake, those artifacts set beside a bank of fountain pens never used. There was only the one rigid chair besides the padded recliner behind Collard's desk. I didn't have to ask to know which seat was for me.

"I don't have much time." He tossed his Stetson onto a prong of mounted antlers. "What you want?"

"I know somethin—" I began.

"I know lots of things," he snorted. "Makes you think you know somethin' I don't?"

"It's about Monk Folsom. Mr. Folsom."

"Don't tell me you miss him."

"I killed him."

Collard swiveled slowly in his highbacked chair. "You what?"

"I killed Monk Folsom. I shot him. With Joe Billy's gun."

He leaned back. The chair squeaked with his weight.

"The State's attorney says different," Collard tapped a Marlboro from a fresh pack. "For that matter so does Joe Billy."

"It was self defense. Sort of," I said.

"'Sort of'?"

So in a chaotic rush I told him everything, that Monk had jumped me alone in Joe Billy's car. That I had seen the belt and at first thought it was J.T. Hewitt's.

"That snake laid on? All silver? But then he leaned inside the car and I saw it wasn't J.T. It was Monk. And then when he showed me the razor I knew it was him that cut me, that castrated Joe Billy, and I was so scared! So scared!"

"Settle down," Collard rumbled. "Take your time."

"Monk, he was mad about the election. Told me he could take me any time he wanted. Said it would be worse than Fort McKoon. Said college wouldn't help, he'd find me anywhere. Then he mentioned the church, in Tallahassee."

"Keep it up," Collard nodded.

"He touched me and said if I told anybody, anybody at all he'd come and cut me again."

"Did he rape you?"

"He was too drunk."

"All right. What happened then?"

"He just showed me the razor and pinched me—up here. I didn't expect him to pinch. My knee slammed into the dashboard and the glove compartment door, it just popped open."

"That's where Joe Billy kept his gun? In the glove compartment?"

"Yes, sir."

"But you didn't shoot him in the car?"

"He was strong! He had a razor!"

"Easy. I'm not judging. I just need a clear picture. So after he threatens you and sexually assaults you, he gets out of the car."

"Yes, sir."

"And you wait 'till he's out of reach."

"He was two, three steps away."

"And then you shot him in the back."

"The first time, yes, sir. Then he spun around and I shot again. I shot, I don't know, three or four times."

"There's a problem with that story, Cilla." The chair groaned as he leaned forward. "There were powder burns on Joe Billy's hand. Shirt, too. Classic pattern."

"He did that for me."

"Beg your pardon?"

So I explained how Joe Billy came stumbling back to the car.

How he saw what happened. How he took the gun and rolled Monk over and shot his lifeless corpse.

"He said you'd be looking for burns," I told the sheriff. "He knew what to do."

A deputy stuck in his head. "Sheriff? Got a call from Abner. Somebody tearing up his deer camp."

"Take it for me. Close the door."

The door swung shut with a squeak of hinges louder than Collard's chair.

"You think you can help Joe Billy? That why you're here?"

"Joe Billy didn't shoot Monk Folsom. He didn't shoot anybody!"

"I figured that. Figured it right off."

My hand must have covered my heart. "You knew? You *know*?"

"I didn't know; I figured. But the only person with a motive to kill Monk other than Joe Billy would be you, and I couldn't figure how you'd get a gun. That business with the glove compartment didn't come up. Joe Billy couldn't mention that, could he? Might have pointed suspicion in your direction." He leaned forward to a phone on his desk. Stabbed a button. "Ronald? Hold my calls till I tell you."

He replaced the receiver on its dark cradle. "You willing to swear to what you just said? In court?"

I affirmed again with a nod and waited for the axe to fall, certain that with this breach my whole dam would collapse and I would be finally and blissfully drowned.

But that didn't happen.

Collard shook his shaggy head back and forth. "If you go out now with this here story folks'll think you're only doing it to protect Joe Billy."

"I'm not!"

"Makes no difference. That's what people—white people, people on a jury—will think."

"But I did it. I shot Monk."

"Sake of argument, let's say you did. But Joe Billy's got a stronger case for self-defense than you do. Fortunately for him there's not a whole lot of forensic evidence. He can probably get away with claiming to have shot Monk in the gut, first, from the front. That's got more of the taste of self-defense than your version. Layin' down on a man with his back turned."

"He said he'd be back! Said if I told anybody it'd be worse than last time! What was I supposed to do?!"

"I ain't talkin' about supposed-to, girl. Far as I'm concerned you had a perfect right to tie Monk to a tree and saw his legs off. Far as 'supposed-to' goes. What I'm talking about is what you *got* to do. And now that Joe Billy's gone this far, you cain't help him."

"I have to!"

"You do and, at best, what will come out of this is both you and Joe Billy will be charged with homicide and a jury will be called to sort it out. Now, I don't doubt for a minute that Joe Billy got knocked upside the head; I saw the scalp wound. But most people will attribute that to some kind of fight or altercation around the car. They'll say Monk was mad about the election, sure. Maybe he even threatened you. Threatened you both. But Joe Billy made a mistake, Cilla, when he was trying to make a case for self defense.

"There was no blood on Monk's razor. It was clean as a whistle. Now, that don't mean he didn't threaten you with it. But if Joe Billy'd thought or been able to cut himself, or if you'd had the sand to cut him, it'd be a lot harder for a jury to discard a plea of self-defense.

"As it is, it's gonna be hard. Gonna be hard for Joe Billy. Would be harder, for you. Don't think there aren't a passel of whites would love to see you fall, Cilla. Would take any excuse to put some uppity nigger back in her place. 'Cause however you see this or I see this, a jury in this county is going to see a dead white man with lots of friends killed by a nigger from Colored Town.

"That's what they'll see. And they won't be buying self-defense when you admit yourself that the man was walking away. That you shot him in the back."

The phone rang. Collard collected the receiver.

"What is it? Tell him I'll call him back."

He hung up the receiver. Folded his hands. "You told anybody anything about this except me?"

"No, sir."

"Not any of your people? Not even Miss Chandler?"

"No, sir."

"So you been carryin' this all on your own?"

"I guess. Yes, sir."

"Well, you're gonna have to carry it a while longer. Now, let me tell you what I'm going to do. Look up at me. Look."

I raised my eyes.

"I am going to do all I can to help Joe Billy. First off, he's charged with two counts, but one of 'em is manslaughter. Big difference between manslaughter and murder in any degree and easier to claim self-defense. I'll tell 'em there was definitely an assault with battery of some kind. I can make the argument that the rain washed all the blood off Monk's razor. That the wound I saw on Joe Billy's head might have come from a swipe of that blade. The State will demonstrate to the contrary, but that will still leave the jury with two opposed opinions. Which they hate.

"That's what I can do. All you can do to help this boy is to keep your mouth shut. I don't have the authority to let him go on anybody's word, most especially yours. And it is my judgment that if you come out like this, the only thing that will happen is that you will be found guilty of some degree of homicide. That means jail. Hard time. No college, no music. No goddamn future.

"Monk Folsom will laugh in his grave if you take up for Joe Billy King. I'm not saying you shouldn't of tried. You brought me some information, as you ought. You did your duty. But you ain't the law, young lady. In Lafayette County, *I* am the law and what I do with your information or anybody else's is *my* call. And my call is this: That justice will not be served by pursuing the information you have given me.

"Joe Billy's got a stronger case to make than you, and easier for a jury to believe. If he goes free, you will have got away with a lie. If the boy is convicted, it will be a sorry day, but no sorrier than seeing you in jail. Or seeing you both in jail. Or seeing the first real hope from Colored Town sacrificed over the slaughter of a fucking Klansman.

"I ain't saying that what you've done is right, or what I'm doing, for that matter, is right. But it sure as hell is legal. Far as I'm concerned you just came in here with a story you made up to protect your boyfriend. If any word whatever of our conversation this evening ever came out, that's exactly what I'd say. 'Girl plays the bassoon, for God's sake. She didn't take no gun to Monk Folsom. You'd have to be a fool to believe that story.' That's what I'll say, or something like it."

"They won't let go, will they? Not Joe Billy. No matter what you say."

That face, so lined, was hard as flint.

"Then you better not let it go to waste."

The next day, I journeyed across the bridge to Suwannee County and Joe Billy's cell. Joe Billy, recall, was not incarcerated locally. It was about thirty miles to the city of Live Oak where Suwannee County kept its inmates. From the time of Monk's murder until the end of July I visited Joe Billy exactly twice. To visit more often would seem suspicious, he said, and with that slender excuse I too readily acceded. But after my confession to Collard Jackson I needed one last attempt to clear my soul with the man who now risked the electric chair on my behalf.

JayBee would be represented by Thurman Shaw, the same attorney who barely a year earlier defended Cody Hewitt for shotgunning road signs. In fairness, I believe Thurman did what he could to help Joe Billy. But even with Sheriff Jackson helping in the wings Thurman was going to have a hard time selling Joe Billy's story—I should say *my* story, or at least the story invented for my benefit.

"Here," I greeted Joe Billy, slipping an RC Cola from beneath my top.

"Bring any candy?"

"Honey Bun."

Conversation turned from those banalities to the coming trial. Depositions and procedures. What he'd be wearing in court.

"Mr. Raymond got you a suit," I told him. "Bought it second-hand at the Thrift Store. You'll look real good."

Eventually my chatter wore thin.

"Ten minutes," a deputy called out.

"Joe Billy."

"Uh huh? Well?"

"I just want you to know I went to Collard. I told him I shot Monk."

I swear he almost turned white.

"Cilla Handsom!"

"No, no," I whispered fiercely. "He wouldn't let me do anything."

"Wouldn't let?!"

"He told me to keep quiet. Said it wouldn't help anything."

"That's for damn sure," Joe Billy grabbed the bars of his cell. "Goddamn, Cilla, you want us *both* in here?"

"I could'n keep it inside! I just couldn't!"

"Never would of guessed you'd pick Collard," Joe Billy shook his head. "Why didn't he arrest you? Didn't he believe you?"

"He didn't come right out in so many words. But, yeah, he believes me. He knows for sure it wasn't you."

"Good to hear," Joe Billy looked like he'd bit off a chunk of lemon.

"I could tell your lawyer, Joe Billy. I could tell Mr. Thurman, couldn't I? Why don' I do that?"

"'Why don't you', Cilla? Why?" And then he looked at me straight and when he did I had no more place to hide. "Because you don't want to."

"But I do!"

"No. You don't, Cilla."

He smiled like one of those clowns at a fair.

"Jesus maybe drank his bitter cup, but you ain't no Jesus. Don't get me wrong, I don't blame you. It's all right, it really is. Remember I'm the one talked you into it. Just think about where you're gonna be this September. 'Cause if you was in here, in my shoes? You'd be on trial for killing a man."

He took both my hands in his.

"You got a chance at college, Cilla. You got your music. You cain't throw that away for no jail time. What kind of scholarship gone be waitin' for a colored girl when she get out of jail? *If* she get out?!

"Get real, sugar doll, you don't want to swap places with me. Your conscience is eating, surely. I can see that. Going to Collard proves that. But the only thing to do is just lay it down. You got to just lay it down, Cilla. I made the decision that put me in this jail. Remember? Me. And I'd do it again.

"Only thing you can do for me is go to Tallahassee and make your mark. Make your mark, baby, and swagger when you do. And when you talk about where you come from, where you been, things you did, you can brag on me. Yes, you can.

"You can tell 'em you knew Joe Billy King."

Chapter twenty-one

"Negroes Excluded From Jury"
— *The Clarion*

One of the last things I did before leaving for Florida State was to fabricate an alibi. Sheriff Jackson insisted. "Nobody's even looking in your direction, Cilla. This here's just to make sure it stays that way." So I signed a statement swearing/affirming that on the night in question I left Betty's Café by myself and was home with my mother and grandmother a little after ten-thirty in the evening. "Simple is best," Collard filed the paperwork. "Just keep it simple. The rest you keep to yourself."

Had I remained in Colored Town I'm not sure I'd have been able to keep that counsel, but by September I was entirely absent from Lafayette County and adjusting to dorm life at Florida State. My roommate at Landis Hall was Cuban, had fled with her family from Castro. She was always on the phone chattering with relatives in a vulgate Spanish, spouting vitriol at any opportunity, railing constantly about the spoiled fortunes of:

her once-wealthy family:

"We drank from silver cups."

her fidelity to Batiste:

"A misunderstood man."

her hatred for Castro:

"Fidel fucks dogs."

While tacking posters of Che Guevara all over our under-
graduate walls.

Despite Dr. Weintraub's best efforts I was not prepared for
college life. There were physical challenges that caught me by surprise. I found, for instance, that for all my hard use in watermelon
and tobacco fields I was not in good physical shape. The rolling hills
around Tallahassee that city slickers negotiated with ease, daily tested
my own endurance. Just getting back and forth between classes left
me winded. I did handle the heat better than most, a not inconsiderable advantage, I suppose. And since I was not accustomed to air-
conditioning, I did not experience its absence as keenly as did the
vast majority of students attending.

I was used to misery.

With the benefit of Dr. Weintraub's summer instruction I was
able to navigate from my dorm on The Green to lecture halls or to
the library. I could find the post office and my chemistry lab and,
off campus, got to know the stores and hangouts convenient along
Copeland Street and Tennessee and Magnolia Way.

The physical terrain was new to me but the cultural topography
was in some ways unexpectedly familiar. It didn't take long to realize
that white students at FSU regarded black people in ways not much
different than Caucasians in my home county. I should not have
been surprised. Florida State's campus body was, still is, comprised
overwhelmingly of students from the South, usually the Deep South.
In '64, these were young people who had always been in positions
socially superior to African Americans. The inevitable stereotypes and
attitudes arising from that segregated milieu were only rarely challenged at the university.

This isn't to say that life as a Negro at Florida State was like life
in Colored Town. It was not. I had many more comforts at FSU than
I ever enjoyed in my childhood home. I ate better. I was healthier. I
was safe from the injuries of overt bigotry, so long as I didn't stray off
campus. And though the academic life at State did not extend much

past college algebra and the poetry of John Crowe Ransom, it was still a life infinitely richer than any I had imagined. Dr. Weintraub was crucial in that development, a mentor as unfailing and wise as Miss Chandler.

Still, now and again, and always at the unexpected moment, I would be challenged with some question or remark that made me feel as though I were back in the heart of Colored Town. Nearly every co-ed in my dormitory, to give the recurring example, found a way to ask how I had gotten admitted into Florida State. Was there a special provision? What string had been pulled? Those students with whom I studied, other music majors, were generally astounded to find I had a serious interest in classical composition. There really aren't any successful Negroes in that field, I would be reminded.

Though I lived on a college campus, I was expected to keep my place. And I honestly didn't mind. I didn't mind eating a little crow, now and then, because it was so much better than eating shit day in and out. I knew how to be a black spot on a white wall, *ende problema*. So it was almost alarming to stumble on a clutch of students who did not care about color at all.

All these women cared about was that I was tall.

I should mention that there were few women of any race over six feet in height on FSU's rolling campus. The only other females close to my size, of which there were three, and only one black, were on the basketball team. I met one of those "ladies", as they called themselves, a little over a month into the semester. I had spread out on the marble bench that was recessed just inside the Music Building. It was a brutally hot September day. Ours was the only centrally-cooled building on campus, recall, and so students who had nothing to do with the School of Music came panting to KMU, clustering around that long marble bench like bees around a honey jar, spreading out homework or term papers that clinged wet to forearms damp with perspiration. Prying apart the leaves of an assigned *Republic*, or Tolstoy, or chemistry text. Or simply pressing sweat-drenched backs to a cool wall.

Anything to beat the heat.

I had cornered part of the marble, spreading out my books and puzzling over some variations of folk music that I'd come across in an anthropology class. The professor had recorded what he described as some "primitive" instrumentals. Somewhere in Brazil, I think it was. Those erotic and persistent rhythms reminded me of the music I used to hear in tent meetings and revivals, and I was taking some time in KMU's Arctic cool to construct a melange of those themes, those shared characteristics. Reclined like Scheherazade on a stone couch.

Making music in my head.

"Do I know you?"

I looked up and saw the Nubian of my dreams, that negress I'd seen on the stairway a summer earlier on my first trip to Talla-hassee. She who was unafraid of uniformed men. A backpack, not ubiquitous in those days, was now slung casually over those broad shoulders. She had traded her short skirt and classy blouse for warm-up slacks and a sweatshirt tied off to offer a peek at a washboard belly beneath. It was daring, those campus days, to show any skin at all. That cream and coffee skin.

"From the stairwell?"

I was still in the Southerner's habit of ending statements in the interrogative even when intending the declarative.

She slid the L.L. Bean off her shoulders.

"There are lots of stairwells."

"Right here. In fact—" I indicated with my hand-sharpened pencil, "right over there? I'd come for an audition. Last summer?"

"So you're a freshman."

"Uh huh."

"Got a name?"

"Sorry. It's Priscilla. Or just Cilla? Cilla Handsom."

She stuck out a hand. A firm grip, not hurried. "Ever play basketball?"

"I play music," I said as if that activity excluded the other.

She laughed. "It's just intramurals, no big thing. We meet each Saturday morning, around nine, at the gym. That's Montgom-ery Gym. You know it?"

"I'm at Landis," I nodded.

"Can't get lost from there, can you? So come on over. It'll be a lot of fun. And I'm guessing you'll find it won't hurt your music."

She turned away.

"Got a name?" I said to her back and she tossed that long, naturally unbrindled hair.

"I'm Kate. Kate Dobson."

"You're not from the South."

She winked. "You got that right. See you Saturday. If you're game."

I never was worth a damn at basketball. But the physical release of sporting activity accomplished in the company of strong, vulgar, and exuberant women was liberating. We'd play for an hour or so, pounding (or, in Kate's case, gliding) up and down the hardwood court to shouts of encouragement from roommates, some of them boys, who came to cheer on the game.

The intramurals at Florida State were optional, of course, completely self-elected. At first I thought that school and music and work would not leave time for Saturday play. But almost immediately I began to look forward to that weekend combat. I was amazed that no one had much to say about my lips or obvious injuries. No one averted their eyes. No one made comments. And everyone seemed to genuinely respect my chosen course of study.

"One of the hardest majors on campus," Kate said proudly, herself a junior interested in vocal studies.

I met a fair number of students majoring in music those first few weeks, most of them as scatterbrained as any teenager, a few, as I was, scared to death and self-absorbed. We were always squirreled away with our instruments, practicing. At any hour freshmen could be found in soundproofed booths, leaning over their piano or oboe or cocked over a violin. But the hard courses for me were the ones that didn't have anything to do with music. I spent hours sweating out biology exams and quizzes in college algebra. Literature just took time; I never got the knack of reading quickly. And then more hours were consumed in a library where Dewey Decimal was the sole search engine.

But the hours I spent performing or researching papers or studying, even when accomplished in groups or in the presence of familiars, was a lonely endeavor. I never got over feeling that I had to prove myself, that my inclusion with other students at the university was not the result of a handout or special consideration. Even in the dormitory I felt the odd woman out.

On the basketball court, however, where I was truly a neophyte, I felt immediately at home. The coeds who slapped me on the back or butt each Saturday seemed cut of an entirely different cloth. They were rowdy. They were sassy. They were smart. My classmates came from Music, or Education, or Pre-med. But my buddies shot hoops.

We showered together afterward. I avoided that exhibition initially, making one excuse or another. One Saturday I was set to sneak away again when I felt an arm drape across my shoulder like a cloak.

"Cilla. What say we get some steam?"

It was Kate. My first impulse was to decline her invitation.

"Naw, I need to get back."

"Are you embarrassed? Is that it?"

The question, directly given, could not be dodged. Her arm remained firmly along my shoulder.

"It's not what you think," I said. "It's worse."

She squeezed me. Just a little squeeze. "Think I can't see? 'cause what I can see looks bad enough."

"I don't know—"

"Cilla, no one is going to make fun of you. Just about everybody here's got something she wishes she could hide."

"Not you," I protested, and she grinned lasciviously.

"I know. Ain't I a bitch?"

The womens' locker room featured spare metal cabinets, long wooden benches and a tiled floor slick as snot on a doorknob. We'd strip in a line before the lockers, tossing pants and only the occasional bra inside, padding then to the showers, our flanks squeezed tight as virgins. Then to reach overhead, turn the chromed faucets on full and hot! To luxuriate in a virtual bath of steam. What a team was there, a gaggle of young, healthy women, pores bursting with perspiration, our voices a constant contralto of teases and curses and other invitation.

The first time I showered in the company of my teammates I contrived to face the tiled walls. But the horseplay around shower stalls and lockers goes a long way to alleviate self-consciousness or absorption. A towel snapped smartly on your rear brings attention vividly to present circumstance. A challenge from a teammate can be terrific diversion from self-pity. It would be naive, certainly, to say that the scars on my lips or between my legs were no different in kind than the acned complexion or sagging boobs variously afflicting my teammates. The signs of my torture would not rinse away in the rowdy communion of that Spartan shower.

But they were largely ignored.

Certainly I saw no one inspecting my genitalia. Any man standing at a urinal knows how to ignore the tool of the fellow pissing next door. Women are no less delicate. It was a tremendous relief to discover that I could stand naked and not be regarded as an object of either disgust or derision. My teammates wanted me under the bucket to break up the fast break. They wanted me to haul down rebounds. They wished to hell I could sink a shot from the free-throw line. They were not interested in a view of my pudenda, and the scars on my lips, open to regard, drew no more comment than those on my closed and private parts.

"Cilla," Kate shouted one day above the pound of stinging needles.

"What?"

"We're going to The Sweet Shop. Wanta come?"

The Sweet Shop was a short walk away, a hangout contrarily named, famous for burgers and beers and other hydration. I could not afford a sandwich or Budweiser, but iced tea was only twenty-five cents and you could get all the refills you wanted. So first came the Saturday games. Then you hit the showers. Then the well-shaded patio at Sweet's.

I was probably a month into that routine before Kate suggested I drop by her room.

"I've got some old forty-fives and a Beatles LP. Be interesting to hear what you think of it."

She had a small garage apartment off Tennessee Street.

The stairs shook on the way up, triggering unsought memories of Joe Billy's roost.

"Here we are."

It wasn't much larger than my dormer, but it was private. An eclectic array of posters and prints. Still-life by Vermeer. Bob Dylan, androgynous with cigarette. Leontyne Price. Magnificent. A bead curtain guarded the loo. A two-burner stove and sink crowded an alcove beyond. One whole side of the place was taken up with sagging bookshelves before which stretched a luxurious futon bed. Kate closed the door with the heel of her foot.

"How you like my castle?"

She dropped her ever-present pack and strolled over to a Dual turntable stacked with long playing records. Suddenly I did not know where I was supposed to look.

"Cilla, it's all right."

I cast around for something to inspect.

"It's all right." She plopped down on her Oriental mattress and pulled her sweatshirt over her head. Her hair was just as I remembered from the first time I saw her on the staircase only damper, now, not yet dried from our recent shower.

"Why don't you get comfortable?"

She patted the bed with her hand.

"We can just spin some records, if you like."

My mouth felt like clay. "...Is that Marvin Gaye?"

"Mmm. Smooth, isn't he?"

"Yes," I said and came to her bed and that is how that started.

First time I had sex was with Joe Billy, I'm sure I mentioned. And if I'd never shared a bed with anybody else that's the only kind of sex I guess I'd have ever known.

Kate was the second love in my life, probably the most selfish, probably the one cared least about me. But in the course of an afternoon in a dorm room in Tallahassee I found pleasure with that girl in a way I never would have imagined possible.

It didn't last, of course. Kate was the woman of my dreams, but I was only the diversion of a moment. She was not as faithful as Joe Billy, but she was a lot better in bed.

And I was a lot better in bed with her.

My society that first semester was literally intra-mural and proved to be great therapy. Basketball provided exercise and release, and, yes, a distraction from concerns related to Joe Billy and his coming trial. In the midst of arduous sport I could forget about truth or treachery. And standing by Kate in a pounding shower I could ignore the fact that though my ordeal appeared to be ending, Joe Billy's had just begun. But not even the distractions of basketball and music and sex could blunt the impact of the subpoena I received at Dr. Weintraub's hand.

My resident advisor delivered the message summoning me to Dr. Weintraub's office in Longmire Hall. A harried man in a jacket spouted a terse rehearsal of instructions given too abruptly to be comprehended, before slapping the subpoena into my hand.

"What's this?"

I turned to Dr. Weintraub after the functionary's brisk departure.

"It's a subpoena, Cilla," she pushed her hair off her forehead. "A summons to court."

"Oh." I stared at the legal envelope in my hand.

"Do you have any idea what this is about?" she inquired.

It didn't take much of a guess.

"Friend of mine killed a man," I truncated the truth. "He used to be my boyfriend."

"Oh, Lord."

I opened the envelope without comment, scanned the summons. "Looks like I got to be at the Lafayette County Courthouse on the eighth of October. Says be there by nine o'clock."

"And so you will," Dr. Weintraub swept her straw hair off her face. "But not without a lawyer."

Irving Statler was a professor emeritus from FSU's Law School, a close friend of Dr. Weintraub's. He took me under his wing *pro bono* without making me feel at all as though I was charged to charity. We met in offices not far from the Music School. Lots of plaques on the wall. Lots of panelling.

"You are being called as a friendly witness for the defense, Cilla, a sympathy witness. I called Mr. Shaw yesterday to see if he'd like to interview you before the trial, but he assures me this isn't necessary. I think you can expect some discussion of your ordeal on the river. Almost certainly there will be questions regarding your intimate relations with the accused. Even if you are embarrassed, it's important to answer simply, forthrightly.

"The State's attorney doesn't even have you on his list. When I called he said the statement provided by the County Sheriff was sufficient for the record."

"Sheriff Jackson, yes, sir," I nodded. "He got a statement from 'bout everybody in Colored Town."

"Don't volunteer information, Cilla," he corrected me gently.

"No, sir."

"Remember our preparation this afternoon: Do not speak except in reply to a direct question. Only answer the specific question you are asked. If you don't know something, just say you don't."

I hesitated.

"Is there anything else you need to tell me, Cilla? Anything at all? Because if there is, now's the time to do it."

I swallowed. "I don't know anything. I wasn't there."

"Right," he said after a moment. "Well, then. I'll see you in court."

I did not sleep the days before the trial. I did not eat. I vacillated back and forth, one moment convinced that there really was nothing to be gained, for Joe Billy or for me, by claiming responsibility for Monk Folsom's homicide, then telling myself with the next pang of conscience that I was a coward, that I should step forward regardless of cost and simply tell the truth. Yes, I shot the man, but I was threatened, wasn't I? I was molested.

I was acting in self defense!

Dr. Weintraub would believe me, wouldn't she? The sheriff

believed me. But would a jury believe me? Would a white jury in Lafayette County believe a mauled nigger girl, and even if they did, would they exonerate Joe Billy King?

Catch a nigger by the toe. If he hollers, let him go...

But would they let their nigger go?

At the time of my courthouse experience I had experienced a month of college life. One month of clean sheets and hot showers. A month of good food and air conditioning and a host of unexpected pleasures. Sports. Sex. I was filled with music, a hunger for knowledge that was daily rewarded. And never, not once, did I have to haul water.

Was I really willing to give that up?

Was I even willing to risk it?

Professor Statler drove me to Laureate on the day of my participation in Joe Billy's trial. Dr. Weintraub wanted to come, too, but I steadfastly refused. I did not want my newest mentor present if the moment came forcing me to choose between the truth and a lie. It would be hard enough with Joe Billy there.

The lawn outside the courthouse looked like a churchyard after a tent revival. Looked like half the town of Laureate had come to see Joe Billy in the dock, a fair number from Colored Town, too. Not to mention the reporters, the cameras. It took a while, in that morass, to locate my high school teacher.

"Miss Chandler," I called out weakly.

"Come here college girl!"

To my absolute amazement Miss Chandler practically ran to meet me, bowling through that pack of hangers-on, wrapping me up in generous arms to that full bosom.

"My, don't you look somethin?"

I tried to meet her eye, uncertain how to behave.

"Now you stand tall," there was the sudden voice of authority. "That's better. We're going to walk in that courthouse and show these people some class."

That was the hardest moment for me, to climb those terraced steps exposed, to enter the court beside its sweeping stairway in full view of the courtiers and the curious and then following the balustrade to ascend on my attorney's arm like a debutante, returning home in a heroine's guise to betray my lover and friend.

So this was class, I thought. A bitter irony, there. Bitter as bad tea.

Chapter twenty-two

I was one of four witnesses scheduled to testify that morning. J.T. Hewitt was familiar to me, tall and dark and hostile in the company of the family's expensively dressed attorney. He had donned one of those string ties, like a country-western star, but had replaced his signature belt with a cowhide substitute. I had no idea what use the court would have for J.T.'s witness.

"King Boy Tried for Murder"—*The Clarion*

"Don't worry about his testimony," Professor Statler murmured. "Just stick to yours."

There waited another witness in the room, a woman with whom I was not familiar. She was dressed like somebody going to Mardi Gras, all bright colors and cleavage. Lots of trinkets, cheap jewelry. A skirt way too short for a woman pushing fifty. I had never met Joe Billy's mother, but Miss Chandler apparently had made some contact.

"Mrs. King? Fanny King?"

"I know you?"

"I'm Joe Billy's teacher. I sent you a letter, few weeks back?"

"Letter? Oh, yes, I remember."

She replied to Miss Chandler, but was staring at me.

"Whatchu lookin' girl?"

"Ma'am?"

"This is Priscilla Handsom, Mrs. King. Cilla."

"So thass you," Fanny clutched her purse. "What they wont you for?"

"I don't know," I was happy to give an honest reply.

"Mr. Shaw says Cilla can help Joe Billy," Miss Chandler amended.

Fanny produced a cylinder of lipstick. "Seem like that girl done help Joe Billy enough."

My heart froze. Did Fanny know? How much had Joe Billy told her?!

"Worst thang ever happen to my boy." She crossed her legs, that skirt hiking up. "Worse thing ever happen to Joe Billy by *far* is that girl over there!"

J.T. Hewitt snorted like a horse.

"Whatchu laughin'?" Fanny turned on Cody's brother. "Whatchu laughin' at me, hah?! I know who you are, you think I don' know? Think you gonna set there and laugh at *me*?!"

I saw the Hewitts' attorney press his hand onto J.T.'s froghopping knee.

"Everyone's a little nervous," the lawyer intervened smoothly. "No offense intended, I'm sure."

"Fine for you to say," Fanny dabbed lipstick off with a napkin. "Fine for you!"

That pretty much killed conversation. There were four witnesses in the room, the attorney, Miss Chandler, three magazines, a pitcher of water and a stack of Dixie cups. It was an hour before the first witness, a deputy, was called. A medical examiner was called next. Then J.T. was taken out with his lawyer.

"Don't think we'll make the noon cut," Miss Chandler remarked, but within minutes the bailiff was returned.

"Priscilla Handsom."

For some reason I had expected Fanny to be called before me.

"Cilla. It's time."

My legs were numb. Professor Statler helped me up.

"Follow me," a bailiff ordered.

Miss Chandler followed as I leaned on my attorney's arm. The corridor now seemed to stretch interminably. I felt as though I were walking and walking and going nowhere. But doors passed by. A water cooler. Then a hard turn and there, dead ahead, was the courtroom. A deputy nodding to the bailiff's unspoken command opened those heavy double doors. Beams of light caught motes of dust spinning capriciously before tall, tall windows.

Heads turned as I entered. A buzz of comment, like bees in a barn. Judge Blackmond dropped his gavel.

"Order in the court."

I took in the room through the filter of a hundred fears, anxieties and distractions. Rows and rows of benches ranged on either side, like pews in a church. So many faces, some friendly, some hostile, nearly all familiar. I saw Garner Hewitt, the mark of Cain below that eye. Cody perched alongside, a countenance without blemish. Mr. Raymond was there too, all creased and cuffed, but up in the balcony where Negroes still segregated themselves.

"Think about your friends." Professor Statler gave my hand a squeeze and I walked the last yards to the stand on my own.

On my right hand was a long table accommodating a trio of prosecutors. In Florida, I should mention, we don't like to call our inquisitors prosecutors, which is what they are, so we call them the State's attorneys; I felt no threat from that quarter. What gave me dread lay at the hardwood table on my left hand. Joe Billy sat to my left, sandwiched between Thurman and some other attorney.

Joe Billy had been moved back from Live Oak to the local jail for the duration of his trial. I would not be expected to visit my old boyfriend under lock and key, but I certainly could not ignore him in court. Certainly I could not appear ashamed of my old friend, or fearful of him. I owed him a nod, at least.

I paused on my way to the stand, and turned. Joe Billy was dressed as I had never seen him, in a white shirt, button down, a narrow black tie, badly knotted, a gray suit. The sleeves were too short; they pulled up past his wrists to display hands clasped together as in prayer, or in handcuffs. Those large eyes, like a deer's, narrowly placed, sought mine. He looked pale. He looked scared to death. Still, he offered a wan smile.

I was ashamed that I could not meet his eyes squarely with my own.

"Over here, please."

I turned to see a white man holding a black Bible.

"Raise your right hand."

It seemed to go up on its own.

"Do you swear to tell the truth…"

It was too fast. It was as though I were present, but a second or two behind.

"…so help you God?""

Just like that. So fast.

"Miss Handsom?"

I turned to the judge's voice.

"Yes, sir?"

"You may take the stand."

I didn't even know I had responded to the oath.

I climbed to that place where you are called to witness. A hard-backed chair waited. I lowered myself onto the seat's firm cushion, trying to find someplace to look that wasn't the floor.

The State's attorney strolled up.

"Miss Handsom, you know the accused?"

"Yes, sir."

Once things got rolling I was almost able to relax. It was simple, really. A piece of cake. I had been agonizing over how I would answer questions directed at my culpability for Monk's killing, but nothing like those kind of question were asked by the State's attorney. The Inquisitor seemed to take my innocence for granted. He was most interested in Fort McKoon, doing exactly what Professor Statler had predicted he would do, reminding the jury of the horror of that afternoon. Feigning sympathy for me while actually establishing for Joe Billy a motive sufficient to murder.

"And did you at any time hear Joe Billy express anger over what happened that day? Was he angry that he had been castrated?"

"More like depressed," I said.

"Then you never heard the accused express anger over what happened to him?"

"Well, certainly, but—"

"It's a yes or no question, Miss Handsom."

"Yes, sir."

"So the accused did express anger?"

"Yes, sir."

"Did he express pain or anguish or frustration over the loss of his manhood?"

Loss of his manhood? How quaint.

"Miss Handsom?"

"He did expreth...express pain and anguish, yes."

"Thank you, that will be all."

The State's attorney turned to Thurman Shaw, then, and I remembered what Collard Jackson told me in his office.

Keep it simple.

"Miss Handsom."

As if roused from dosing I looked up to see Thurman before me.

"You need some water? A little time?"

"No, thank you."

"All right, then, let's start by calling the court's attention to State's evidence, Item Number 43 Baker."

I hadn't the faintest notion what he was talking about, but I didn't like the puzzled expressions on the faces stacking the State's bench.

"This is an application to Florida State University, Your Honor. This application was submitted by and notarized for Priscilla Handsom. Right at the top you'll see that Miss Handsom's birthday is given. That would be October the 31st, 1945. Born on Halloween, if memory serves."

The prosecutor opened his hands wide.

"Your Honor, these facts are neither in dispute, nor relevant."

"Will speak to motive, Your Honor."

A buzz in the court got rapped short.

"Proceed."

"Miss Handsom."

There was no comity in Thurman's voice.

"Yes? Yes, sir."

"When did you first meet the defendant?"

"At the train station. Summer before our junior year in high school."

"You became involved sexually?"

I swallowed. "Yes."

"A fling? Or was this a sustained romance?"

"Sustained, I suppose."

"You 'suppose'? Wasn't Joe Billy very close to you? Intimate with you?"

"Well, yes."

"Did you love him? Miss Handsom, did you love Joe Billy?"

"I'm...not sure what you mean by love."

A titter arose from the gallery and I knew I'd mis-stepped.

"He was my first," I came back firmly. "We were together a lot."

"Ever think of marriage?"

"We never talked about it."

"Why not? Would it have interfered with your plans? College, for instance?"

The judge leaned from his high place.

"You are leading the witness, counsellor."

"Apologies, Your Honor."

Mr. Shaw paused before returning to me.

"Did Joe Billy's mother support your relationship with her son, Miss Handsom?"

"I never met her 'til today," I answered, glad to have firmer ground.

"In a statement written for this court, Mrs. King insists that her son is incapable of killing anyone. Do you agree with that?"

"Unless it was self defense," I qualified. "I mean, no, Joe Billy wouldn't just go out and kill somebody. But he was threatened. Monk threatened him with a razor."

"Objection."

"Sustained."

Thurman turned toward the jury casually, perfectly at ease.

"Miss Handsom."

"Yes, sir?"

"Did you kill Monk Folsom?"

That's how the question came, abrupt, unexpected, like a hook to the jaw when coming out of a clinch.

The gallery gasped in collection.

Joe Billy about came out of his chair.

"Sir?" I stalled, which I had not intended to do.

"It's pretty simple, Miss Handsom. Did you shoot Monk Folsom on the night of your graduation, below the water tower in Town Park?"

"OBJECTION!"

"Overruled. Witness will answer the question."

I looked at Joe Billy. I wanted to believe he was begging me with his eyes to lie, imploring me to stay the crooked course we had set.

"I've never killed anybody," I declared with a conviction I did not feel. "Not Monk Folsom. Not anybody."

Thurman consulted his pad of paper.

"Did you see Joe Billy King the night of your graduation party?"

Keep it simple.

"No," I answered.

"Isn't it true that you did see Joe Billy? That in fact you sat on the back porch and drank iced tea with him?"

"No, it is not."

"Your Honor!"

This time the State was on its feet.

"I'm challenging the witness's alibi, Your Honor," Thurman responded, without waiting for a framed objection. "I surely have the right to do that."

"Within reason," Blackmond allowed, and Thurman set about doing whatever he could to discredit the story that I had rehearsed for months.

I could tell that Joe Billy was stunned at his lawyer's tactics. Clearly, Thurman had not cleared this defense with his client. You could see Thurman's second chair anchoring JayBee to his hard seat as Thurman did his best to make me a likely perpetrator of Monk Folsom's homicide. I expected most of his questions. I was prepared to keep it simple. To stick it out.

How long was I at the graduation party?

Had I danced?

With whom?

Did I pass the tower on the way home?

Those questions were not hard to field. I mostly just told the truth—so far as I was able. But there was one question I did not anticipate and it almost stumped me:

"Miss Handsom, in your statement to Sheriff Jackson you maintain that you got home fairly early. Very early for a young lady celebrating her graduation, I would say. A little after ten-thirty?"

I told him that was correct.

"Do you own a watch?"

I felt a sudden need to do something with my hands.

"No."

"Any clocks at your home? Timepieces of any sort?"

"No, sir."

"Then how can you know when you got home, Miss Handsom? Where did you get the time?"

Where could I get the time? Where?!

"Miss Handsom?"

"The radio!" I blurted it out.

"Radio?" Thurman looked as though he'd got hold of a sour peach.

"Mr. Raymond and the men were listening to his radio," I nodded happily, "and when I walked by I heard it was thirty minutes after the hour and I knew it wasn't nearly eleven when I left Betty's so I know I got home just a little after ten-thirty."

Thurman took a pencil to the yellow pages of his outsized pad. He hadn't counted on Raymond's radio, a source impossible to either validate or refute.

Judge Blackmond leaned forward in that interval.

"Are we ever going to get back to the birthday, counselor?"

"Yes, your Honor. But I will need to cross examine Mrs. Fanny Meadows King for that purpose."

"No objection, Your Honor," the prosecutor seemed content to let Thurman wander. "She's next on the list."

"Fine." Judge Blackmond turned to me. "Miss Handsom, you may step down."

The moment I had rehearsed and dreaded had come and gone with a banality I could never have imagined. I stepped off the witness stand relieved to have survived Thurman Shaw's unexpected attack. I expected Joe Billy to be relieved, too, but when I looked over he would not look at me. No smile, no indication of closure or encouragement. Instead, as I passed, Joe Billy cradled his head in his hands, his gaze fixed, apparently, on the laces of his shoes.

But I had done well, hadn't I?

I had done what he told me to do.

Fanny King entered the courtroom as I groped toward the pew where waited my attorney and Miss Chandler. I brushed past Joe Billy's mama on the way to my seat, she swaying down that long aisle, a heavy waft of *ode de cologne* following, hips rolling with invitation. Smiling broadly, like a singer at a nightclub to a gathered lounge of favorites, or some sidewalk harridan.

Passed right by me as though we'd never met.

"You did fine," Miss Chandler whispered as Fanny raised her right hand. "Just fine."

The prosecutor treated Joe Billy's mother with sympathy bordering on the obsequious, managing in that time to point out that her son was a dropout from his Tallahassee school, never steadily employed, and dependent for income on the sale of guitars which even Fanny allowed were "pretty kinky."

Having used the mother to discredit her son, the State stood aside for Thurman's cross.

"Are you close to your son, Mrs. King?"

"Oh, yes, very close."

"How many times have you visited your son since his incarceration for this homicide?"

"Well, I live in Tallahassee, it's hard to get down."

"Hard to get down, I see. Then how many letters have you written your son? Or is the Post Office similarly impaired?"

"Objection."

"Overruled. Witness will respond."

Thurman looked up from his legal pad. "How many letters, Miss King?"

"You cain't tell how much a mama love her children by no letters."

"You can't?"

"I love Joe Billy. He's my child. My only child."

"Your only child?"

"God only give me one."

"But that's not true. Is it, Mrs. King?"

The court stilled with Thurman's calm contradiction.

"Whatchu mean?" Fanny's smile wavered. "I don' know whatchu sayin'."

Then Thurman paused, and it was like a thunderstorm, how it goes calm. Right before it breaks.

"Mrs. King, when was your son born?"

"You know when. Seventh of November. 1945."

"Born according to your affidavit in Valdosta, Georgia, is that right?"

She squirmed in her seat. "That's what I tole' the man in Tallahassee."

"Sworn to that effect, yes. But there is no birth certificate, is there, Mrs. King?"

"Not ever'body born in a hospital. I'm a midwife. Was, anyhow. I should know."

"Yes, you should."

Thurman made no pretense, now, of consulting his yellow pad.

"Mrs. King, where were you employed from, say, June of 1944 through October of the following year?"

"I was at Dowling Park, ever'body know that."

"You were a midwife."

"I worked in the orphanage."

"And you also were a midwife, were you not? Delivered according to Park records some eleven children during your tenure there?"

"Eleven sound about right."

"You delivered Priscilla Handsom, didn't you? Her mother, Corrie Jean, had been in your care nearly six months."

"She was simple. She couldn't have no baby by herself."

"Lucky to have you, then, wasn't she? Eleven children brought into this world? Heavens to Betsy. And all healthy?"

"Ever' one."

"But you and your husband had at the time no children of your own, isn't that correct, Miss King?"

"I was pregnant with Joe Billy. Our first pregnancy. Not that we hadn't tried. Oh, Lordie!"

That got a chuckle from the gallery. Fanny primped and smiled. Hamming it up.

"My husband wanted a boy," she was pleased to amplify. "'Course we would have taken a girl. Anything, really. Anything healthy. We were just excited to finally be pregnant."

"Is it accurate to say that you would have hated to lose that child? That after trying so hard, for so long, having a husband desperate for a son, that there was a lot riding on this pregnancy? Would that be accurate, Mrs. King?"

Joe Billy turned in his seat. Our eyes met through a lane plied between rows of skulls.

"I'll withdraw that question for the time being. Your Honor, I would draw the court's attention at this time to Defense Exhibit 11B, previously introduced, a record of treatment for the witness signed by a Dr. Leon Purcell on October the 19th, 1945 at Dowling Park. Note especially the prescription of antibiotics. It had to do with a miscarriage, didn't it, Mrs. King?"

"Don' know whatchu talking about."

A murmur rippled through the court like wind over a pond.

"Mrs. King, is it not the case that less than two weeks before your last paying day at Dowling Park you lost your baby? That you lost, in fact, a little boy? Isn't that true?"

Fanny just smiled to the jury, as if the question had been addressed to someone else. As if she were not involved in this discussion at all.

Judge Blackmond leaned over the stand.

"Mrs. King?"

"Why, yes, yo' Honor."

"If you refuse to answer questions put to you by counsel I will find you in contempt and will put you in jail."

"Jail?!"

Fanny seemed astounded at the prospect.

"I'm glad to have your attention. Now allow me to rephrase counsel's question. Did you miscarry at any time during the fall or winter of 1945? Did you lose your child?"

"It watn't my fault I lost him. I was holdin' two jobs. Plus taking care of a retard!"

"A retard, yes," Thurman mused. "That must have galled."

Fanny extended a trembling hand toward Joe Billy, as if she could touch him from her hard chair.

"I wasn't looking for no baby. But when I got him I raised him. Raised him good as anything."

"But where did you *get* him, Mrs. King?"

Thurman swatted the stand with his legal pad.

"Who is Joe Billy's mother? Where was he born? *When?*"

"I ain't gonna say nuthin' more. I don' have to!"

"Yes, you do, Mrs. King."

This from the judge.

"You are under oath. You will answer truthfully before this court or find a cell with the County."

Thurman tucked his pad beneath his arm. "You have claimed a mother's love, Mrs. King. Well, now show it. Joe Billy's life may depend on it."

Fanny clutched her cheap purse, her lipstick wet and smearing.

"It was Clifford's idea, all of it. I weren't lookin' for no kind of baby in the first place. And then I liked to of died with ours, but Clifford, he kept after me, 'The Lord takes away, Fanny. But He gives, too.'"

The gathered court seemed to inhale in unison, heads turning to find me, back to Joe Billy. I felt sick to my stomach. Miss Chandler took my hand.

"The Lord gives," Thurman acknowledged gentle as a lamb. "Yes, he does. And sometimes, when we want something badly enough, we help Him along."

"Objection!"

"Withdrawn."

Thurman returned to Fanny, but smiling, now, approaching her like a preacher eager to absolve every sin, remove every stain.

"Joe Billy was not born in Valdosta, was he, Fanny?"

"No."

"He was born in Dowling Park, wasn't he?"

She nodded dropping her eyes like stones to her lap.

"And his birthday—it wasn't in November, was it?"

"No."

"Isn't it true that Joe Billy was born in October of 1945?"

"Yes."

"When in October? We're almost there, Fanny. Now, tell this court the day in October when the defendant was born."

Her eyes dragged up to find mine.

"It was Halloween," she admitted finally. "Last day of October, the thirty-first. Joe Billy came around six in the morning—right after his sister."

Chapter twenty-three

"Trial Brings Shocking
Revelation"—*The Clarion*

I left the courtroom unable to feel the floor beneath my feet. Miss Chandler guided me past the salacious gaze of onlookers as my attorney answered the puerile inquiry of reporters. I was now the Hester of my community. Worse than Hester—incest registered with far more repugnance among my people than adultery. And thanks to Mr. Shaw, I was doubly lettered, people on both sides of the tracks now pondering whether a nigger sorry enough to sleep with her brother might also have killed Monk Folsom.

"You were ambushed," Professor Statler was furious. "I should have known there was something behind that subpoena. I should have seen it."

Miss Chandler was terribly upset, made no attempt to disguise that. Kept shaking that hound's head, back and forth.

"How could Thurman imagine you a killer? And what made him tie you to Joe Billy? What on earth?!"

Professor Statler said not to worry on that count, that once things settled everyone would know that the only reason Mr. Shaw pointed his finger at me was to keep Joe Billy out of jail.

"It's the attorney's job to cast doubt." Professor Statler spoke with conviction. "But in the end the gun was in Joe Billy's hand."

It was in my hand first, I could have said.

But I didn't.

The jury began its deliberation Thursday afternoon. Thurman Shaw did everything he could for his client, closing before the jury with the admonition—"You cannot condemn this boy for trying to protect his sister!" After barely an hour's sequestering, the jury's foreman sent the judge a note asking for instruction in the nuances differentiating manslaughter from first-degree murder. Twenty-three hours later a verdict was announced in court. My brother was found not guilty of murder with premeditation, nor with malice. He was convicted instead of simple manslaughter. The conviction for manslaughter protected me from further investigation. Provided, of course, that I stifled my mouth and any pang of conscience. Joe Billy could expect to pay for my freedom with five years in the penitentiary at Raiford. Five years, that is, with good behavior.

"...and still a young man," the sheriff had said and it looked as though, once again, Collard had called it right.

I had planned to stay the weekend with Corrie Jean and Grandma, but elected to leave early. Even Grandma was suspicious that I was somehow involved in Monk's killing. "I don' remember you comin' home that night," she said, and I did not reply.

What could be simpler than silence?

I knew that rumors would grow the longer I stayed and I knew that if I lingered the shame attached to me would associate with my small family. There were too many rumors now unleashed in Colored Town which I could not allay or answer. Too many hostile or averted stares. Miss Chandler agreed to board Dr. Statler overnight so that I would have a ride back to Tallahassee.

The next morning I rose early, very early, so that I might haul water unobserved. Then I made some eggs, took care of Mama, and walked over to Miss Chandler's house. Professor Statler was waiting. I embraced Miss Chandler briefly,

"Write me," she said.

I promised I would and then stooped to enter the Cadillac. Once inside it was as though a sudden bile of fury and disappointment, rage and guilt, boiled up inside and I vomited a stream of vile invective.

"FUCK THESE PEOPLE!"

I pounded the dash of my counselor's car.

"FUCK THESE PEOPLE!"

He waited patiently for me to finish.

"Is there anything else?" he said finally. "Before we leave?"

We crossed the tracks separating Colored Town from Laureate and I did not look back. But I couldn't leave without seeing Joe Billy. The desk sergeant worked hard to pretend he didn't see me as I pushed through the single door opening to the street.

"May I see him?"

Another deputy lazily waved a scrap of paper.

"Sheriff said let her in if she came."

The desk sergeant returned to his *Field & Stream*. "You take her, then."

One more trip to the county cells. One more passage through that forbidding portal dull and gray, that pad of keys, the buzzer raucous and abrupt. I walked down, down to the seventh circle. My guide abandoned me half way.

"You'll find him."

The sheriff had given Joe Billy the suite cell. The commode had a lid. There was a sink with faucets in repair. He even had a radio, a portable. Some deejay was going on about a British invasion. Joe Billy switched off that transistorized miracle as soon as he saw me.

"Joe Billy…"

I couldn't think of anything to say.

He stood up and wrapped his hands around the bars. "It's awright."

I shook my head. "No. It's not."

"Cilla, it was right before. It's more than right now. Look at me, girl—you my sister. How could I let my sister wind up in a place like this?"

"You shouldn't be here, either."

"You sound like Thurman."

"Thurman's right."

"Right don't always win out, Cilla. If life was right colored folks wouldn' get cut by Klansmen. Wouldn' get set on with dogs or hoses. Wouldn't get they churches burned to ash, or hung on dogwood trees."

You know how light changes? I mean the light of the sun, how it changes from nadir to zenith through the seasons, the shadows getting longer and longer from summer when it's bright all the time to winter when it's dark before you can haul your water? It must happen slowly, that gradation into the diurnal.

But the thing is, when you notice it, you notice it all at once. That's the way it was with Joe Billy. He had changed, I could see that clearly. I saw it all at once.

"Did Thurman tell you before the trial?"

"Tell me what?"

"You know what."

"That you was my sister? Naw. He din' tell me nuthin."

I clutched myself. "I feel dirty."

"Don't," he reached out a hand to comfort me. He, in jail, awaiting a term of damnation, comforting me. "You din' know. Ain't no sin less you know."

"I know you didn't kill Monk Folsom," I replied. "But I'm letting you take the blame, aren't I? Lied in front of God to do it. Under oath! Isn't that a sin?"

"Prob'ly," he allowed. "But it's my sin, too. I'm the one tole' you to do it, Cilla. And if I had it to do over? I'd do the same thing. 'Specially now, knowing we're kin. Do it every goddamn time."

"They blame me for it, anyway." I wiped my eyes on the sleeve of my Seminole sweatshirt. "Ever'body. They hate me."

"They get over it," Joe Billy squeezed my hands. "I get out, I'll *tell* 'em to git over it, how's that?"

That boy! He could get a laugh anywhere.

Sheriff Jackson pulled up in his cruiser as I left the jail. That big, bronze-painted star on the door. The car slowed to a stop and the window rolled down.

"You see Joe Billy?"

"Yes, sir."

"How's he doing?"

"Holding up."

"Uh huh. How 'bout you?"

"I'm fine," I told him, and then, "Not really."

"No," he shook his head. "It ain't never gonna feel good. But you did what you had to do. Only thing surprised me was, well, about you and Joe Billy."

My cheeks burned. The sheriff shook his head.

"You'd think a place this small I could know every hair on every head."

I swallowed. "What do they do to you, Sheriff? In jail?"

He tapped the accelerator with the toe of his boot. "He's young. He'll be fine."

Then he pulled away. The window rolled up, the car purred past me and around the corner toward the chain-linked entrance protecting the county compound. I salved my own conscience that day with the pithy mantra that five years of a man's life, though not desirable, was better than the dreaded Chair. I knew that Raiford was a dangerous place, but I told myself that Joe Billy would be protected, at least. I did not want to think what might happen to a castrated man, a boy, really, in the company of hardened felons. I don't think I could have imagined what would happen to Joe Billy in that Sodom of sodomites.

I just told myself that he'd be all right. He'd be fine. Maybe they would even let him illustrate his guitars. And I would help, I would. I'd send batteries for the radio. Cards and letters. I would not neglect my brother in prison. Not for five years.

I walked from the jailhouse to the opened door of my attorney's automobile and an hour and a half later was back in Tallahassee. I left Florida State within the year for a scholarship at Juilliard. I left New York for the concert in Manila. From there I took my bassoon to Berlin, then back to New York before recording in Los Angeles and Rome.

During those travels Joe Billy was raped by an inmate, starved by guards, and felled by heatstroke on a chain gang.

Thurman Shaw called me once, through my agent, with an urgent request to appear as a character witness on my brother's behalf, at a parole hearing. It would have meant giving up the Berlin tour. I made do with a letter and a videotaped plea for clemency. My manager assured me it was just as effective as going in person. Better use of time, he said.

I was performing in Vienna the day Joe Billy's parole was denied. It was not long afterward that JayBee made the first of two attempts to escape from Raiford. On the second attempt he killed a trustee, one of the inmates who'd raped him. Cut the bastard's throat with a razor. With that act of defense or justice Joe Billy lost any chance at parole. His eighth year in Raiford he was jumped in the laundry room. A pair of inmates held him down while another pried out his eyes with a spoon. Joe Billy never got out of prison. And until I returned to bury him I never again saw my brother's sightless face.

I checked my watch.

Until tonight.

Chapter twenty-four: Homecoming

*I*t took a funeral to return me to the community of my childhood. I left the mortuary in my rented Lincoln, hooked a left on Highway 27, which doubles as Main Street, and on the way to my motel spotted the water tower. The only thing changed was the latest addition of grafitti—

LHS SENIORS, 1993

Cindy's Motel remained unchanged in the shade of live oaks just behind Shirley's Café. A message was waiting for me when I checked in. Edward Tunney had located dogwood blossoms in quantity and hoped I would be pleased. The message also assured that "the body" was ready for transport from the funeral home to Mr. Raymond's residence.

Mr. Raymond assumed that responsibility in my absence. Yet another debt accrued to my account.

I did not sleep well that evening. I rose late, showered and walked in the damp, languid air to Shirley's place. I looked for distraction in my coffee, the morning paper. But finally the moment could not be delayed. I left Shirley's Café and the motel sometime before noon, turning onto a freshly paved street that took me to City Park, a place still shrouded in Spanish moss and memory. My rented towncar seemed pulled as if by some invisible hand over the railroad tracks and suddenly I had left the paved streets of Laureate and entered the shaded and sandy avenues of Colored Town.

I was looking for Mr. Raymond's home, but the sandy ruts that had been the boulevards of Colored Town were now converted to blacktop, those old latitudes and longitudes shifted to some unfamiliar Mercatur. Other landmarks I used to take for granted had been razed or renovated beyond recognition.

The houses I used to see every day on my way to Kerbo School were gone, those framed boxes of pine and tin largely replaced by doublewide trailers presiding over what looked like used-car lots, the rusted hulls of Nissans and Mitsubishis replacing the chassis of the Fords and Chevrolets which for generations were the only vehicles to be seen in Colored Town.

The fences of field wire or split rails that were once friendly perimeters around boisterous playgrounds were now forbidding boundaries bereft of children, reinforced by rebar and barbed wire and field fence. Dogs now patrolled the playgrounds of Colored Town, those mange-ridden sentries snarling at any passerby, their tails tucked into their anuses.

I rolled right past Mr. Raymond's, had to double back on a strip of splintered asphalt to find that once-familiar residence.

It was not the home I knew from teenage years, but at least it wasn't a trailer. The exterior was most altered, asbestos shingles now lapping over the ageless cypress whose warps and grooves always before pleased my eye. The porch had a new roof but the pump, the hated hand pump remained, seized in rust.

The yard about the house was gone to seed, the sandy ground once meticulously raked and weeded now grown over with briars and sandspurs. But heaving out of my luxury car I did see one thing that remained familiar; bleach bottles broken and amber and strung by their necks on the field fence defending Mr. Raymond's home.

For as long as I can remember my people have used bleach

bottles to mark a grieving house. Bleach takes the stain of Death away, if not the sting. It disinfects, it makes white. Purity is still identified with the absence of color in Colored Town. It is hard in Laureate to make black beautiful, even for black people. Colored folks from my region know that when you've got something isn't clean, it needs to be bleached, to be made sere.

The broken bottles of Clorox ringing Mr. Raymond's yard cordoned off an area now purified and sacred. Older people would simply say the bleached necklace wards off evil spirits, by which they meant darker malignancies, those succubi inhaled in moments of sin, concupiscence or, as in my case, when afflicted by a malformed or guilty conscience. Within the bottles' defended perimeter the soul of the deceased enjoys a final evening with his family and friends before being subsumed into the bosom of a Savior always depicted with ivory white skin.

I knew that somewhere in Mr. Raymond's house I would find a casket and Joe Billy. It used to be common, bringing the dead into your home. Before the insinuation of funeral parlors we always laid out our dead in their own houses, or homes of kin, in open coffins. Ed Tunney and an industry of undertakers begging to save that inconvenience now offered a viewing room of the deceased in return for a down payment toward interment. In the older custom those "passing on" were carried without expense to a bedroom or out front. To the living room, so called. People filed by to grieve, or at least to affect symptoms of grief appropriate to one's distance from the deceased: Husband, wife, son, daughter, grandparents, if applicable, uncles, aunts, first cousins—and so on.

Following the family's expressions came those of friends or neighbors. And of course there was a final group of mourners, not inconsiderable, who only passed the corpse on their way to the kitchen. Anytime you saw a coffin in a house there was food, my Lord, and the stricken family was not allowed to prepare a thing, not even a pot of coffee. Everything eaten for three days before a funeral and three after came potluck from relatives and neighbors and in generous quantity.

When I was younger I felt perfectly at ease eating before a

corpse. It was one of the few occasions I could have my fill and not feel as though it came from charity. And I was never alone; there might be a hundred people, or more, gathered to respect the passing of the most humble soul in our community. We all came. It was expected.

But entering Mr. Raymond's protected yard I saw no throng of mourners. A handful of men palmed smokes at the porch, their conversation lost in undertones. A few children played tag out front, their voices high and empty of grief. I was not recognized as I crossed the yard or even when I mounted the newly manufactured steps to Mr. Raymond's porch. The doorbell was there, but on this occasion was not to be used. It was impolite, in these circumstances, to require anyone inside to abandon his cup, plate, or corpse for the simple purpose of opening a door. I rapped the knuckles of my hand lightly on the postern anyway, as if for luck. The door opened easily. I stepped inside.

Pudding Reed saw me first.

"Well, well." He held a Ball jar filled with iced tea. "Somebody said you was back."

No hint of Romeo, here. The long soft body hanging heavy with flesh. A fold of belly over his belt.

"Pudding," I put on a big smile. "It's good to see you."

Heads turned with that opener. Mr. Raymond was there to preside, seated at the same deer-hide chair that used to preside over the porch, formal, as usual, the crisply creased trousers sharp as any conductor's.

"Cilla. Been expecting you." He did not rise from his seat.

"How long you been back?" Another and younger challenge. I swiveled to locate a black woman in cornrows and a loud florid warp and almost did not recognize Shirley Lee. "I say 'How long you been back?'"

"Just since yesterday."

"Been a while since we've seen you."

"Yes, it has," Pudding answered for me.

"And where is Chicken?" I asked jovially of Shirley Lee's brother. "Where is that Chicken Swamp?"

Shirley Lee's face seemed to stretch over a picture frame. "Chicken's been dead for years, Cilla. Died in Viet Nam."

"Cambodia," Pudding corrected her. "But then that cain't be right, can it? 'Cause we never had a war in Cambodia."

"Now, Pudding—" I turned to find Lonnie Hines. This could not be the boy who huddled behind my desk at Kerbo school! This could not be the boy I let cheat off my tests! Lonnie had grown tall and fit. He was wearing a suit that I could tell had been tailored. A Ralph Lauren shirt. Rolex watch. "Good to see you, Cilla."

Pudding reached past Lonnie to get a leg of chicken. "You'd of called or wrote anytime the last twenty years you'd of known about Chicken."

"Pudding, let's don't take it out on her. Joe Billy wouldn't want that."

"You got that right," Pudding took his white meat and headed for the kitchen.

"It has been a long time," I tried to ameliorate the tension. "But it's good to see you-all. And Lonnie Hines, look at you! What have you been up to?"

"Got a store over in Live Oak. Auto parts, tires and batteries."

"Much business?"

He shrugged modestly. "Depends. Got a county contract now that's good."

"'Till they take it away from us," Shirley Lee joined.

So they are married. Something else I did not know.

"So what you been up to, Cilla?" Johnny Boy Masters joined Lonnie and Shirley Lee to pose that question, or challenge. He seemed diminished, shrunken, with terrible pallor, but I was too embarrassed in the moment to inquire after his health, unwilling to present yet another piece of evidence that I had lost touch, a delicate euphemism, with my Kerbo classmates.

"Johnny Boy."

I offered my hand like a politician. He regarded it a moment. "You been up to?" he asked again, pumping me once, briefly.

"Just working. Just like you-all."

"Oh, I doubt that."

I don't know what I expected. Not effusion, certainly. Not a party. Not the nodding adoration of fans or sycophants. I certainly did not expect things to be the same as when I left; you cannot go to that home again and should not want to. But I suppose I had imagined or hoped that years of absence would be seen in light of the success I had enjoyed. Had earned. I supposed I imagined that my life away from Colored Town would at least kindle curiosity. I am after all a *cause célèbre* in Paris and Rome and Manila. Toast of the town on rainy Tuesdays in New York and Milan and Berlin. But not here. The hero known in these quarters lies somewhere beyond the smell of pot roast and pilau and pound cake.

"Seem like you kind of petered out." Pudding returned with a beer. "What somebody tole me. Say you ain't put out nothing new in a while."

"I'm working on something."

"Not what I heard."

"Pudding, show some manners." A voice got old still carried authority. I turned to find my first and best teacher at my shoulder.

"Miss Chandler!"

"Come here."

She wrapped me up in her arms and for a moment I would give anything to be a girl again, to be a maid and innocent, sitting by my mama at church before an upright piano. Content to hear the music my mother plays.

Content to turn the pages.

"He's out back," Miss Chandler released me and I followed her, past whispered comment, to Mr. Raymond's back porch.

"Fancy, isn't it?"

The rear-facing veranda was now screened in. I saw Mr. Raymond's ancient pickup rusting on blocks out back. A satellite dish was anchored with cement blocks alongside.

"Raymond calls it a 'Florida room'," Miss Chandler drew my attention back to the altered porch. "It's the only room big enough for a casket, really."

I saw a set of blinds erected near to hand. They reminded me of the curtains pulled on rings around the beds in hospital rooms. But these flimsy screens were framed in wood, screened in silk, some indefinite sylvan pattern.

"Is that him?"

"Behind them, yes."

I felt Miss Chandler's hand squeeze my arm.

How many times had she done that? Urged me on with that strong hand?

"Go on. Go to him."

I edged past the silk-rendered forest to find Joe Billy waiting. I had admonished Edward to put JayBee in the most expensive suit he could obtain and found myself irritated, even there, even as I should have been feeling grief for my brother, to see a half-inch of Joe Billy's wrists protruding like pods of okra from a cheap Arrow shirt and off-the-rack jacket.

"Joe Billy."

The stitch was fixed, that sloppy repair about his glass eye now invisible to mourners. His hair was combed back just like when he was a teenager. Just like Sammy Davis, Jr.

"He's still got his hair," I remarked to the air.

He appeared to have all his teeth, too, though I later learned that this was the mortician's compensation. Joe Billy lost a number of teeth over the years fighting guards or other prisoners.

"It's all right," Miss Chandler stood beside me. I don't even know how she got there. "You can touch him," she said.

She always could read my mind.

I followed the lapel of his suit to timidly reconnoiter the terrain of his chest, his throat, his cheek, face.

His lips.

They were not entirely closed. I imagined he was trying to speak. Trying to tell me something.

I leaned forward. "...Yes?"

There was nothing.

Then it came. The thing I feel so often, that knot in my chest, like a pair of socks? Working its way up, up, up.

It was to my throat. To my voice box. And then it swelled in my mouth. Gorging it. Forcing it. My mouth opened as if pried with tongs and I bayed to the faltering moon. I howled, I slobbered over my brother. My poor brother.

"JOE BILLY! JOE BILLY—"

I squalled over and over.

"I'M SORRY!!"

My wiry head sank to his white-shirted chest.

"I AM SO SORRY!!"

The ritual that helps my people cross their river Jordan normally serves as well to comfort those remaining. A wife or husband, brother or sister, can expect to be enveloped in the moments after lamentation, physically wrapped in the arms of her community once the grief has rent her garment or heart. That is the ritual. You let them alone. You hear the awful imprecations against chance or death or agony. Then when they come stumbling from the kist you wrap them up, as in a blanket, or swaddling clothes, as if the grieving sister, say, were being received fresh from the womb, which in a real sense she was, the swaddling and unwashed flesh of neighbors and friends, their arms, their lips and legs and buttocks pressing, suffocating nearly—and then released so that the living kin experience a sudden lightness, a sudden sensation of light, a baptism, the kitchen then offering succor like a mother's tit, the chatter of children signifying hope, their selfish and carefree play once an irritation now a sign like God's rainbow reminding us of His promise.

There will be no more flood.

There will be no more Death.

Only a passing.

A passing from the entrapment of flesh to weightless immortality. That is how the ritual works, that is its power, but when I returned composed from behind Joe Billy's casket there were no arms save Miss Chandler's to comfort me. My schoolmates remained occupied with their potluck. They turn to the coffee pot, the pilau, or the mindless situation comedy all but black-faced that drones on Raymond's television. No one came to me. No one spoke my name.

The voices of children in the yard remained distant and disinterested, a nuisance, no more.

330

"Why don't you stay?" Miss Chandler, again, reading me like a book. "Stay and eat."

"No," I declined bravely. "I can't take the time."

"I'll walk you out," Miss Chandler's assent, coming quickly, confirmed what I did not want to believe.

Which was that while I was acknowledged as Joe Billy's surviving sister, I was not welcome here. Mr. Raymond did not rise from his primitive chair. Shirley Lee offered a sorority-girl smile. Lonnie's sympathy was genuine, if restrained.

He opened the door for me. "So sorry for your loss, Cilla."

"Thank you."

"Take care of yourself."

Well, I had learned to do that. Hadn't I?

Out the door, onto the porch. The yard beyond glowed white and bare beneath a wont of clouds and a full moon. I saw in the sand the footprints of children who disappeared like elves.

"I'm sorry about Chicken Swamp; I didn't know."

I offered that apology to my old mentor.

"People want to be remembered, Cilla. But that's only partly it."

My stomach wrenched. "What's the rest, then? Is it because I have a life they don't? Is it resentment? Jealousy?"

"Those exacerbate, I believe," Miss Chandler sighed. "But the biggest thing they resent, Cilla, is that when it counted, you did not trust them. You did not trust me. Not any of us."

I swallowed. "Trust you with what?"

"Cilla, don't you think it's about time you laid this burden down?"

I leaned heavily on the roof of my borrowed car. Miss Chandler's nostrils widened, detecting some pleasant aroma. The hyacinth, probably.

"When you left for Tallahassee I had no doubt that you were blameless, baby. But then you quit communicating. The letters stopped. The phone calls. You never came home, Cilla, not even on holidays. Joe Billy called me from prison asking me why his letters to your dormitory were being returned. You had not even told your own brother that you'd be finishing school in New York. Why this withdrawal, I wondered? Why were you pulling away from Joe Billy? From me? From all of us? There had to be a reason. Had to be."

The yard behind me was white and bare. "What was I supposed to do, Miss Chandler? Put yourself in my position. What would you have done?"

"I don't know. Perhaps the same as you. But then I would have come to my people and told them to pray for me. For I had sinned. I would have told my preacher and my teacher the truth of what I had done, and by so doing I would give my neighbors and friends and classmates the opportunity to understand my hard choice, to show grace, to forgive."

"They wouldn't have forgiven me," I shook my burly head. "I know they wouldn't."

"Oh, Cilla." I could see the moon in my teacher's eyes. "That is where you are so, so wrong."

*   *   *

Joe Billy was laid to rest in a twelve thousand dollar casket a little before noon in a yard of sand. The blossoms of dogwood trees wreathed the coffin, those white blossoms also strewed around the gravesite, spilling even into the loamy maw that received my brother's box. It was a humble resting place, segregated entirely by race, just a swell of topsoil set off beneath clumps of cypress by a green picket fence badly in need of painting. The graves, all for black people, reflected their origins in an impoverished population. Most of Colored Town's interred could not even afford tombstones. I saw many crosses carved of wood. Sometimes a metal marker.

The graves were scattered between stands of cypress. Joe Billy would be buried next to his mother. His mother and mine. Next to Corrie Jean. A stump away from Grandma's grave. I didn't handle the arrangements for Grandmother Handsom. I was away when she died. I was away when mother died too, for that matter, but I did make arrangements for their markers.

Joe Billy's headstone was cut from pink granite. I wasn't sure what to inscribe for my brother's surname. We never knew who our father was. In the end I decided to leave Joe Billy the same *nomen* for perpetuity that he joyfully and tenaciously used during the run of his life:

—JOSEPH WILLIAM KING—

There had been some hesitation over the selection of the stone's attending inscription and iconography. For the former, Ed Tunney suggested a variety of aphorisms precut into polished slabs, "Rest In Peace," say, or, particularly apposite, "Greater Love Hath No Man."

"Something along those lines is always nice." Him smiling like a midway barker. "Or how 'bout some Scripture? Scripture's always popular. I like Corinthians."

"And will there be a design to go with it?" I asked. "Some kind of etching on the stone?"

"Oh, yes," he nodded enthusiastically. "We have a wide selection. Doves, angels. Angels' wings. Or olive branches. Those are symbolic."

It's a hell of a thing trying to decide what symbols to risk on a dead man's stone. In the end, I just did what I thought Joe Billy might like.

"Engrave a guitar," I directed.

"A guitar? On the headstone?"

"Yes. Two of them. To frame his birth and death. Find me some paper, I'll make you a sketch."

"And the inscription?"

"Let's go with this."

I took out my Mont Blanc pen. The epitaph was quickly rendered:

—JOSEPH WILLIAM KING—
October 31, 1945–April 17, 1993
Born in Dowling Park
Buried in Colored Town

333

"Ashes to ashes, dust to dust…"

It was a graveside funeral. I endured a sonorous sermon rendered by an anonymous cleric whose spliced assurances of salvation and succor were for me tiresome, if not meaningless. But others believed them, I reminded myself, or wanted to believe. Finally, Joseph William was interred. The sun was high and hot by the time I knelt at the jaws of the pulleys and spars spanning my brother's damp pit.

"You can rest, now, Joe Billy."

I dropped a single pearly blossom onto the lid of his coffin. It landed with a plop that seemed comical. Time, then, to stand and accept the mumbled condolences of the perhaps twenty or so persons attending. The same schoolmates and one-time neighbors who frostily greeted me the evening before now filed past my brother's open grave, paying their respects in genuine coin to Joe Billy, offering counterfeit consolations to me. Which was fine. As it should be, probably.

Finally, it was finished. Miss Chandler accompanied me as I left the yard.

"Could you use a ride?" I asked her.

"Thank you, I could."

I drove Miss Chandler home in silence. I got out to help her from the car. I didn't walk her inside. Just to the gate.

"There is no way to thank you, is there, Miss Chandler, for all the things you did for me? For Joe Billy?"

She squeezed my arm. "It's good seeing you, Cilla."

That was it. No parting speech or pearls of wisdom. It wasn't until her gate opened on protesting hinges and Miss Chandler stiffly mounted the still-wooden steps to enter her home that I fully appreciated how old my teacher had become. How near to the grave she herself had to be. How much she had spent on my behalf. How much could possibly remain?

I waited for the front door to close before I climbed back into my air-conditioned car. Then I drove as if making for the railroad station, but then turned back to my brother's grave. I wanted to be alone with Joe Billy for awhile with no one to see me. No prying eye to judge or censure my expression of grief, or lack thereof.

I wanted to say goodbye properly.

By the time I returned to the cypress-shrouded yard, Joe Billy's grave was covered, his marble monument looking over a mound of sand and the flowers offered at the site by those attending, day lilies being the dominant addition to the blooms of dogwood. Both fruits signifying in varying ways the agony or hope of resurrection.

The diggers were already gone. They use tractors, now, you know, to score the earth and then to fill it. Makes for quick work, especially in the soft loam near the coast of northern Florida. I parked my car and angled for the gap in the cemetery's badly painted perimeter. "Tunney's Mortuary"; the reminder was stitched in white over the green canopy that rippled as the sail of a boat. I didn't see any automobiles other than my own at the cemetery, but as I approached the fresh grave I saw someone seated in a folding chair outside Tunney's canopy. A white man, I could tell that, though his back was to me and his torso was shielded by a tangled trunk of cypress. He was dressed in a suit that must have been bought in the fifties. The trousers bagged about what I could only imagine were bony legs. The jacket was faded gray and rumpled as a pillow. The shoes by contrast appeared newly purchased, Fieldings, probably, plain-toed Oxfords, black, low-quarter. Spit-shined as if for military inspection.

I smelled something acrid and familiar. It was borne on the wilting breeze, twining up through the branches of the shielding trees. Tobacco? A *cigarette?* What was this, a white man smoking at my brother's grave?!

The short heels of my shoes sank into the sand as I marched straight over.

"Sir," I challenged him as I approached the canopy. "Sir, do you have business here?"

He rose with my tone and turned and then I saw that the man with the shoes and cigarette was Sheriff Collard Jackson.

"Cilla," he leaned against the flimsy chair. "Ain't you somethin'?"

His face was by now deeply etched and cratered, a lunar land-scape. The eyes recessed deeply into sockets that now seemed frail in the large cranium. The hair thinning. The frame bereft of muscle, gone nearly to bone. Flesh hanging loosely in his sleeves, in his trousers.

"Sheriff Jackson. Good Lord!"

He squinted at me genially. "I missed the service."

"You didn't miss much."

He took a drag from his cancer stick. "Why don't you set a spell?" He reached behind to lurch a chair over.

"All right."

The legs of our folding chairs stabbed like spears into the soft earth. Collard extricated a handkerchief from a vest pocket.

"You may be the only white man's ever set foot in this yard," I observed.

"Without a doubt," he mopped his brow.

"You really could have attended, Sheriff. No one would have said anything."

"Not out loud, no."

"I'm not so sure," I rejoined. "You're practically family."

"I 'spose."

There was something in the way he said it, some note of despair or irony. I couldn't quite make it out.

"I hope it's not guilt," I finally managed. "I hope you didn't come here out of guilt."

He turned those deep set eyes into mine. "Well, if I did, I expect it's something you and me have in common."

"I'd be a liar to deny that."

He stirred the sand with the toe of a leather shoe. "I was read-ing somethin' 'bout you just the other day."

"Better to be in the news than not, I suppose."

A breeze gusted suddenly. The flaps of the canopy reported like a flag. Collard crushed his cigarette into the bone-yard sand. Fished a fresh one from its pack.

"Those things are going to kill you," I said.

"Gave 'em plenty of chances. They ain't done it yet." He leaned sideways to fish out a box of matches. "I been in this yard one other time. For Corrie Jean."

"Nobody told me when she died," I said. "Nobody called."

"Nobody knew how," Collard grunted. "Watn't like you was over in Perry or Live Oak. We couldn't keep her in deep freeze."

"No. Of course not."

"I remember taking your mama to Dowling Park. Raymond came and got me. I was sleeping off a drunk. It was cold, raining. Corrie Jean had a melon in her belly."

"Two melons," I corrected.

"Right," he grunted. "Right."

"Do you have any idea who our father was, Sheriff?"

"Nobody knows. My guess'd be Lester, be just like that sumbitch to take a retard. No offense. But I don't know. Maybe I shouldn't say."

I beheld my brother's grave. "I shouldn't have let Joe Billy go to prison."

"You didn't let him go anyplace. A white jury sent him to prison and there's nothing in hell you could of done to stop 'em."

"I could have spoken up. I should have."

"You think you'd of finished school and done your music and all the rest with Monk's murder hanging around your neck?"

"It does hang, Sheriff. It has hung. Like a lodestone. An albatross. You have no idea. Sometimes I think it's dragging me to the grave."

"Don't let it." The old command was back in his voice. "You think this don't stick in my craw, too? I'm the one told you to shut up. I'm the one sat by and watched an innocent boy put behind bars. But I wasn't about to see Corrie Jean's daughter go to jail for something I'd of been proud to do myself."

I pressed my hand to my temple.

"I got to be going," Collard announced. He had to use the tent pole to pull himself up. "He was a good boy," Collard declared, facing the silent stone. "He had sand."

That eulogy delivered, the man who used to be sheriff of

Lafayette County limped away from the graveside, alone, in the heat. Didn't take ten steps before he lit up another cigarette.

Chapter twenty-five

I "It's Just One Of Those Things…"—*Peggy Lee*

don't know exactly how long I remained at my brother's grave. A few minutes? A half hour? Not long. Not compared to eternity, certainly. I needed to get back to New York, but even allowing travel there were hours to kill before my flight out of Tallahassee, plenty of time to change clothes, to indulge in a long, cold shower.

I drove from the grave to my motel, stopping along the way at a convenience store for bottled water and munchies.

"Paper or plastic?" I was given a choice of bags.

"Paper," I replied. "Always."

Cindy's Motel nestled beneath a shade of oaks not fifty yards from Betty's still-existing café. The room was not much larger than the dorm at Florida State, but frigidly air-conditioned. My suitcase opened wide on a double bed to expose the essentials for travel.

The television was useless, its coaxial ripped from the wall, but there was a radio in the room, vernier tuned. I dialed that pleasantly old-fashioned receiver past National Public Radio to find an FM station and Vivaldi's Spring Movement, shucking my sand-filled shoes and clothing on the way to the shower. I emerged refreshed from the sting of water and while changing into a light skirt and blouse saw the message light winking on the touchtone phone.

"Cilla, it's me…"

That would be my latest inamorata. Veronica.

"Listen, when you get back we need to talk."

I skipped the rest. When a younger woman wants to talk it always means the same thing. She's found another interest, a better deal, a more fantastic orgasm—who knows? And she wants to tell you she's moving on without hurting your feelings, which is patently impossible. Or it could be she just wanted money.

I swear it's enough to make you want to go back to men.

The only other call of import came from my agent at ICM. Green light for a film. Big budget. "John says he's got to have you on the track." By which he meant the sound track for the film's score. I wasn't sure I knew who John was, but his enthusiasm for me was relayed through Syd who I was assured was so totally close to Rene that the deal was as good as done.

My bassoon, naturally, was to be featured.

"It's schlock," Syd's voice always sounded like tin over the phone. "But the money's filthy."

Filthy money, yes. I'd got used to it.

But there were clean sheets in my suitcase just waiting to be scored. I had a pen, and time. So I decided, as I had on countless other occasions, to sit down and make myself write. Just sit, quietly, and compose.

To once again make music in my head.

I gave it less than an hour, and still barren, gave up. It was time to leave these haunts. I tossed my pad in the overnight and collected my pharmacy of medicinals and fiber. My bill was prepaid in plastic. Within ten minutes I was ready to turn my back on Laureate and Colored Town. All I had to do was gas up the car.

I was surprised to find Charles Putnal's full-service station pretty much as I remembered it, and Charles, too. He was beneath the hydraulic lift in his garage when I drove up. Even from the pump I saw a full head of hair, a posture still as casual and powerful as an athlete's. His arms still filled the shirts I recalled from childhood and there was no gut hanging his oil-stained jeans. He saw me from the garage, came out bareheaded. Unlike most local men Charles never preferred the bib of a cap, squinting into a west-falling sun like some sailor of old, the creases thus laid into his face deep and abiding and honestly got.

I buzzed my window down.

"Fill her up?" he asked.

"If you would, please."

He paused for a moment at the pump, squinted inside my rental. "I know you?"

"It's Cilla, Charles. Cilla Handsom."

"I will be damn, Cilla! Sorry I didn't recognize you."

"It's been twenty years. More."

"Still, I bet perfect strangers come up to you at airports or concerts, *they* know who you are. Hell, I ought to. We ought to."

"That's nice of you to say, Charles."

"Will that be regular or high test?"

"Your call."

"If you're renting, I'd go cheap," he advised and reached for the low octane.

I used that chance to get out of the car.

"'Long you in town?"

"Leaving now. I just came for Joe Billy."

He set the pump's nozzle, shaking his head on to way to my windshield.

"We heard all kind of stories. Was he killed up there?"

"Suicide, they're saying. Guard found him hanging."

"He deserved better."

"Yes, he did," I found my eyes going down to the ground.

"Juanita was asking about you couple of weeks back," Charles remarked.

"Juanita Land?"

"You got time you ought to go see her."

"I'm sure Juanita wouldn't want me dropping in unannounced."

Charles stopped his labor to regard me.

"She's at Dowling Park, been a nurse out there for years, the Infirmary. And for what it's worth, you can't never be sure about what people want. Hell, half the time we don't know ourselves."

I heard the nozzle chunk with the backflow of gasoline.

"Be seventeen dollars, eighty-three cents," he announced and I handed him a twenty.

"Get your change," Charles said and I knew better than to suggest otherwise.

My itinerary for travel did not include reunions with high school class-mates unless they were black, and my reception at Mr. Raymond's did not encourage a widened scope of exploration. I had not expected to hear at all from Juanita Land, could not believe she had not flown her small-town coop as soon as she was able. I always imagined Juanita in Tampa or Miami, married to some wealthy scion, or perhaps a good-natured halfback with a trust fund. I could not imagine the richest and most vivacious girl in the county nursing the dead and dying at an old folks' home. She might as well be a missionary.

Was she a missionary?

Was she married?

Did she have children?

What had Charles said, exactly? That she had asked about me? Or that she asked *for* me?

It was not yet three o'clock in the afternoon when I saw the tower supporting the cables that span the Hal W. Adam Bridge. I crossed high above the Suwannee River, turning off the hard road four miles later to the patched and broken two-lane that leads to Dowling Park. I was amazed to see a roadside gas station familiar to me from my youth. The scenery was equally familiar, pastureland broken with hickory and pine and, yes, the bright spring blossoms of dogwood trees. The sign marking the entry to Dowling Park is large and metal and raised for easy sighting. The tires of my hired car rumbled over a cattle-gap, a relic of the days when dairy cows grazed the grounds.

My mother had endured two hard labors here, the first to give life, the second to give up living. I used to be able to walk up to the place where Corrie Jean brought me into the world, a small, tin-roofed farmhouse down from the dairy. But the dairy and orphanage and other buildings familiar to me were long gone, entirely replaced now by retirement homes and geriatric facilities. I saw wheelchairs where once I saw children.

Bounded by a high bluff overlooking the Suwannee and by pastureland once attached to an active dairy, the Park's growing community spread uncluttered between original growths of oak and pine and rosebud trees. Lining the drive were groupings of photina and juniper and hedges of azalea. Wild flowers and palmetto, all well tended.

There were bungalows nestled beneath the trees that were reserved for the Park's staff. The larger homes at the outskirts were owned by retirees buying or building under the Park's aegis. Extended care was managed from a hospital set in the middle of the complex, on the site of what had been the Park's orphanage. Apartments nearby were intended for what has come to be called assisted living.

A caduceus mounted in stainless steel on the brick face of the building marked the entrance to Dowling Park's pharmacy. A community center abutted that facility; the infirmary and emergency room were accessed directly behind. I entered via the pharmacy, going directly past that apothecary and through a pair of swinging doors to reach the infirmary beyond. The infirmary at Dowling Park was a medium-care facility which with pharmacy, x-ray room, and e.r., served all of the Park's residents. There were probably no more than eight or ten rooms in the sick bay itself, fifteen or twenty beds. The nurse's station was no more than a countertop shoehorned along a modest hallway.

"Can you help me locate Juanita Land?" I asked a young woman the size of a newt in a uniform starched stiff as boards. "I won't keep her long."

"Of course," she nodded pert and professional. "She's in room one nineteen."

I proceeded down a linoleum-tiled hallway in the indicated direction, wondering idly what kept a woman working for years in a place so near death's door.

There was room 119.

I turned my hand to rap knuckles lightly on the door.

"Come in."

I entered, to find Juanita cranked up in a hospital bed. Her hair was loose, something I had never seen. And she was not tending anyone. I realized suddenly, with shock, that my old friend was herself a patient. A physician leaned over her partly bared chest, that pale skin, some white man in a snowy white lab coat flapping open over Gucci slacks and weejuns. He handled a stethoscope and a somber demeanor. A bag of fluid distended by a tube from what looked like a hat rack to the needle in my schoolmate's arm. She smiled at me.

"Cilla! I'm so glad you came!"

"What is this?" I steadied myself on a side rail. "What have they got you in here for?"

"Cilla, this is my doctor, Dr. Larry Hall. Larry, this is Cilla Handsom."

I barely acknowledged the introduction.

There was some kind of gauze or dressing about her breast.

"Oh, Lord," my hands went to my own. "Oh, Lord."

"It's all right, Cilla. It's just chemo."

Just chemo?

"Oh, Jesus."

I sank to the side of her bed. The doctor excused himself quietly and I was left with a woman I had always thought impervious to age or infirmity.

"I almost didn't come," I confessed straightway.

"Glad you changed your mind."

She reached over and squeezed my hand.

"How was the funeral?"

"Terrible."

Her laughter was so pure, so unaffected. Here she was facing death herself and yet unchastened, apparently, by any wisp of mortal fear. A peal of pure mirth. We talked small for a while. She had married a boy from Gainesville, it turned out, not a wealthy scion, not a halfback. There was a divorce. No children. Halfway through nursing school Juanita learned that her father had mort-

gaged the family store to finance a real-estate deal in South Florida
that totally collapsed.

"Wasn't long after daddy filed Chapter Nine I came out to the
Park," she smiled. "Been here ever since."

"Charles told me you worked out here. He didn't say anything
about you being sick."

"I didn't want him to, Cilla. I wouldn't want you coming out
here on that account. I think about you often, though."

"You do?"

"Mmmhmm. But you had pretty much forgot about us, hadn't
you, honey? Or tried to?"

"Guilty on both counts," I replied, unable to dissemble before
such artless candor.

She folded my hand into hers. "So how's life in the big city,
girlfriend? How you doin'?"

I paused a long moment. I had wanted, for so long, to have
someone take my hand like this. But now the moment was here and
I felt myself preparing the canned response. What did it matter, anyway? But then Juanita looked up to me, pale and small.

"Cilla, I don't have that much time. Let's not waste it."

I looked into her eyes. There was nowhere else to look. "I'm
not doing so good," I blinked. "I'm scared. I'm running out of money.
I buy things I can't afford. I had to take in a roommate to keep my
apartment in New York, and I'm damn near positive when I get back
she'll be gone. But the worst is, I haven't written anything worth-
while in a year. I keep wanting to break into jazz with my bassoon,
try something original, but every time I do I come up dry.

"I used to get concerts. I used to get invited to Berlin, to Vienna.
Now I do soundtracks for horror movies."

"Is that what they call writer's block?"

"I don't believe in writer's block. I don't believe in blocks of
any kind."

"Then what's holding you back?"

That was the question, wasn't it? That was the disturbing,
unnerving, frightening question.

And I did not know the answer.

"I have something for you," Juanita leaned over her nightstand to retrieve a tattered cigar box.

"We were cleaning out one of the old residences the other day and found this squirreled away in a closet. It was your mother's, Cilla. I'm sure of it."

I hesitated before the humble box.

"Go ahead. You need to see."

The cardboard lid came off in my hands. First I saw was a photograph, an old one, black and white.

"Good Lord."

I brushed the photo with my fingertips as if to make certain it was real. A mature man and a lanky teenaged girl held their backs to the camera, smiling broadly, each of them, over the shoulder. I recognized myself in the grainy likeness, a gawky, tall, chocolate-skinned teen. The player beside me was also tall, six feet at least, and slender. He had thick hair, groomed back a lot like Joe Billy's. His fingers were preternaturally long, you could see them in the picture splaying across eight octaves of keys. He could probably have held a basketball in either one of those hands. A black man, a musician in his prime, dressed to the nines in suit and tie.

"That's you, isn't it, Cilla? On the bench?"

"Yes, Joe Billy took the picture. And that's Alex McBride."

I sat with the photograph, holding it as if to soak the emulsion into my eyes, my mind. He had changed my life, that man. In the space of an afternoon he showed me a new path.

"I was seventeen years old," I said.

There were a few other mementos hoarded away. A locket, cheaply engraved. A postcard, one of the few I sent home while on the road. Some newspaper yellow with decomposition papered the bottom of my foundling box. I picked up a clipping.

"Local Negro at Carnegie," ran the headline.

"You all right, Cilla?"

"I'm fine," I said and returned my inheritance carefully to its flimsy keep. "Is this why you sent word to Charles?"

"You're my friend, Cilla. You will always be my friend. I didn't need a reason."

She lay open as a book before me. That modest, firm architecture of bone and muscle. Hair aged and splendid and spreading like linen. I leaned over and pressed my lips to hers. Juanita smiled up at me. Not a hint of embarrassment or censure.

It was like kissing an angel.

I emerged from the smell of disinfectant and bedpans into a summer breeze redolent with ozone and the admonitions of a coming storm. I had long missed my flight out of Tallahassee and was surprised to find that I was untroubled by that failure. I could take a room overnight in the capital city, after all. Make a connection through Atlanta to New York or Newark in the morning.

Syd, or John, or whatever his name was, could wait.

I remained on the grounds of Dowling Park, lingering about the place where I was born, to hear wind shaking the cymbals of leaves, to anticipate the flicker of sheet lightning. I strolled away from the infirmary, pausing outside some open commons to see a group of aging residents rapt before a widescreen television, their faces slack and passive before that lambent hearth. There was a piano in that open room, unused. I tried to imagine my mother still among them, how they might crowd about her perfect performance animated and active, recalling the lyrics of some long-ago song, rekindling in Corrie Jean's untutored play the music of a durable youth.

Double your pleasure. Double your fun.

I tried to imagine what it must have been like for Corrie Jean dying here, no mother of her own to hold her hand, her daughter uncomprehended and a continent away, a son never imagined. Did she know I had deserted her? I hoped not. Thank God Juanita had been here to care for Mama; thank God she forgave me for running away.

I hoped Joe Billy forgave me, too.

By the time I picked my way back to my car, leaves and twigs were whirling off the pebbled path in ominous dervishes. Sliding beneath the wheel, I saw a faint glow from an infirmary window.

I would call, I promised myself. I would write.

It was almost eleven o'clock when I re-crossed the Suwannee.

Not a hint of moon showing. I could not see the water churning darkly below, nor the sky above. I hit a thunderstorm near Perry, turned north soon after to take the wide four-lane leading to Tallahassee. My car rocked with fresh buffets of wind. The rain slapped my windshield in heavy sheets. It was now as dark as the inside of a cow, impossible except in brief flashes of lightning to see anything along the road, though through the interval of my wipers' arms there would appear brief and distant flickers of light. Just small winks of illumination, well off the pavement. Trailer homes, probably, intruding onto what were once fields garnished exclusively in islands of dogwood.

Without the stimulation of scenery the radio was even more welcome than usual. I tapped the scanner of my car's digitized receiver and picked up a publicly funded station.

The overture to Von Weber's *Oberon* is instantly recognizable. It has been often observed that the opening themes find a concrete link, sometimes even repetition, in narrative details later encountered. The overture's opening horn, for instance, calling soft as a lute, provides the tune played by Puck's magic horn. The violins that climb quickly and with energy in the *allegro* will later run with the lovers to their waiting ship. The fairy kingdom itself, that ambiance, that mood, (especially when accompanied by wind and storm) is mostly the product of wind instruments; the woodwinds in particular descend on a steep staircase to establish a musical constellation for Puck's fairyland, and when the bassoons came in I instantly recognized my own.

To that point I honestly do not believe I had ever heard a performance of my own over the radio. In studios, yes, many times I have listened to my recordings. On CDs as well, or tape. But not on a radio, certainly not traveling. And this was not one of my solo performances. I was barely a neophyte at the point in my career when this work was conducted, a day-laborer in ensemble with others.

I turned up the volume, siphoning out Planche's English libretto, and then something happened that had not happened to me for a long time. I was not only hearing the music, I was seeing it *as written*. Each instrument's score flashed before me, each note. I imagined each score as code, a rune guiding the transformation of sound to electricity to analog to discreet digits of information—and then back again, the code broken, a pulse of magnets transmogrified to the flight of fairies, a composite of percussion and string and wind coursing invisibly through the integrated circuits, reproduced with fidelity through woofs and tweeters that niched like elves in the cage of my luxury car.

What kingdom could be more fantastic? And what fairy was telling me to write it down? It seemed silly. Why would you write down other people's music? Why would you do that? From where did this impulse derive?

Then I remembered Colored Town and Mr. Raymond's porch side pump. The red wagon. Hauling water. Mr. Raymond always said you couldn't get any water until you first primed the pump. How long had it been, I wondered, since my pump had been primed?

I rummaged around the console, feeling for the barrel of my pen. But what to do for paper? My legal pad and stationery were packed away in the car trunk. Was I really willing to rescue those parchments in the assault of rain and wind and lightning?

Then I saw the bag.

It lay there, brown and dry on the floorboard of my car, emptied of Perrier and potato chips. Within moments I was pulled off onto the shoulder of the road, scribbling measures of *Oberon* on a grocer's parchment smoothed over the console between my bucket seats. I wrote as fast as I could hear. I'd pick up the cellos for awhile, then the flutes, the clarinets. The solo clarinet. I wrote until I ran out of space. I wrote until there was no more bag to write on. Then I looked at the music in my lap, a mess of notes and instruments, folded it in squares, and got back on the road. The storm was spent by the time I reached Tallahassee. I stopped at a Seven-Eleven and purchased coffee bitter as bark.

"There be anything else?"

"Yes," I said.

I checked into a Holiday Inn and rose early the next morning to turn on the radio. I tuned in a jazz station, a pop station, back to the station I had heard the night before. Jazz, pop, classical, I did not discriminate. I just scored samples from every song, symphony, or jingle

I tuned in. Anything with a melody in it I scratched down. An hour or so into that activity I paused to book a flight out of Tallahassee.

Then I called my agent.

"I'm going to be late."

"Columbia's waiting."

"They can wait a few weeks longer."

"The hell are you doing, Cilla?"

I board a plane in Tallahassee and spread my scores on the seat tray. I am no longer writing down the music that someone else has rendered. I am not writing down the tunes I hear from a radio, nor from the aircraft's digital store. For the first time in a long time I am rendering the notes and chords and melodies for a composition that only I can hear, a work that exists only in my imagination.

It comes so quickly I can scarcely keep up.

"What is that?"

The passenger beside is bemused.

"It's music," I reply, thinking that ought to be obvious.

"No, no," he folds his *Journal*. "What is *that*? That you're writing on."

"Oh," I smile. "It's a grocery bag."

Not white paper. Not pure. Not regular, either. Not an eight-by-eleven tapestry, no. My vellum is dark and coarse and brown, an unruly citizen in the world of paper. Not pristine. Not elite. It is working class and ragged. It tears unevenly. Its folds are ravines for my scrawling pencils. I can wad it or stretch it or tape it to the wall. Or spread it with other bags on the floor.

"I like the color."

I am not certain at first where I am going, so long has it been since I successfully composed. But as I write I begin to hear the sounds again, and see them. I nearly miss my plane in Atlanta so busy am I scoring my brown paper bags. I determine to remain in New York, or at least nearby, for weeks of labor and composition. I will listen to Joe Billy's music, to blues and jazz. I will listen to Mozart and Beethoven and the White Album and Charles Mingus. I will listen to my mother, even in my dreams. And I will wrestle with angels hip and thigh until

I fuse the music of Colored Town with classical ode to tell the story of a boy who painted guitars dirty and became a king.

I am going to write this thing, I know now that I am, and there will be no pause. The dam is broken and I must haul water 'till the barrel's filled. And then I will have to gather my crew, my musicians. Mend those fences. And then to find a producer. Someone willing to take a chance. I'll use my own money, if I have to. Even if I lose it all. And when it's done I shall find a radio and I shall listen to the work I have created. I will think of Joe Billy. I will remember Mama. I will write Miss Chandler, long letters, full of appreciation. And Juanita, too, I will write. I will tell her I am through wasting time. Go to her bedside to tell her.

But not right now...

As soon as I am finished.

THE END

Acknowledgments

Thanks go to the Department of Music, Florida State University, and to the many performers who contributed to this novel. Special encouragement and support for my research along other lines came from educators, particularly Rev. Carolyn Demps and Mr. Taylor McGrew, whose courage, wisdom and generosity I am proud to acknowledge.

The fonts used in this book are from the Garamond family

About the Author

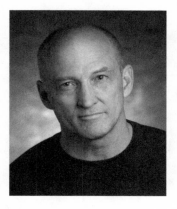

Darryl Wimberley

Darryl Wimberley is an author and screenwriter who resides with his family in Austin, Texas.

Other works by Darryl Wimberley
available from *The* Toby Press

A Tinker's Damn

The Toby Press publishes fine writing,
available at bookstores everywhere. For more information, please
contact *The* Toby Press at www.tobypress.com